Rhys Bowen is the *New York Times* bestselling author of the Royal Spyness Series, Molly Murphy Mysteries, and Constable Evans. She is a recipient of the Agatha Best Novel Award and an Edgar Best Novel nominee.

Praise for Rhys Bowen

'The latest addition to Molly's case files offers a charming combination of history, mystery, and romance.' *Kirkus Reviews* on *Hush Now, Don't You Cry*

'Engaging . . . Molly's compassion and pluck should attract more readers to this consistently solid historical series.' *Publishers Weekly* on *Bless the Bride*

'Winning . . . The gutsy Molly, who's no prim Edwardian miss, will appeal to fans of contemporary female detectives.' *Publishers Weekly* on *The Last Illusion*

'This historical mystery delivers a top- notch, detail- rich story full of intriguing characters. Fans of the 1920s private detective Maisie Dobbs should give this series a try.' *Booklist* on *The Last Illusion*

'Details of Molly's new cases are knit together with the accoutrements of 1918 New York City life. . . . Don't miss this great period puzzler reminiscent of Dame Agatha's mysteries and Gillian Linscott's Nell Bray series.' *Booklist* on *In a Gilded Cage*

Also by Rhys Bowen

THE MOLLY MURPHY MYSTERIES
Murphy's Law
Death of Riley
For the Love of Mike
In Like Flynn
Oh Danny Boy
In Dublin's Fair City
Tell Me Pretty Maiden
In a Gilded Cage
The Last Illusion
Bless the Bride
Hush Now, Don't You Cry
The Face in the Mirror
Through the Window
The Family Way
City of Darkness and Light
The Amersham Rubies
The Edge of Dreams
Away in a Manger
Time of Fog and Fire

HER ROYAL SPYNESS SERIES
Masked Ball at Broxley Manor
Her Royal Spyness
A Royal Pain
Royal Flush
Royal Blood
Naughty in Nice
The Twelve Clues of Christmas
Heirs and Graces
Queen of Hearts
Malice at the Palace
Masked Ball at Broxley Manor
Crowned and Dangerous

HUSH NOW, DON'T YOU CRY
~ A Molly Murphy Mystery ~
RHYS BOWEN

Constable • London

CONSTABLE

First published in the US in 2012 by Minotaur Books, an imprint of St Martin's Press, New York

First published in the UK in 2014 by C&R Crime, an imprint of Constable & Robinson Ltd
This edition published in Great Britain in 2016 by Constable

A CIP catalogue record for this book
is available from the British Library.

ISBN 978-1-47210-311-6 (paperback)

Typeset in Times New Roman by TW Type, Cornwall
Printed and bound in Great Britain by CPI (UK) Ltd, Croydon CR0 4YY
Papers used by Constable are from well-managed forests and other responsible sources

This book is dedicated to Maxine and Bill Everest, with thanks for their friendship, their terrific hospitality, and the fun we've had at their lovely condo in Kona.
And also a special dedication to Catherine Swan Gallinger, who has kindly lent her name to one of the characters.

Toora loora loora,
Toora loora li
Toora loora loora,
Hush now, don't you cry.
Toora loora loora,
Toora loora li
Toora loora loora.
It's an Irish lullaby.

One

October 8, 1903

'We should not have come here!' I shouted over the howl of the wind. Rain swept in great squalls off the ocean, snatching the words from my mouth. It was not a night to be standing on a clifftop in complete darkness. Our umbrella had given up the unequal struggle with the storm on the way from the station and now lay in a rubbish bin, its ribs sticking out like a large dead spider. Daniel had deposited it there despite my protests, stating that it was past all hope of repair.

It was a long walk from the station and not one that should have been attempted on a stormy night. But we had little choice. The directions we had been given were for a delightful afternoon stroll along a cliff path, with blue ocean below us. We had not anticipated that Daniel would be delayed with a last-minute problem at headquarters and that what the locals called a nor'easter would arrive at the same time as ourselves.

After changing trains in Providence, then again to a branch line in Kingston, we finally pulled into Newport station, at almost ten o'clock. There was not a hansom cab or any kind of conveyance to be found. The town appeared to be battened down in anticipation of the coming storm. We'd set off bravely enough under Daniel's big umbrella but once out of the town center, heading toward the clifftop footpath, the full force of the wind had turned the umbrella inside out and ripped it to shreds in minutes.

'Damn and blast it,' Daniel had muttered, no longer apologizing if he swore in my presence now that I was married to him. 'We should have waited for the morning. I should not have listened to you.'

'What, and missed a whole day of our honeymoon?' I demanded as I struggled to take off my new hat. It was a jaunty little concoction piled high with ribbons and lace and I certainly didn't want to lose it over the cliff. I stuffed it into my carpetbag, probably not doing it much good in the process but at least preventing it from sailing off into the ocean. 'Cheer up. I'm sure it can't be far. Newport is only a small seaside town, isn't it? Just a few cottages, I was told.'

Daniel had to chuckle at this and put an arm around my shoulders. 'You wait until daylight and then you'll see the extent of the cottages.'

In my mind's eye I pictured a long road like the one leading into Westport in Ireland, with simple whitewashed cottages stretching along the side of the road facing sea. It would be nice to be spending my honeymoon in a place that reminded me of home, I had thought when Daniel told me of this opportunity.

The walk turned from an annoyance into a frightening experience. We tried to follow a dark little street called Cliff Avenue, but it ended in a pair of high, locked gates, forcing us back to our original route along the cliff – not what we would have chosen on a dark night. No lights shone out through the storm and we could hear the pounding waves crashing onto rocks below us. That cliff path seemed to go on forever and even I began to doubt the sense of wanting to reach our cottage tonight. Luckily the wind was blowing in from the ocean or I should have worried about being swept over that unseen cliff edge to our deaths.

'Are you sure this is the right way?' I shouted, grabbing on to Daniel's arm. 'Are there no roads in this place? Is this cottage not on a proper street?'

'Obviously,' Daniel said tersely. 'But it never occurred to me to ask for foul weather directions. I assumed there would be a cab if we needed one.'

I peered into the blackness. 'There are no lights. We can't be near any cottages. Surely the whole population of Newport doesn't go to bed by nine o'clock?'

'It's October. None of the cottages are likely to be inhabited at this time of year,' Daniel shouted back. 'They are only used in the summer.'

The thought of being the only people in a remote seaside village had seemed desirable when Daniel had presented it to me, our original honeymoon plans having fallen through when Daniel was summoned back to work two days after our wedding. I had borne this with remarkable patience for once, understanding that this was to be the lot of a policeman's wife. I think Daniel had been impressed by my stoicism and had promised me that we would escape from the city as soon as his work permitted. So when the offer of a seaside cottage had come up, he'd jumped at it. Of course October was a little late in the year for beaches and bathing, but we had other activities in mind anyway. And this part of the country often experienced what they called an Indian summer, with glorious sunny days and glowing fall colors. Just not this year, it appeared.

'Nearly there, I think.' Daniel propelled me forward, his arm still around my waist. 'Then a bath and a hot drink will soon bring us to rights. Ah, this way. I believe we follow this wall and it will lead us to the gate.'

As Daniel took my hand and guided me away from the cliff path, there was an ominous rumble of thunder overhead. A few moments later a flash of lightning lit up towering wrought-iron gates. Daniel felt for a latch but the gates refused to open.

'Blast and damnation!' he shouted. 'These infernal gates must open somehow.' He shook them in frustration but they refused to budge.

'They knew we were expected today, didn't they?' I asked. 'I don't see any lights.' I was soaked to the skin, my teeth chattering now, my hair plastered to my face, and my clothes clinging to me. All I wanted was to get indoors to a fire and a cup of tea.

'I don't understand it. I know the family is not usually here at this time of year, but there has to be a caretaker on the property,' Daniel snapped out the words. 'But we have no way of alerting anyone, unless we walk back into town and see if we can reach the place by telephone.'

This suggestion didn't seem too appealing. 'Everything seemed to be closed for the night in town. Besides we can't walk all the way back,' I said. 'We're already soaked to the skin. I don't suppose it's any good shouting.'

'No one would hear us with this infernal racket going on.'

Thunder growled again and once again the scene was illuminated with a lighting flash. It revealed a long driveway behind those gates and in the distance the great black shape of what seemed to be an enormous castle. I stared in amazement.

'I thought you said it was a cottage.'

'I wanted to surprise you,' Daniel replied in an annoyed voice. 'The wealthy who own summer homes in Newport call them cottages but they are actually mansions. This one is called Connemara.'

'Holy mother of God,' I muttered. 'We're not getting a whole mansion to ourselves, are we?'

'No, we've been offered the guest cottage on the property. If only we can find a way in.' He rattled the gates again angrily.

I had been experiencing a growing sense of anxiety. It wasn't just the howl of the storm and the flashes of lightning. God knows I'd seen enough storms on the west coast of Ireland. It was something more. 'Daniel, don't let's stay here,' I blurted out suddenly. 'Perhaps we should go back into town after all. There is bound to be a hotel or inn of some sort where we can spend the night. The house clearly doesn't want us.'

Daniel gave me a quizzical smile. 'The house doesn't want us?'

'I'm getting this overwhelming feeling that we shouldn't be here, that we're not wanted.'

'You and your sixth sense,' Daniel said. He was still prowling, staring up at the gates and the high stone wall. 'You'll feel differently when we're safely inside. I am determined to find a way in, even if I have to scale that wall.'

A great clap of thunder right overhead drowned out his last words and simultaneously the world was bathed in electric blue light. I was staring up at the house and I saw a face quite clearly framed in an upstairs window. It was a child's face and it was laughing with maniacal glee.

I let go of the bars of the gate as if burned. 'Come away!' I shouted. 'We shouldn't be here.'

Two

'Easy now.' Daniel grabbed me as if he sensed I was about to bolt like a spooked horse. 'I didn't think a wild Irish girl like you would be frightened of a little storm.'

'Didn't you see it?' I asked.

'I can't see a blasted thing,' Daniel said. 'It's pitch dark.'

'The face at the window. I saw a face at that window in the turret, Daniel.'

'Then at least the place is occupied,' Daniel said. 'Let's hope the person saw us and is sending down someone to unlock the gates.'

'It was a child and it was laughing. A rather alarming face, actually.'

We waited. No lights shone out. The storm raged on, the wind howling through the trees and making them dance crazily. I kept staring up at that turret, waiting to see the face again.

'I'm damned well going to scale that wall if I have to.' Daniel eyed the solid eight-foot stone speculatively.

'And what good would that do? If the gates are locked, you won't be able to let me in and I certainly can't scale a wall like that.'

'I thought lady detectives could do anything a man could do. Didn't you tell me that once?'

I was in no mood to be teased. 'I'm going back to town,' I said. 'If we stay out in this much longer we'll catch our death of cold.'

'Give me a boost up,' Daniel said, ignoring me. 'I think I could climb it right here.'

'And if you can't open the gate or get back over? You propose to spend the night on one side of the wall with me on the other?'

'Don't worry. I'll rouse someone in the main house.'

He started to climb the rough stone of the wall.

'Come on, give me a push.'

'Don't tempt me,' I snapped. He laughed. I relented and pushed. It seemed strange to have my hands on a gentleman's person, even if we were alone in the darkness. He heaved himself higher with a grunt then swung a leg over the top of the wall. A moment later he disappeared and I heard a yell.

'What happened? Are you all right?'

'Holly bush,' came the faint words. Then he appeared on the other side of the gate.

'Ah, I see!' he shouted. He bent to raise some kind of pin from the ground and miraculously the gate swung open with a loud groaning sound.

'Let's just hope they don't have watchdogs patrolling the grounds,' I said as Daniel retrieved our bags and helped me through.

'They'd have shown up by now. Besides, we are expected. They would have locked up the watchdogs.'

'Not exactly what I'd call putting out the welcome mat,' I said. 'Who exactly was it who said we could stay here? One of the servants?'

'Alderman Hannan himself,' Daniel said. 'It's his house.'

'Alderman? I didn't realize you hobnobbed with aldermen.'

'Ah. There's still a lot you don't know about me,' he replied with a hint of that typical Daniel Sullivan swagger that I had found in turn attractive and annoying.

We made our way cautiously up the gravel drive toward the dark looming shape of that castle. Not a single light was visible and I hesitated to go up the steps toward that imposing front door.

'You said we're supposed to be in the guest cottage.' I grabbed Daniel's arm and held him back. 'Shouldn't we try to locate it?'

'Amid acres of woodland?' Daniel replied and I could hear the tension rising in his voice. 'We're likely to blunder over the cliffs.'

'Then what do you propose we do?'

'This,' Daniel said. He went up the steps, lifted the knocker, and hammered insistently. We heard the sound echoing inside but there was no response.

'Now what?' I said. A thought struck me. 'Are you sure we've got the right place? It wouldn't be hard to take a wrong turning in all this darkness.'

'Yes I'm sure,' Daniel said, not actually sounding very sure. He stepped back from the door and peered up at the house. 'Yes I'm sure this is it. I've seen pictures. I'll try knocking again.'

'Someone must be with that child in the turret,' I said. 'I suppose a nursemaid could have gone to sleep by now and the child wouldn't realize that we wanted to get in.'

'We can't stand on the doorstep all night,' Daniel said irritably. 'Really, this is too bad of old Hannan.'

'Maybe he forgot to inform the servants,' I said.

Daniel started prowling around again, glancing first up at the house and then out into the blackness of the night. If anything it was raining even harder now – a solid sheet of rain bounced off the gravel of the driveway. Thunder still grumbled overhead.

'There has to be a coach house somewhere,' he said. 'A place for their automobiles.'

He disappeared into the storm and then called to me. 'Over here! There is a coach house. Let me see if . . .' I heard him rattle a door. 'The stable appears to be open. Do you mind spending the night with the horses?'

'Anything is better than this.' I ran through the curtain of rain toward him, although I don't know why I bothered to run as there was no way I could be any wetter. My skirts, now heavy and sodden, wrapped themselves around my legs as I tried to move and I almost stumbled. Daniel reached out to take my hand and then ushered me inside. There was a faint smell of horse but the stalls proved to be empty. No horses in residence. Rain drummed on the roof and thunder still growled, but farther off now.

'Ah, this will do nicely,' Daniel said. 'Clean straw. What more do you want?'

'A hot meal, a bath, and a fire would be lovely,' I muttered through chattering teeth. 'But anything is better than being out in that rain. I don't ever remember feeling so drenched.'

It was pitch dark in the stable and we felt our way forward until we came to an empty stall lined with straw.

'You better take off those wet clothes,' Daniel said. 'Let's hope some of the things in our valises have remained dry.'

My hands were freezing. I fumbled with the clasp of my valise and found what I hoped was my nightgown. It felt damp, but that might just have been my cold wet hands. I was now shivering uncontrollably and felt near to tears. I swallowed them back. There was no way I wanted to expose a weakness to my new husband. I tried to undo the ribbon that tied my cape at my chin. My fingers refused to obey me and the knot had become sodden and immovable.

'It's no use. I can't do it!' I shouted angrily.

'Do what?' Daniel asked gently.

'Take off my cape. I can't undo the knot.' I must have sounded like a small helpless child because he put his arms around me.

'It's all right,' he said. 'We're safe now. And you have a husband who is happy to undress you.' I felt his hands at my throat. 'Blasted knot,' he muttered after a struggle. 'I'll just have to break the ribbon.'

I started to protest. It was my new traveling outfit, part of my trousseau. But then I didn't want to wear it all night either. Daniel yanked and pulled and I heard fabric ripping as the sodden garment fell away from me. 'That's taken care of that,' he said, throwing it to one side. 'Turn around.' Then his hands moved from my cape to my dress, patiently undoing all the hooks. 'Thank God you don't wear a corset,' he muttered. 'I think that would be beyond me.' His hands lingered on my body. 'My God, you're cold,' he said. 'Get something dry on you quickly.'

'My nightdress is completely damp,' I said. 'I don't know what else to wear.'

I heard the click of his valise. 'Here, take my nightshirt.'

'Then what will you wear?'

'I'll be all right. I expect my underwear is dry enough.'

I heard him struggling to take off his own clothes, then he said, 'Come here,' and enveloped me in his arms.

'You're as cold as I am,' I said, feeling his half-naked body pressing against me.

'We'll soon get warm now.' He pulled me down with him into the straw. I lay against him, resting my head against his chest.

'Now this reminds me of another time,' he added. 'Do you remember?'

'Of course.' It had been long ago now. A similar storm, a lonely barn, and the first and only time I had let down my guard enough to give in to Daniel's lovemaking. A lot of water had passed under the bridge since that night. Then I wasn't sure he would ever marry me. And now I was his wife, lying in his arms quite legally. I snuggled up to him, feeling better already.

'I'm glad this isn't our actual honeymoon,' Daniel muttered. 'It would be one hell of a way to start our marriage, wouldn't it?'

'Oh, I don't know,' I whispered. 'Rather romantic, if you ask me.'

'If you don't mind this dratted straw scratching and tickling and the wind whistling through the cracks in the door.'

'I know a way to take your mind off it.' I nuzzled against him. Daniel needed no second invitation.

I awoke to a shaft of bright sunlight falling on me and to a vast figure standing over me.

'Holy Mother of God!' a voice muttered. 'What have we here? Gypsies? How in heaven's name did you get onto the property? Go on, be off with you immediately before I call the police.'

Daniel sat up, eyeing the figure blearily. 'Good morning,' he said. 'I take it that you're the housekeeper, and I also take it that you're either deaf or a sound sleeper.'

'What for the love of Mike are you blathering about?' She spoke with a thick Irish brogue, sounding almost like a vaude-ville stage Irishwoman.

I was now awake enough to notice that she was a large elderly woman dressed entirely in black, and she was standing with her hands on her hips.

'Only that we stood hammering at the front door last night and nobody let us in,' Daniel said. 'So we had to resort to sleep-ing in the barn.'

The woman removed her hands from her hips and raised them in a gesture of horror. 'Jesus, Mary, and Joseph! Don't tell me that you're Mr and Mrs Sullivan.'

'We are indeed,' Daniel said. 'So you were expecting us. And yet the gate was locked and nobody answered our knocking on the front door. A fine welcome if you don't mind my saying so.'

'God forgive me,' she said. 'I waited for you until past nine o'clock and then I didn't think you would possibly come so late and in that storm. I'd been told to expect you early afternoon, so I assumed you'd been delayed and would be arriving today. So I locked up as usual. I don't sleep on the premises while the family is not here, you see. I go back to my own little house in town. And the master is very particular about everything being locked safely for the night.'

I sat up too, aware that I probably looked somewhat immodest with my legs showing below Daniel's nightshirt. 'So you're telling us that that there was nobody in the house last night? But I saw a face at the window – a child's face.'

'A child's face?' I saw the color drain from her cheeks as she gave me a momentary look of alarm. Then she forced a smile. 'It must have been a trick of the light, my dear. There's nobody in the house. Certainly no children. But where are my manners?' She became spritely again. 'I'm Mrs McCreedy. And it's a terrible welcome to Connemara you've had. Let me take you to your quarters and I'll cook you a nice hot breakfast.'

She stepped outside discreetly while we tried to locate enough items of dry clothing to dress ourselves, then we followed her past the looming rough stone walls of the castle and down a path to a small cottage nestled among trees. What's more it looked like my definition of a cottage this time, whitewashed and thatch roofed, just as one would find in Ireland.

The trees that surrounded it were already turning gold and red so that it made a charming picture with the blue ocean beyond. I gave a little gasp of pleasure.

'Reminds you of home, does it?' the woman said. 'I know. I get quite homesick myself every time I look at it. I'm from Galway myself, and I can hear that you're from that part of Ireland too.'

'A village near Westport,' I agreed. 'And Alderman Hannan must be from the region himself if he called his home Connemara.'

'He is indeed,' the woman said. 'The family fled from Galway in the great potato famine. He came to America as a young child. Both his parents died when he was twelve years old and he's been supporting the family ever since. I wouldn't say he'd done badly for someone who came with nothing, would you?'

I turned back to look at the castle. In daylight it was not quite so foreboding, but it had been definitely built to look like an old bastion, such as one would see in the Irish countryside. The walls were of rough-hewn stone, partly covered with ivy and Virginia creeper that had turned to a delightful shade of red. The windows were arched and recessed, there were crenellated battlements along the roof and in the corner a turret rose – with a window in it. A window at which I could swear a child's face had appeared last night. All around it were perfectly manicured grounds, with stands of trees, flower beds, a tennis court, an ornamental fountain. The whole scene was framed by blue ocean beyond.

'The grounds are beautiful,' I said. 'I'm not sure it would be my choice of house.'

'Nor mine,' she said. 'I'd go for comfort myself and the way the wind whistles down those high hallways in winter makes the place impossible to heat.'

Daniel, I noticed, had not been contributing to the conversation. I suspected he did not like being caught out in such a disheveled state. His pride and dignity had been hurt and they were important to him. The housekeeper seemed to realize at the same moment that she and I had been ignoring Daniel. She turned back to him. 'So you're a friend of the alderman, are you, sir?'

'Not a friend but the alderman and I are acquainted. And when he heard that our honeymoon had been ruined, he was kind enough to offer me the use of this place.'

The woman's face broke into a smile. 'Oh, yes, he's a kind and generous man. As softhearted as they come when he wants to be, although I hear that in business he's as ruthless as a tiger.'

'Is he now?' Daniel said.

We had reached the front door of the cottage.

'And it is your honeymoon too. Fancy that,' Mrs McCreedy said. 'Well, that nasty old storm has passed now. You can set about enjoying yourselves.' She opened the front door and stood aside for us to step into the hallway. The house certainly didn't smell like a cottage from home. For one thing there was no lingering smell of peat fire, nor that combination of damp and furniture polish that one equates with old houses. This was a new house made to look old, which was confirmed when Mrs McCreedy said, 'You'll no doubt be wanting a bath. There's a lovely bathroom upstairs with the bedrooms. And plenty of hot water too.'

We needed no second urging. Half an hour later we came downstairs looking civilized to find eggs and bacon waiting for us. The horrors of the night before were forgotten.

'Well, I'll leave you to it then,' she said, wiping down her apron and giving a satisfied nod. 'The larder should be well stocked, but if you need anything I'll be up at the big house. They'll all be coming this weekend so there's plenty to be done with bedrooms to be aired out and supplies to be brought.'

'"They'll all be coming"?' I asked. 'The alderman's family, you mean?'

'The whole lot of them.' Mrs McCreedy gave us a look of complete vexation.

I looked enquiringly at Daniel. 'I thought you said the cottages were not used at this time of year.'

'Nor are they normally,' Mrs McCreedy answered for him. 'Everything is usually shut up for the winter by now, but I gather Mr Archie is taking part in some kind of boat race this weekend and the alderman has invited the whole family down. But it's not mine to reason why. He gives the orders and I carry them out. And I'd best get moving if I'm to have everything ready by the time they get here.'

'Are there no other servants?' Daniel asked. 'It's a big establishment for only one woman to run.'

She nodded agreement. 'Of course they bring their personal maids and valets, and the alderman always brings his personal chef. Very particular about his food, the alderman is.'

'I could come up and give you a hand if you like,' I suggested.

She looked horrified. 'A friend of the alderman giving me a hand? That would never do. But you've married yourself a warm and generous young lady, sir.'

'Definitely.' Daniel smiled at me. 'Always likes to keep herself busy, this one.' I took in his double meaning. We had debated for months about my abandoning my career when we married. I'd had to agree to give up my detective business – understanding, somewhat grudgingly, that it might compromise Daniel's position in the New York Police Department. But I'd also made it quite clear that I was not prepared to sit idly and devote myself to housewifely pursuits.

'We do bring in local girls to help out with the cleaning when the family is here,' Mrs McCreedy paused in the doorway. 'Do you need me to arrange for one of them to do your cooking and cleaning while you're here?'

'Oh, no. I'm sure we can manage,' I said. 'I'm used to doing my own cooking.'

'Well, let me know if you need anything. And I'd make use of the solitude now if I were you because things are going to be pretty lively come Friday.'

With that she departed, leaving us alone.

Three

I waited until the door closed behind her, then I turned to glare at Daniel.

'Did you know that a whole lot of people were going to be here with us?' I asked.

Daniel shifted uncomfortably under my questioning stare. 'No, I didn't.'

'Then why exactly did this alderman invite us here at the same time as his family? Surely it wasn't the best of times. And a man like that must have had a reason, other than the goodness of his heart.'

Daniel chuckled. 'You're too sharp for your own good. All right, I suppose there must have been a motive, other than the goodness of his heart.'

'I knew it!' I said angrily. 'I knew there was something fishy about this. Important men don't do things out of the goodness of their hearts – not unless they want something. So what does this alderman want you to do for him? You're not here to work on a case, are you?'

Daniel put his hands on my shoulders. 'Calm down, firebrand. I'm not here to work. He wanted to speak to me about something – something that was troubling him, he said. He thought he might have got it wrong.'

'Got what wrong?'

'He didn't say. He just said he valued my judgment and he'd like me to see for myself. That's all I know.'

'So you've worked with him before? You know all about his affairs?'

Daniel smiled. 'I doubt that anyone knows all about his affairs. If anyone could be said to have a finger in every pie, it would be Brian Hannan. He and his brother own a big construction company, as you probably know. They only take on important jobs now – bridges, tunnels, that kind of thing. You might have heard that they're currently building the subway under the streets of New York. And you know that he's also involved in politics – he's been a big noise at Tammany Hall for years and recently got himself elected alderman. And now he's after even bigger things, so we hear. I think he's got his eye on a state senate seat, but he doesn't want to give up his control of Tammany Hall, to make sure he has all those votes in his pocket.'

'Goodness,' I said. 'A busy man indeed.'

'Maybe he's finally bitten off more than he can chew,' Daniel said. 'He's handed over the day-to-day running of Hannan Construction to his brother. And to tell you the truth, we've had our eyes on Hannan Construction for quite a while. They sail close to the wind, but we've never managed to nab them yet.'

'What kind of sailing close to the wind?'

'Contract fixing, that kind of thing. With the help of Tammany, of course. But Tammany elections are coming up soon. Brian Hannan wants to make sure his candidate wins. But the rank and file seem to favor a guy called Murphy. So Hannan's political ambitions may have lost him his influence here. City alderman means that he's now part of the establishment. That doesn't always go down well with Tammany. Should be interesting.'

'Do you think he's invited you here to bribe you?' I asked.

'We'll just have to see, won't we?' Daniel smiled again. 'And in the meantime we'll make the most of his hospitality. Let's see if he's left us a well-stocked wine cellar.'

'Daniel!' I gave a nervous laugh. I was only just understanding the ramifications of being a New York policeman's wife. There were rules, but those rules could be successfully bent at the right time and place, so it seemed. At least I didn't have to worry about Daniel being crooked like some of his fellow officers.

We conducted a quick tour of our little guest cottage. It was simple but adequate – the downstairs consisted of a living room, dining room and kitchen, and two bedrooms upstairs with the bathroom between them. The larder was well stocked and to Daniel's satisfaction there was a barrel of beer and some bottles of wine. 'Let's go for a walk. The sun is shining,' Daniel said.

'We need to clear away the breakfast things first,' I said.

'I wonder if they have a newspaper delivered up at the big house?' Daniel looked around.

'Don't think you're going to get out of doing your share of the housekeeping while we're here, Daniel Sullivan,' I said. 'You didn't marry a drudge. Here, stack up those plates while I go and run some hot water.'

Daniel sighed but didn't protest. Half an hour later we were walking through the lovely grounds, enjoying the warm sun on our faces. The occasional downed tree limb and drifts of fallen leaves were the only signs of last night's fury. Today the air was balmy enough to allow us to walk with no overcoats and the breeze from the ocean was gentle and tinged with just enough saltiness to be delightful. I slipped my hand through Daniel's arm, still enjoying the new feeling of being a couple. Marriage wasn't so bad after all. I don't know why I had protested for so long.

Our route took us away from the big house, through a stand of

Scotch pine trees and rhododendron bushes. Suddenly we came out to find ourselves at the top of the cliff with wicked-looking rocks on the shoreline below. There was no fence or wall and Daniel grabbed my arm, dragging me back. 'Don't take another step,' he said. 'We don't know if the edge is overhanging.'

'I'm glad we didn't blunder too far last night,' I commented. 'We might have wound up on those rocks.'

We stepped back as a particularly big wave crashed onto the rocks and the sheet of white spray came up toward us. But the cliff was too high and it didn't reach us.

'Do you fancy a swim?' Daniel asked wickedly.

'I swam in wilder seas than that when I was a child,' I replied, meeting his gaze. 'But that was a long time ago now. I think I'll stick to more sedate occupations. And I'd like to take a look inside the big house while we still have the place to ourselves, wouldn't you?'

'It might be interesting to see if Hannan has acquired taste along with money,' Daniel agreed.

We completed the circle by walking past the tennis court, a croquet lawn, and then the fountain. There was even a pretty little gazebo, hidden among trees.

'This place has everything,' Daniel said. 'I wonder if Hannan has ever allowed himself enough time to enjoy it. Men like him devote their lives to making money.'

'We are definitely going to allow enough time to enjoy ourselves, aren't we?' I tugged on Daniel's arm.

'If I remain a policeman our life will certainly not be devoted to making a fortune like Brian Hannan, that's for sure,' he said. 'And I've warned you that I have to work all hours of the day and night.'

'You make it sound so appealing,' I said dryly, making him laugh. He put an arm around my shoulders and pulled me close to him. 'We will make time to enjoy ourselves. I promise.'

We came around to the front of the house and my eyes were drawn again to that corner turret. From which window had I seen the face? Was there even a window facing the main gates?

'Are you coming?' Daniel interrupted my reverie. I followed him up those imposing steps to the front door. This time it stood half-open. Daniel peered around it. 'Hello!' he called. 'Anyone home?'

Nobody appeared as we stepped inside a towering oak-paneled foyer decorated like an old castle with swords and banners hanging from walls.

'I wonder where he picked those up,' Daniel said, peering up at the walls. 'Irish castle or theater prop shop.'

'Hush, Daniel, someone will hear you,' I whispered. I shivered, wishing I had brought my wrap. The entry hall felt cold and unfriendly after the bright sunshine outside and I wondered why anyone would choose to build a house to feel old and uncomfortable.

'I wonder where that housekeeper has disappeared to,' Daniel said, pacing impatiently.

'It's a big place.' I looked around, my eyes following the broad curved staircase that led to a dark gallery. 'She's probably upstairs making beds. We should go out again and ring the doorbell to let her know we are here.'

'Nonsense,' Daniel said. 'We can look around without her. Hannan wouldn't mind. It's not as if we're going to pocket the silver.'

'I'm not sure that's the right thing to do,' I said. Since I stepped into the entry hall I had been feeling a growing sense of uneasiness. I found I was looking over my shoulder, as if unseen eyes were watching me with disapproval. But Daniel was already walking ahead of me, through an archway and into an impressive salon. This room had quite a different feel to it – spacious, light, and opulent with brocade sofas and ornate gilt tables and mirrors. We had gone from Irish stronghold to French château in a couple of steps. Daniel looked around with amusement.

'I wonder if he had this lot shipped over from Versailles,' he said, voicing my exact thoughts. 'These aren't copies, they are the real thing. And the paintings aren't shabby either. These look like genuine Italian old masters, I think.'

'That one's a Raphael, I believe,' I commented.

Daniel looked surprised and impressed. 'Now how do you know that?'

'I'm a well-educated young lady.' I gave a smug little smile. 'You don't think you married a peasant girl straight from the bogs, do you?'

My eyes were drawn to a collection of silver-framed photographs, grouped on a glass-topped table. 'I suppose these are the family,' I said. 'Look, this one is a group picture. They're a handsome bunch. Which one is the alderman? There seem to be three men who look very similar.'

'Hannan has a brother who runs the business these days, and there may well be another brother besides. Let me see.'

He came to look at the photograph over my shoulder. There was something strange about it. The top and bottom had a white border but the sides of the photograph disappeared under the silver frame, almost as if they had been cut off.

'Look at this,' I said, pointing at the sides of the picture. 'Doesn't it seem that there were more people in the picture when it was taken – look, to the left of that little boy. Isn't he holding someone's hand? And the right side has been cut off too. Why would anyone do that?'

As I held out the photograph to Daniel a voice spoke right behind us, making us spin around guiltily. 'Captain Sullivan! How on earth did you get in? I didn't hear the doorbell.'

Mrs McCreedy was standing there looking almost flustered.

'The front door was ajar,' Daniel said, replacing the photograph on the table. 'We called out and nobody came, so we thought you were probably busy elsewhere.'

'Indeed I was,' she said. 'And I've no idea how that wretched door came to be open. The master wouldn't be at all happy to hear that folks could walk right in off the street and help themselves to his things.'

'We were interested to see the house before the family arrived,' I said, not liking this insinuation. 'I assure you we weren't about to pocket anything.'

At this she became even more flustered. 'Indeed no. I wasn't insinuating anything of the sort. You're the alderman's guests and of course he'd want you to be welcome in his house. Any other time I'd be happy to show you around – it's just that right now I'm up to my eyes in work, so if you don't mind . . .'

And she tried to usher us toward the front door, like a large sheepdog.

'We can take a look around by ourselves if you're busy,' Daniel said.

'Oh, no. That wouldn't do at all,' she replied hastily. 'I'd rather everything was as it should be before you see it.'

It occurred to me that perhaps she had been lax in her cleaning while they were away and was now rushing to make up for her laziness.

'That's no problem at all,' I said. 'We have all the time in the world. We'll leave you to get on with your work now, and you can let us know when you've a minute free for a tour.'

'I will do that. Thank you kindly.' I could see the worry leaving her face.

As we crossed that gloomy entrance hall I felt a sudden cold draft on the back of my neck and that strange feeling of being watched. I couldn't help glancing up the stairs again. 'Tell me, Mrs McCreedy,' I said. 'Is this house haunted?'

'Haunted?' She laughed. 'Oh, no, ma'am. This house is much too new to be haunted. Only finished in 1890 it was. That's too young to have acquired a ghost or two, even if the master might have liked a resident ghost to add a little atmosphere to his castle. Now back in Ireland I've seen my share of haunted places and I expect you have too. We had a castle ruin near our village and the local people used to swear that they saw a white figure on the battlements. Well, one night my friends and I went there for a dare. As we got close we heard this unearthly moan and we all ran for our lives. I suspect, looking back on it, that it must have been a cow.' She paused, laughing. 'Ah, well, no time for gossiping now. I've work to be done. But come back at tea time and you can sample my freshly baked soda bread. I'll be baking a batch for the master. He's particularly fond of his soda bread, he is, and he says I'm a dab hand at baking.'

With that she almost pushed us out of the front door and shut it firmly behind us.

Four

'She was certainly in a hurry to get rid of us, wasn't she?' Daniel looked back at the house.

'I rather suspect she had been slacking on her chores and now has found herself with too much to do,' I said.

'She could always bring in local girls to help her,' Daniel dismissed this. 'What was all that about the house being haunted?'

'I was thinking of that face I saw last night,' I said. 'I know what I saw, Daniel. I didn't imagine it. And I felt something today. Standing in that hallway. It was almost as if a presence was watching me.'

'Are you always going to be this fey?' Daniel asked. 'I saw no faces last night and felt nothing evil today. The only mysterious thing was where that dratted woman came from. She certainly didn't come from the hallway and I didn't notice a door behind us, did you? Perhaps she is your ghost herself and she can appear and vanish at will.' He looked at my worried face and chuckled. 'Come on, let's go and explore Newport while the sun is shining.'

And so off we went. I could hear the click of shears and noticed a gardener at work on the rose bushes, and the big iron gates slid open easily. First we turned away from town and followed the street to our left. One lovely estate followed the next, each one grander than the one before. Through tall gates we glimpsed marble palaces and stately homes that made the Hartleys' manor house that I had always looked up to as the height of elegance look small and ordinary. One of these so-called 'cottages' stood on the cliffs like a very posh hotel, one had a marble portico with columns like a Roman temple. I was overawed into silence as we glimpsed one after another. In fact I had never seen anything so grand in my life.

'And these are just summer homes?' I demanded. 'Look at them. You'd expect to find a king living in each of them, wouldn't you?'

'Well, they are owned by Vanderbilts and Astors, which is almost the same thing here in America,' Daniel replied. 'They don't need to count their pennies.'

'But to build such places for just a few weeks in the summer, it seems criminal, doesn't it?'

'They do a lot of entertaining,' Daniel said, 'although I understand that most of them are built with few bedrooms. They expect their guests to own their own cottages.' He smiled.

'I wonder what the Vanderbilts and Astors think about having Alderman Hannan as a neighbor.' I paused to stare through ornate gilded gates. 'He's not exactly one of the Four Hundred, is he?'

'No, I don't suppose he gets invited to dinner very often,' Daniel said. 'But I expect they snubbed him in a very polite and well-bred manner. That may be one of his reasons for wanting to get into politics. Becoming an alderman certainly helps. If he becomes their senator he'll find a lot of doors open to him. Everyone will want to be his friend then.'

The road petered out at the end of a point. We stood for a while looking out at the ocean. There were yachts sailing in the stiff breeze, and a ferry crossing the Bay. Suddenly I found that I was enjoying myself enormously. Several days with nothing to do except making the most of sea and sun and fresh air was not something I'd experienced in my life before, although I knew that the wealthy went away for holidays all the time. I was beginning to see that being married to Daniel might have its benefits!

'We should go on a boat trip,' Daniel said, again as if reading my thoughts. 'Do you feel up to walking into town and seeing what we can find there?'

'I'm no little delicate flower.' I looked up at him, smiling. 'I walk miles every day when I'm following someone in the pursuit of my profession.'

'*Walked*,' Daniel said. 'Past tense, remember. Now you will have no need to wear out your shoe leather, and you can take a pleasant stroll around Washington Square instead.'

'Before I go back to my embroidery?'

My giving up my profession as a detective had been a bone of contention between us for a long time. I had finally come to realize that Daniel not only worried about my safety, but also that it could compromise his own position with the police force. Since he was to be the breadwinner, I had agreed that I would take no more cases. As yet I hadn't had time to see how I would handle boredom and domesticity. We'd just have to see.

We turned and followed the street back into town, moving from the fantasy world out on the point back to reality. Soon mansions gave way to ordinary older homes, of a more colonial appearance, then to a little seaside town of plain clapboard houses with views beyond of a harbor and fishing boats.

Daniel looked up at the street sign and grunted. 'We could have followed this Bellevue Avenue all the way from town last night and saved ourselves an adventure on the cliffs.'

'We'd have ended up just as wet I suspect,' I said. 'Anyway it was an adventure and no harm done.'

'I'm not so sure about that,' Daniel said. 'My throat feels

scratchy. I think I may have caught a chill from that wetting last night.'

'Typical man,' I said scornfully. 'I'm feeling hale and hearty myself. Ready for a good lunch at one of these little cafés maybe.'

'I wouldn't say no to some lunch,' Daniel agreed. 'They do say feed a cold, don't they?'

I grinned and walked on ahead. We chose a place on the waterfront that advertised locally caught lobster, but my enthusiasm waned when I found I had to choose my lobster from those swimming around in a tank on the waterfront.

'It seems rather brutal to select my food alive and have it killed in front of me.' I stared down at them, feeling pity.

'Most of the food that you eat was alive at some stage,' Daniel pointed out. 'Did you not catch crabs and mussels when you were a child?'

'I suppose that I did,' I agreed.

'Well then. Go ahead and select yourself a nice meaty lobster. Or do you want me to do it for you?'

'You do it. I'd rather not look.'

'And this is the woman who has taken on murderers single-handedly.' Daniel chuckled.

I stared down the quayside, watching the fishermen unloading their catch while Daniel made the selection and not long after the lobsters appeared on a plate with crusty bread and a knob of corn beside them. And I have to confess that after the first mouthful I was tearing mine apart with no conscience whatsoever.

After lunch we resumed our walk around town. There were pretty old churches and fine brick colonial buildings. Altogether a charming place and one that made me a little homesick for Ireland, since it felt so old and peaceful.

'This place is really old,' I said, staring up at a house that bore the date 1631. 'Even in Ireland that would count as old. I doubt we've many buildings of that vintage in Westport.'

'Rhode Island was one of the earliest settlements,' Daniel said. 'I find the simple styles of these old houses rather attractive myself. I never was one for extravagance.'

'Which is why you chose a nice simple Irish girl,' I said.

'I don't know about that.' He laughed.

'Let's go down this street.' I attempted to steer him. 'It has a row of quaint little shops.'

'Women and their shops,' Daniel muttered. 'Can they go nowhere and just admire the architecture? Must any outing include shopping?'

'But of course,' I said, pausing outside a leaded glass window crammed full of souvenirs – china lighthouses, wooden fishing boats, and of course saltwater taffy. Because of Daniel's remark I contented myself with looking on this occasion, then moved on to the next shop window. One of the old cottages had been turned into an art gallery and as I peered in through the window a painting on the rear wall caught my attention.

Daniel was already walking on ahead of me, having tired of my gazing in shop windows.

'Wait, Daniel! We have to go in here.' A bell rang as I pushed open the front door then stood staring at the painting. It depicted a lovely little girl with a mass of blonde curls seated amid flowers, holding a lamb in her lap. She was smiling as if she was sharing a huge joke with someone we couldn't see, standing off to her right.

'What is it?' Daniel came in behind me. 'We're not about to buy paintings.'

A man appeared from a backroom. He was dressed in a blue fishermen's sweater with smudges of paint on it. 'Can I help you?' he asked.

'That painting.' I pointed at it. 'Do you know the name of the child in that painting?'

'I didn't paint it myself,' he said. 'It's one of Ned Turnbull's. He has a cottage down by the harbor, if he is not out somewhere painting.' He turned to examine the picture. It was small and dainty compared with its neighbors depicting seascapes and storms. 'Pretty little thing, isn't it? Just right for a lady's boudoir wall. I wonder if Ned used a local child as a model or just created the whole thing from his imagination.' He leaned closer. 'Oh, wait. He's written it here – Miss Colleen Van Horn, May 1895.'

'Thank you.' I turned to go.

'Are you interested in the painting? I could hold it for you,' he called after me.

I shook my head and managed to stammer out a thank you as I stepped out into the sunshine.

'What was that all about?' Daniel asked, noting the expression on my face.

'That child in the painting – there was something about her face. I know I've seen her before.'

'Are you suddenly turning fey on me?' Daniel asked with amusement. 'Seeing ghosts and children's faces everywhere we go?'

I grabbed his arm. 'That's it. That's why it looked familiar, Daniel. I think it was the same face that I saw in that turret window.'

Daniel sighed. 'You've already been told that there was nobody in the house that night.'

I shrugged. 'If it was a ghost that I saw, it couldn't have been this child. Van Horn obviously belongs in another of the mansions, not an Irishman's castle.'

'Van Horn.' Daniel repeated the name. 'I've come across that name somewhere. It will come back to me. So have we taken enough exercise for one day? I'm ready to head back to our little cottage.'

'Very well.' We set off in that direction. I was still looking around with interest, wanting to examine every church and monument we passed. Daniel had grown silent and unenthusiastic and I was about to allow myself to be led home when I spotted something.

'Daniel, that old churchyard. We have to take a look at that before we go home. I find old cemeteries fascinating, don't you?'

'On occasion,' he said. We pushed open the rusty gate and wandered between moss-covered stones. I read off dates and names, commenting on each one. 'Look, Daniel, this man had three wives and they are all buried with him. And this woman had fourteen children. Fourteen – imagine!'

'I seem to remember reading that this was one of the places where they used to put bells above the graves,' Daniel said, now showing interest. 'You don't suppose there are still any to be found?' He started poking around in deep grass.

'Bells – what for?'

'If the person wasn't really dead and had been buried by mistake he could tug on the string and the bell would alert people that he wanted to come out.'

'Don't.' I shivered. 'That's horrible. Buried alive by mistake. Surely that didn't happen?'

'In the old days they couldn't tell the difference between a coma and death. Maybe sometimes they didn't want to.'

'Let's go. I've seen enough.' I took his arm to lead him away. Then my eyes were drawn to a lovely marble monument in the classical style with an angel standing guard and cupids frolicking. I read the inscription and stood staring silently: COLLEEN MARY VAN HORN. BORN FEBRUARY 12 1891. TAKEN FROM US JUNE 15 1895.

'Look, Daniel, how sad,' I said. 'It's the little girl in the painting. She died a month after it was completed.'

Then I read the rest of the words carved into the white marble. OUR LITTLE ANGEL HAS BEEN TAKEN FROM US. BELOVED DAUGHTER OF ARCHIE AND IRENE VAN HORN. BELOVED GRANDCHILD OF BRIAN HANNAN, AND FREDERICK AND MARIE VAN HORN.

'I was right, Daniel,' I said in a shaky voice. 'It was her face I saw at the window. There is a ghost at Connemara.'

Five

We walked back to the cottage in silence. I couldn't stop thinking of that adorable little girl, dead at the age of four. I suppose that now I was married the next logical step was children of our own and I tried to imagine how it would feel to lose a beloved child so young. Of course it happened all the time. So many childhood diseases, so many dangers in life. Daniel sensed my thoughts. 'It's not as if we knew her. Children die all the time. It's a fact of life. One has to accept it.'

'I could never accept losing my own child.' I went to say more but swallowed back the words. Actually I had lost my own child, an early miscarriage that Daniel had never known about. I had no hope of marrying him at the time, in fact he had been in prison when I found out, and even though it had never been a baby I had held in my arms, I still thought about it and mourned it in my way. I had wanted to tell Daniel about it but there had never been a suitable moment. Now it hung between us as a secret and I wondered if I would ever tell him.

'Cheer up.' Daniel opened the gate for me. 'We've just time for a rest before we have tea and soda bread to look forward to.' He put his hand up to his throat, rubbing it as he spoke.

'Your throat is bothering you?'

'Yes, it hurts like the devil. Let's hope I haven't caught a

33

chill from last night. But I'm sure a cup of tea will make it feel better.'

We reached the front gates and I stood staring up at the big house. Daniel went to walk ahead then saw me standing there.

'Come on. What are you doing?' he called.

'I'm wondering if the face I saw was the little girl's ghost,' I said.

'There is no such thing as ghosts.'

'I can tell you never lived in Ireland. Everyone you ask would tell you of at least one encounter with a ghost.'

'Which would then turn out to be a mooing cow, like the one Mrs McCreedy told us about.' Daniel went ahead of me up the flagstone path to our cottage.

I hurried to catch up with him. 'But how then do you explain that I saw a face at a window of an empty house and that the face I saw was that of a child who died eight years ago?'

Daniel shrugged. 'I'm sure there is a logical explanation.'

'For example?'

'I can't think of one right now,' he said shortly. 'I'm going to put my feet up and read the newspaper until tea.'

He opened the front door, holding it open for me to pass through. Then he went straight into the little drawing room, selected an armchair for himself and opened the newspaper he had bought. I was going to sit at the writing desk and write to Gus and Sid, my neighbors and dearest friends who had made me promise that I would write to them every day. But the sun was streaming in through the cottage window and I couldn't bear to stay indoors on such a lovely day. I found pen, ink, and paper in a pretty little lap desk, then I carried it outside. The grass was still wet from last night's storm but I found a garden chair that had been dried by the sun and dragged it to sit on the grass in the shade of a big beech tree. Its leaves had already turned to gold and many had fallen in last night's storm. I sat in the midst of a golden carpet and began my letter to my friends.

You cannot imagine the beauty of the scene that I am now admiring, I wrote. *I am sitting in the midst of a carpet of golden leaves while beyond me stretch perfectly manicured lawns that end with the blue ocean. However, our arrival last night was not quite so serene.* I proceeded to describe our harrowing walk along the cliffs. *You have never seen two more veritable orphans of the storm,* I wrote. *When we reached the 'cottage' which turned out to be a large stone mansion built like a great castle, the full fury of a thunderstorm broke forth over our heads. I looked up at a window and* . . . I was going to say that I saw a face but I couldn't bring myself to do so. They were both such educated worldly women. I could imagine them smiling to each other about dear Molly's Irish fantasies. So I left it out and went on, *and we had to follow up our ordeal with a night spent in a stable, snuggled down in the straw, which proved to be surprisingly warm. But we must have looked complete frights when the housekeeper came upon us in the morning. I suspect she thought we were a pair of tramps.*

I went on to describe the town and the mansions before I remembered that such things were old hat to them. This kind of life was not unusual to them. Gus was really Augusta Walcott of the Boston Walcotts. In fact they had stayed with Gus's cousin in one of those mansions, although Gus had described it to me as a cottage.

I sealed the letter and was going to take it inside ready for posting. But the sun had moved and its warm setting rays now shone in my face. I leaned back and closed my eyes. I could hear the sound of the waves and smell the last of the honeysuckle and freshly mown grass. I heaved a sigh of contentment and must have drifted off to sleep, because I dreamed that I heard a child's voice singing sweetly in a language that made no sense to me and a girl in a white dress stood looking down at me. I opened my eyes to find myself alone. As I brushed my hair from my face I recoiled in horror as my hand touched something. I brushed it away and jumped up as the thing fell into my lap. I thought it to be a bug of some sort, only to find that the things that had fallen from my hair were a perfect yellow leaf and a honeysuckle blossom.

I stood there with my heart beating rather fast, scanning the lawns. But nothing moved and I was forced to admit that my dream and the honeysuckle had nothing in common. Leaves fell at this time of year and the honeysuckle had been deposited in my hair by a gust of wind. I collected my things and went in search of Daniel. He had indeed fallen asleep in an armchair by the window, the newspaper unread on his lap. I stood looking down at him with affection. 'Mrs Daniel Sullivan,' I said to myself, then I tapped him gently on the shoulder.

'Time for tea,' I said.

This time Mrs McCreedy greeted us warmly. 'I hope you don't mind eating in the kitchen,' she said, 'but it seemed rather silly to bring a tray all the way to the drawing room just for the three of us and the kitchen has a delightful view.'

So we followed her in the opposite direction from our last visit, down a long hallway and then through a traditional baize door that led to the servants' quarters. The kitchen was a big light room with sparkling copper pans hanging over the stove and a large table in its center. There was a blue-and-white checked tablecloth on the table and a tray containing a simple blue-and-white tea service. Clearly she had decided that we were not fancy enough folks to warrant the good china. The whole place smelled delightfully of fresh baking.

'Sit yourselves down facing the window, so that you can enjoy the view,' she said.

'You're right, it is lovely.' I took a seat, looking out over lawns to the ocean beyond. There was a sailing ship with red sails passing and a large steamer in the distance, heading out to sea.

'I'll just cut the soda bread,' Mrs McCreedy said and put it on the table. 'There's plenty of butter and homemade jam so help yourselves.'

'You have been busy,' I said.

'I certainly have. Eight bedrooms and a nursery to get ready, as well as all this,' she sounded proud but indignant.

'Eight bedrooms?' I said. 'All those people are coming?'

'I've no idea how many of them will turn up. Nobody bothers to tell me. I was told the family would be coming so I was to get the house ready. And eight good bedrooms there are, so eight beds I've made. And all alone without a scrap of help too.'

'I thought you said that you brought in local women to help.'

'In the summer I do, but one is having a baby and another has her aged mother to nurse, and we were all caught off guard, weren't we?'

'So a visit from the family is unexpected at this time of year?' I asked. I was still curious about exactly why Alderman Hannan had wanted Daniel to be at his summer home to coincide with his family. The timing couldn't be accidental. If I was looking forward to a pleasant stay at the seaside with my family, the last thing I'd want was strangers on the premises. I looked up at Mrs McCreedy, realizing that she was thinking along the same lines.

'It certainly is. They never come here after Labor Day as a rule. You could have knocked me down with a feather when the master wrote out of the blue and told me that the whole family was coming.'

'Is it some kind of anniversary then? Some kind of celebration?'

'Not that I know of.' She frowned. 'There's no family birthday in October. The master said something about Mr Archie

37

wanting to compete in a yacht race but the rest of them wouldn't want to make the journey just to watch that, would they? It's not as if they all live in New York either. Mr Patrick has to come all the way from the Hudson Valley. That's quite a trip for a couple of days by the sea.'

'Mr Patrick, is he one of the brothers?' Daniel joined in the conversation, making me realize that he had kept quiet until now. 'I don't think I know about him. He's not involved in the company?'

'Oh, no, sir.' She rolled her *r*s in that very Irish way. 'Mr Patrick's a holy priest. He used to have a big parish in Albany but it was too much for his health and now he has a small country parish up on the Hudson somewhere. He never was as robust as Mr Joseph and the master, so I understand.'

She poured cups of strong tea as she spoke and handed them to us, then passed around a plate of sliced bread. It was still warm and dotted liberally with currants. For a while there was silence.

'So which family members do you expect?' I asked. Daniel shot me a warning look as if I was being too nosy, but I suspected that Mrs McCreedy liked to gossip and was starved for company.

'Well, let's see,' she began easily enough, 'the master and Mr Joseph, that's for sure.'

'And their wives?'

'Mr Joseph's wife rarely comes with him,' she said slowly. 'Doesn't like the ocean. And the master's a widower. Been without a wife ever since I've known him. In fact he's raised his one child alone since she was small. That's probably why he doted on her so much and spoiled her if you ask me.'

'And who is she?'

'Miss Irene. She was a rare beauty in her time, and she's married well too. Mr Archie comes from one of the best fam-il-ies in New York. She's done well for herself.'

I remembered the names on that monument. 'Do they have any children?' I asked cautiously.

'Two little boys. Master Thomas and Master Alexander. Grand little fellows but full of mischief. Their nursemaid has her hands full with them, especially in a place like this.' She broke off, staring out of the window.

I decided to take the bull by the horns. 'Tell me about Colleen,' I said.

She dropped the spoon she had been holding as if it had burned her. 'Wherever did you hear about her? Who has been talking?'

'Nobody. We were exploring the town and I saw her grave in the cemetery. It named her parents and her grandfather. And I saw a portrait of her in a gallery in town.'

'A portrait of her?' She was still looking stunned.

'Sitting in a field of flowers, holding a lamb. I was drawn to it because she was such a pretty child. So I was quite shocked when I saw her grave in the cemetery and saw that she'd died only a month after the portrait was painted.'

'The master gave that picture back to the artist after her death,' she said angrily. 'He wouldn't be pleased to hear that the man was trying to sell it again. He'd already been paid for it once. But the master wanted no trace of her around the house. It was just too painful for him to look at her likeness.'

'What happened to her? Did she die of a childhood illness?'

'Oh, no, ma'am. She was found lying on the rocks at the bottom of the cliff. God rest her little soul.'

Involuntarily my hand went to my forehead to make the sign of the cross with her.

'How tragic,' I said.

Mrs McCreedy nodded. 'Such a lovely little thing she was too – a beautiful child with a beautiful nature too. Everyone adored her. When she died the light went out of our lives, especially the master's.' She lifted the corner of her apron and wiped

39

quickly at her eye. 'But let's not mention her name again. We are all forbidden to speak of her anymore. Now, were you still wanting your tour of the house?'

'I'm sure we don't want to inconvenience you when you are so busy,' Daniel said, giving me a nudge with his knee under the table.

'We could take a look at the main rooms by ourselves, now that you've got them all ready, couldn't we?' I added. 'I'm sure you deserve a rest.'

'No rest for the wicked, isn't that what they say?' She got to her feet and brushed crumbs from her apron. 'I'll take you around.'

'You should not have insisted upon this,' Daniel hissed in my ear. 'The poor woman has enough to do.'

'Daniel, I have to take a look at that tower,' I whispered back.

Daniel rolled his eyes. 'You think the ghost will be waiting to greet you, do you?'

'Come along then. Let's start in the dining room through here,' Mrs McCreedy called to us, already on her way through the door. We followed her into a room dominated by a long polished table over which hung two impressive candelabras.

'Why, this is long enough to feed the five thousand,' I blurted out, obviously demonstrating to her that I was not used to such rooms.

'The table came from the refectory of a monastery in France,' she said. 'The master had it shipped over. And the candelabras were from the chapel of a convent in Spain. I'm not sure that I like the idea myself – looting holy places, even though I'm sure he paid a fair price for them – but it's not my place to comment. I just dust and polish. But you have to admit that they raise the tone of the place.'

'They certainly do,' I said. 'It must be a sight with the candles all burning.'

'Maybe the alderman will invite you to dinner when they are all here and then you can see for yourselves,' she said. She led us through to a morning room overlooking the lawns, a writing room, a music room with grand piano and harp, a library full of old books the alderman had had shipped from a stately home in England, the salon we had seen before, and even a ballroom with great crystal chandeliers dotting the ceiling and French windows along one side, facing the ornamental garden and fountain. Every room was finely furnished, with heavy brocade drapes, impressive paintings on the walls, vases, statues, and every kind of objet d'art in niches and on tables, so that the effect was like walking through a museum.

'Alderman Hannan certainly has a lot of lovely things,' I said.

'He certainly does. They are his pride and joy. He never forgets that he came from nothing, you see. The family was near to starvation all the time he was growing up, so he needs to remind himself that he can afford anything he wants.' She paused, adjusting a drape that wasn't hanging properly. 'But it's more than that. He needs to be surrounded by beauty. He's a perfectionist at heart. Everything has to be just so. He insists that the family dress properly when they are here – formal wear for dinner every night, you know.'

She nodded, emphasizing the point. 'And woe betide any family member who doesn't measure up to the alderman's standards.'

As we went up that curved stone staircase I felt the same shudder of apprehension as I had experienced that morning. Whatever she said, there was definitely some force or malevolent spirit in this house that didn't want me here. We did a perfunctory tour of bedrooms, all of them with splendid views across the bay, then Mrs McCreedy started toward the stairs again.

'And up on the next floor?' I asked.

'Only servants' rooms, box rooms. The family doesn't go up there,' she said.

'What about that old turret? How do you get to that? I should think there is a wonderful view of the town from up there.'

Daniel shot me another warning look.

'I daresay there is, but nobody goes up there. The rooms were never finished. The master only added it for a kind of folly, you know. If anyone had a mind to climb up there, they'd have to climb a ladder through a hole in the floor because there's no proper stair. The master's nephews used to do it when they were boys but nobody's been up there for years now – and I'm certainly not dusting and sweeping up there! You wouldn't catch me up a ladder.' She chuckled wheezily and started toward the stairs again. I loitered behind her, trying to locate the position of the tower, still horribly curious and wanting to decide if I felt anything as we walked down the long hallway toward the front of the house.

I didn't and we came out to the gallery that ran around the staircase – I noticed a door in the front right corner and wondered if it led to the tower. I stood looking up.

'Mrs Sullivan?' Mrs McCreedy called to me as she started down the stairs. I jumped guiltily and hurried to catch up with her. Her gaze went to the direction I had been staring. A look of horror spread across her face.

'Wait a minute. You said you saw a face at a turret window – it was Miss Colleen's face, wasn't it?'

'Yes, it was,' I said.

'She thought she saw,' Daniel corrected. 'My wife has a vivid imagination.'

'No, I believe her,' Mrs McCreedy said. 'I can tell that she has the sixth sense. It was not so unusual at home in Ireland. And I have to confess that I've felt her presence myself in the house. For some reason her poor little soul can't find rest.'

Six

'You see,' I said triumphantly as soon as Daniel and I had left the house and were walking back to our cottage. 'I knew it. I was right. Mrs McCreedy feels her presence too, poor little thing.'

'In that case I'm keeping you well away from that house,' he said. 'I'm here to enjoy myself and so are you, not to worry about dead children or to keep an eye out for ghosts.'

We went back to the cottage and I set about preparing an evening meal. Daniel slumped in an armchair and opened the newspaper again.

'You're certainly a scintillating companion tonight,' I said dryly as I laid the table.

'I'm sorry. I'm just not feeling up to par,' he said. 'First it was a sore throat and now I'm feeling achy all over. I knew I was coming down with something.'

I felt his forehead and it was slightly warm, so after dinner I made him some hot milk and packed him off to bed. When I had cleared away supper and turned in myself he was fast asleep. Hardly the honeymoon I had imagined. I snuggled closer to him and his arm came around me.

'That's nice,' he murmured.

I was just drifting off to sleep, listening to the smack and hiss of the waves on the rocky shoreline, when I heard the sound of a door opening. Instantly I was awake and alert. We had not locked the front door, feeling ourselves to be safe on an estate with a high wall around it.

'Daniel,' I whispered, 'I think someone's trying to get into the house.'

Daniel still lay in blissful slumber. I wondered if I had imagined the sound until to my horror I heard voices – a man's voice and then a light female laugh. I sat up, not knowing what to do next. Surely burglars did not chat and laugh as they went about their business? I fished around in the darkness for my robe, but before I had time to act I heard heavy feet coming up the stairs. The bedroom door was flung open and the electric light was turned on. A large man stood in the doorway. He was gray haired and middle aged, big boned rather than fat, but with the unmistakable round red face and shock of hair of a typical Irishman. I was also aware of someone standing in the shadows behind him. That much I took in as I sat blinking in the bright light, clutching the bedclothes to me to preserve something of my modesty.

'What the deuce?' The man looked as startled as I did. 'What is going on here?'

Daniel had stirred and grunted in his sleep at the bright light in his face. Now he sat up suddenly at the sound of a strange voice. 'What's all this?' he demanded.

My first thought was that the man was Alderman Hannan in person, but that notion was dispelled when he roared, 'Who the devil are you?'

'I could ask you the same thing, sir.' Daniel was now wide awake and in fighting spirit. 'Or do you make a point of bursting into people's bedrooms in the middle of the night?'

'As to that, I am Joseph Hannan, and you are trespassing on my family's property. Thought the place would be empty for the winter and you'd have a nice quiet spot to entertain your fancy girl, did you, my boy?'

Daniel got out of bed and took a step toward Joseph Hannan. He was several inches taller and stood face-to-face with the man. 'In the first place she's my wife and not my "fancy girl," as you so crudely put it,' he said. 'In the second my name is Daniel Sullivan and I am here as a guest of Alderman Brian Hannan, whom I was expecting to see tomorrow.'

'My brother didn't let me know that there would be any outsiders present,' Joseph said, sounding a trifle defensive now.

'Ask him yourself if you doubt my credibility,' Daniel said. 'But I can assure you that, if I wanted a few days away with my wife, the last thing I'd consider doing is sneaking into someone else's house when I can afford to pay for a perfectly good hotel.'

'Then may I ask why my brother invited you to come here at the same time as the family? You're not some relative I don't know about, are you? Some lost kin from Ireland he's tracked down? He never invites outsiders.'

'He was doing me a good turn. I was at a meeting with him the other day and he heard that I'd had to abandon my honeymoon after only a couple of days due to urgent business in New York. So he most kindly offered me the use of his guest cottage.'

'But surely not at a time when the family was coming?'

'I think he assumed that the family would stay at the main house,' Daniel said.

Joseph scowled. 'Damned inconsiderate of him. He knows I often choose to get away from the others and have the guest cottage to myself.'

I thought I witnessed the shadow in the background start to tiptoe back down the stairs. And I remembered Mrs McCreedy saying that Joseph Hannan rarely brought his wife with him. *He's got a lady friend in tow*, I thought with a smile. That's why he's come up early and wants the privacy of the guest cottage.

Joseph Hannan noticed my expression and annoyance flushed across his face.

'The family wasn't expected until tomorrow,' Daniel said. 'At least that is what Mrs McCreedy told us.'

'Then my brother is not here yet? I was hoping for a word with him before the hordes descend. It's downright impossible to talk to the man in New York, now he's rushing all over the place with his political aspirations, leaving me to run the business alone.'

He stood scowling at us.

'There must be more to this. My brother is not noted for his generosity to outsiders. Something to do with Tammany Hall, maybe. He wants to make sure he can sway the election his way.' He studied Daniel's face. 'Am I close to the mark? You've influence at Tammany and he wants you to get him votes?'

Daniel said nothing so Joseph Hannan went on. 'That would be more like Brian than a simple act of kindness to a newly married couple.'

'Why don't you ask him yourself?' Daniel said.

'I will, as soon as he damn well gets here,' Joseph said. 'You can bet your boots I will. He's not the only Hannan brother, you know. Damned dictator – summoning us all here, as if we were his lackeys. And it's bad enough having the whole family present without a horde of outsiders.' He paused, looking from Daniel to me.

'So I suppose I'll have to rethink my plans for tonight,' he said as neither of us showed any inclination to move.

'I gather there are two bedrooms,' Daniel said. 'You're more than welcome to the other one.'

Joseph Hannan took a belligerent step forward then thought better of it. 'Downright inconvenient,' he said. 'I don't like having my plans upset. It's too bad of my brother. Never bothers to consult the rest of the family about a damned thing.'

Daniel just stood there, arms folded.

'Mrs McCreedy has all the beds made up and ready in the main house,' Daniel said. 'I don't know whether she'll be sleeping there tonight, but as you're a family member, I'm sure you'll have a key. Now if you don't mind, my wife and I would like to go back to sleep.'

Joseph Hannan snorted, then turned on his heels and stomped down the stairs. I picked up a hint of whispered conversation and then the front door slammed.

'The arrogance of the man,' Daniel said. 'I really think he expected us to slink out and leave the place to him.'

'He had a lady with him,' I said. 'I heard her voice while you were asleep.'

'Ah, so that explains why he didn't want to be with the rest in the main house. I don't suppose Brian would have welcomed Joseph's mistress with open arms, not if he'd a wife he left at home.'

He climbed back into bed. 'This is almost becoming farcical,' he said. 'Are we never to have a peaceful night's sleep as man and wife?'

'Daniel,' I said as he turned out the light and climbed back into bed, 'why didn't you tell him that you were a police officer?'

'I decided that now was not the right moment,' Daniel said. 'More interesting to listen to what the man had to say when he didn't know I was with the police. Ah, well, let's get some rest. I hope to sleep off this damned chill or grippe or whatever it is. I'd like to be at my best when they all arrive.'

With that he pulled the covers over his face and promptly fell into a deep sleep. I lay awake, still disturbed by the nocturnal visit and by the events of the day. I listened to the crashing of waves onto the shore and my thoughts turned to that poor little girl. I pictured her body lying on those rocks and I snuggled up closer to Daniel. There were so many dangers in life and no way to prevent them. I was now married to a policeman. Danger was to be part of our lives. When I had been living alone and running my detective business I had found myself in danger several times. To begin with it hadn't worried me but lately it had preyed on my mind. I suppose that, now that I had Daniel, I didn't want to lose him.

Seven

Eventually I fell asleep but my dreams were troubled. A little girl dancing on the lawn with a lamb until a great shadow loomed over her and a voice said, 'Now the light has gone out of our lives.'

By morning the sadness melted away and I awoke quite cheerfully to another day of brilliant sunlight. Daniel awoke not quite so cheerfully, acting like most men with a cold – in a thoroughly bad temper. I tried to remind myself of my recent vows of in sickness and in health, made him hot tea and a boiled egg and tucked a rug around his shoulders.

'What would really help is a mustard plaster,' he said. 'And something to steam. That's what my mother always did for a cold. Friar's Balsam, I believe.'

'And what did you do for a cold when you were not with your mother?' I asked, trying to keep my expression sweet and caring.

'Nothing. I never had time to be ill so I just kept on going.'

'Would you like me to walk into town and see if I can find a chemist who stocks the things you want?' I asked.

'That would be wonderful.' He reached out his hand and took mine, looking up at me with gratitude, making me glad that I had acted like a dutiful wife.

I left him with a rug over his knees, sitting in the sunshine, while I put on my cape and hat and went into town. The gardener was working near the gate and he dropped his tools and ran ahead to open it for me. 'You're walking, are you, miss?' he asked. 'You don't need anyone to summon you a carriage or a cab? I'm afraid we've no coachman or chauffeur here until the master arrives.'

'I'm happy to walk. I'm enjoying the fresh air and sunshine, thank you,' I said. 'It's a treat after living in New York City.'

'Are you a relative over from Ireland?' he asked.

'No, not a relative. My husband knows the alderman. I've never met him.'

'I understand he's coming later today, or tomorrow, so you'll have your chance.'

'What's he like?'

'Not my place to say, ma'am. He's a tough man to work for. Likes his orders carried out instantly and to the letter, but he pays well. Nothing stingy about him. And he's very good to his family, so we hear. Supports the lot of them.'

'Does he?'

'Oh, yes. Mr Joseph is the only one of them who does an honest day's work from what I can tell.' He looked around as he held open the gate. 'But I shouldn't be talking like this. And I've work to do. There will be hell to pay if there's a single dandelion left in this lawn.'

With that he ushered me through the gate and shut it hurriedly behind me.

On the opposite side of the street was an ordinary brick colonial house, and as I looked at it, I noticed a lace curtain twitch back into place as if someone had been watching me. I set off at a brisk pace into town, found a chemist, and came back laden with a chest rub – Friar's Balsam – a tonic guaranteed to put people back on their feet instantly, and some grapes to make

Daniel feel better. I found him reading and he seemed to have perked up quite nicely, eating a good healthy amount at lunch.

But he still declined to come with me down to the seashore in the afternoon. 'I think I'll take a nap after I've inhaled some steam,' he said. 'If you could just boil me some water and find me a towel to put over my head.'

I did as he asked, leaving him swathed like a fortune-teller.

'Don't take any risks or climb over rocks, do you hear?' he called from under the towel. 'I don't want to find your body lying there where you've slipped and hit your head.'

'No, Daniel,' I said with mock meekness, making him laugh. I laughed too then. 'Do you realize that I went out almost every day over the rocks to gather seaweed when I was a child.'

His face appeared from the towel. 'Yes, but I suspect you were not wearing fashionable shoes and a tight skirt in those days,' he said.

'You're right about that. I was mostly barefoot. But don't worry, I'll be careful. I've no wish to slip and ruin my new clothes.'

So off I went. I looked toward the big house before I crossed the lawns, feeling something of an interloper. Wouldn't the rest of the family give us the same hostile reception as Joseph Hannan when they arrived? I kept going until I came out of a group of rhododendron bushes to see the ocean below me. At this point the ground fell a sheer forty or fifty feet to rocks below. I looked for a way down but couldn't find one. Further around the point the cliff turned into a tumble of rocks where there had been a landslide at some stage, but I wasn't about to attempt that either in my good clothes. So I started along the cliff path, back in the direction of the town. As the path turned a corner I was rewarded with a flight of narrow steps going down the cliff, leading to a little patch of beach. I went down and found a flat rock to sit on. After looking around to make sure nobody was watching I removed my shoes and stockings, then hitched up my skirts and waded at the edge of the ocean. The feel of gentle waves running over my toes took me back to my childhood. I walked along the edge of the water, peering into rock pools, looking for crabs and starfish, delighting in gently waving anemones as I had done as a little girl.

I lost all consciousness of time or place and it was only as a big wave rushed in, catching me unawares and completely soaking the lower half of my skirt, that I realized where I was and that the tide was coming in. At the next instant I realized that I was now cut off. The narrow strip of shoreline along which I had come was now underwater. I was going to have to find a suitable spot to scramble up the cliffs. I soon realized that this was not going to be achieved in a ladylike manner. There were places when the slope was more a tumble of rocks, but it would still require serious clambering. Not that I found this as daunting as other young ladies would have done, having done more than my share of clambering.

I tried to assess exactly where I was in relation to the estate above me. I wanted to come up at a spot where I could slink to the cottage unseen. I was well aware that the members of the Hannan family were due to arrive this afternoon and I certainly didn't want to run into any of them with my skirts sodden and probably torn by the end of the climb.

As I picked my way gingerly over the rocks, clutching my shoes and stockings, I heard a voice saying, 'No, it can't be a mermaid, can it?'

I looked up and saw a young man perched on an outcropping high above me. He was dressed in the sober suit of a city gent with a stiff collar and black ascot, but he sat on the cliff edge with his legs dangling over like a large child. The first thing I noticed about him was that he was a most attractive young man. Yes, I know I was now a married woman but one does still notice these things. He had light-brown hair that waved just the right amount, a neat little brown mustache, and a good, firm jaw. He also had dark eyes that were now alight with amusement.

'Don't tell me you have been cut off by the tide and need rescuing. How delicious. I've always wanted to be a hero and save a maiden in distress, but opportunities to do so have been denied to me until now.'

'Thank you, but I don't need rescuing,' I said primly.

'Ah, but you do,' he said. 'If you're not a mermaid, and intending to swim back out to sea – and I perceive no tail – then you'll have to climb up this cliff and will find yourself trespassing on a private estate where trespassers are shot on sight. Fortunately for you, I am a member of the family and can save you from a rapid and horrible death.'

With this he scrambled nimbly from his perch to a lower rock and then came down the rest of the way with remarkable agility to my side.

'I said I didn't need help,' I said. 'And I am afraid I'm not about to be shot either. I'm a guest on the estate, just like you.'

His face lit up. 'A new family member I haven't heard about? Has one of my disreputable cousins finally done the decent thing and married you?'

'Not at all,' I said. 'I'm not connected with your family. I'm a guest of the alderman.'

He looked at me now with great speculation. 'Are you now? The old dog. So he's finally tired of widowhood and is thinking of marrying and recapturing his lost youth.'

'You make a remarkable number of speculations, don't you?' I said. 'When I said I was a guest of the alderman, I meant just that. My husband and I are staying in the guest cottage at Mr Hannan's invitation.'

'Oh, no, don't tell me you are married. Why is it the pretty ones are always taken? Just my lot, I suppose. But then you have a roguish twinkle in your eye. You might not be the horribly faithful kind.'

'I've only been married three weeks,' I said. 'Even the most unfaithful kind is hardly going to look for dalliances during the first month.'

He laughed then. 'I like you. A woman of spirit, indeed. And all that Irish red hair. Delectable.' He held out his hand. 'I'm Terry, by the way. Terrence Hannan.'

'And I'm Molly Murphy – Sullivan, I mean.'

'Molly Murphy Sullivan? That's surely a surfeit of Irish names.'

'Actually it's Molly Sullivan now. I just haven't become used to the name yet.'

'Well, Mrs Sullivan, allow me to assist you back to civilization before we're both swamped by the incoming tide.' He held out his hand to me. I took it and he stepped from rock to rock, ably assisting me up to the estate above. There was something like a path at this point up a sloping tumble of rocks, and we reached the top with no problem. He released my hand a trifle reluctantly, I thought.

'Well done, Mrs Sullivan. You managed that without a single swoon.'

'I am not the type of woman who swoons,' I said, 'and I grew up climbing rocky shorelines.'

With that I tried to walk away with dignity, until I realized that my shoes and stockings were still in my other hand.

Eight

We came out onto the lawns close to where the stand of Scotch Pines reached almost to the cliff edge.

'Now you are surely in need of a little brandy to calm your nerves,' Terrence said. 'Come over to the house for a drink.'

'I hardly think I'm in a fit state to come to the house,' I said. 'Look at me – shoeless and sodden.'

He looked me up and down and then laughed. 'Yes, I do see your point.'

'If I cut through the pine trees, can I make it back to our cottage unseen, do you think? I really don't want to encounter any other members of your family while I'm in this state.'

'Oh, absolutely. We've come up at the perfect spot. You'll notice that you can't be seen from the house here, and I'll be happy to escort you through the pine wood. There is a little path. I find it very convenient myself for times when I wish to come and go without attracting attention.'

'I'm afraid I need to put my shoes on first,' I said. 'I'm out of the habit of walking barefoot, so I'd be grateful if you'd point me in the right direction and then leave me.'

'I can wait while you put your shoes on.'

'I daresay you can but it wouldn't be proper, would it? I don't think your family would approve of my exposing my bare ankles to you.'

He laughed. 'But I already observed them, when you stood at the edge of the surf. And very pretty ankles they were too.'

'All the same, I'm not going to sit down and put on shoes with you watching, so please go.'

'I'll be gallant and turn my back,' he said. 'See, there's a convenient log over there you can sit on and I promise not to watch.'

'I don't think I can trust you,' I said.

He laughed again. 'I am cut to the quick. All right. I'll stand here behind this large shrub. Does that reassure you?'

'I suppose so,' I said. I picked my way over to the log and lifted my wet skirts enough to put on my shoes. I wasn't about to attempt stockings.

'So you're a friend of our esteemed patriarch, are you?' Terrence asked as I pulled on first one shoe then the other.

'I've never met him,' I said. 'It was my husband who received the invitation and I'm not sure how they are connected. Daniel's family lives out in Westchester and knows a lot of influential people.' I remembered that Daniel had avoided mentioning his profession and thought it wise to follow suit.

'Sullivan,' he said thoughtfully. 'I don't think we've ever met. But then I rarely find time to get out to Westchester. I am expected to keep my nose to the grindstone, slaving away at the family firm, which I am supposed to take over some day – even though I keep pointing out that my father's generation kept their noses to the grindstone precisely so that I wouldn't have to. But the word leisure is considered obscene in this family.'

I stood up, my shoes now safely on my feet and my skirts hiding the offending ankles. The way that he stepped out to meet me convinced me that he'd been peeking the whole time.

'Are you Brian Hannan's son?' I asked as we set off together through the pine wood. 'I thought he only had one child.'

'He does. The exquisite Irene. You haven't met her yet then? I think I saw her arriving a while ago. Oh, yes, an only child and raised like one to have everything she wanted. A spoiled little miss and hasn't changed. Can still arrange the odd temper tantrum like a two year old if she doesn't get her own way – even though she's now past thirty.' He grinned at me wickedly. 'Of course she has received her just desserts – married to the horribly boring Archie because she wanted his distinguished name. The man hasn't an interesting or novel thought in his head and has never done a day's work. It's all about polo and sailing and the occasional flutter on the gee-gees. All the expensive sports and luckily Irene's money allows him to live in the lifestyle to which he is accustomed.'

'Isn't his family rich in their own right?'

'Used to be. Bad business decisions and too many idle sons like Archie. Oh, no, it was a marriage of utter convenience to both. He got the money, she got the name and the stature that goes with it. So both, we hope, are satisfied and deserve each other.'

'So if you're not Brian Hannan's son—'

'Joseph's my father,' he said. 'But it's Uncle Brian who pulls the strings in this family, and controls the purse strings too. When he tells us to jump, we jump, even my father who is technically a partner in Hannan Construction. Of course he lacks in Uncle Brian's fanatical work ethic. And his tastes are more expensive. I seem to have inherited that weakness—' He broke off. 'I say, I shouldn't be revealing the family skeletons to a stranger, should I?'

'My lips are sealed,' I said, making him laugh.

Suddenly we heard a voice calling 'I think I see them!' and a young woman came running through the trees toward us. She was dressed in a severe dark-blue dress, almost looking like one of the Salvation Army ladies and had an equally severe pale and haughty face. She looked startled then stared at us in disgust.

'Oh, it's you. I didn't think that even you would stoop as low as going off into Uncle's woods with some woman.'

'How lovely to see you, Eliza,' Terrence said. 'And as usual you've gotten the wrong end of the stick, seeing degradation where there is none. This lady is a guest of Uncle Brian's and I have just risked life and limb climbing down the cliff to rescue her from being cut off by the tide.'

The haughty face flushed. 'Oh, I am so sorry. It's just that my brother – well, his behavior is not always what one would wish and when I saw you I naturally assumed . . .' She held out her hand. 'I'm Eliza Hannan.'

'This is my dear sister,' Terrence said. 'As you can see from her clothing, she has taken after our mother and has devoted her life to good works among the poor.'

'Molly Sullivan,' I said frostily. 'And I really must examine the way that I dress, since this is the second time I've been taken for a lady of ill repute since I arrived on this property.'

'Oh, no, there is nothing wrong, I assure you,' she gushed, her face bright red now. 'It was a hasty judgment knowing the wild ways of my brother. I'm sorry you've had an ordeal on our beach. The tide does come in quickly, doesn't it?'

I nodded, still unwilling to let go of this latest slight. I hoped the rest of the Hannan family would not be so unwelcoming as these first members.

'Mrs Sullivan's skirts are cold and wet, so if you'll excuse us, Liza dear. I'm escorting her back to the guest cottage, where she and her husband are staying.'

'Of course,' Eliza said. 'Off you go, then.'

'What were you shouting about anyway?'

'Thomas and Alex. They are missing and Irene is in a terrible state, after – well, you know.'

At that moment there was more blundering through the bushes and crunching of leaves and a man came running up to us. 'Have you found them yet?' he asked breathlessly, then he noticed me and looked at me inquiringly.

'No, we haven't seen them,' Terrence said. 'But we were down on the seashore and there was no sign of them there.'

'Thank God,' the man said. He was immaculately dressed, hair perfectly parted in the middle, and had the pale face and light hair of Dutch ancestry, drawing me to the conclusion that this was indeed Archie Van Horn, the boys' father.

'Little devils,' he said. 'That new nursemaid cannot control them. Absolutely hopeless. They run rings around her and poor Irene is distraught.'

'I'll help you look, as soon as I've escorted Mrs Sullivan back to the guest cottage,' Terrence said.

'Oh, please don't concern yourself about me,' I said. 'I am quite able to find my own way. It's more important that you look for the missing boys.'

'Mrs Sullivan and her husband are Uncle Brian's guests,' Terrence said, noticing Archie's questioning stare.

'She got caught by the tide,' Eliza added. 'And Terrence rescued her.'

'Dashed dangerous place,' Archie said. 'Don't know why we come here. I don't know why Irene's father still likes it here so much, and insists on our joining him. But Irene will never disobey her father. Just because I'm planning to compete in a yacht race this Saturday he insisted we all come up to watch. Frankly I'd rather have come up alone and stayed at the yacht club. Whoever heard of using the cottage in October? Ridiculous idea. We are probably the laughingstock among the usual crowd.'

'Have you found them yet, Archie?' a high voice floated through the woods and an exquisite creation in pale-blue silk joined us. Her red-blonde hair was piled on her head in tiny curls and her wide blue eyes looked terrified.

'Not yet, my dear, but don't worry. They can't have gotten far. They've only been gone a few minutes.'

'A few minutes is enough,' Irene said. 'How could that incompetent woman let them slip away from her? She only has one job and that's to guard my boys. You must fire her as soon as we get home, Archie.'

'I will, my dear. But in the meantime . . .'

I had moved away from the group feeling awkward and superfluous in such an intimate family setting. As I walked through the undergrowth, I thought I heard something. It could have been a bird, but it sounded like a giggle. Up in an old oak tree I spotted a foot.

'You'd better come down right away. You've frightened your poor mother,' I said sternly. 'Come on. Quickly now or it will be straight to bed with no supper for you.'

Two little boys slithered down sheepishly. They looked to be about eight and ten years old and they were dressed in identical sailor suits that were now the worse for wear.

'Here they are!' I called. 'They were hiding in a tree.'

Irene rushed over to them, her arms open. 'Thank God, thank God. You naughty, naughty, naughty boys. You made Mama so frightened.' Irene enveloped them in a big hug, holding them to her bosom and rocking them fiercely.

She looked up at her husband as he strode angrily toward them. 'Speak to them, Archie. Make them understand that they must never do this again.'

'You'll get a damned good thrashing if you ever do that again, do you hear?' Archie said in a not-too-threatening voice, as Irene released her hold and the boys wriggled free.

'Yes, Papa,' the boys muttered.

'Archie, they are just little boys. Be gentle with them,' Irene begged, trying to embrace them again.

'They need discipline, Irene. They are running wild.' He wagged a finger at the boys. 'Now off to the house with you and get cleaned up before you meet your grandfather. You look a disgrace.'

'Yes, Papa,' the boys chimed in unison, but I got the impression that they knew no threat would ever be carried out.

They ran across the lawn toward the house.

'Thank God,' Irene said again. 'When I couldn't find them, I thought—'

'They are boys, Irene,' Archie said. 'They need some freedom. You can't keep them wrapped in cotton all their lives.'

'I can and I will. If I have to follow them every second we are here, then I'll do it to keep them safe.' And she started after them across the lawn. She stumbled on the wet grass. Archie took her arm to steady her but she snatched it away as if burned.

'I think I'd better let you go back to the house. I can find my own way from here,' I said to Terrence and Eliza who were watching with expressions both pained and embarrassed. 'I had tried to avoid meeting the family in this disheveled state. I'd prefer not to come face-to-face with Alderman Hannan himself, so if you don't mind . . .'

And without waiting any longer I took my leave.

Nine

As I approached our cottage a procession was coming down the drive – a cart piled high with boxes, valises, and baskets – followed by an open carriage full of male and female servants. An automobile was sitting outside the front door. It appeared that the family had arrived in force.

Daniel had been sitting in the bay window and jumped up as I opened the front door.

'Where have you been? You've been gone for hours. I've been worried about you.'

'I'm sorry. I thought you'd be sleeping. I was on the seashore and then I met some family members and joined in a search for two little boys, whom I found hiding in a tree.'

'Such adventures,' Daniel said. 'I'm sorry I missed them. So these boys – they were the alderman's grandsons?'

'They were. Thomas and Alex. Nice little chaps from what I could see. Their mama was most distressed.'

'Well, she would be, wouldn't she? If she'd already lost one child over that cliff. So did you meet the alderman too?'

'No, thank heavens. I wouldn't have made too good a first impression with my skirt in this state, would I?'

'You're soaked. What have you been doing to yourself?' he demanded.

'Only got a little wet while I was wading in the ocean. Nothing serious,' I said. 'So stop scowling like that. I'd better get to work right away sponging out the saltwater or it will leave a mark.'

Daniel shook his head. 'Who else's new bride would spend her first day on a great estate getting herself half drowned in the ocean?'

'It was nothing like half drowned. I was looking into a tide pool and I was caught unawares by a particularly big wave.' In his current state of agitation I thought it wiser not to let him know that I had allowed myself to be cut off by the tide.

'Now that you're back, I'd like some hot tea,' he said. 'And could we maybe light a fire? This place is cold and damp. I'm shivering.'

'It doesn't feel that cold to me,' I said, going over to feel his forehead. He actually felt quite warm to my touch. 'But I'll light a fire if you like. There is a log basket all ready and we'll have a nice cozy evening.'

Half an hour later we were sitting by a crackling blaze with hot tea and toast. I looked across at Daniel and the thought struck me – this is what I have to look forward to – cozy afternoons doing nothing in particular, just enjoying each other's company. It was a pleasant prospect.

'So I told you that I met some of the family, Daniel,' I began brightly, because I wanted to cheer him up.

'Did you?' he asked without great enthusiasm.

'I did. The alderman's daughter, Irene – very lovely and dressed in the height of fashion, and her equally suave and dashing and upper-crust husband, Archie. I also met their cousins Terrence and Eliza, who are Joseph's children. Terrence is a likable rogue, I suspect. Typical Irish gift of the gab with an aversion to work, and his sister is quite the opposite – looks like a Salvation Army lass and does good works.

So does their mother, I understand, which might explain why she's not here.'

'And why Joseph brings a younger diversion with him.' Daniel chuckled. The chuckle turned to a hacking cough. I looked at him with concern.

'That cough sounds terrible. You really have caught a bad chill.'

'And I always pride myself on my strong constitution.' He put his handkerchief up to his mouth as he coughed again.

I got up. 'I'll go up to the big house and see if they have a chicken or stewing beef,' I said. 'You need a good strong broth,' I said.

'Don't bother. I'm sure I'll be right as rain in a day or so,' Daniel said. 'It's just a question of letting these things work their way through the system.'

'Nonsense. I want you back to your normal self as quickly as possible,' I said. 'I'm missing out on my honeymoon. It's no fun without my husband to share it with me.'

'It's almost dark. Go carefully then,' he called after me.

The temperature had dropped with the sunset and I grabbed a shawl for my shoulders before I set out across the lawns. Lights were now twinkling from the big house, making it no longer so intimidating. Nevertheless, I had no wish to encounter the alderman or any of the family members again without Daniel present so I veered around the side of the house, looking for a servants' entrance. As I made my way past the fountain, I heard the click of a lock and turned to see someone coming out of one of the French windows that ran along that side of the house. In the half darkness all I saw was a tall slim shadow of a man. He hesitated, looked around, then strode purposefully away from the house and into the darkness. *Terrence slipping out for a drink before dinner at a local watering hole*, I thought.

Eventually I came upon a back door, opened it, and entered

to find myself in a dark, narrow passageway. Good cooking smells led me to a door on my left and I found myself in the kitchen where we had taken tea. The room was empty but pots were bubbling away on a stove.

'Hello!' I called. 'Anyone there?'

Nobody appeared. I looked around for a larder. There was no pantry door inside the kitchen so I went back out to the passage again and started opening doors. The first was a broom closet. The second was locked, the third was a servants' dining room, unused and in darkness. I encountered nobody as I poked around. Where had they all disappeared to? I found myself glancing nervously over my shoulder as I worked my way down the hall. A fourth door was recessed into the wall. I opened it and gave a little scream as I encountered a face literally a few inches from mine. I stepped back with a gasp of horror as the apparition said in an angry voice, 'Mrs Sullivan. Whatever were you doing?' And Mrs McCreedy stepped into the hallway. She was breathing heavily and her hand was on her large bosom as if she too was recovering from a shock.

'I'm sorry,' I said. 'I didn't mean to startle you. I was looking for the larder.'

'The larder?' She was eyeing me suspiciously. 'Was the icebox over at the guest cottage not well stocked then? I thought I made sure you'd have all you needed.' She was still gasping as if she had run a race.

'Yes, thank you. The food is wonderful,' I said. 'It's just that my husband has come down with a bad chill and I thought some kind of broth might be just what he needed. So I came over to see if you had a chicken maybe or some stewing beef or even some bones.'

'Bones?' She was staring at me impassively.

'To make a broth. I believe we already have onions and carrots at the cottage.'

'I'll see what I can do for you,' she said coldly.

'Do you do the cooking when the family is here?' I asked, trying to melt the icy freeze that seemed to have developed between us. 'There are some wonderful smells coming from that oven.'

'I'm cooking the meal tonight but I expect the alderman will be bringing his own cook from the city. He has a French chef, from Paris, you know. Very particular about his food, he is.' She walked ahead of me back into the kitchen and then opened another door behind a curtain. This one led to a scullery containing an enormous icebox. 'I've chickens here but they are for tomorrow night's dinner,' she said. 'I suppose I might spare you one.'

'I'd appreciate it if you could. I'll go into town and buy one tomorrow to replace it,' I said.

'Well, all right. They are only little poussins and I expect I have enough here for one each for the meal, if more family members don't turn up out of the blue.' She reached in and lifted out a pathetic-looking little body. It hung limply in her hand, the head still attached and drooping to one side. Then she opened a drawer with the other hand and brought out a piece of greaseproof paper.

'I hope your husband feels better,' she said, wrapping it deftly and then tying it with a piece of string.

'I won't trouble you any longer. I can see you're busy.' I started toward the back door again.

'Mrs Sullivan,' she called after me.

I turned back.

'What are you really doing here?' she asked. 'Did somebody send you?'

'What are you talking about? I told you that the alderman made the invitation to my husband.'

'I see,' she said. 'It's just that, well, yesterday I caught you snooping around the house on your own and now again today. And I certainly don't expect to find guests of the master poking around in the servants' quarters.'

'We have no servant to send over for me. I came to the back door because I didn't want to encounter family members before we were formally introduced,' I replied. 'I called from the doorway, but nobody came. So I thought I'd try to locate the larder.'

'And help yourself to our food? What if you had taken a chicken and I was then one short?'

'I would never have taken anything without permission, and I don't take kindly to your insinuations,' I said hotly. 'Now if you'll excuse me, I must get back to my husband. I'm concerned about him and about the fever he caught because there was nobody around to let us in when we arrived, even though we were expected.'

With that I stalked out, in high dudgeon. The woman had practically accused me of coming here to steal things, hadn't she? I was almost tempted to throw her chicken back at her and tell her we'd do without, but my concern for Daniel outweighed my pride.

I was just turning onto the path to the guest cottage when I heard a voice calling, 'Hey miss. Over here.' I could make out the figure of a man peering in through the bars of the gate.

I went up to him. 'Oh, dear, have they locked the gates again? We were shut out the other day. Let me see if I can find the way to let you in.'

'I don't want to come in,' he said. 'Not right now in any case. I just wanted to make sure – this is the house of Brian Hannan, isn't it?'

'Yes, it is,' I said.

'And Mr Hannan is in residence?'

'I gather he hasn't arrived yet,' I said.

'That's funny. Are you sure?'

'I don't know, actually. We're not staying at the big house.'

'I'd swear I saw him at the station in New York. Very well, then. I'll be back. Thank you.' He let go of the bars of the gate he had been holding.

'You're not another family member, are you? Because a lot of them have already arrived.'

'Oh, no, nothing like that. Far from it.' He was starting to move away. 'I'd better go then.'

'Would you like me to tell the family that you called, Mr—?' I shouted after him.

'No, thank you. Let's keep it a surprise, shall we?'

With that he melted away into the darkness, leaving me to pick my way home to the cottage.

Ten

I did not sleep well that night. Daniel tossed and turned with a hacking cough. Having just become accustomed to the advantages of sleeping in the same bed as my husband, I was now finding out the disadvantages. I got up to fetch him water and make him hot tea and in the end I chose to curl up on the sofa with a rug over me. I had just drifted off to sleep as the birds were twittering with the dawn when there was a thunderous knocking at the front door.

I got up, reached blindly for my robe, and went to the front door, first pausing to make sure the robe was tied decently. Really this nightly interruption was becoming less of a joke each time it happened. I opened the door to see a policeman standing there.

'Good morning, ma'am.' He touched his helmet to me. 'I am sorry to bother you so early, but I'm afraid I have to ask you to get dressed and come over to the big house as soon as possible. My chief would like to talk to you.'

'About what? Is it my husband you're wanting?' I pulled my robe closer around me, conscious of his interested stare.

'No, both of you, and I couldn't tell you what about. Just that it's urgent and you are requested to come straightaway.'

'Very well. We'll come as soon as we're dressed,' I said shortly.

I went upstairs to rouse Daniel. He looked decidedly the worse for wear – hollow eyed and still flushed with fever.

'What the devil do they want now?' he growled. 'Are we not to get a minute's peace in this place? I rather wish I had not accepted the invitation. A stay on Coney Island next to the new Luna Park would have been quieter than this.'

'Maybe you should stay in bed. The early morning air will not help your condition. I can go in your stead and give your excuses.'

'No, that wouldn't do at all,' he said. 'I'll be all right. I just hope for their sakes that the matter warrants dragging us out of bed like this.'

He sat on the bed, breathing heavily, as he dressed. His breathing sounded ragged. I went off to dress myself, noting gratefully that I had succeeded in eliminating the saltwater stains from the skirt of my dress. As I put up my hair I tried to think what a policeman could want with us at this hour. Surely Mrs McCreedy had not reported me for trying to steal a chicken? And if she had, the alderman would certainly have arrived by now and would have vouched for us. A chilling thought crossed my mind – those little boys, mischievous and lacking control – surely something hadn't happened to them?

I followed Daniel down the stairs and out across the dewy lawn. I took his arm, feeling that he might need me to steady him as much as I needed his support. Toadstools had appeared overnight in the damp grass and there was a decidedly autumnal chill in the air. Seagulls wheeled overhead mewing. The policeman who had summoned us was standing at the front door of the castle and ushered us inside, across that cavernous main foyer, down a gloomy hallway until he paused outside a door at the far end. He knocked and pushed the door open for us to go in. We stepped into one of the lavishly formal drawing rooms on the north side of the house. It was decidedly chilly at this early hour with no fire lit in the grate.

I started with surprise as we entered because the room was full of people. The entire Hannan family appeared to be assembled in various stages of undress. Pajamas were visible under silk dressing gowns. Irene was in a feather-trimmed negligee, but her hair fell over her shoulders and clearly had not been brushed. They were posed, unmoving, almost like a tableau in the popular party games – their unkempt appearance and motley attire in sharp contrast to the fine furnishings and decorations of the room.

My first impression was of this incongruity and I tried to imagine what had brought them all so hurriedly from their beds. They looked at us as we entered, hollow eyed and almost as if they were in a trance. A thought passed through my head that these were people who were in shock. Then of course I remembered the incident of the day before and realized that the little boys were not part of this gathering. *Please God let it not have anything to do with those boys*, I found myself praying.

I glanced around the group, recognizing Irene and Archie Van Horn, Terrence, Eliza, Mr Joseph Hannan as well as a few people I hadn't seen before. One was a plump, motherly looking older woman; one a skinny youth. He was perched on the arm of her chair, a study in contrasts, making the rhyme about Jack Sprat and his wife spring into my mind. The third person was a thinner, younger, somehow softer-looking version of Joseph, presumably the third Hannan brother, the priest. And the only one standing was a portly florid man in a policeman's uniform with enough braid on it to indicate he was someone important.

'Ah, here they are now,' he said as we came in. 'Mr and Mrs Sullivan, isn't it? Please take a seat. I am Chief Prescott of the Newport police.' There were two upright chairs near the door and we sat. It felt as if we had been called to an inquisition and tried to imagine what we were to be accused of.

'Mr and Mrs Sullivan. I am told you are supposedly here as guests of Alderman Hannan.'

'Supposedly?' I began, but Daniel put a hand on my arm to restrain me.

'May we ask what this is about?' Daniel demanded. 'Exactly why have we been dragged from our beds at this ungodly hour on what is supposed to be our honeymoon? If this is some kind of family gathering then obviously we do not belong here.'

'Precisely,' Mr Joseph Hannan said, pointing a finger in our direction. 'Exactly what I told you, Chief Prescott. What are they doing here at the same time as us? That was the first thought that went through my mind – and the other family members as well.'

'We are here because Alderman Hannan invited us,' Daniel said.

'You're a good friend of the alderman, are you, sir?' the policeman asked.

'No, I don't know him socially. We have crossed paths professionally.'

'See, what did I tell you?' Joseph Hannan began again. 'None of us had any idea they'd be here. None of us has ever heard mention of them before.'

'You say you don't know the alderman socially, and yet he invites you to his house at the same time as his family. Didn't that strike you as odd, sir?' The police chief took a step toward us in a menacing way, as if he was expecting us to break down and confess all. I studied his face. It must have been handsome once, but the jawline was starting to sag and those red cheeks betrayed too much liking for alcohol. And the way he was looking at us was making a flush of anger rise to my own cheeks.

I could keep quiet no longer. 'Look, if you believe we are

gate-crashers here, and obviously that is what you are insinuating, why don't you ask the alderman himself? I'm sure he must have arrived by now.'

I saw a quick glance pass between several people seated in the room.

'May I ask when you last saw the alderman, sir?' the police chief asked.

Daniel frowned. 'A couple of weeks ago.'

'You haven't seen him since?'

'I just told you,' Daniel snapped, then drew out his handkerchief as the words turned into a bout of coughing. Prescott waited until he had finished.

'I must apologize,' Daniel muttered. 'I seem to have caught a chill after being drenched in that storm the other night.'

'You say you cross paths professionally,' the policeman said. 'What kind of profession would that be, sir?'

'I'm a policeman, like yourself,' Daniel said. 'If you want to know the details, the alderman and I were chatting and when he learned about my ruined honeymoon, and that he was partly to blame, he made the kind offer of the use of his guest cottage, and suggested this date.'

'He was partly to blame? What do you mean?'

'I'm talking about the tunnel collapse last month. The new subway system that Hannan Construction is building in the city. I'm sure you must have read about it. If not, Joseph Hannan can tell you. He runs the business these days, isn't that right, Mr Hannan?' He looked at Joseph.

'There was a cave-in,' Joseph said coldly. 'Bound to happen from time to time, given the unstable nature of the soil under Manhattan and the many streams that crisscross it.'

'It was a bad cave-in and several men were killed, weren't they?' Daniel continued. 'And I was called back from my honeymoon to see if there was any evidence of foul play involved.'

73

'Foul play?' Joseph demanded, half rising to his feet. 'What are you getting at?'

'An attempt to sabotage your construction, Mr Hannan. That's what I'm getting at.' He and Joseph stared at each other for a long moment then Joseph sat down again.

'You're a detective of some sort, are you then?' Chief Prescott asked. The tone was hostile, almost insulting.

'Captain Sullivan, New York police,' Daniel said. 'Senior detective at Mulberry Street.'

'I see, sir.' I noticed a slight shift in attitude. 'Could you tell me why Mr Hannan specifically invited you here at the same time as his family?'

'He mentioned this date and we accepted.'

'So he never said why he wanted you here at this particular moment? Didn't that strike you as a trifle odd?'

'I had no idea he was planning to hold a family reunion at the same time. It came as a surprise to me, too,' Daniel said. 'We came here expecting the place to ourselves and a quiet time.' I stared down at the carpet, not wanting to catch Daniel's eye. But he went on calmly enough, 'Where is the alderman, anyway? Why this meeting without him?'

'The alderman's body was discovered lying half submerged in water on the rocks below the cliff this morning,' the police chief said evenly.

Daniel was instantly on his feet. 'Who found the body?'

'Young Samuel did,' the plump woman said. 'Came back to me in a terrible state.'

Daniel focused his gaze on the skinny youth. 'And you are?'

'Sam,' the boy said. 'Sam McCloskey, sir.'

'A member of Brian Hannan's family?'

'He's my grandson,' the large lady said. 'I'm Mary Flannery, and Joe, Pat, and Brian are my brothers – were my brothers,' she corrected and crossed herself. 'Samuel is the oldest of my daughter's children. She married herself a no-good drunkard and she's trying to raise eight children more or less single-handed so Brian had taken young Sam under his wing. Very fond of him, he was. And the other way around too. The boy has been quite beside himself all morning.'

Indeed young Sam was ashen faced and did look as if he was in shock. But then they all did. Irene's eyes were red and swollen as if she had been crying. Now she just sat perfectly still, not moving a muscle and staring blankly at the unlit fireplace.

'You found the body at what time?' Daniel asked, moving toward the youth.

'I don't know the exact time, sir.' Sam muttered. 'I think I heard the grandfather clock chime six before I went out.'

'What were you doing out at that hour?' Daniel asked.

'Excuse me, Captain Sullivan,' Chief Prescott cut in, 'but may I remind you that we are not in New York City and this is not your case. If anyone asks questions it will be me. Is that clear?'

'Certainly,' Daniel said, going back to his chair. 'I'm sorry. Force of habit. I'll let you get on with it then.'

'What were you doing out alone at that hour, son?' the chief asked.

'Going fishing,' the boy said. 'My grandpa taught me how to fish. He said early morning was the best time.'

'My late husband, he means,' Mary Flannery said. 'He taught the boy to fish off the docks in the city. We lived near the East River.'

'So you were going fishing,' the chief went on. 'Go on.'

'I went and got a rod and line from the shed and then I decided to go down to the rocks and get some mussels for bait. I got to the edge of the cliff and I saw something on the rocks. To start with I thought a seal or a whale was lying in a tide pool. It wasn't quite light, you see. I was really excited. I'd never seen a seal or a whale close up like that before.' He looked around for confirmation.

'Go on, boy,' Chief Prescott said.

'And then I saw the hand floating in the water and it was a human hand. So I ran along the cliff until there's the place where we can climb down and – well, I just thought it was a body fallen off a boat or something. I never expected . . .' He broke off as his voice choked. 'Then a wave came in and lifted the head and I saw that it was Uncle Brian.'

'What did you do then?'

'Tried to help him, of course. In case he was still alive. I made my way out to him through the waves. But then I saw his eyes, just staring and his face all beaten up and I knew he was dead.'

He put his hand up to his mouth and tried to swallow back the sob.

'Pull yourself together, boy,' Joseph said. 'You're almost a man. Men don't cry.'

'Hush up, Jo. The boy's had a horrible shock. You know how fond he was of Brian,' Father Patrick said gently. 'It's all right, boy. It's good to grieve for those we loved.' I looked at him – a softer, kinder face than Joseph's but also one that had known suffering, I decided.

'We've all had a shock,' Joseph said. 'A terrible shock.'

'And we've all lost someone we loved,' Irene said. 'But then some of us more than others. He was my father, you know.'

'We're not debating who has the greatest claim to love him,' Joseph said shortly.

'Please, please.' Chief Prescott held up his hand. 'Ladies and gentlemen, we're just trying to get at the facts here. Go on, boy. What did you do after you saw it was Brian Hannan and he was dead?'

'I came running straight back to the house and I woke my grandma.'

'And I got dressed and went to see for myself, because the boy has been known to pull a prank or two before now,' Mary Flannery said, patting the boy on his knee for reassurance. 'And there he was, the poor man, lying in the surf, just like the boy said. I came straight back to the house and went to wake my brothers.'

'Has a coroner or a physician been summoned?' Daniel asked.

'He has,' Prescott replied. 'Not that there's anything we can do for the poor fellow.'

'So we don't yet know how long he'd been lying there,' Daniel said.

'I presume he must have gone for an early morning walk and miscalculated the cliff edge,' Prescott said, dismissing Daniel by turning away from him.

'But he never arrived last night,' Archie pointed out. 'We waited dinner for him and he never showed up. So we all thought he'd been detained on a business or political matter and that he'd come this morning. We did think it odd that he didn't telephone. He had a telephone put in the house, you know. He liked to stay abreast of matters.'

'So it's possible,' Chief Prescott said, this time turning to look back at Daniel, 'that he did arrive last night, and fell off the cliffs then, before he could make his presence known.'

'That hardly seems likely, does it?' Joseph interrupted before Daniel could comment. 'My brother arrives at his own house, doesn't come in to meet anyone or to let his servants know he is here. Instead slinks off to the cliff edge and falls over.'

'He wouldn't have done that.' Irene's voice was full of emotion. 'You know how careful he was. You know what he thought about that cliff, after what we'd all gone through.'

'You mean the little girl?' Prescott said.

'Of course that's what I mean. My daughter. My precious little daughter.' Irene's voice cracked.

'Now don't distress yourself, my dear,' Archie said. He frowned a warning at the police chief. 'We don't mention her anymore.'

'But I still think about her,' Irene said. 'I still think about her every day, you know. She is still a raw wound that will never heal.'

'Uh, quite.' Chief Prescott looked embarrassed. 'So you believe your father would not walk near the cliff edge because he had already experienced one tragedy?'

'Of course,' Irene said. 'Especially not in the dark.'

'We do know it was dark when he arrived, do we?' Daniel asked. 'If he had fallen and been killed earlier yesterday evening, for example, would anyone have seen him?'

'I might have,' I spoke up, making them all stare at me. 'I was down on the seashore in the late afternoon. And Mr Terrence Hannan had to assist me because the tide had come in and I was caught unawares. We could tell you there was no sign of anyone else near the beach then.'

'But that was some time before sunset,' Terrence said. 'The servants and the luggage arrived just after I got back to the house, so I suspect we were all inside sorting out who was sleeping where and then dressing for dinner when it actually became dark.'

'Has anyone spoken to the servants yet?' Daniel asked. 'Has Mr Hannan's valet not come to attend to him?'

'Brian still had the egalitarian outlook of our forebears,' Joseph Hannan said. 'He saw no reason to have someone else hanging around to dress him. He employed servants only for things he couldn't do himself. He kept a butler and housemaids and a cook at home. But no gentleman's gentleman.'

'That wouldn't have gone down well with his Tammany pals, would it?' Terrence said dryly and was rewarded with a sharp look from his father.

'And Mr Hannan would have come by train and not by automobile?' Daniel went on.

'It is a long uncomfortable trip by automobile,' Joseph said. 'Most of it on unpaved road, you know. Certainly not worth the effort for a few days. I'm sure he was intending to come by train.'

'Who would have met him at the station? Would not one of the servants have been sent?'

'It depended if he had notified anyone of the train he was planning to catch,' Joseph said. 'He could have telephoned from the station if he wanted someone to come and fetch him. He was just as likely to have taken a cab. Brian didn't like fuss.'

'So we have no way of knowing whether he took the train and at what time he arrived here?' Daniel said.

'Not at this moment,' Joseph said.

'I met someone who had seen him in the station in New York yesterday and was surprised that he hadn't arrived here yet,' I said.

They all looked at me with interest again, as if they had forgotten about my presence.

'And who was that?' Chief Prescott asked.

'I don't know. He wouldn't give his name. He was standing outside the main gate yesterday evening after dark and of course the gate had been locked for the night. He called out to me and asked if Alderman Hannan was in residence. I said that I didn't know if he'd arrived yet. I asked him if he wanted to come in, or to let the family know that he was here, but he said he wanted it to be a surprise and he went away again.'

'Aha. Now we're getting somewhere,' Chief Prescott said. 'Can you describe this man?'

'Not really. It was dark. He was young, I'd say. Slight of build, and a voice that didn't sound educated. Oh, and I believe he had a mustache.'

'That describes half the population of this country,' Joseph Hannan said.

'I'm sorry. In the dark one doesn't see colors or facial features,' I replied haughtily.

'Were any of you expecting another guest? Any family members who are not here?' Prescott asked.

'Only Aunt Minny and Aunt Agnes,' Terrence said. 'And we certainly weren't expecting them.'

'My two sisters who are in the convent,' Mary Flannery explained. 'They haven't been outside the walls for years. And the only other family members are my daughter and son-in-law and their other children. My brother Brian didn't approve of her marrying him against his wishes, so they are not invited here.'

'Could the husband be the man that my wife encountered last night?' Daniel asked. 'Uncouth, thin, with a mustache?'

'Possible,' Joseph Hannan said, 'but why on earth would he show up here? He knows he's not welcome.'

'To touch Uncle Brian for money?' Terrence suggested with a grin.

'Then why come here? It would be more convenient to see him at his office in the city, any day of the week,' Joseph said. 'They only live a stone's throw away.'

As I watched him, an idea struck me. The whispered conversation at our cottage. The shadowy figure on the stairs and the feminine giggle. Joseph Hannan had conveniently forgotten to mention that he had brought somebody with him – someone who was not here now.

Eleven

'Your wife is not here, I believe, Mr Hannan?' I said innocently and was glad to see a flash of annoyance cross his face.

'My wife never comes to family gatherings,' he said. 'She is of a nervous disposition, easily upset by noise and too many people.'

I thought that someone who did good works among the poor, as described by Eliza, would quite often encounter noise and bustle in the slums of the Lower East Side. It was one of the noisiest places on Earth with the pushcart vendors shouting their wares and all the facets of life taking place in such close quarters.

I thought Eliza was going to say something but she glanced at Terrence and then looked out of the window.

'Is there anything else we can do to help at this moment?' Joseph Hannan went on. 'I believe we've established that nobody saw Brian or knew that he had arrived. Now I don't want to sound callous but I could do with some hot coffee and breakfast. So could we all. We're all in a state of shock. You're welcome to join us, Chief Prescott.'

Joseph rose to his feet. Other family members also got up. So did Daniel. He held up his hand. 'One more question, if you don't mind. Exactly why did Brian Hannan invite his family here in the middle of October? Not exactly the season, is it? And a long, awkward journey for all of you.'

'We asked ourselves the same thing,' Terrence said. 'Didn't we, sissy?'

'It was most inconvenient,' Eliza said. 'I had volunteered to take part in a suffragist rally and I had to let them down.'

'Maybe that was why Uncle Brian did it.' Terrence grinned. 'You know his feelings on giving women the vote.'

'Not amusing, Terrence. Your uncle is dead,' Joseph said. 'Show a little respect, please.' He turned to Daniel and me. 'And I take it you'll have the decency to vacate the guest cottage and leave us to our private grief, given the circumstances.'

'Unless Chief Prescott would like us to stay.' Daniel looked across at the other policeman.

'Why would he want to do that?' Joseph asked.

'I don't think that will be necessary,' Prescott said hastily. 'The family will surely want to arrange for the burial, but that would not concern you. I see no reason that you'd not be free to go.'

'So you've completely ruled out the possibility of foul play, have you?' Daniel asked.

'Foul play?' Joseph asked. The other occupants of the room jerked their heads up as if they were puppets on strings.

Daniel nodded. 'Mr Hannan was a very rich and ambitious man, after all.'

'You're hinting at murder?' The color drained from the police chief's florid face. 'Surely we're talking about a tragic accident. Mr Hannan took a wrong turn in the darkness and fell off the cliff. It's easy enough to do here, as you all know too well.'

There was an uncomfortable silence among family members.

'And if he was pushed off the cliff, I don't know how you'd

ever prove it without a witness,' Prescott continued. 'It's not as if there would be a handprint in the middle of his back.'

'What an awful thing to say,' Mary Flannery gasped. 'Who would want to kill dear Brian? The kindest man that ever lived, God rest his soul.'

'He's a political figure and I'm sure that such a man has enemies,' Daniel said.

'If he did, would he be likely to meet with them near the edge of the cliff?' Terrence asked, again with a hint of amusement in his tone. 'Uncle Brian certainly wasn't stupid. What I want to know is why he didn't come into the house and greet us when he arrived. He usually loves to have the family around him. That does seem odd, doesn't it?'

'Where is his bag, if he didn't come to the house?' Daniel asked. 'Surely he would have traveled with luggage?'

'As to that, I expect the servants would have brought it,' Joseph said. 'And they traveled separately from us.'

'Ah, yes, the servants. Maybe one of them can enlighten us as to why Mr Hannan arrived at his house but didn't come in,' Daniel suggested.

'What about that strange man Mrs Sullivan encountered at the gate?' Joseph said. 'If we are to suspect that my brother met his end unnaturally, then this fellow is someone we need to talk to. A stranger, hanging around the property after dark, wanting to know if Brian had arrived. You need to find him, Prescott. Find out if he stayed in a boardinghouse in town overnight and if he was seen at the station.'

'I believe I know my job, sir,' Prescott said primly.

'Let's hope it does turn out to be him,' Terrence said, 'because if not, everyone else on the property was a family member.'

'What a ridiculous thing to say.' Archie Van Horn rose to his feet. 'Are you suggesting it was one of us?'

'Some day you'll go too far, boy,' Joseph said. 'It's about

time you learned that your idea of amusing talk might be taken seriously. It was an accident, I tell you.'

'And if it wasn't?' Terrence challenged his father. 'What then?'

'Anybody could get into the property if they were serious about it,' Joseph said. 'It would be simplest matter in the world to come in during the day when the gates are not locked and hide out in the shrubbery. I told Brian we should have the grounds patrolled by watchdogs, but he didn't like the idea.'

'Wouldn't the gardeners have noticed someone trying to enter?' Eliza said. 'They always seem to be around when I'm outside.'

'Not necessarily.' Archie gave her a withering look. 'In case you haven't noticed, it's a big property and when we're not here who knows how much work they do.'

'They were much in evidence yesterday,' Daniel said. 'It would be worth questioning them with the rest of the servants.'

'I'll decide whether anybody needs to be questioned,' Prescott said. 'So far we have a body lying on rocks below a cliff. Nothing to suggest that anyone else was involved or even witnessed what happened.'

I had been sitting quietly, like a dutiful wife, but a thought had been growing in my head and I thought it was about time I spoke up. 'If someone did try to kill him,' I began, making all faces turn toward me again, as if they'd only just remembered that I was in the room, 'they were taking an awful risk. I've been at the bottom of that cliff. It's not that high, as cliffs go. And the tide was coming in when I was on the beach so it would have almost covered the rocks last night. Surely there was a chance that Brian Hannan would not have died at all. He might have been injured, but live to point the finger at his accuser?'

They all stared at me as if I was a creature from another world. Irene put her hand to her breast as if she might swoon.

84

'You must forgive my wife,' Daniel said hastily. 'Having asso-
ciated herself with me and my police work, she doesn't have the
normal feminine sensibilities. But what she says is correct. It
is not at all a given fact that a man would die from such a fall.
Especially if the tide was up on the rocks. A well-timed wave
would have broken his fall and he would have lived. If someone wanted to dispatch him and he was wandering alone in his
grounds in the darkness why not shoot him or stab him?'

The Hannan family members shifted uncomfortably.

'I think we're getting into the realm of fantasy here,' Chief
Prescott said. 'Until I hear differently, I'm treating this as an
accidental death. Let's hear what the coroner has to say, shall
we, before we start making any wild speculations? And even
then, we may never know.'

'I agree,' Joseph said. 'I find it highly unlikely that an enemy
followed him all the way out here with the intention of killing him. It was a tragic accident, that's all. Brian arrived and
decided to do the rounds of his property. He was very proud of
this place, you know. Perhaps he was enjoying the solitude and
the sound of the ocean after a busy week in the city. He lost his
way in the dark and made a fatal mistake.'

At that moment the door opened and Mrs McCreedy stepped
in cautiously. 'Begging your pardon, sirs, but will you be wanting your breakfast as normal?'

She had clearly been crying and was fighting to maintain her
composure.

'We're just coming, thank you, Mrs McCreedy,' Patrick
Hannan said gently. 'It will do the servants good to have something to keep them busy.'

'Then I'll tell the chef, sir.'

'So Mr Hannan's chef did arrive last night?' I asked.

She shot me a suspicious glance. 'Yes, he came with the rest
of the servants, just like I told you he would.'

'Mrs McCreedy, isn't it?' Chief Prescott said. 'I believe you're the housekeeper here?'

'Have been since Mr Hannan first had the place built thirteen years ago, God rest his poor soul.'

'So maybe you can shed some light on the events of last night,' Prescott said. 'Did you see Mr Hannan when he arrived?'

'No, sir. I did not,' she said firmly. 'I was concerned if you want to know because he had told me that the family would all be here in time for dinner, and he was very particular about punctuality for meals. They all waited for him last night but by eight o'clock the food was spoiling, so finally they sat down to eat without him. And then when I locked up for the night and he still hadn't come, I started to get worried. I felt sure he would have let us know, you see.'

'There's a telephone in the house, isn't there?' Prescott asked. 'Did you expect him to telephone you?'

'Oh, no, sir.' Mrs McCreedy shook her head vehemently. 'There would be no sense in telephoning me. I don't hold with contraptions like that. I'd never get up the nerve to answer it. It don't seem natural, does it? I wasn't even happy when they had electricity installed a few years back. I don't trust this tampering with nature and when they're not in the house the lamps and candles are good enough for me.'

'So Mr Hannan would not have telephoned even if he was running late, you think?' Prescott continued.

'My brother had the line installed primarily so that he could stay in touch with our business in New York when we are here. I am rarely in the main house and, as Mrs McCreedy has just said, the servants are unlikely to answer it,' Joseph Hannan said.

'So you'd have had no way of knowing if Mr Hannan was expecting to arrive that evening or not.'

'He'd have let us know one way or another. He'd have sent a telegram, sir, if he wasn't planning to come,' Mrs McCreedy said. 'He was considerate in matters like that. This whole thing was odd, very odd indeed. Bringing the family here for a weekend in October – it's never happened before. And then these people arriving out of the blue.' She pointed at us. 'I'd like to know what it was all about.'

'So would we all,' Joseph said. 'Unfortunately Brian kept us all in the dark, Mrs McCreedy.'

'And it may have cost him his life,' Daniel said.

Mrs McCreedy frowned at us. 'What does he mean?' she asked.

'Nothing. We'll go through to breakfast now,' Joseph said. 'Come along, everyone.' He ushered them out of the room, like a large sheepdog rounding up sheep.

As we left the room I heard Mrs McCreedy saying in a low voice to Chief Prescott, 'If I were you, I'd find out more about those Sullivans and what they are really doing here.'

I grabbed Daniel's arm and drew him into an alcove near the door. It was dark and half hidden by a velvet drape. Daniel looked at me as if I had gone crazy but I put my finger to my lips. The police chief and housekeeper were still standing just on the other side of that door. Daniel stifled a cough, pressing his handkerchief to his mouth.

'They've been acting peculiar and snooping around,' Mrs McCreedy went on in a voice that was little more than a whisper.

'But you were expecting them? Your master did notify you that they were coming?'

'Well, yes. I got one letter from the master to say that the family was coming for a few days and to have everything ready for them, just like in the summer. And then a separate letter arrived to say that Mr and Mrs Sullivan would be occupying the guest cottage at the same time, so please make sure that it was well stocked and comfortable for them.'

'And it was written by Mr Hannan?'

'Oh, no, sir. He very rarely wrote his own letters. It was written by a secretary. It said Alderman Hannan wishes me to inform you that . . . And I can't say I recognized the signature.'

'So anybody could have written it,' Chief Prescott said.

'My thoughts exactly,' she muttered in a low voice. 'I was waiting for the alderman to arrive to see what he'd have to say about the couple in the guest cottage. Clearly Mr Joseph knew nothing about them and was quite upset, since he likes to stay there himself.'

'Interesting,' Chief Prescott said. 'Thank you for letting me know about this, Mrs McCreedy. I'll certainly have my men look into it.'

And they came out into the hallway, walking right past us without seeing us standing half hidden in the shadows of the alcove.

'Bates,' Chief Prescott called out as he approached a constable standing at the far end of the hallway.

'Bates, I want you to send a telegram to the police headquarters in New York City,' he said. 'The message should say, "Verify whereabouts of Captain Sullivan."'

With that he and the constable went out through the front door. We waited until the sound of their footsteps on the gravel had receded before we emerged from our hiding place.

'The damned cheek,' Daniel exclaimed. 'That trumped-up little popinjay, full of his own self-importance. Let him go ahead and solve his own case without help. The most challenging case he's probably had until now is to locate a missing cat!' The words turned into a bout of coughing again and he stood there, holding on to me and gasping for breath.

'Daniel, you sound terrible,' I said. 'You shouldn't have

88

come. Now back to bed with you and you're not moving again today, whatever those rude people say.'

'Am I in for a lifetime of being dictated to?' he asked, attempting to make light of it.

'Only when it's good for you. Now come along. I'm taking you back to the cottage.'

As we made our way down the long hall we heard the sound of voices coming from behind a half-open door, along with the chink of plates and scraping of chairs. The family was sitting down to breakfast.

And Joseph Hannan's voice came clearly to us. 'What were you thinking, opening your big mouth and making that suggestion that it could have been one of the family who pushed your uncle. Are you out of your mind?'

'It was meant to be a joke. To lighten the occasion,' Terrence's voice answered.

'Some joke. After what we went through. Have you no thought for Irene?'

'Oh, come on, Father. That was long ago. Anyway, it was quite different, wasn't it? Besides, we were all in the house together after dark, weren't we?'

Were they? I thought. Someone had come out of the French doors and stalked off into the night and that somebody looked remarkably like Terrence himself. But then why would he take the trouble to put the idea into their heads if he was responsible? Why not insist that it was an accident?

I moved closer to Daniel. 'You heard that, didn't you?'

He nodded. 'Interesting. Do you think they were referring to the death of the child or was there perhaps another occasion we don't know about? When we get back I'll look into—'

'Ah, Captain and Mrs Sullivan.' Chief Prescott appeared around the side of the house just as we stepped out of the front door. 'I know the family members have indicated that they would like you out of their hair as soon as possible, but please don't plan to leave just yet.'

'So you think you might need my help after all?' Daniel said. 'Or are we the prime suspects?'

I tried not to smile.

'Of course not. Nothing of the kind. It's just that – I'd rather everyone stayed in place until we've conducted a thorough investigation – as a matter of principle, you understand.'

'Oh, yes. We understand very well, don't we, Molly?' Daniel said. 'We'll be at the guest cottage if you need us, Prescott. If not, we may be lurking at the top of the cliff, or snooping around. Come, my dear.'

We did not wait for his reply.

I tried to put Daniel back to bed when we reached the cottage but he was having none of it. I suppose a possible murder for a detective is like the scent of a fox to a hound.

'I'd dearly like to get a look at that body for myself before they go and spoil things,' he said, pacing to the window and back. 'They have probably moved everything and destroyed every clue by now.'

'I don't think that police chief would welcome you with open arms.' I put my hand fondly on his shoulder. 'We are under suspicion, remember.'

'Damned fools,' Daniel muttered.

'I could go and look,' I said. 'An inquisitive woman is not seen as a threat.'

'You're a threat to that housekeeper,' he said with a grin. 'It was you she was glaring at when she launched into her tirade about suspicious people arriving out of the blue.'

'That's because she caught me snooping around the passage behind the kitchen when I went to see if I could find a chicken for you. I opened a door and found her on the other side of it. I can't tell you which of us was more startled.'

'Why was that, I wonder?' Daniel said. 'I suppose she was used to having the servants' quarters to herself.'

'No, it was more than that. She looked – well, shocked, scared.'

'Guilty, maybe?' Daniel suggested.

'Possibly.'

'Then she was up to something she shouldn't have been doing. I wonder if that door led to the butler's pantry or the wine cellar and she'd been helping herself to a tipple?'

I smiled almost in relief. It could have been something as petty and simple as this that had turned her against me. She was afraid of being reported to the master and losing her position. Daniel started coughing again.

'Come on,' I said to him. 'Back to bed, young man. I'll bring you up tea and a boiled egg.'

'I may grow used to this,' Daniel said as he headed for the stairs. 'Breakfast in bed every day, a wife who attends to my every need. Yes, marriage may prove most satisfactory.' But the sentence finished in a barked cough. I looked at him with concern.

'For the love of Mike go to bed and stop talking. It's doing you no good to keep coughing like this. You take it easy and I'll be up with the food.'

'I wish I could take it easy,' Daniel said. 'But I'm itching to be out there taking a look at that body before they cart it away. I know that little oaf is going to make a mess of the investigation.'

'No you don't,' I said. 'For all we know he might be a first-class detective. Looks can be deceiving, you know.'

'Not in his case,' Daniel growled. 'Any first-class detective would welcome outside expertise, especially in the form of a man from New York. He jumped a mile when he thought I might be stepping on his toes.'

'You did rather try to take over his investigation,' I pointed out.

'What if I did? It hadn't even occurred to him that we might be dealing with foul play here, or at the very least that someone assisted him in falling over that cliff.'

'We don't know it is any more than an accident,' I said. 'We only have their word that he wasn't likely to be near the cliffs in the dark. What if he made a point of checking out his estate each time he arrived here? And besides, how would you or anyone prove it if he were a victim of a crime?'

'I might be able to prove it,' Daniel said. 'There was a storm recently, remember? A lot of rain means the ground is still soggy. There would be evidence of a second person – a footprint in a patch of mud, the fiber from clothing caught on a bush, and above all, signs of a scuffle on the clifftop.'

'Even Mr Prescott would notice signs of a scuffle, I suspect,' I said dryly.

'That Prescott fellow wouldn't know a clue if it jumped up and bit him.' Daniel started slowly up the stairs. Then he turned back to me. 'I feel it in my bones that this is more than a simple accident, Molly. All the instincts of my training tell me so.'

'And why is that?'

'A man arrives at his property for the first time in months. His family and servants are inside and yet he doesn't pop his head in the door and say, "Good evening one and all, I'm just about to inspect my grounds." He goes to the edge of the cliff and falls over? Not good enough, Molly. For one thing his family has pointed out that he was cautious about the cliffs and for another he wasn't likely to lose his way in the dark. The house is fitted with electricity. There would be light streaming from all the windows. He'd have had enough light to see by, and

HUSH NOW, DON'T YOU CRY

what's more there is a fountain, a tennis court, formal flower beds – plenty of landmarks by which he could orient himself. He could only have lost his way if he was on the fringes of his property where there is more of a wilderness, and surely even then the sound of the surf would have warned him he was getting close to the cliffs.'

I nodded in agreement. 'It does seem rather odd,' I said.

'And there is one more thing that convinces me.' Daniel paused at the top of the stairs.

'What is that?'

'He asked me to be here at the same time as his family.'

With that final statement he went into the bedroom.

Twelve

When I came up with a breakfast tray, Daniel was standing at the window, leaning forward to get a better view, his face almost pressed against the pane like a young child watching a parade go by.

'The damned fools are attempting to bring up the body already.' He did not turn back to address me. 'No sign of a police photographer and I doubt they made any proper observations of the crime scene. That Prescott fellow probably thinks that only Sherlock Holmes approaches a case in a scientific manner.'

I put the tray down on the bedside table.

'Daniel, I've been thinking,' I said. 'You said that the fact that Mr Hannan invited you here at the same time as his family was important. Do you have an idea why Mr Hannan wanted you here with his family? You claimed ignorance before but I wondered if you hadn't wanted to tell me all the facts at that time. So do you know what this might be about? Did he suspect he was in danger?'

He turned around now and shrugged. 'I really don't know, Molly,' he said. 'He said he wanted to show me something and then he said something like, "I think I might have got it wrong."'

'Got what wrong?'

'He didn't tell me. I thought it might have to do with misman-agement of company funds, that sort of thing, and he was going to show me balance sheets. Of course I could be quite wrong. Now we'll probably never know.' He went over to the bed and sat down, taking the tray onto his lap. 'By the way, that was a most astute observation of yours about the fall from the cliff not being guaranteed to kill someone at high tide.' He chuckled. 'I must say you caused quite a stir. They looked positively horrified that such a statement should come from a lady's delicate lips.'

I nodded. 'Yes, I thought Irene was about to swoon. It would have been high tide about six or seven. Of course if he didn't arrive until much later then the rocks would have been exposed again. Can you tell exactly how long someone has been dead?'

'My colleagues at Mulberry Street could. I can't answer for their expertise here.'

'Would it be harder if the body had lain in cold water overnight?'

'Harder but not impossible. Rigor mortis follows a certain pattern, you see. The progression would be slower if the body was chilled, but . . .' He looked up from his toast. 'Now why am I telling you this? This is not the sort of fact you will be needing in your future life as my wife.'

'You may want to discuss cases with me. You never know.'

'Oh, no. That would never do. A police officer does not dis-cuss his cases with his wife.'

'Most wives aren't equipped to be able to help,' I said. 'If I were a police detective, I would seek help wherever I could get it, especially from a smart and experienced female detective who has solved some most tricky cases single-handedly.'

He glanced up at me and shook his head, smiling. 'I can see you're not going to adapt easily to tea parties.' Then he looked down again and started tapping the top of his boiled egg, took a bite and gave a sigh of contentment. 'This is just what I needed.

To tell you the truth I was feeling completely washed out as we walked across that lawn. I felt as if I might keel over at any moment. This wretched cold. I am so angry with myself.'

'Don't be silly. You can't help catching a chill. We were both frozen to the marrow that night and you gave me your dry clothes. It is I who should feel guilty.'

'But I feel that I've spoiled our honeymoon. I wanted it to be a special time for both of us and now you're having to look after an invalid.'

'Get on with that egg and hush up now.' I patted his shoulder. 'I'll be up again with the linctus for that cough and the mustard plaster for your chest. And then you should take a little nap.'

'It sounds delightful,' he said dryly. I grinned as I left the room.

Outside the front door I heard the sound of horses' hooves and raised men's voices. I went to the sitting-room window and saw a bevy of policemen loading what was obviously the body, now on a stretcher under a tarpaulin, into the back of a police wagon. Chief Prescott was nowhere to be seen and the job was not going smoothly. At last the back door was closed and the wagon took off at a lively gallop. I was thankful the corpse was already dead – otherwise he certainly wouldn't have enjoyed that ride. I sat down to eat my own breakfast and then did the washing up.

When I went to clear away Daniel's breakfast things, he had fallen asleep, half sitting propped on the pillows. I pulled the coverlets over him and tiptoed downstairs again. Now that he was asleep, I was going to go for a morning stroll and take the sea air. And if I happened to have a look around the crime scene at the same time, then I was just being a typical woman, indulging her curiosity. I put on my hat and cape, securing the former well with any number of hatpins, because the wind was sharp and blustery, and went out.

Clouds were racing across the sky and the air was full of twirling leaves. The moan of the wind through the pines and around that house competed with the thump of the waves onto the sea shore. Seagulls hung in the air, being tossed around like scraps of paper. I wondered if this heralded the arrival of another storm and whether we would still be here when it hit. It wouldn't take long for Chief Prescott to receive a reply to his telegram, confirming that Daniel was who he said he was. And then for sure the chief would want us out of the cottage and out of his hair as quickly as possible. So it was likely that we'd be back in our own house by nightfall, Daniel probably chafing because he wasn't able to help at the scene of the crime – if it was a crime. I really didn't want to go, being as curious as Daniel was and enjoying this delightful setting, but I reasoned that he'd make a better recovery in his own bed at home.

I crossed the lawn without seeing anyone. A smart new automobile was standing outside the house, presumably belonging to Chief Prescott as I had seen no auto the evening before. But of the chief himself there was still no evidence. As I came toward the clifftop, the wind picked up in force, almost snatching the hat from my head, and I could taste the salt of sea spray on my lips. The ocean was angry today, slapping in over rocks and sending up sheets of spray. If there had been any clues to what happened to Brian Hannan, then they would have been surely destroyed or washed away by now. I looked down at the shore below. The body was gone and the police with it. There was no indication as to where it had been lying. Rocks, seaweed, tide pools glinted in the morning sunlight.

I continued along the edge, taking care that I was not close enough that a sudden swirling gust of wind could send me over too. As I walked I checked the ground at my feet. It was all manicured lawn, right up to where it dropped away and I wondered how the gardeners managed to maneuver their lawn mowers in a spot like this. Perhaps they clipped the very edge by hand. Disappointingly there were no muddy patches revealing a clear, condemning footprint. Nor was there any sign of the turf being disturbed in a struggle, nor of the cliff edge having recently collapsed, thus sending Brian Hannan hurtling to his death. In fact the whole scene was peaceful and serene – a gentleman's manicured country estate as one might see in a picture postcard.

I thought about the man I had seen leaving through the French doors the evening before and striding out into the darkness. If that person had been Terrence, and it certainly was someone of his build and height, then where could he have been going in this direction, away from the main gate and the bright lights of the bars in town. I looked around the grounds. On this side of the house were the formal gardens – the fountain and the tennis court. Among the trees I caught a glimpse of a gazebo and then the estate became a wilderness of shrubs and bushes. Nothing to entice a young buck like Terrence Hannan. I wondered if I'd be reckless enough to ask him about it, if I got the chance.

'There's nothing you can do, Molly Murphy,' said the small, warning voice in my head. 'It is not your case. You just mind your own business, look after your husband, and stay away from the Hannans.' I had felt that the house hadn't wanted us when we arrived. Now a great tragedy had occurred but it was nothing to do with us and the best thing we could do would be to leave these people to their grieving. Maybe Daniel and I had only stirred things up and given more grief by even suggesting that Brian Hannan's death was more than an accident.

I stood examining the clifftop, where the trees came close to the cliff edge. Why would Mr Hannan ever have wanted to come here in the dark? Unless – another disturbing thought crossed my mind – unless he had wanted to do away with himself. I had heard how he grieved for his beloved grand-daughter. Maybe he held himself somehow responsible for her death and had decided he could no longer live with the guilt, so he flung himself from the cliffs in the same spot that she had plunged to her death. Only that didn't concur with what I had heard about Brian Hannan. He was an egotist who thought highly of himself, who liked to play the benevolent dictator, the puppet master who pulled the strings. Described as kind and fair and yet with enough power over his family to know that they would make the uncomfortable journey from New York to Rhode Island at this strange, unfashionable time of year when he summoned them. Such men usually believe that they are always right and would not consider killing themselves. But then he had said to Daniel, 'I might have got it wrong.'

What might he have got wrong? And did it have anything to do with his family?

I looked down at the crashing waves. No, I couldn't see a man like Brian Hannan had been described flinging himself over that cliff. It would not have been guaranteed death and more likely would have resulted in messy maiming. From everything I'd heard about him, he would not have wanted to survive as a cripple. If he was going to kill himself he'd have done it efficiently and neatly – a shot through the head in his own New York house, along with a written note explaining his actions.

As I turned away from the cliff I spotted something glinting among the rocks below. I made my way back to the place where descent was possible, even if not too gracefully. Indeed it did involve sitting on my bottom for part of the way, but I did check first that nobody was watching and arrived without incident on the shore below. The tide was receding and the seaweed-covered rocks were wet and slippery. I made my way cautiously to the spot where I had seen the glinting object. I was half hoping to find a jewel or something incriminating like a cigarette case with telltale initials on it, but it turned out to be nothing more than several pieces of broken glass. They could have lain there for any length of time, of course. But they hadn't come from a passing ship. Their edges were still wickedly sharp. Some pieces lay among the rocks, some in a tide pool. I used my handkerchief to retrieve as many as I could, knowing that the larger fragments might contain a valuable fingerprint. Then I wrapped them in the handkerchief before I attempted the scramble back up the cliff to the gardens.

The glass was quite thick and obviously curved. I wondered if the autopsy might reveal that Mr Hannan had been hit over the head with a bottle as he stood on the cliff. I also wondered why Chief Prescott's men had not picked up the pieces themselves. I made it successfully to the top of the cliff, brushed off sand and dirt before walking back through the grounds. As I passed the French windows I paused, again trying to decide where the man who had left the house that way in the dark could have been heading. Perhaps there was a gate in the wall on that side of the property, where a person who did not wish to be seen could slip out unnoticed. But then why walk all that extra distance if one was going into town? Unless one wanted to meet somebody and didn't want the family to know. My thoughts turned to Mr Joseph Hannan and the woman who had been with him. What had he done with her, I wondered, and was tempted to go into town to find out if she had gone back to New York or was staying on in one of the small hotels.

Then I told myself that she was none of my business either. If Joseph Hannan chose to leave his wife at home and brought another woman with him instead, then it wasn't up to me to snoop into their affairs. And surely her presence here could have nothing to do with Brian Hannan's death. I paused, considering this, and made up my mind that I would go into town to see if I could find out any more about this mysterious Miss X.

Thirteen

As I came close to the back of the house I heard voices. I moved closer, taking the path that ran along the side of the house. A kitchen window was open and inside I glimpsed a row of black-and-white uniforms. So the servants were assembled in the kitchen and from the way those backs stood unmoving I suspected that Chief Prescott was grilling them. I dearly wanted to listen in but there was no convenient bush or obstruction near the window behind which I could hide. I went around the corner where there was a blank wall and flattened myself against this, praying that nobody would come, as I couldn't think of any logical reason I should be standing in this spot. Certainly not to be out of the wind as it was about the most exposed corner of the house and buffeted me as I stood there. It also snatched away the voices that floated out through the window so that I only caught snippets of conversation. Not enough to make sense of what anyone was saying.

In the end I gave up in frustration and had just decided to move away when the back door opened and three men came out. I stood still against the wall, hoping that they wouldn't turn and look back in my direction, but fortunately they stood for a moment outside the door, then started walking away from me. I recognized one of them as the gardener to whom I had spoken – a pleasant-looking lad.

'Well, how about that, then?' he said to the other men. 'Poor old geezer, what a way to go.'

'What do you mean, poor geezer?' a larger, big-boned cart-horse of a youth said. 'Why should we worry about him? What about us, that's what I want to know? Who gets the property now? What if they decide to sell it?'

'I suppose it goes to Mr Joseph, doesn't it? He was the master's partner in business,' the pleasant lad said.

'We'll just have to wait and see, won't we?' An older man stepped in between them. 'It's not our place to speculate and until we're told otherwise we get back to raking leaves and pulling weeds. Got it?'

'Yes, Mr Parsons,' the boys muttered.

'You know what I think,' the gardener I had spoken to said. 'I think there's more to this than they are saying. The way they grilled those New York servants – they aren't sure this was an accident, are they?'

'Watch your mouth, boy,' the older man hissed. 'Nothin' to do with us. We keep our mouths shut and stay well out of it.'

'Lucky for us we go home before dark, that's what I say,' the bigger youth said, nudging his friend. 'They can't pin nothing on us.'

'Not so lucky if they find out that you haven't got rid of those brambles over on the far side like you was supposed to,' the older man said.

'How was I to know they'd be coming here in October,' the boy complained. 'Ain't natural, is it? Whoever heard of a family coming up in October?'

'So you'd best get moving now, or you'll be looking for another job,' the older man said. 'We've already lost enough time today answering his danged fool questions.' And he stomped off in the direction of the stables. The younger gardeners exchanged a grin and then went their own ways. I paused until they were out of sight, thinking. Daniel had mentioned something about scraps of clothing fiber being caught on bushes. If there were lots of brambles in that far wilderness, maybe I'd turn up a valuable clue. I wasn't sure why I was so keen on finding clues to an incident that had nothing to do with me – perhaps I wanted to show Daniel how competent I was, but perhaps it was more that I wanted to impress Chief Prescott. A little of both, I suspect. I've always enjoyed a good challenge and I had nothing else to do at that moment.

I set out across the formal garden, veering to avoid the fountain that was sending out a mist of spray in that fierce wind until at last I reached the part of the grounds that had been allowed to grow wild. A white painted gazebo was half hidden among tall shrubs. A flagstone path led to it. I went up the steps and peeked inside. It was a simple structure, six sided with a wooden bench running around the walls. There was nothing special about it, except for its location, hidden away from the main house but with a delightful glimpse of the cliffs and ocean through the arched entrance. A drift of red maple leaves had accumulated on the benches and floor and it had an abandoned feel to it. I almost turned away again, then something caught my eye. On the bench just inside the entrance was a tray containing a decanter and a glass, half filled with a brown liquid – brandy or whiskey, I surmised.

Of course my first thought was why the police had not come across this or chosen to remove it for testing. What if the whiskey had been tampered with? Had Brian Hannan been here? Had he decided to have a quiet drink before facing the family? Of course it could easily have a more simple explanation. Maybe Terrence or Joseph, or even Father Patrick, may have needed to escape for an occasional tipple. There was nothing wrong in this and they'd have no problem confirming their presence in the gazebo. But the tray must have been placed there recently, as there wasn't a single leaf on it, whereas the bench beneath it was littered with them. So it was definitely worth mentioning to Chief Prescott. I changed direction and walked firmly around to the front of the house.

There was no longer a constable standing at the front door, but it was ajar and I stepped unchallenged into the foyer. Nobody was in sight and the hall still had that cold, unfriendly feel to it. I shivered and involuntarily glanced up the staircase. I didn't care what Mrs McCreedy had said, there was some sort of presence in this house. Almost as if a curse lay over it, claiming first the beloved child and then the master. But this was the twentieth century and it was America, not Ireland and people no longer believed in curses.

I stood waiting for someone to come, listening for voices but the house remained silent, apart from the wind that moaned softly down a chimney. Chief Prescott had been in the kitchen with the servants so I started down the passage that led to the rear of the house. Halfway along this hallway I heard men's voices coming from behind one of the many doors. I put my ear to the door, trying to discern whether one of those voices belonged to Chief Prescott. I thought I recognized Joseph Hannan's blustering manner and hesitated to barge in on him, when he had made it so clear that he wanted Daniel and myself off the premises as soon as possible.

I jumped guiltily as I heard footsteps behind me and spun around to see a footman coming toward me, carrying a tray containing a silver coffeepot and cups. He looked at me curiously.

'Can I help you, miss?' he asked in a voice that still had a trace of Irish brogue.

'I was trying to hear whether Chief Prescott was in this room,' I said. 'Are you bringing that coffee for him?'

'I believe he is in there with Mr Joseph,' the young man said, staring at me impassively. I could see him trying to judge from my appearance whether I was a guest or someone of lesser rank and whether he needed to treat me with deference. Of course I had been out in the wind and up and down a cliff so I'm sure the first impression was not too good.

'Is he expecting you, miss?' he asked flatly. 'Do you have a message for him?'

'I wish to speak with him immediately concerning the alderman,' I replied in my haughtiest voice. 'Kindly announce me when you take in the coffee.'

'Whom shall I say is calling?' he asked.

'Mrs Sullivan. My husband and I are staying in the guest cottage. We were invited by the alderman himself,' I said. 'And I have already made the acquaintance of Police Chief Prescott this morning.'

His fair Celtic face flushed. 'Very well, ma'am. I'll ascertain whether he and Mr Joseph wish to be disturbed. If you'll just wait here.'

He opened the door. 'A Mrs Sullivan is here and wishes to speak to Chief Prescott,' he said grandly.

'What does she want? We're busy,' Joseph Hannan said.

I wasn't going to stand meekly in the passage while they discussed me and what I might want. I walked into the room. It was a gentleman's study, with leather chairs, a mahogany desk, and a wall of leather-bound books. It looked so perfect that I couldn't help wondering whether Brian Hannan had purchased the whole thing from an English stately home and had it shipped across. Joseph Hannan and Chief Prescott were sitting across from each other in leather armchairs. They both looked deci-dedly displeased to see me.

'This won't take a moment of your time,' I said, addressing myself to the police chief. 'But I've discovered something that may be important for your investigation.'

'You have? What is it?'

'I was taking a stroll around the grounds,' I said, 'and the wind became rather strong so I decided to take refuge in the little gazebo. Imagine my surprise when I saw a tray on the bench. There was a decanter on it, and a glass, half full. I presume your men must have mentioned it to you, but on the off chance that they hadn't, I thought I'd better.'

'Yes, well thank you, Mrs Sullivan,' the police chief said. 'Good of you.' His expression made it clear that nobody had told him about it but he wasn't about to lose face by admitting it.

'A tray with a decanter on it, you say?' Joseph Hannan asked.

'And it looks as if it had been placed there recently,' I added.

'And how would you know that?' Joseph Hannan asked in what I took to be a patronizing voice.

I still kept my gaze directed toward the police chief as I answered. 'Because there are a good many leaves lying on the bench and none on the tray. So I wondered who might have gone to have a quiet drink alone there, and when that was.'

'Interestingly enough, that ties in with what I was just telling you,' Joseph Hannan said to the police chief. 'That would make perfect sense. Brian arrived last evening and the first thing he needed was a drink before he faced us. But he didn't want any fuss from us so he took it off to the gazebo where he could drink in peace.'

My gaze went from the police chief to Joseph Hannan and back again.

'Mr Hannan had just this minute mentioned to me that his brother had begun drinking rather heavily and that the family was trying to stop him before it was too late,' Chief Prescott said.

'Nobody enjoys a good Irish whiskey more than I do,' Joseph Hannan said, 'but with Brian it was beginning to take over his life. Threatening all he'd worked for all these years – the business, his political ambitions. Naturally we tried to help him. My wife and daughter are part of the temperance movement so you can imagine how they lit into him any time they saw him with a glass. Poor man, they gave him hell.' He gave a wry smile.

'So if he arrived last night and wanted a drink, he must have got it from somewhere,' Chief Prescott said. 'Where would he have helped himself to a decanter and glasses without being seen? Or one of the servants must have brought him the tray, which is strange, because none of them mentions having done so. In fact they all swear that they didn't see him arrive.'

'Ah, well, I think I can shed some light on that,' Joseph said. 'Shed being the operative word. Brian knew his drinking wasn't well received in the house, so he kept a little stash in the shed by the stables. That's where this probably came from.'

'Thank heavens for that,' Chief Prescott said. 'I was fearing we'd be in for an investigation, given that Mr Hannan was such an important man in New York. But this explains it all, doesn't it? You say Mr Hannan drank too much. Didn't know when to stop. He sat there in the gazebo last night until he was drunk and then in his drunken stupor he walked the wrong way, over the cliff. A sad ending to a great man, but not entirely unexpected would you say, Mr Hannan?'

'It's what we've all been fearing,' Joseph said. 'What a waste. Just when his future had never been brighter.'

Chief Prescott nodded. 'Better in a way than the suspicion of a crime hanging over the family.'

'I suppose it is. And that means there is no reason for Mrs Sullivan and her husband to stay on any longer, is there?' Mr Joseph put the question to Chief Prescott. 'They'd be free to leave now, wouldn't they?'

'I suppose so.' The police chief was hesitant. 'Let's just wait and see that the autopsy confirms what she has just told us. We should hear their initial findings later today with any luck.'

'And if you don't mind, I'd appreciate it if we could stay at least until tomorrow morning,' I said. 'My husband is not at all well. He needs a day of rest before we attempt the journey home.'

'I'm sorry to hear that,' Chief Prescott said. 'I noticed he was coughing this morning. Caught a chill, has he? The wind can be fierce at this time of year.'

'He'd recover better in his own bed at home,' Joseph Hannan said. 'That's the first thing I want when I'm ill. My own bed.'

'I'd prefer they didn't leave at this very moment,' Chief Prescott said. Then he actually extended his hand to me. 'Thank you, Mrs Sullivan. You have been most helpful and most observant. No doubt our autopsy will reveal the presence of alcohol in his system and we can close this case.'

And he escorted me to the door then shut it firmly behind me.

Fourteen

Daniel opened his eyes as I came into the bedroom.

'Oh, there you are,' he said wearily. 'I wondered where you had gone. I'm so thirsty, I needed a drink of water, but I didn't feel like going all the way downstairs to fetch one.'

'I'll get you one,' I said and did so. He drank as if he'd been lost in a desert for days. I put my hand on his forehead. 'You're rather hot,' I said.

'And my head aches like the devil,' he said.

'I'll go into town and get you some aspirin from the chemist if you like,' I said.

'Thank you, if it's not too much trouble.'

'What else do I have to do?' I looked down at him fondly and stroked his hair. 'I want you to get well as soon as possible, don't I?'

Having left Daniel with a carafe of water and a glass at his side, I put on my hat and cape again and set out on my errand. As I joined the main driveway close to the gate I saw my gardener from yesterday working nearby.

'Morning, ma'am,' he called. 'You've heard the terrible news, no doubt.'

'I have.' I didn't need a second excuse to go over to him. 'What an awful thing to have happened. The whole family was in shock this morning.'

109

'I can imagine. The servants were pretty cut up too, I can tell you. Especially Mr Hannan's own servants he'd brought from the city. Couple of maids bawling their eyes out and even his cook looked as if he'd been crying – but then he's a French guy so you expect that kind of thing from foreigners, don't you?'

'How many staff actually came from Mr Hannan's house in the city?'

He sucked through his teeth, thinking. 'Not many this time. It wasn't worth bringing up the whole household like he does in the summer. Let me see. The French chef, for one. Mr Hannan never leaves him behind. He was fond of good food and frankly Mrs McCreedy's cooking isn't too wonderful. What you'd call Irish basic, I think. And usually the butler comes up in the summer, but this time he stayed behind. And who else was there – Mr and Mrs Van Horn brought their personal servants. They have a maid and valet who look after them, like in all the good households. But the master just brought a couple of maids and a footman to serve at table, oh, and his chauffeur. He keeps an automobile here to run him around and he has another one in the city. Imagine – two automobiles, and I hear he has a very fine carriage and pair too. Nice what money can do, isn't it?'

'No use to him in the end though, was it?' I said.

'True enough. We're all wondering what's going to happen now.' He looked around before speaking again. 'We don't know if the whole kit and caboodle will go to Mrs Van Horn, seeing as how she's his only child. Or to Mr Joseph as his business partner, or whether the fortune will be shared between all the family members. If it's Mr Joseph he may not even want to keep on this place. He doesn't really like it here. He's a city gent. He doesn't even stay in the house most times – he sleeps out in the guest cottage where you are now.'

'And I have a good idea why,' I said. 'He arrived unexpectedly a couple of nights ago and brought a woman with him.'

'That's what we've heard.' The boy lowered his voice even though there was nobody within sight. 'He and his wife don't get along. He only married her for her money, of course. That's what we hear. And she's very religious and into charity work and he – well, let's just say that he likes a bit of fun, if you know what I mean. They say he has a regular mistress – all set up in a house of her own and everything. But the master didn't approve so I suppose Mr Joseph kept her away from prying eyes in the guest cottage.' He laughed in disbelief. 'He's got a nerve, hasn't he? The way rich folk carry on.'

'So tell me,' I said, steering the conversation back. 'What did the servants have to say to Chief Prescott? Anything interesting?'

'Nothing much at all. He asked us whether Mr Hannan was definitely expected last night and what orders he'd given to his staff. They all said that he sent them ahead and told them he'd got a spot of important business to take care of and he'd be coming up on a later train. The footman had brought the bags and had unpacked his master's clothes – laid out his suit for dinner, so he was definitely expected by then.'

'But nobody saw him arrive?'

'That's the funny thing, isn't it?' The boy put his head on one side, like a sparrow. 'House full of people – you'd think someone would have seen him. You'd think he might have said hello to his family before he went off walking in the dark.'

'It's all very strange,' I agreed.

'You know what else was a bit strange,' he continued. 'Mr Parsons, he's the head gardener. He said someone had been in the shed. Moved things around.'

'Ah, well, I think I can explain that,' I said. 'Two people in fact. Mr Hannan's grandson Sam went out fishing early this morning and I gather the fishing tackle is kept in the shed, and also I was told that the master kept a bottle of whiskey and a glass in the shed, in case he wanted a tipple without anyone seeing him.'

'So that's why nobody saw him.' He looked relieved now. 'He went off for a quick drink in private.' Then a frown crossed his boyish features. 'All the same, that don't explain how he wandered the wrong way and went over a cliff, does it?'

'No, it doesn't,' I said.

He lifted his shears again. 'Ah, well, it's no business of mine. I'd better get back to work. Mr Parsons is a stickler about slacking off and I'm lucky to be one of the ones they keep on all winter. In the summer they take on five gardeners. In winter it's just down to three.' And he went back to digging up dying plants.

I continued out of the gate and followed the road into town. As I passed the solid redbrick colonial I glanced up and thought I saw a figure half hidden behind the drapes again. Someone in that house had nothing better to do than to sit and watch the road. I wondered if this observation continued after dark. If so the person might prove very useful to the police chief – but then he'd already decided that this was an accident caused by drunkenness, hadn't he?

I went over this as I walked on. I'd been trying to form a picture of Brian Hannan in my head and what I'd heard didn't add up. A man who was the clear head of the family, who could summon them, knowing they would all come. I'd gotten the impression they were all a little afraid of him. I'd heard how they had to be well dressed for him, how the staff were not allowed to slack off. And yet this man, the owner of the estate, a powerful politician and businessman, had apparently not wanted to face his family without taking a drink first. He had slunk off to a gazebo with a bottle he'd kept hidden away in a shed. That didn't make sense. Surely a powerful, confident man like Brian Hannan would have said, 'To hell with

the lot of you. I'm going to take a drink in my own house.'
He would have announced his arrival and expected his family
to gather around him to pay their respects. The only reasons
I could think of for this secret drink in the garden was that
he was ashamed of his own weakness, or . . . He was meeting
someone he didn't want the family to know about. And my
thoughts went to the man who had stood outside the gate and
said, 'Don't tell him. I want to surprise him.'

Had the surprise been to push him over a cliff?

I decided to keep an eye open for him when I was in town. I
also thought that I might find out whether Mr Joseph's ladylove
was staying somewhere close by. I went first to the chemist
shop. The young man behind the counter remembered me.

'And how is your husband today?' he asked. 'Did the medicines make him feel better?'

'Not yet,' I said. 'In fact he is now suffering from a headache
and a fever. I know how well aspirin works so I thought I'd
bring him some.'

'Good choice,' he said. 'I've got some packets already made
up. You just need to stir them in water. I always find a spoonful
of jam helps take the bitter taste away. And I've a good tonic to
help build him up – it's made with Fowler's solution of arsenic
and Culver's root. Powerful stuff. Do you want me to make you
up a bottle of that?'

'Let's just try the aspirin first,' I said, having reacted to the
word arsenic. 'I think it's just a nasty cold and needs to take
its course.'

I came out of the shop with my packets of aspirin powder
and stood looking out at the blue waters of Narragansett Bay.
A line of white sails stretched across the horizon, obviously
the yacht race in which Archie was going to compete. I thought
how pleasant it would be to take another stroll through the
town, to sit in the sun on the harbor, and watch the boats. But I

wanted to get the aspirin back to Daniel. Maybe if he slept after lunch I'd go for another walk.

I did keep a lookout for the man I encountered at the gate last night and I visited a couple of small hotels on the main street to ask if a single lady had been staying there. No such brazen ladies had darkened their doors, but one establishment did say that a lady and gentleman had come in very late a couple of nights ago, saying that they had missed the last train back to New York and would have to stay until morning. A Mr and Mrs Joseph. She had done most of the talking. He'd stayed in the background – big fellow with an impressive bushy mustache. They'd left early the next morning, without even waiting for breakfast for which they'd paid. The woman sounded amazed that anybody would do anything so foolish. 'They must have been in a real hurry to get back to the city,' she'd added.

That sounded as if I'd hit on something. A Mr and Mrs Joseph? And he'd stayed in the background, and worn a big fake mustache. As a disguise it was always successful because the mustache was always the one thing that people remembered, not the face, the expression, or the voice. So it appeared that Joseph's ladylove had taken the first train back to the city. That was probably correct, given the small size of Newport and the prejudice against a woman alone trying to stay at a hotel. Not that it could have any relevance to Brian Hannan's death. I hardly thought that Brian Hannan's brother would shove him over a cliff because his mistress was not welcome at Connemara. But something had made Joseph Hannan uneasy. It couldn't just be suspicion of outsiders that had made him so anxious to get rid of us.

I gave one last regretful look at the bustling harbor scene and made my way back to the cottage. It was harder walking back with that wind full in my face and I was quite out of breath by the time I entered at the main gate. There was no sign of the gardener. No sign of anyone, in fact. I glanced up at the tower window and started as I thought I saw a movement. But then a second later a dove flew down and I realized that it must have been sitting on the windowsill.

Daniel was sound asleep and snoring noisily, so I need not have hurried back after all. But it was close to lunchtime so I heated up the soup I had made the night before and carried him up a tray with a hunk of bread. The bread was now getting stale and I didn't like to repeat last night's fiasco by visiting the kitchen for more. Crumbled into the soup it wasn't so bad. I woke Daniel and he made a halfhearted attempt at eating. Then I gave him the aspirin mixture to drink and he made an awful fuss about the taste. Really men are such babies when it comes to sickness and medicine!

After lunch I decided against going back into town. There were clouds on the horizon that promised rain later. Instead I remembered that I had promised to write to Sid and Gus, so I took the little lap desk and went to sit in the gazebo. I noticed that the tray had been removed and big policemen's boots had trampled the leaves on the floor. I wondered if they had searched for clues, then wondered what those clues might be. How did one detect whether one or two people sat on a bench, or stood together in a gazebo, when the place was littered with leaves? But then Chief Prescott was now treating this as an accident, wasn't he? The case was closed as far as he was concerned.

I cleared a portion of the bench to sit down. It was dusty and damp, the leaves having been rained on recently. Not at all appealing as a place to write letters. I had just decided to give up and go back to write in the pleasant warmth of the little sitting room at our cottage when I heard footsteps tramping through the undergrowth. They were coming closer and closer – a heavy, measured tread.

Fifteen

I was on my feet instantly, my heart beating rather faster than normal. I hadn't imagined it. I could definitely hear the sound of footsteps over the whistle of the wind in the trees and the crash of the waves. Then I told myself that it was broad daylight and I had nothing to alarm me. It was probably just one of Chief Prescott's men been sent to patrol the area once more. The footsteps came ever closer, that same slow measured tread that was alarming in itself. It was the footfall of someone moving cautiously, but with purpose. I looked around me but could see no one. When the bushes parted just outside the gazebo, a few feet away from me, and a face poked through, I leaped back, stifling a scream, until I saw it was Terrence. He laughed and pushed his way through the undergrowth.

'It's all right, it's only me,' he said. 'I heard rustling in the gazebo so I thought I'd creep up and take a look.'

'Some creeping. I heard you coming a mile off.' I replied with as much bravado as I could muster, ashamed now of my weak and female reaction to his sudden appearance.

'Then why did you look so startled when I poked my head through the foliage?' he demanded, coming up the steps to join me in the gazebo. 'Who did you think I was? The Jersey Devil moved north for the winter?'

'No, but you have to admit that one doesn't expect a face to appear suddenly through the foliage like that. Among civilized adults, that is.'

This made him laugh even more. 'But then, my dear, this is the jungle and I've never been a civilized adult. Ask my parents. My mother has completely given up on me and spends long hours on her knees in front of statues, praying that I'll see the light and start acting like a God-fearing and sensible human being. My father has tried everything and has now also pretty much given up on me in disgust.'

'You don't seem so uncivilized to me,' I said. 'What is it that has made them despair of you?'

'My riotous living, I suppose. Wine, women, and song. Especially the wine, of course. You've heard no doubt that mother is a big noise in the temperance movement. Beware the demon alcohol and all that.'

'Yes, I did hear something of the sort.' I found that I had to return his smile. There was something unmistakably likable about him, whatever his failings might be. 'So what were you doing creeping through the undergrowth?'

'I couldn't take it in the house another moment,' he said. 'It was getting too much for me.'

'You have felt it too,' I said. 'I sensed it right away.'

'Sensed what?' he asked.

'You said you couldn't take it in the house another moment so I wondered if you also found it – oppressive?' I phrased it carefully, not wanting to use the word 'haunted.'

'Oppressive? More like depressive. All that weeping and gloom and doom. I mean, I miss the old fellow as much as anyone, but weeping and wailing won't bring him back, will it? And those steely-eyed policemen everywhere watching us. Enough to give one the shivers and make one confess to something one hasn't done.'

And he gave a slightly forced gay laugh.

'But you still haven't told me why you were creeping through the undergrowth,' I said. 'If you wanted to come to the gazebo, there is a path directly from the house.'

'If you really want to know, I wanted to check that it was unoccupied before I emerged,' he said.

'Really? Why was that? You didn't want to risk encountering one of those policemen?'

'Exactly.' He grinned then lowered his gaze like a schoolboy who is on the carpet before the headmaster. 'All right. I have a confession to make. I won't be giving it to the priest so I'll make it to you. My reason for coming this way was not entirely honorable.'

'Really?' I tried not to sound too interested.

'I heard my father talking about a decanter and glass that Uncle Brian must have left in the gazebo last evening before he plunged to his death. Since my sister and father watch the booze in the house with hawk eyes, I thought I'd take a stroll on the off chance that the decanter might still be here. But alas I see it isn't.'

'You'd have been taking an awful chance,' I said.

'Of being caught by Eliza?'

'No, of coming to a bad end,' I said. 'Did it not occur to you that if your uncle had fallen to his death after drinking in this gazebo that maybe the drink had been tampered with?'

The smile faded. His mouth opened wide in surprise. 'Good God. You're suggesting that the old boy was poisoned?'

'I'm suggesting it is a possibility we should consider, given that you all think it unlikely he'd just have blundered over the cliff by mistake. Poisoned or drugged. What if there was something in the liquor to make him drowsy or to disorient him?'

He hit himself on the side of the head. 'I never thought of

that. Stupid of me. I might have been lying at the bottom of that cliff by now if you hadn't been here.'

'Hardly, since the decanter and glass have been taken away.'

Terrence sat down and patted the bench beside him for me to join him. 'So tell me, Mrs Sullivan,' he said in an intimately low voice. 'Do you really think that my uncle was murdered?'

I sat. 'What do you think?'

'Me? I really don't know what to think. I don't think I'd go along with his being drunk enough to walk over a cliff. My observation was that he held his liquor pretty well. Unless he was well soused before he got here, which I suppose is possible. But if he had drunk that amount, wouldn't he have been more likely to have passed out, rather than gone blundering around in the dark? And as you pointed out, there is a perfectly good path back to the house.'

'Do you have a more plausible explanation?'

Terrence shook his head. 'I really don't. If someone tried to kill him – well, he was a big burly fellow. Kept himself in good shape. He'd have fought back. The police would have come across signs of a struggle.'

'Can you think of anyone who might want to kill him?'

At this Terrence had to chuckle. 'Want to kill him? Oh, I'm sure there are plenty of those around. Let's just say that the Hannan company doesn't always play fair and straight. In fact they play downright dirty to get contracts and to knock out competitors. And Uncle Brian's involvement with Tammany Hall – he never wanted the control himself but he liked playing kingmaker, and puppeteer. Yes, I think that described him well. He liked jerking the strings and making the rest of us dance to his tune.'

He fell silent while the wind rustled dead leaves and made branches creak around us. I wanted to take this one step further, to ask him whether his uncle had pulled on his strings and made

119

him dance recently. I also wanted to ask where he had gone when he left the house the prior evening, but until this was ruled an accident he was a suspect like everyone else in the house. So instead I asked, 'What does the rest of your family think?'

'As to that, I can't tell you. We're a reserved bunch. Keep our feelings and thoughts to ourselves. My father wants desperately to believe that it was an accident, brought on by Uncle Brian's weakness for alcohol. Eliza is ready enough to go along with that. Irene is still in shock, I should say. She's never had the strongest constitution and another body lying at the foot of the cliff is one too many for her to handle. Especially her adored papa who spoiled her horribly and kept her protected from the big bad world.'

'What about your other uncle, the priest? What does he think?'

Terrence shrugged. 'Who knows? He's a quiet, withdrawn sort of fellow. A little naive as most priests tend to be, especially when they are sent off to the seminary at fourteen as he was. So it probably hasn't entered his head that it could be anything but an accident. He was saying to my father this morning how Brian's drinking was grieving him and how he had hoped to speak to him about it while they were here.'

'And your aunt?'

'Not the brightest of souls, you know. And had no education to speak of. Hasn't exactly come up in the world like the rest of us. So she'd be prepared to believe anything, especially if it was on the headline of some penny rag. Of course she doesn't believe in the basic goodness of mankind like Father Patrick. She's seen her share of the other side – drunken husband who knocked her around and now her daughter's married to a lout of the same sort – always out of work, always drunk, always getting into fights. If he'd been anywhere near she'd have been all too keen to believe that he threw Uncle Brian over a cliff.'

'But you don't think he was the one who showed up at the gate last night asking if Mr Hannan had arrived?'

Terrence kicked at a pile of leaves with his well-polished shoe. 'Frankly I don't think he'd have the brains to find his way here. He's probably never been out of the city in his life – certainly never had to change trains. Besides, he wouldn't have had the money for the train fare – in addition to which it's already been pointed out that he lives within a block or so of the company office. He could have seen my uncle whenever he wanted. And I know Uncle Brian occasionally could be tapped for money, so why kill the golden goose?'

Why indeed? I thought. That same reasoning would apply to all the family members. They all benefited from his beneficence and if he'd left his fortune to his only daughter, then the rest of them would be worse off now than they had been.

Terrence reached into his pocket and took out a cigarette case and a lighter. 'Do you mind if I smoke? Irene makes a frightful fuss if I do it in the house. I don't suppose you'd like one yourself, would you?'

'Uh, no thank you,' I said. 'And I really should be getting back to my husband. He's not well, so I should be keeping an eye on him.'

'Not another victim of poisoning?' Terrence asked.

'No, just a normal chill,' I replied. 'At least I think it's a little worse than a normal chill. It's turned into a full-fledged grippe. However, I suspect that it's partly a case of men making terrible patients. Women just get on with it and know they have to recover quickly or else.'

'That's us men. Weak and self-centered creatures.' Terrence took a long drag on his cigarette and blew out a perfect smoke ring. 'Give my regards to your husband.'

My encounter with Terrence had left me feeling uneasy. I started to walk away quickly and had to resist the urge not to look back over my shoulder to see if he was watching me or following me. I told myself I had no reason to be afraid. He had done nothing to threaten me in any way. In fact he had been open, frank, and chatty with me. What's more, I liked him. He was witty and charming. He reminded me of my playwright friend Ryan O'Hare. But I knew quite well that criminals and even murderers could be charming. And his story about coming to the gazebo on the possibility that he might be able to help himself to a drink – surely that was a thin excuse, wasn't it? There would obviously be a drinks cabinet in the house where he could sneak a drink unobserved if he put his mind to it. It seemed more likely to me that he had wanted to come to the gazebo because he wanted to check it out. Perhaps he was concerned that he might have left something there – something that could be used as evidence against him. The truth was that I suspected that Terrence had something to hide.

I emerged into the full force of the wind as I came out onto the lawn and battled my way back to my cottage as quickly as possible.

Sixteen

'Molly, is that you?' Daniel called in a croaking voice as I came in through the front door. I went up and found him lying propped up in bed exactly as I had left him. He looked up at me, hollow-eyed and pathetic as only a man with a minor illness can look.

He held out his hand to me. 'I woke up and you were nowhere around. I wondered where you had gone. I was worried about you.'

I look his hand. It felt hot and clammy. 'I just went to sit in the fresh air to write a letter, although I didn't get much of a letter written. Terrence Hannan joined me and wanted to chat.'

'I don't like the thought of your wandering around out there,' he said. 'For all we know a murder was committed here last night.'

'Just because someone wanted to get rid of Brian Hannan doesn't mean that I'd be in any danger,' I said. 'I've nothing to do with the Hannan family.'

'No, but your presence could be taken as snooping. You made a couple of astute observations this morning, and it is now known that I'm with the police. You could be seen as posing a threat to a murderer.'

'I think you're exaggerating, my love.' I patted his hand as I held it. 'Besides the house and grounds are full of servants and even the occasional policeman. I'm not stupid, Daniel and I've learned not to be reckless either.'

'Oh, no,' he said. 'I can think of some fairly recent examples of your recklessness.'

'Nonsense. They were just bad luck not bad judgment,' I said. 'And anyway, I'm only prone to recklessness when I'm on a case.'

'Was on a case,' he corrected.

'Yes, dear,' I said dutifully, making him smile. 'Are you feeling any better?'

'I think I am,' he said. 'I should be all right by morning.'

'Which will be good, because Joseph Hannan has emphasized that he wants us out of here as soon as possible.'

'That's interesting, isn't it?' Daniel said. 'Is it just because he wants to bring his ladylove back to the guest cottage or does he think we'd be doing some investigating into Brian Hannan's death?'

'Not the ladylove,' I said. 'She caught a train back to New York the next morning.'

'Now how do you know that?' He sat up, staring at me.

'I thought it might useful to find out if she was still staying in town. And I discovered that a Mr and Mrs Joseph had stayed one night at an inn quite near the railway station. Arrived very late and left at crack of dawn. The landlady was amazed that they'd gone without the breakfast for which they had paid.'

'Not bad for a lady detective,' he said. Then he ducked. 'No, don't hit me. I'm on my sickbed.'

'I'll make us both a cup of tea.' I smiled as I went downstairs. It was good to see his energy returning. Maybe he would be well enough to travel in the morning. Frankly I couldn't wait to get away. The atmosphere of this place was beginning to weigh on me. I had just put on the kettle and was cutting some bread to toast when there was a knock at the front door. I was surprised to see the police chief standing there.

'Mrs Sullivan, I'm sorry to disturb you. Is your husband at home?' he asked.

'He is.'

'Then if I might have a word?'

'He's been taking a rest, but if you'll go into the sitting room, I'll see if he feels up to receiving a guest.' I ushered him inside. As I went up to the bedroom I found Daniel already struggling into his jacket.

'Are you sure you're up to it?' I asked.

'I want to hear what he has to say,' Daniel said. 'He wouldn't have come back if he hadn't information on the case.'

'Maybe he's come to arrest you as prime suspect,' I muttered.

'I think that's highly unlikely.' He paused to examine his reflection in the dressing-table mirror. 'God, I look awful,' he said. He ran a comb through his hair before heading downstairs. I didn't follow him into the sitting room, since the chief had specifically asked to speak to my husband, but I lingered at the doorway.

'Would you like a cup of tea, Chief Prescott?' I asked. 'I've a kettle about to boil.'

'Thank you. Most kind.'

I went through to the kitchen. At least I'd have an excuse to join them when I brought in the tea tray. The kettle was boiling. I made the tea and got out an extra cup and saucer. Then I carried in the tray.

Chief Prescott looked up as I came in. 'I came over because I owed your husband an apology,' he said. 'I received a telegram confirming that he is indeed who he claimed to be.'

'Well, that's nice to know,' I replied.

'And also because the two of you immediately assumed that there was more to Mr Hannan's death than a simple accident. It would appear you may be right. A doctor's initial examination revealed—' He broke off. 'I'm sorry, Mrs Sullivan, but this conversation is probably not something for a sensitive lady's ears.'

Daniel laughed. 'I should tell you that my wife has run her own detective business for several years and has seen more blood and gore than most men I know. I don't think you'll easily turn her stomach.'

'Really? Good gracious.' Chief Prescott looked at me as if I was a strange specimen at a zoo.

'I've sat in on an autopsy or two,' I said, not admitting that they had indeed turned my stomach.

'Very well then,' the chief said. 'If you wish to stay and hear this, I've no objection. A preliminary analysis of the stomach contents and the blood do show the presence of alcohol, but certainly not enough to draw the conclusion that Mr Hannan was too drunk to know what he was doing. And there is something else – our doctor thinks he detects the presence of some chemical poison in the bloodstream. He's taken samples to the hospital in Providence where they have better means of testing, but we should know tomorrow.'

'Interesting,' Daniel said. 'Poison, you say. It will depend if it turns out to be slow acting or fast acting. If it's the former then the lethal dose could have been administered even before he left the city. That would make it much harder.'

The chief nodded. 'Virtually impossible, I'd say. It could have been dropped into a cup of coffee on the train, for example.'

'Which would bring it down to motive,' Daniel said. 'Who had a reason to kill him?'

'That's why I've come back to see you,' Chief Prescott said. 'I wondered if you could shed any insights into this matter.' He paused, looking down at the pattern on the carpet.

'You're asking my assistance with this investigation?' Daniel asked.

'Well, not exactly. I wondered if it was more than coincidence that Mr Hannan invited you here this weekend. Because everything I've heard about Mr Hannan does not cause me to think that he was a warmhearted and generous soul who would invite a relative stranger to join his family gathering. And the fact that you are a policeman – a senior officer with the New York police – is significant. So can you shed any light on this? Did he suspect he was in danger and want protection?'

'I wish I could shed more light,' Daniel said. 'I gathered that I was being asked here for a reason. He said he had something he wanted to show me and then he added that he thought he might have got it wrong.'

'Had got what wrong?'

Daniel shook his head. 'He didn't elucidate and I didn't see fit to press him at that point. I had the impression that Brian Hannan was the sort of man who would tell you what he wanted to tell you, when he wanted to.'

'So you had no idea what it could have been?'

'No,' Daniel said. 'I surmised it might be something to do with finances. I don't know why I thought that. Maybe something he said about difficulties running a family business.'

He paused, coughing. I remembered that I had brought in the tea tray and poured two cups, handing one to the police chief and one to Daniel. The latter nodded gratefully and took a sip. 'You'll have to excuse me,' he said to Chief Prescott. 'I'm not at my best today. Nasty chill, I'm afraid.'

'So your wife told me,' Chief Prescott said. 'Well, I won't bother you much longer, but I had to know whether you got the impression that Mr Hannan knew he'd be in danger here.'

'I did not get that impression,' Daniel said. 'Quite the opposite. He waxed eloquent about how delightful it was and what a perfect spot for my delayed honeymoon.'

The chief took a drink of his own tea. 'Did he tell you why

127

he'd invited his family this particular weekend? None of them seems to know. Something about his son-in-law taking part in a yacht race, but surely there was more to it than that. It's quite unheard of for owners of cottages to come here after the season.'

'I realize that now,' Daniel said. 'Frankly at the time it never crossed my mind that there was anything unusual about it. I'm not often invited to mix with the Newport elite.'

'It had to have been planned for a purpose,' Chief Prescott said. 'I did hear from Mr Hannan's family members that they had been issued the royal summons and felt that they had to come. But not one of them had any idea about what it could mean.'

'Maybe he was planning to change his will,' I suggested, making them both look in my direction as if they had forgotten I was in the room.

'Now there's a thought.' Chief Prescott put down his teacup. 'And a good motive, if it turns out to be murder. If one of them was about to be cut out of a fortune . . .'

'I don't think that was about to happen,' I said. 'One thing I have noticed was that they all speak warmly of him. They were concerned about his recent drinking but that was because they were fond of him.'

'Fondness can change if one discovers one is being cut out of an inheritance,' Prescott said. 'Especially among people like this who are used to enjoying the good lifestyle. And that would explain the tray in the gazebo.' He smiled with satisfaction. 'He knew he was going to tell them something unpleasant. He wanted to fortify himself before he faced them, so he carried out the decanter and a glass and had a quiet drink.'

'I presume you've had the contents of the glass and the decanter tested if you suspect he might have ingested poison?' Daniel asked.

'Again, an initial testing. Frankly our facilities here in a small town like Newport are not the best. We've sent them to Providence with the blood sample.'

'And were traces of a poison present?'

'Not that we could detect,' Chief Prescott said. 'The glass and decanter seemed to contain nothing but Irish whiskey.'

'What about fingerprints?' I asked.

Again he looked at me in surprise. 'Your wife is certainly up-to-date in her methods, isn't she?' He said with a nervous chuckle. 'Yes, we'll have them tested for fingerprints.'

'I have something else that might be of assistance,' I said. 'Wait one minute.' I left the room and went to collect my handkerchief containing the fragments of glass I had picked up on the rocks. I returned and opened it on the table in front of them. 'Here,' I said. 'I found these earlier today when I was walking on the clifftop above where Mr Hannan was found. I saw the glint of something shining in the sunlight. I thought it might be important, so I climbed down to retrieve it.'

'Good gracious,' the chief said again.

'And it turned out to be these pieces of glass. At the time I thought they could have lain there any amount of time or even fallen from a passing ship, but now I'm wondering – was there a second glass on that tray? Was Mr Hannan holding it when he drank and fell?'

They said nothing so I went on. 'I picked them up with my handkerchief as carefully as possible, so that I wouldn't disturb any fingerprints, but I'm afraid the waves will probably have washed away any trace of what the glass contained.'

'Mrs Sullivan, you astound me,' Chief Prescott said. 'You've got yourself a clever little woman there, Sullivan. She'll no doubt be a big help to you in your profession.'

'So I keep telling him,' I remarked dryly.

Daniel wisely said nothing.

With that the interview came to an end. The police chief stood up.

'I'm sorry to have disturbed you, and wish you a speedy recovery,' he said, shaking Daniel's hand. 'You have been most helpful. A tricky business, Captain Sullivan. A prominent family – lots of money, influential in politics. I'll have the eyes of the country on me when this gets out. I can't afford to make a mistake. I keep thinking that maybe we're reading more into this than actually happened. What if it was an accident?'

'But the poison?'

'What if it turns out to be something his pharmacist prescribed that has toxic qualities. Many medicines do, don't they? There are plenty of tonics containing arsenic or mercury.'

'A competent physician will be able to tell you whether any substance was in his bloodstream in sufficient quantities to kill him,' Daniel said. 'And his physician will vouch for what he prescribed. So all we have to do right now is watch and wait.'

'That's it.' Chief Prescott headed for the door. 'Watch and wait.'

As I opened the door for him he said in a low voice. 'And Mrs Sullivan, your own observations have been most useful, but I have to warn you: leave this to the police from now on and devote your energies to looking after your husband instead.'

'Go back to my rightful place, you're saying,' I commented. 'And leave the real work to the men?'

'Not at all.' He shook his head. 'I'm saying that if what we fear turns out to be true, then someone on this estate killed a man in the proximity of many other people. Such a person is extremely dangerous and would not hesitate to dispatch you, should he consider you a threat.'

He stepped out into the slanted evening sunlight, blinking slightly as it shone into his face. He stared up at the brooding shape of the castle. Then he put on his hat, gave me a curt little bow, and walked over to his automobile.

When I came back into the room Daniel was standing up, one hand on the back of an armchair. 'I thought I'd go back to bed, if you don't mind,' he said. 'My head's still throbbing like the devil.'

'What do you feel like for supper?' I asked, taking his arm to escort him up the stairs. 'Anything I can tempt you to?'

He managed the ghost of a smile. 'Normally I could answer that in the affirmative. This evening I can't be tempted by anything except my bed and sleep. Oh, and another of those disgusting aspirin powders.'

'But you must eat something.'

'Just some more of that broth. That's all.'

'That's easy then. I don't need to cook.' I helped him off with his jacket. 'Why don't you get undressed properly and into bed?'

'I should probably stay like this for now, in case somebody comes from the big house. I'll just lie with a rug over me.' He brought out the words one by one, and with difficulty as if the climb up the stairs had winded him.

I draped the rug over him, then kissed his forehead. 'I'll be up with the aspirin then. And a spoonful of jam this time. That's what the chemist said. It makes the bitter taste go away.'

He nodded, lay back, and closed his eyes. Then as I was leaving the room he said, 'Molly, what made you say that about changing his will?'

'I don't know. I was trying to think of a reason he'd want his family assembled in a remote place.'

'You might have hit close to the mark,' Daniel said. 'Remember I said I surmised it was something financial. We'll have to find out from his attorney whether any such change had been planned.'

'Or implemented already,' I said.

Daniel nodded. 'If he was poisoned then one has to think that the most likely suspect would be a family member. Who else would know the alderman might have a quiet drink away from the house? And he was a wily old fox. He'd not have let a stranger get near enough to slip something into his glass.'

'We'll know more when the doctors in Providence have examined the evidence,' I said.

'I hope they are more competent than that Prescott fellow,' Daniel grunted. 'The problem is that most police forces outside of New York are hopelessly antiquated in their methods. No scientific approach to speak of. They rather try the witch trial approach – set fire to the suspect and if he doesn't burn he's a witch.' He lay back and closed his eyes. 'You could see that the idea of fingerprints was a novelty to Prescott. He probably will have no idea how to lift them from a surface and to preserve them as evidence. Of course, most of the judges in this country are no better. They've never yet been admissible in court. But that will have to change.' He coughed again – a rasping, rattling cough that shook his body.

'Stop talking and rest now,' I said. 'You heard Chief Prescott. He made it quite clear that he doesn't want your help with his case. You get better and then we'll go home.'

'He'll just bungle everything and a murderer will walk away a free man.'

'Or woman,' I said.

He opened his eyes in surprise. 'You yourself said that poisoning was a woman's crime,' I pointed out. Then I tiptoed out of the room.

A little later the stew was warming on the stove and I finally had time to write my letter to Sid and Gus. The wind had dropped and the sky was bathed in pink light. I sat at the open window of the sitting room, enjoying the tangy ocean breeze and the gentle thump and hiss of waves. Birds were calling from the treetops. It was a peaceful scene and I tried to blot out the disturbing events of the day. I started my letter by telling my friends of the alderman's death.

I know you are no friends of his, I wrote. *Nor of his politics. I remember when he was elected you were disgusted that Tammany Hall should wield such power and that yet another man had come to power who was only out to feather his own pocket and had no sense of justice.*

I paused, thinking about what I had written. It was funny, but I had forgotten all about that particular conversation until I started writing. Now it came back to me quite clearly. Sid and Gus sitting out in their lovely little conservatory, surrounded by potted palms, drinking their morning coffee while Gus read from the *New York Times* of the election results. They had hoped a more moderate candidate would win a seat on the city council. But Brian Hannan had used the normal dubious Tammany Hall voting methods to bring himself and Tammany Hall to power. Sid and Gus had been angry.

'If only the laws were not so stupidly archaic, I'd have run for the office myself,' Sid said. 'And I would actually have done something for the workingmen and women of this city. I'd have improved the conditions in the sweatshops. I'd have made sure that newsboys got proper food and an education.'

'And all he will do is to award his own company more contracts, take kickbacks from all and sundry and make sure it's more jobs for the boys,' Gus said indignantly.

'You'd have been brilliant,' I agreed. 'Too bad half of us have no say in the running of this city.'

I went back to my writing, finding that I was unable to speculate in writing as to whether it was a murder or an accident. If they picked up any hint that I might be looking into a suspicious death myself, they'd be down on me like a ton of bricks. They had

133

long being trying to persuade me that I was running unnecessary risks. *A full autopsy is being conducted,* I wrote, *and we should know more soon. In the meantime my time is fully occupied in looking after Daniel. No, he is not demanding that I become the little wife and attend to his every need. But he has come down with a nasty chill or grippe and I'm a little concerned about him. Still, I expect a good night's sleep will do wonders and he'll be better in the morning. How is life in the city? I expect—*

I broke off as I heard voices coming through the trees. I couldn't see the speakers but the voice that came to me was male.

'It's a rum do, and that's for sure.'

'You know who'd come to mind instantly if circumstances were different, don't you?' another male voice said softly.

'You mean they are suspiciously similar?'

'Of course. Exact same spot, if you ask me.'

'She's safely far away, isn't she? Of course she'd be the most convenient. Tie the whole thing up nicely.'

They drifted away without my ever being able to see them, but they left me wondering – 'she?' Which *she* could they mean? The only family members I knew of who were not present were Joseph's wife, Mary Flannery's daughter – the one with the loutish husband and all the children – and the two sisters who had been in the convent for years.

But then I realized that I didn't know how many years they'd been 'safely far away' in a convent. I wondered why the person they only referred to as 'she' would have tied the whole thing up nicely. One thing was evident – those two men were not prepared to believe that Brian Hannan's death was a random accident.

I finished off my letter, blotted it, and sat watching the sky as the sun sank in the west, making the stone at the top of the castle, peeping over the treetops, glow bright red. It was not a pleasant red of warmth but rather of blood. I stared at it, frowning, wondering if this image in my mind was only brought on by my current mood and by Brian Hannan's untimely death. But I had sensed the negative currents emanating from that house from the moment I first stood outside the gate. It was a place of hostility and of secrets. I glanced up at that turret window again, thinking about the child's face. But it winked in the setting sunlight and I couldn't see beyond the glare.

My thoughts turned to the beautiful little girl that nobody mentioned anymore. Her death had obviously affected the family and shrouded them since it happened. Then I remembered the words spoken by the two men who passed my window. 'Exactly the same spot.'

I sat up straight, dropping the pen I had been holding on the table. Had Colleen's death not been a tragic accident? Had there always been a suspicion among family members that it too was murder?

Seventeen

Daniel hardly touched his supper. Right after, I helped him undress, made him a mustard plaster for his chest, and put him to bed.

'I'll be fine by the morning' were his last words before he fell asleep.

I cleaned up, sat and read, and waited for the time when I too could go to sleep. I felt lonely and uneasy. Outside an owl hooted and the wind made tree branches around the cottage creak and crack, while the crash of waves on rocks echoed up from the shore. I suppose I have inherited that Irish sense of the fey, of portends, of the thin veil between the natural and supernatural worlds, but I can tell you that I felt very uneasy that night. The weight of something about to happen hung over me. I thought about Colleen and Brian Hannan. I worried about those two little boys whom I hadn't seen for the whole day.

At last I gave myself permission to go to bed. Daniel was still coughing and tossing in his sleep so I elected to curl up with a rug on the couch again. I drifted off to sleep and was awoken by a loud bump. I was on my feet instantly, heart thumping. My first thought was that Daniel had fallen out of bed. I ran up the stairs and was relieved to see his shape still lying in the bed. Then, of course I wondered if the noise had been someone trying to break into the cottage. I lit a lamp, then went around cautiously from room to room, but everything seemed safe and secure. I was just about to go back to bed, because the night was cold and my bare feet were freezing, when I decided to check on Daniel once more.

The moment I stood over him I knew that something was wrong. His breath was coming in ragged, rasping gasps. I reached for his forehead and he was burning hot. Even as my hand touched him he threw out his arm, making it thump against the wall and he muttered unintelligible words. I ran downstairs to bring up a wet flannel to sponge his face. He knocked me away.

'Keep it away from me,' he moaned. 'It's coming closer.'

'It's all right, my love,' I said. 'You're just having a bad dream.'

But even as I said it I knew it was more than that. He was hallucinating in his fever. I tried to lift up his head and give him a sip of water, but it was impossible. He fought off my touch. I began to feel frightened. This wasn't just an ordinary fever such as one might have with a cold or a grippe. It was more serious than that. I felt horribly cut off and alone. I dressed hurriedly and ran across the grounds to the castle. The moon was out, throwing crazy tree shadows across the lawns like long bony fingers reaching out to grab me. I ran up the front steps and hammered on the door.

Nobody came.

I hammered again, louder this time, pounding with my fists. The house had electricity – was there no electric bell? I searched but couldn't find one in the darkness of the porch. A window, I thought. There must be a window open somewhere. I started to walk around the castle, peering up at the walls in the moonlight. No window that I could see was open. Stark blank walls frowned down at me. I came to the side of the house with the French doors. I tried them, one by one, rattling each door with growing frustration. I reached the back of the house and the back door too was locked. It seemed I had only two options – one was to run all the way into town myself to try and find a doctor, the other was to break a window and wake someone to help me. I remembered how deserted the town had felt when we arrived that wet and windy night. How would I ever find help there?

So instead I went to the nearest flower bed, prized up one of the rocks that bordered it and, after a second's hesitation, hurled it through a kitchen window. The crash of breaking glass should have been loud enough to wake the dead, but no lights came on upstairs. I punched out enough of the broken glass to reach through and undo the catch. Then I hauled myself inside.

The house was completely dark and still and I groped around the walls for a light switch, eventually locating one. I flipped it down and the room was instantly bathed in harsh light from a naked bulb overhead. I came out of the kitchen, wondering whom to wake. The family slept upstairs and I had no idea where the servants' bedrooms were. Probably up in the attics. I couldn't find a light anywhere in the passage and made my way along it by feel until I sensed, rather than saw, the vast emptiness of that front foyer. *The telephone*, I thought. The telephone must be somewhere around here. Moonlight made narrow stripes on the tiled floor as it came in through thin arched windows over the staircase. It did little to illuminate, rather added to the unreal atmosphere of the place.

Suddenly I couldn't stand it any longer. There are times when decorum has to go out of the window. 'Help!' I shouted. 'Wake up! Somebody help me!'

My voice echoed as if in some vast church. For a moment nothing happened, then there was the sound of feet above me and an electric light was turned on in the corridor above.

'What's going on?' a male voice asked.

'Down here!' I shouted.

Then Mrs Flannery and Father Patrick appeared at the top of the staircase.

'What is it? What's happening?' Mrs Flannery asked.

'Is that you, Mrs Sullivan?' Father Patrick's calm voice called to me.

'It's my husband. He's dangerously ill,' I called up to them as they made their way cautiously down the stone stairs. 'He needs a doctor right away. I know there's a telephone some-where here.'

They reached me. Father Patrick put his hand on my shoulder. 'Don't worry, my dear. I'm sure it will be all right. Now where is that telephone? I know I've seen it somewhere.'

'Don't ask me,' Mary Flannery said. She had taken longer to reach me and was puffing with the exertion. 'I agree with Mrs McCreedy. I don't hold with such contraptions myself.'

'Mrs McCreedy would know,' I said. 'Do you know where she sleeps? Or does she still go home for the night?'

'Go home for the night?' Mrs Flannery sounded surprised. 'As far as I know she stays on the property year round. I think her room must be up with the rest of the servants.'

'I have a feeling the telephone is in Brian's study,' Father Patrick said. 'Let's go and look, shall we?' He led me down one of the halls and finally opened a door. 'Ah, yes, I was right. Do you know how to use it?'

'I'm not sure,' I said. 'I've tried a telephone before. You just wind the crank, don't you?'

'Go on then. Give it a try,' he said.

I had just picked up the receiver when a voice behind us demanded, 'Jesus, Mary, and Joseph, what is going on here?'

And there was Mrs McCreedy herself, breathing heavily as if she'd just been running.

'Mrs Sullivan's husband has taken a turn for the worse,' Father Patrick said quietly. 'She needs to telephone for a doctor.'

'That won't do much good,' Mrs McCreedy said. 'Dr Wilkins is the old-fashioned kind. Hasn't taken to the electricity yet, nor the telephone.'

'Then what am I going to do?' I demanded. 'Daniel is running a dangerously high fever. He's delirious.'

'We'll have to send somebody for the doctor,' Mrs McCreedy said. 'Too bad the master didn't bring his chauffeur this time. Can that footman boy drive the automobile?'

'I've no idea,' Father Patrick said. 'But I have driven a vehicle a couple of times in my life. I expect I can manage it. Give me a minute to get dressed and I'll go and fetch the doctor myself.'

'Thank you. Thank you.' I was on the verge of tears.

'You'll find him on Spring Street,' Mrs McCreedy said. 'White clapboard house just up from Narragansett Street. You'll see his brass plate outside.'

I watched him go back upstairs. 'I must get back to Daniel,' I said. 'But I don't know what to do.'

Mrs McCreedy patted my shoulder tentatively. 'Don't you worry, my dear,' she said. 'I'll come over to the cottage and stay with you until the doctor arrives.'

'Thank you.' I muttered again, feeling a tear now trickling down my cheek. Their kindness was almost too much to bear.

We helped open the gates, then went to the cottage. I heard the sound of cranking, then the *pop-popping* sound as the engine came to life. The big vehicle jerked forward in a rather hesitant manner as if its driver was not the most skilled, but at this stage I didn't care. Mrs McCreedy followed me in through the cottage door. I picked up the lamp and carried it up the stairs. I could hear Daniel's ragged breathing a mile away. So could Mrs McCreedy.

'He sounds terrible,' she said. 'I reckon it's turned to pneumonia. That's how my poor husband went, God rest his soul.' And she crossed herself.

I went over to Daniel and touched his burning forehead. He moaned again. All I could think was that I had made light of his illness when he had probably been rather sick for the past two days. It felt as if I had somehow brought this on myself.

'I'll make you a cup of tea,' Mrs McCreedy said, going down the stairs and leaving us alone.

It seemed an eternity before I heard the sounds of a motor again and the scrunch of tires on the gravel. Then I heard the front door open.

'Hello?' a voice called.

'Up here, Doctor,' I called and heard footsteps coming up the stairs.

'Now what have we got here?' he asked. 'I hope it's serious. I'm getting too old to be dragged from my bed at three in the morning.'

Before I could answer he looked at Daniel and shook his head. 'My, my. That doesn't sound good, does it?'

His manner changed and he was all business. He undid Daniel's nightshirt, brought out his stethoscope, and listened to Daniel's chest. He took Daniel's temperature, making little *tut-tutting* noises. Then he looked up at me. 'I'm afraid I've no good news,' he said. 'As you may have gathered, your husband has developed an inflammation on the chest. To put it shortly, pneumonia. There's not much we can do for him but make him comfortable and hope for the best. In my early days in medicine we'd have tried a purge or even a bloodletting, but both those are *pooh-poohed* in these days of modern medicine. All I can suggest is to keep the windows closed. Keep him bundled up and try to sweat it out of him. If he can drink give him water.'

'That's all? Would something like aspirin help?'

He gave me a cold stare. 'I'm still suspicious of these new-fangled medicines, young lady. From all I've heard, aspirin is helpful for headaches,' he said. 'I've no doubt he's got a whale of a headache at this moment but it's the least of his problems. No, I'm afraid all you can do is make him comfortable, let him ride it out, and pray.'

He gathered up his things and stuffed the stethoscope into the black bag. 'I'll return in the morning,' he said. 'And in the meantime—' he put a hand on my arm. 'I'm afraid you should prepare yourself for the worst. The chances of survival are not ever the best with pneumonia.'

'Would he be better off in a hospital?' I asked, trying to keep my voice steady. 'Would they be able to do more for him there?'

'There's nothing they could do for him in our small hospital,' he said, 'and the ride to Providence over bumpy roads could well finish him off. But he looks like a fit and active fellow. So we won't give up hope, will we?' He attempted a positive nod that didn't exactly come off as sincere. Then he patted my arm and left.

Eighteen

'You'll be all right alone with him, will you?' Mrs McCreedy asked, setting a tea cup down beside me. 'I should be getting back to the big house. I don't like to – I mean it will soon be dawn and I need to make sure those girls are up to light the fires in the bedrooms.'

She gave me a sympathetic smile.

'Thank you. There's nothing you could do anyway,' I said, 'except say a prayer for him.'

'I'll do that, my dear. I'll say a rosary. We'll put him in the hands of Our Lady. She'll take good care of him.'

I nodded, wishing I had her faith. Presumably she'd said a rosary when her husband was dying of pneumonia and it hadn't helped. She got as far as the door, then turned back. 'Look, I'm sorry I was short with you the other evening,' she said. 'When you came about the chicken. I had no idea your man was so poorly. You startled me, you see. I wasn't expecting to see anyone.'

'I understand,' I said. 'You gave me a turn too when I opened that door and saw your face on the other side.'

'I've been a bit jumpy these last few days,' she said. 'This whole visit didn't seem natural from the beginning, and then you and your man turning up like that.'

I nodded again, wishing she would go. Frankly I had no desire to sit chatting with her while my husband tossed and turned in his fever.

'And now that the master has been taken from us – well, I'm all of a tizzy. I don't know what's going to happen to us.'

'I'm sure it will all turn out just fine.' I put a tentative hand on her shoulder. 'Whoever inherits the house will want you to stay on.'

She nodded. 'Ah, well,' she said at last. 'I'd best be going. I'll send one of the local girls round in the morning to look after you. You'll not be wanting to cook and clean with your man lying in this state.'

'Thank you,' I said. 'I'm sorry to have disturbed your sleep.'

'Don't worry about me. I'm often awake during the night.' She went quietly down the stairs as if trying not to wake a sleeping child and I got the impression that this was a woman whose nerves had been on edge for some time – long before Brian Hannan had announced that he was bringing his family to the cottage for an October stay.

I turned my attention back to Daniel and sponged his forehead. 'Can you try to take a drink, my darling,' I whispered and attempted to lift his head. Again he fought me off, thrashing so that he kicked off his covers. Dutifully I replaced them. Another bout of coughing followed, then more rasping breaths. He was fighting for air now.

As I sat on the bed beside him, watching him, other pictures flashed into my mind. I saw myself as a fourteen-year-old standing at my mother's bed, watching her die. And the Irish patriot Cullen Quinlan dying in my arms as he spirited me to safety after the failed Dublin uprising. And each time that feeling of utter hopelessness, of anger and frustration that I wasn't God and I couldn't save them, whatever I tried. Now the thought struck me that I was to be a widow before I even had a chance to learn what it was like to be a wife, before Daniel and I really learned to love and appreciate each other, before there were children . . .

I had resisted marrying Daniel, even though I knew I loved him, because I wanted to savor my independence for as long as possible – thinking, of course that we had all the time in the world. And now I knew with absolute clarity that I didn't want to be alone and independent anymore. I didn't want to struggle and deal with danger. I wanted to be part of a joint life, with someone at my side, someone on my side. I squeezed back tears. I was not going to cry. I had been strong in situations as tough as this and I was not going to give in now.

'You can beat this, Daniel,' I said loudly. The sound echoed around the small room, bouncing back at me from the slanting ceiling. 'You're a strong man. Fight it. Keep fighting, do you hear?'

I looked around and started in terror as a tall figure in black with a skeleton's face stood in the doorway watching me. My first reaction was that it was Death, come to claim Daniel. But then he said softly, 'I didn't mean to frighten you, but the door was unlocked so I thought I'd let myself in and save you the trouble of coming downstairs.'

He stepped into the circle of lamplight and I saw that it was Father Patrick, dressed formally now in his priests' robes and wearing a stole. 'I came to see if I could be of any comfort,' he said, 'and to offer the last rites to your husband.'

'He's not going to die,' I said fiercely.

'Let us pray that he won't, but knowing the terrible reputation of the disease would you not want him anointed anyway, just in case, so that his soul goes straight to his maker?'

A battle raged inside me. I had renounced my religion long ago when I had clashed with narrow-minded, judgmental priests, seen the injustice and suffering in the world and all those prayers going unanswered. But Daniel's Catholicism meant more to him. He had insisted that we marry in a church. And I got the feeling it wasn't just to please his mother and the family friends. Deep down I felt that he still believed. So could I deny his soul the right to be washed clean of its sins? Could I condemn him to years of purgatory because of my stubbornness?

I took a deep breath. 'Very well,' I said. 'It's probably what he would want.'

'I think you'll find there is a lot of comfort in the sacrament – for the receiver and for those who witness it,' he said and brought out a little silver box, opened it and set out various little vials. Then he made the sign of the cross and commenced to mutter the prayers. The familiar Latin words hung in the air like incantations. I kept expecting Daniel to open his eyes, sit up and say, 'What the deuce do you think you're doing?' but he didn't. He didn't react at all when Father Patrick anointed him with the holy oil of the sick. The sacrament was finished. He started to put the vials of oil back in the silver box, then stepped back.

'His soul is now at peace,' he said. 'At least we've done one good thing for him, haven't we? It's always good to know we've done everything we can to make up for . . .' He looked at me with eyes that were incredibly sad. Of course I remembered then that he'd just lost his brother. Brian Hannan's death had been pushed from my mind in this crisis.

'I'm so sorry about your brother,' I said. 'I can tell that you're grieving.'

He took a deep breath. 'My brother was a good man,' he said. 'It was a terrible waste that he had to die now. He could have accomplished many things.' He went to say more, then closed his eyes. 'A sad loss for the family.'

I took a deep breath. 'I never had a chance to thank you for fetching the doctor, Father. It was good of you to think

of us at this sad time, and to bring the sacrament to my husband when you were not able to do the same for your poor
brother.'

He nodded. 'It was the least I could do.' He placed the last of
the sacramental vials back in the box and closed the lid with a
sharp little snap.

I couldn't take my eyes off Daniel. He seemed to be breathing more irregularly now. 'Do you believe that the souls of the
just go to Heaven? That there is such a place?' I asked.

'Yes I do. I most definitely do,' he said.

'And the souls of the damned go to Hell if you die in mortal
sin? You believe in that too?'

'Yes,' he said quietly. 'I'm afraid that I believe that there is no
pardon for the damned.'

'And last rites can make a difference?'

'It is always good to die in a state of grace,' he said. 'It's what
we all hope for.'

At least I had done that for Daniel. I sat staring at him, listening to his rasping breath.

'Is there anyone you'd like notified?' Father Patrick asked.
'Friends or family? I would be happy to have telegrams sent
for you.'

'You're very kind,' I said. 'Yes, I suppose I'd better let his
mother know.'

'Then write down for me what you want to say and where it
has to go.'

I went downstairs to find a piece of paper and noticed the
letter to Sid and Gus lying on the hall table. I couldn't send that
to them now. Suddenly I decided that I wanted them to know.
I had to send them a telegram too. I wrote: *Daniel pneumonia outlook not good.* Then I copied down the addresses of his
mother and of my neighbors onto a sheet of paper. I wondered
if I should send a telegram to police headquarters but I decided

147

there would be time for that later, after – I stopped that thought before it was allowed to take shape.

Father Patrick had come down the stairs behind me. I handed him the piece of paper. He took it without saying a word, then nodded. 'His mother lives out in Westchester County, I see. Not too far from my present assignment.'

'You're in the Hudson Valley? I assumed you were a priest in New York City,' I said.

'I had to leave the city years ago, for my health,' he said. 'Since then I've been in smaller parishes in rural settings. More to my liking, away from the dirt and noise of the city. I'm currently at St Brendan's in Granville. Do you know it?'

I shook my head, wishing he'd stop talking and go away when all I wanted to do was be at Daniel's bedside.

I held out my hand. 'Thank you again,' I said. 'You're most kind. Especially when you're grieving the death of your brother.'

'It's my priestly duty,' he said. 'At least I try to do that.'

I watched him walk back toward the house. As he went I looked up and thought I saw a light winking in a turret window. I blinked, stared again, but the light had gone and the turret loomed as part of that great shape in the darkness.

I went back to Daniel. He did seem to be sleeping a little more peacefully now and I hoped that somehow he had felt the presence of the sacrament. I perched on the edge of the bed beside him and took his hand. It felt hot and dry, and a memory flashed back to me unbidden of being handed a baked potato fresh from the oven by my mother. His lips looked cracked and I tried again to tip some water through them. He coughed and spluttered as the liquid ran down his throat.

I looked across at the packets of aspirin lying on the dresser. That old doctor had dismissed it as newfangled, but my friend Emily had brought it for me from her pharmacy when I had come down with a bad case of influenza and it had definitely helped. I was going to try, regardless of whatever that doctor had said. I went downstairs and mixed a dose with water. Then I hesitated for a moment before adding a second packet.

I carried it to the bedside. I glanced out of the window. The first rays of dawn were streaked across the Eastern sky. It was almost day. Outside my window a bird began to chirp – tentatively at first and then more confidently. It all seemed so calm and serene and normal, almost as if that bird was mocking me. Was this to be the last day of my present life? That thought flashed through my mind. I looked at the tumbler in my hand.

'I'm not going to let you die, Daniel Sullivan!' I shouted at him. 'Do you hear that? I will not let you die.'

I lifted his head, forced his mouth open, and tipped the liquid down his throat. He coughed and retched and fought, then fell back like a dead thing. Immediately afterward I was scared at what I had done. But it was too late. He had swallowed most of it.

'On fire,' he whispered. 'I'm on fire.'

Again I didn't hesitate. I pulled off the bedclothes. I ran to get a wet wash cloth, then I lifted his nightshirt and I began to sponge him down. He moaned, tried to sit up, then collapsed again. He lay so still that I thought for a moment I had killed him. I covered him with the sheet and heard him take a faint breath. At least he was still breathing. I rested my head on the pillow beside him. 'I love you,' I whispered. I took his hot hand in mine and closed my eyes.

The next thing I knew a shaft of bright sunlight hit me full in the face. I woke with a start, wondering for a moment where I was and why my neck hurt like billy-o. Then I saw Daniel lying on the bed beside me. His breath was no longer ragged and his face looked peaceful. I touched his hand and it was cool. I sat there, staring at him unblinking. *Dead*. The word tried to force its way into my head, however hard I tried to push it back. Daniel was dead. He had died while I had slept. I hadn't even had a chance to say good-bye to him. A great bubble of rage and despair came into my throat.

'No!' I shouted. 'No. No.'

Daniel's eyes flickered slowly open. 'What's all this racket about?' he murmured in a husky voice.

Nineteen

For a moment I thought my eyes were deceiving me. Then his eyes focused on me and he smiled with recognition.

'Daniel. You're alive.' I threw myself on him and covered his cheek and forehead with kisses.

'What have I done to deserve such a display of affection?' he asked, bringing the words out with difficulty as if it was a big effort to talk.

'You nearly died, you idiot,' I said. 'I've been up with you all night. The doctor was here and he had pretty much given up hope. And the priest gave you the last rites.'

'That's funny. I seem to remember hearing Latin and I kept telling myself that I was late for church and I'd get into trouble. I believe I thought I was still an altar boy.' He turned away and stared up at the ceiling. 'I had all kinds of bad dreams. People trying to kill me. Monsters trying to swallow me alive.'

'I know. You were hallucinating. You kept thrashing around and kicking the covers off.'

'I was too hot.'

'I know you were. That doctor told me to keep you covered so that you'd sweat out the disease, but I couldn't stand to see you as hot as that. I took the covers off and sponged you down.'

'Typical Molly, doing exactly what she was told not to.' He gave me a tired smile and closed his eyes again.

'I was scared that I'd killed you,' I said. 'I was so scared, Daniel. I thought you were going to die.' And a great hiccupping sob escaped from my throat.

He reached up and stroked my cheek. 'There, there,' he said. 'Don't cry. I'm still here and everything's going to be just fine.'

'Yes,' I said, unable to stop the tears now. 'Everything will be just fine. I'll go and make us both a cup of tea.'

Daniel had just fallen asleep again when there was a tap at my front door and Mrs Flannery was standing there. 'We've just come back from church, so I thought I ought to stop by and see how you were doing,' she said and she came into the front hall without being invited.

'Oh, church. Is it Sunday?'

She nodded. 'A terrible business. They go so quickly with pneumonia, don't they? But at least my brother gave him the last rites, and that's a comfort, isn't it?'

'Mrs Flannery, he's fine. That is, he's not fine yet, but he's much better. The fever broke. He's breathing almost normally again.'

Her face lit up. 'Well, that's a miracle, isn't it? I'm so happy for you, my dear. Mrs McCreedy was going to send over one of the local girls to help you out but I'll be happy to cook you a good breakfast. What would you say to ham and eggs and maybe some flapjacks? Perhaps your man could take a lightly boiled egg?'

I was going to turn her down but then I realized how drained I felt. 'If you're sure you don't mind,' I said.

She took off her hat, hanging it on the peg. 'Nonsense. I've been used to hard work all my life,' she said. 'It doesn't come easily to me to have servants fussing around and me not lifting a finger. Why I cooked and cleaned for the six of us when our parents died and I was just eleven years old. Brian went out to work at twelve to support us all but I had to become the mother.'

'I had to do the same thing,' I said. 'My mother died and I had to stop my schooling to look after my little brothers.'

'Did you now? At least it makes us stronger people, doesn't it? More able to handle trouble and tragedy.' She went through into the kitchen.

'It was good of you to come,' I said.

'To tell the truth I was glad to get away for a bit. I can't take the atmosphere in that house. Suspicion and innuendo and snapping at each other. What's more, they're already arguing over where poor Brian's to be buried. Joseph wants him to have a grand funeral with all the trappings in New York. He says Brian would have wanted it, being a public figure and all. But Irene thinks he'd want to be buried here, beside his beloved granddaughter. She says he loved this place and he was happy here for the first time in his life.'

'So who will win?'

She shrugged. 'I couldn't tell you. I suppose it will come down to who is his heir. And Brian may well have left instructions for his final resting place. He was the sort of man who liked to organize everything. For all I know he may have a funeral plot all picked out, and even the hymns they're to sing in St Patrick's.'

'You can still have a memorial service for him at St Patrick's even if he's buried here, can't you?' I suggested.

'I don't see why not. The boys at Tammany Hall put on a grand funeral for their members. They'd go to town for Brian.'

'I'm sure they would.'

She bustled around my kitchen, knowing with the instinct of one who has cooked and cleaned all her life where to find things. 'I told them all this bickering over the funeral is premature, seeing that the police won't release the body to us yet.'

'No, I suppose you'll have to wait until after the autopsy results are known.'

She took a knife and started slicing bread, holding it to her breast and cutting it toward her as my mother had always done. Frankly I had always been scared that she'd slice into herself but she never had. And Mrs Flannery looked as if she knew what she was doing as well.

'A terrible business, isn't it? I can't stop thinking about him. If ever there was a man full of life, it was Brian. Full of energy, always had one grand scheme or another.'

'A great tragedy,' I said.

'A great tragedy or a great crime,' she said. 'I can scarcely believe that someone deliberately tried to kill him, but that's what that policeman seems to think, doesn't he? I mean, who would do such a thing?'

'Someone with a grudge against your brother.'

'But who would come all the way out here, to this remote spot to do it?'

'Maybe it was easier to find him alone out here,' I said. 'Or someone didn't originally mean to kill him but seized the opportunity.'

'If it wasn't an outsider, then it had to be one of us,' she said quietly. 'That's the thought I can't get out of my mind. One of our family. But it couldn't be. Just couldn't.'

'I'm sure the police will find the person who did it,' I said, although I was not at all sure.

'My poor little Sam is so cut up about it,' she said. 'Hardly said a word since it happened and not eaten a thing either, which is shocking in itself if you knew Sam. Eats like a horse that boy. Always has. Skinny as a rake too. I don't know where he puts it sometimes but he sure loves to eat.' She smiled for a moment then her face became solemn again. 'I don't know what will happen to him now. He was starting to run wild until

Brian took him under his wing. With a no-good father like that and my poor daughter burdened with a new baby every year it's no wonder that no one had time for the boy. He started running with the wrong crowd – going with a gang, you know. Junior Eastman, he called himself.'

'I know the Eastmans. In fact I've met Monk Eastman more than once.'

'Holy Mother – have you indeed?'

'I used to have my own detective agency. Sometimes it took me to the less savory parts of the city. And Monk recruits them young. Your Sam is well out of it.'

'Brian stepped in as soon as he found out,' she said. 'He brought the boy to live with him and started him working for the company as messenger boy. Made sure he worked him hard too so that he had no time for bad companions. But now what? I'd take him in, of course, but he doesn't listen to an old woman. And Joseph – well, Joseph only cares about himself and money. And a fine sort of example he'd be for the boy. Look how Terrence has turned out.'

'He seems a pleasant enough young man to me,' I said.

She sniffed. 'My dear. I can't tell you the number of times his father has had to pay his bills – gambling debts, unpaid wine bills, girls he's got in the family way. His mother has washed her hands of him, I can tell you. And even Brian could do nothing for once, because Jo wouldn't let him take over the boy. They almost came to blows over it.'

She lifted the egg from the boiling water and found an eggcup. 'You'll no doubt want to take this up to him yourself,' she said.

I agreed and carried the tray upstairs. Daniel roused as I came into the room and I helped him into a sitting position. He was as weak as a kitten and lay back gasping as I propped pillows behind him.

'Try and get some of that egg down you,' I said. 'You need building up now.'

'I can't think how I let something like a little cold get the better of me,' he said. 'And look at you – the picture of health.'

'Just you remember who the strong one is,' I said, smiling.

I paused, hearing a knock at the front door, then Mrs Flannery's voice.

'I hope that's not Prescott again,' Daniel said. 'I don't feel in any state to speak to him now.'

Words were being exchanged downstairs. I couldn't make them out but then I heard heavy footsteps coming up the stairs. I stepped out to intercept the visitor and found that it was the doctor.

'Mrs Sullivan,' he said. 'I've just been told the good news about your husband. So the fever broke by itself, did it? Oh, that is a relief. I have to tell you that I was expecting the worst this morning. I didn't think the poor man would make it through the night.'

'Not only made it through the night but is currently eating breakfast,' I said and ushered him into the bedroom.

'You are a fortunate young man, sir,' he said to Daniel. 'You clearly have a strong constitution to fight off the disease when it had such a grip on you.' He took out his stethoscope and started listening to Daniel's chest. When he'd finished he nodded.

'Not out of the woods yet by any means,' he said. 'There's still a lot of fluid on the lungs. So no exertion, no excitement for a while yet. You're not to move from this bed until I say so, and that's an order.'

I followed him down the stairs. 'Thank you for coming out in the night like that,' I said. 'I'm so relieved. If I write out a telegram, I wonder could you arrange to have it sent from the telegraph office when you go back to town? I don't want to leave him yet but I'd like his dear ones to know that he's not going to die.'

The doctor shook his head and at first I thought he was refusing to send the telegram, but then he leaned closer to me. 'I'd wait a little longer if I were you. He is not out of the woods yet. A relapse is all too possible with a disease like pneumonia. I've seen it many times. So hold off sending your good news for a while and make sure you keep him in bed, keep him quiet, on an invalid diet.'

'I will, don't worry. You'll be sending us the bill, will you?'

'I most certainly will. Extra money for being woken from my beauty sleep.' He smiled and patted my hand before he put his hat on his head and departed.

A young woman called Martha arrived soon after and Mrs Flannery went back to the bickering at the big house. Daniel was asleep when I came to collect his tray, so I left Martha busy in the kitchen and went outside. I felt that I needed a breath of ocean air in my lungs after everything I'd been through that night. It was another perfect day for sailing, with a stiff breeze and puffy white clouds racing across a blue sky. I expected that Archie Van Horn was miffed that he couldn't compete in his yacht races.

There was no sign of the family, nor of the gardeners and I strolled through the trees and down to the ocean front. Then I sat on a log and watched the sea birds and the waves. The sound of feet on gravel made me look up and there came the two little boys in their identical sailor suits, marching side by side at a great rate down the path, while their nursemaid struggled to keep up with them, gasping every now and then, 'Slow down, boys. Do you hear me? Slow down.'

As the boys came closer to me I stood up. 'Are you two in trouble again?' I asked.

They stopped and grinned at me. 'We're not allowed to play,

you see,' the older one (*Was it Alex?*) said. 'Because of grand-papa. And it was so boring sitting in the house and reading on a fine day that we begged Mama and she said we could walk around the grounds if Bridget stayed with us, but we weren't to run.'

'So we weren't running,' the younger one (*Thomas, if I remembered correctly*) joined in. 'But we were seeing how fast we could walk.'

'You boys will be the death of me,' the nursemaid said. 'You don't do a thing you're told. Well, your father is going to hear of this.'

'But we weren't running, Bridget. It's not our fault if you only have little legs and we have long ones,' Alex said.

'I don't believe you're allowed anywhere near the cliffs,' I reminded them. 'You know what your mother feels about that.'

'We thought we'd take a look for ourselves at the place where they found grandpapa's body.' Thomas said. 'We won't go really near the edge.'

'You'll go nowhere near it. I'll walk you back to the house,' I said. 'The last thing you want to do right now is give your poor parents more worry. Your mother has lost her father. She's nat-urally very upset. You should try to be good boys and comfort her. I expect you miss your grandfather too, don't you?'

'I suppose so,' Alex said. 'We didn't see him very much and he was rather bossy. We always had to mind our manners with him.'

'He was your grandfather,' I pointed out. 'It's up to you to show respect to his memory.'

'Yes, ma'am,' Alex said. Then his face lit up again. 'You'll never believe what we saw last night – we saw a ghost. Mama won't believe us, but we did.'

Thomas also looked excited. 'It was a white lady and she wafted across the lawn and then she vanished.'

'I'm sorry to disappoint you,' I said, 'but I suspect that was me. I ran across to the big house in the middle of the night. My husband was taken ill and I ran across wearing a shawl over my night clothes, so I was your white lady.'

Alex shook his head. 'No. This white lady didn't go any-where near the front of the house. She ran to the tower at the side where there is no door. We tried to look down by hanging out of our window, but she had just vanished and there was nowhere she could have gone.'

'It was a ghost,' Thomas agreed. 'We think we've heard ghostly noises before in this place but nobody believes us.'

'You believe us, don't you?' Alex asked.

'That's enough nonsense,' their nursemaid said. She took them both by the arm. 'Ghosts indeed. Back into the house right now. March. On with you.'

They gave me a regretful look as they were borne away. A white lady who wafted across the lawn and then vanished. I didn't like to tell them that I was inclined to believe them.

Twenty

I stood looking up at that turret as I made my way back toward the house. It stood solid and windowless at one corner of the castle, its stone sides covered in dense ivy looking incredibly old and foreboding. It was only at the very top, where the turret rose above the level of the battlements that there was a window – in which I had seen a strange child's face. But the face I had seen had definitely been that of a child, and they were talking about a white lady. Was there more than one ghost that haunted this castle? It didn't seem possible in a building so new.

I went back to Daniel and persuaded him to try a little broth.

'What news on Hannan's death?' he asked. 'Have I missed anything?'

'We've heard nothing more,' I said. 'But I've had interesting chats with some family members. Mrs Flannery, Brian's sister, can't believe that it would be a family member, but then she mentioned her grandson Sam who had become a Junior Eastman before Brian took him over.'

'And he was the one who supposedly discovered the body when he went out early to go fishing.' Daniel said the words thoughtfully. 'I'd be interested to hear the coroner's report on the time of death. Maybe the body hadn't lain there since the night before after all.' He tried to sit up. 'I wish I'd had a chance to—'

'Lie back. You're not going anywhere,' I said firmly. 'You heard what the doctor said. Absolute rest and quiet because of the possibility of a relapse.'

Daniel sighed. 'It's not easy to be at the scene of what could be an interesting murder and to watch it probably being bungled by a small-town cop.'

'Such prejudice.' I smiled. 'You New Yorkers really do think you're the bee's knees, don't you?'

'I just happen to be a top-notch detective who has solved any number of murders.'

'I seem to remember when we first met, you were about to throw me in jail for a murder I didn't commit,' I reminded him.

'Well, you had guilt written all over you. And I got it right in the end, didn't I?'

'Only just.' I pushed back the dark curl that had fallen across his forehead. 'Anyway, I want you to go on being a brilliant detective for many years to come. So rest now. I'm going to take a little nap myself. I didn't get much sleep last night.'

Daniel's hand closed around mine. 'You did a splendid job, Mrs Sullivan.'

I went downstairs and lay on the sofa with the rug over me. I was just drifting off to sleep when there came a light tap at the front door. *What now?* I thought. No peace for the wicked. I paused to smooth down my hair before I opened the door. Irene Van Horn was standing there. The last time I had seen her she had been in her night attire with hair spilling over her shoulders and eyes red with crying. Now she was back to the perfect vision of loveliness I had seen the day before, except that the dress was dark-green shantung – the closest to black that she had brought with her, I suspected. Her face still looked pale against the dark fabric – like a delicate porcelain doll that might shatter easily.

'Mrs Sullivan. How is your husband doing?'

'Much better, thank you. His fever is down and he seems to be making good progress.'

'I am glad.' She gave me a tired smile. 'I was just talking to my husband and he commented how distressing it must be for you to have your honeymoon turned into such chaos. I'm sorry but with our own grief we have not given much thought to you and your needs until now.'

'That is quite understandable, Mrs Van Horn. May I say how sorry we are about your father. I could see how distressed you were yesterday morning and wished I could have done something to help.'

'Most kind,' she said. 'But there's nothing you or anyone can do. He's gone. I'll never see him again.' She put her hand up to her mouth, then composed herself. 'My duties are now to the living. We would have invited you to dinner, but we suspected you would not want to leave your husband for that length of time.'

'No, I think I should keep a close eye on him for the next few days.'

'So we hoped at least you'll come out and take tea with us on the lawn. It's a lovely afternoon and tea on the lawn is something of a tradition at Connemara. My father's chef is famous for his scones and éclairs.'

'Thank you. I'd like that,' I said.

'In about half an hour then.' She smiled again then walked away. I watched her go, wondering if I would have been so composed and gracious after the shocking death of a beloved father. She might have been spoiled but she had been raised with perfect social graces.

I went back into the house, splashed cold water on my face

to revive me, then went upstairs to make myself presentable. Daniel was sleeping, but Martha was in the kitchen, having started work on our supper. I asked her to keep an eye on him and went off to take tea with the family.

The whole family assembled on the lawn next to the tower, seated in various poses in an assortment of wicker chairs. Elegant and unmoving, they created almost a replica of yesterday's tableau, only this time they were suitably dressed: the men in dark suits, Mrs Flannery in black, and Irene in dark green. The only differences were that on this occasion the two little boys sat on stools at their father's feet. Also two maids in white caps and aprons stood by a white-clothed table, laden with a silver tea service and cake stands piled with various delights.

Mrs Van Horn saw me coming and reached out a hand to me, thus breaking the tableau effect. 'Mrs Sullivan. Welcome. Do come and sit down.' She gestured gracefully to a wicker armchair beside her. 'Alice, bring Mrs Sullivan a cup of tea. Do you take oolong or Earl Grey, Mrs Sullivan?'

I'd tried oolong but wasn't so sure about the other. Still it was time to broaden my horizons. 'Earl Grey, thank you.'

Tea was poured for me and luckily milk was offered. I knew that Daniel's mother took her Chinese tea with lemon and I wasn't so fond of that. I took a sip and was somewhat startled by the scented taste. Really the upper classes did eat and drink the strangest things.

'And how is your poor husband, Mrs Sullivan?' Mrs Flannery asked.

'Much better, thank you. Definitely on the mend.'

'That's good news,' Joseph said. 'You'll no doubt be wanting to get him home as quickly as possible. I'm sure we could arrange transportation for you.'

'That's kind, but the doctor stressed that Daniel was not to be moved for a while, at least until he says so.'

I noticed a flicker of annoyance cross Joseph's face. I wondered why he was so very keen on removing us from the premises. The thought crossed my mind that we had accidentally seen him arriving early with his ladylove and perhaps he wanted that fact concealed from the family. I wondered if he had any other secrets he didn't want universally known.

'Of course the poor man can't be moved yet, Jo. What were you thinking?' Mary Flannery said sharply. 'It's not as if they're bothering you, stuck away in that poky little cottage.'

'It's a very comfortable little cottage,' Joseph said. 'As you know, I enjoy staying there myself.'

'And we well know its attraction for you,' Terrence said smoothly and got a look of venom from his father. Terrence turned to me without batting an eyelid. 'Do have a scone and jam, Mrs Sullivan, or would you prefer to start with a sandwich? They're watercress or potted shrimp, I believe.'

I took a shrimp sandwich, feeling awkward now – the cuckoo in another bird's nest – and wished I hadn't accepted their invitation. I could easily have said that Daniel couldn't be left alone and now here I was sitting among people who clearly didn't want me there. I nibbled at my sandwich.

'What I want to know is how long we're expected to hang around here, doing nothing,' Joseph said. 'I should be back in the office tomorrow, especially now I'll have to take over Brian's share of the work too.'

'You know we can't go anywhere until the police have released Irene's father's body,' Archie said. 'And we still need to come to a decision on funeral arrangements.'

'That's another reason for being able to go back to the city tomorrow,' Joseph said. 'A visit to his attorney and the reading of his will should clear up a lot of things for us. Until then we can't proceed.'

'It would be funny if he'd left the whole kit and caboodle to the least likely of us,' Terrence said, with his customary grin. 'To young Sam, maybe.'

Sam blushed bright red. 'Don't be silly, Terry,' he said. 'You saw what he thought of me. I was the messenger boy. At least you got an office, even if you never worked in it.'

'Hey, none of your cheek, young fella,' Terrence said. 'Some of us are not cut out for the daily grind. I've got the brains, others can have the brawn.'

'Then it's about time we saw a demonstration of the use of those brains,' Joseph said coldly. 'Frankly the way you've been acting recently would indicate to me that you have no brains at all – or at least no common sense.'

'Please, please.' Irene held up her hand. 'None of this bickering. We have a guest and my father is not yet resting in his grave. Don't you think I've had enough to upset me recently?'

Archie put a hand on her shoulder. 'There, there, my dear. Do not distress yourself. Have another cup of tea.' He glared at Joseph and Terrence. 'You should know how hard it is for Irene even to come to this confounded place. Every time she's here it's a reminder of what she lost. And now her father lying dead in the same spot. Well, have a little consideration please.'

There was an uncomfortable silence. I looked out at the sailboats on the ocean, wishing I were somewhere else.

'Mama, when can we start playing again?' Alex asked. 'We're bored.'

'And you'll learn to show a little respect too, young man,' Archie snapped. 'One does not play nor make merry in any way when there is a death in the family. We are in mourning.'

'Well then, shouldn't we be eating gruel or dry bread rather than these éclairs?' Terrence asked. 'They are sinfully good.'

'One day, Terrence, you'll go too far,' Eliza said.

'As you and Mama have often told me.' Terrence deliberately took a big bite of éclair. 'I wish that dratted policeman would return with some news. Was he or wasn't he? It's quite putting me off from eating a second éclair.'

'If he was, then you would be a prime suspect,' Eliza said.

'Me? What on earth makes you say that?' Terrence demanded. 'I was always the soul of politeness to the old boy.'

'Even after he gave you that ultimatum last week?' she asked sweetly. 'I seem to remember your language was quite colorful.'

Terrence flushed uncomfortably. 'I didn't like being spoken to as if I was a child.'

'None of us did,' Joseph said. 'But Brian thought he had the right to lay down the law.'

'And he did have the right,' Irene said. 'He created this pleasant existence for all of us. He worked jolly hard all his life so that we could live like this and it's not right to try and run him down after he's dead.'

'Nobody is running him down,' Terrence said.

Father Patrick stood up. 'We're all a little on edge, aren't we? Brian was a fine man and at this moment we should be praying for his soul and reflecting on the good he achieved in his life.'

Suddenly Terrence got to his feet beside his uncle. 'There is an automobile outside the gates. I believe the moment we've been anticipating has arrived. That pompous policeman has returned and now maybe we can all go home.'

The auto contained three policemen as well as Chief Prescott. One of the men was in the process of dragging open the big gate so that Chief Prescott could drive through. As the auto approached the house he spotted us seated on the lawn. He left the car and strode purposefully over to us. 'Ah, good. I'm sorry to interrupt your little tea party, but I have news for you.'

'You do? What is it?' Joseph said. 'Have you discovered that we were right all along and the poor blighter had simply drunk too much and fallen?'

'Not exactly, sir.'

'Then what, for God's sake?' Joseph blustered. 'Speak up, man. Don't keep us in suspense any longer.'

'I'm afraid I'll need your servants out here too.'

'Our servants?' Archie said indignantly. 'What right have they to be privy to matters that don't concern them.'

'I'm hoping that they can shed light on a few facts,' Chief Prescott said. He saw me sitting there. 'And Mrs Sullivan – could you fetch your husband. I'd like him to hear what I have to say.'

'I'm afraid that won't be possible,' I said. 'My husband has been gravely ill. He almost died of pneumonia last night and he is not to be moved or excited. You'll just have to tell me and I'll pass the news on to him.'

'I see.' Chief Prescott frowned as if he wasn't sure I was telling the truth.

'My brother Patrick had to give him the last rites,' Mrs Flannery said. 'It's a miracle he's alive at all today.'

'Of course. I'm sorry. Please give him my best,' the chief said gruffly. He turned to address the maids. 'Would one of you girls go to summon the rest of the servants?' The girls looked uncertainly at Irene.

'It's all right, Alice. Do as he asks,' Irene said. The maid scurried across the lawn toward the front door.

'And your gardeners. I don't see any of them around today.'

'It's Sunday,' Archie Van Horn said brusquely. 'They don't work on Sundays.'

'I'll need to speak to them as well,' Chief Prescott said. 'If you could give me their home addresses, I'll have one of my men go and round them up.'

'You make them sound like escaped cattle,' Terrence said dryly.

'You'll have to ask the housekeeper for their names and

addresses,' Joseph said in a clipped voice. 'She handles everything to do with the servants around here.'

'Then go and fetch the housekeeper, please,' Prescott said to the other maid. 'Tell her we need to speak to her right away.'

The girl took off like a frightened rabbit. We continued to stare at the police chief.

'Now, for God's sake tell us what you've found,' Joseph bellowed the words. 'Don't keep us in the dark any longer.'

'Very well.' Chief Prescott looked around the assembled group with a certain amount of satisfaction. 'Mr Brian Hannan did indeed have alcohol in his blood, but not enough to have made him drunk.'

'Then what killed him? Was it an accident?' Joseph demanded.

'No accident, sir. What the physicians doing the autopsy did find was the presence of potassium cyanide.'

Twenty-One

Nobody moved. We stared at him, trying to comprehend what he had just said. Then Archie stood up. 'Alex, Thomas, go to your room immediately and stay there until I tell you that you may come out.'

'Oh, but, Papa,' Alex complained. 'We're old enough to hear this. And just when it's getting exciting.'

'Now, young man.' Archie pointed dramatically at the door. 'Where is that nursemaid of yours? Why does she never seem to be around when she's needed? Go on. Go.'

The two boys shuffled off reluctantly with a few backward glances.

As they retreated there was silence. Nobody moved. The tableau had resumed, with each person staring down, wrapped up in their own thoughts.

'You mean Brian was deliberately poisoned?' Mary Flannery asked at last.

'That's exactly what I mean.'

'And the poison was in the whiskey?' Archie asked.

'No, there was no trace of poison in either the glass or the decanter,' Prescott said.

'But cyanide is a fast-acting poison,' I pointed out, making them look at me suspiciously.

'Precisely. The amount of cyanide he had ingested would have killed him immediately.'

'Then how and when was it administered?' Joseph asked.

Chief Prescott turned to me. 'Thanks to Mrs Sullivan, we found shards of a shattered glass at the bottom of the cliff, matching the one on the tray. One has to surmise that Brian Hannan was planning a quiet drink with someone. A tray with two glasses on it. The other person came prepared.'

'But if Mr Hannan had drunk from the glass containing cyanide, he'd have keeled over and died right there in the gazebo,' I pointed out, 'and there are no signs of a body having been dragged to the cliff.'

Prescott nodded. 'Which must mean one of two things. Either the two people were actually drinking together somewhere near the cliff and the tray was carried to the gazebo later to make it look as if Brian Hannan had been drinking there alone, or Hannan was lured by some pretext close to the cliff edge once he had consumed a drink or two. His attention was drawn to something on the shore, or out to sea, maybe, and the moment he looked away, the cyanide was dropped into his glass. A bold and daring move. A person prepared to take great risks. That's who we're looking for.'

'Do you have any idea who that could be?' Archie Van Horn asked. 'What about the fellow Mrs Sullivan spotted, standing at the gate and asking if Mr Hannan had arrived yet. Has he been tracked down?'

'No, sir. We've had no luck with him. Any number of men matching his description were seen boarding trains back to New York. He doesn't appear to be staying anywhere in town, that's all I can say. Naturally I'll speak with the New York police and ask them to take this matter further, but I'm not prepared to speculate until we hear what the servants have to say on this matter.'

'Fingerprints,' I said, waving my own finger at him. 'Did anybody test the tray and glass for fingerprints?'

'They did, and you know what? They discovered something interesting. Brian Hannan's prints on the tray and decanter, but nobody else's. And those prints were smudged as if someone had attempted to wipe the items clean.'

'My betting is on one of the gangs,' Joseph said.

'Gangs, sir?'

Joseph folded his arms. 'In our business we are subject to constant demands for protection money, and threats if we don't pay up. Brian refused to be intimidated. In fact this accident, the tunnel cave-in a few weeks ago, was highly suspect, in my opinion. The police were investigating and it's possible that Brian named names. Gang leaders don't like squealers. This might have been payback.'

'Interesting, sir.' Prescott scribbled in his notebook. 'I'll definitely bear that in mind. Because if it's not someone convenient like a gang member, then it has to be someone highly inconvenient – like a family member, for instance.' He looked around us – deliberately, slowly. 'So if any one of you knows the real reason that Brian Hannan assembled you here at this time, it would be wise to tell me right away, because I will find out eventually.'

Silence. Again the family members looked down, not wishing to meet another's eye. I studied them, noticing Father Patrick's gaze go from Joseph to Terrence and back again. Maybe Daniel had been correct in his supposition that this gathering had something to do with money, squandering of funds. Had Joseph and his son been cooking the books, or in some way betrayed Brian's trust, so that he was about to announce he was cutting them out of the family business? Joseph knew about Brian's fondness for drink. Had he placed the tray where he knew Brian would find it?

And Terrence – someone who resembled Terrence in stature

had crept out of those French doors at about the right time for a rendezvous with his uncle in the gazebo. Terrence who was clearly considered to be a black sheep in this family. It was Joseph who spoke first.

'The accusation is preposterous. You would not find a more close-knit family than ours. Brian was the patriarch. He earned and received love and respect from each of us. We'd still have been living in a fourth-floor tenement on Cherry Street if it hadn't been for his hard work and enterprise. Do you think we're not mindful of that?'

'I'm sorry, sir. I'm sure this is very hard to hear, but in my profession we are taught to start with the obvious. And to me the obvious is that Mr Hannan summons his family here at a strange time of year and he is poisoned. What would you think if you were in my place?'

'I'd think it was time to start looking beyond the obvious,' Joseph said sharply. 'Find out who wished my brother ill, who had a grudge to settle, especially among the criminal classes.'

We looked up as one of the maids came running back across the lawn, the ribbons in her cap flying out behind her. 'Alice is bringing the rest of the servants, ma'am,' she said to Irene, 'but I couldn't find Mrs McCreedy anywhere. Nobody's seen her.'

I felt a jolt of fear go through me. I remembered all too clearly when nobody had seen Mr Hannan, although it was supposed he had arrived. And I'd come to appreciate that Mrs McCreedy was a woman living on her nerves. Something had severely rattled her even before Mr Hannan had died. I suspected she knew something she hadn't told us about this visit and had feared something might go wrong.

'Might she have stepped out?' Police Chief Prescott said. 'It is, as you pointed out, Sunday afternoon when servants do like to visit their families.'

'But she helped to carry out the tea things,' Eliza said, 'and we've been out here since. We'd have seen anybody going past toward the gate.'

Eliza turned to the maid. 'Go and look again, Sarah. Perhaps she is taking a nap in her room. She does get up extremely early.'

It struck me that this was an unusual thing for a woman of her station to say. I'm sure the thought never crossed Irene's mind that servants might need to take naps or indeed had to get up awfully early.

I got to my own feet. 'I'll go and help her, if you like. It is an awfully big house.'

I think Joseph was about to protest when Chief Prescott said, 'Good of you, Mrs Sullivan.'

So I went. As well as my nagging fear that something had happened to her, I realized that this would be my one chance to look around the house for myself. I don't know exactly what I expected to find, but I was still morbidly curious about that tower. As the maid and I went in, we passed the other servants filing out through the front door.

'Has any of you seen Mrs McCreedy?' I asked.

'I have. She helped carry out the table about half an hour ago,' the footman said.

'But since then?'

They shook their heads.

'She may be in her room,' one of the local girls said.

They went on their way, out toward the lawn. I looked at the maid. 'Where is her room, Sarah?'

'I'm not quite sure, ma'am. Up on the top floor with the rest of the servants, I presume.'

'Then you go straight up and see if you can find her. I'll search the rest of the house systematically.'

'Very well, ma'am,' she said not too graciously. She was a hefty girl and I could tell that she wasn't charmed with the idea of climbing all those stairs again.

'Off you go then,' I said as she still lingered. 'Up on the top floor, correct?' I indicated the grand staircase. She blushed. 'Oh, no, ma'am. I shouldn't use that staircase. I have to use the servants' stairs at the back.' And with that she set off down the long dark hallway to the back of the house. I wondered if the servants' staircase had been behind that door I had opened when I had so startled Mrs McCreedy. That would explain a lot of things – if maybe she had been up in her room, taking a nap when she shouldn't and had just hurried down several flights of stairs. I knew that not everything has to have a sinister meaning. I just prayed that the girl would find Mrs McCreedy asleep.

I was going to follow her, to check out that staircase for myself, but I decided that an empty house and permission to search it was an opportunity too good to miss. So I worked my way through the ground-floor rooms. She wasn't in the salon, the drawing room, dining room, morning room, music room, or library. I half expected to see her feet sticking out behind a bookshelf in the library, but all the rooms lay calm and serene in the afternoon sunshine. I went through a swing door to the servants' part of the house. I found the back staircase off a side hallway. I also found the door behind which I had seen her startled face, but it was locked. There was nobody in the kitchen, nor in any of the closets, scullery, or anywhere else.

I stood looking out of the back door, realizing that she could have come out this way without being noticed. A picture of her lying dead at the foot of the cliff flashed into my mind. I'd leave that search until I'd been through the whole house. I went up the servants' stairs and peeked into the bedrooms one by one. Behind one door I heard shrieks. I flung it open to see two little boys jumping on beds with toy guns in their hands while the nursemaid was standing with a look of despair on her face.

'I'm so sorry,' she said. 'I told them they weren't allowed to play but they don't listen to a thing I tell them.'

'You know what your parents told you,' I said, wagging my finger severely. 'No playing out of respect for your grandfather. If you want to do something fun get out some paper and write an adventure story. Take yourselves up the Amazon.'

Two sets of eyes lit up. 'The Amazon? That's where you find anacondas,' Alex said.

'I can't spell "anaconda,"' Thomas complained.

'Your brother will help you. And don't forget the illustrations.'

They rushed to get to work. The nursemaid gave me a grateful smile.

'Did you want something, ma'am?' she asked.

'I was looking for Mrs McCreedy. I don't suppose you've seen her?'

'Not recently,' she said. 'And why don't you write in pencil, Thomas. We don't want ink spilled on this carpet.'

I left them and finished my tour of the bedrooms. The main staircase did not go any higher so I went back to the servants' stairs, up another flight, and found myself on a bleak and bare landing.

'Hello, Sarah?' I called. 'Any sign of Mrs McCreedy up here?'

She appeared further down a hallway. 'Not yet, ma'am. She's not in her room. I don't know where else to look. There's an awful lot of box rooms and spare rooms up here.'

'Check them all,' I said.

She looked puzzled. 'What would she be doing in box rooms? I've called her name enough. Surely she'd have heard.'

'Check anyway.'

I went to the other end of the hall. It opened to a landing with doors all around. Some were locked. I found a key in one and tried the other doors. Some opened, some didn't. What I found were empty rooms. But one on the far right opened into a narrow passage. It was dark and I couldn't find an electric light switch. I

175

went down it cautiously and found myself in a round area like a rotunda. As far as I could make out in the dim light it was nicely paneled in dark wood, with statues in niches around the walls. This must be the tower, I realized and looked for a door that might lead me higher. There was none. No door of any kind. So I had to conclude that Mrs McCreedy had been telling the truth – it was just a folly, an unfinished area. I looked up at the ceiling and could make out what looked like a wooden trapdoor in the plaster. Mrs McCreedy had said that you could only get up there with a ladder, so that must be the entry. But it was firmly closed and there didn't appear to be a string that one could pull to open it. I stood there for a moment, trying to work out if the tightness in my chest that I felt was as a result of worrying about Mrs McCreedy or if I was experiencing that same feeling of dread that had overcome me the first time I entered the house. I found myself looking around nervously, but no ghost appeared.

'I've done looking up here, ma'am,' Sarah called. 'And she's not anywhere.' She hesitated and then shouted with alarm in her voice, 'Where are you, ma'am?'

'I'm coming,' I called back. I saw the relief in her face when I reappeared. I wondered if she sensed my alarm or had her own reasons to be uneasy up here. 'I think we'd better check the grounds. She's nowhere in the house.'

We went back to the staircase and walked down one flight then the next.

'Should we go and see first whether she's turned up outside?' Sarah suggested, clearly not welcoming a long search around the estate.

'I suppose that might be a good idea,' I agreed. We reached the cavernous foyer at the front of the building. As we crossed it we heard footsteps. We looked up as someone came down the main stair toward us.

'Was someone calling my name?' Mrs McCreedy asked.

Twenty-Two

'Where were you?' I asked. 'We were looking all over for you.'

'We searched the whole house,' Sarah added.

Mrs McCreedy was obviously flustered but trying not to show it. 'I don't know what all the fuss is about,' she said. 'I've been here all the time. Up and down taking the clean laundry up to bedrooms. There's never a moment's peace in this house. You say you've been looking for me? We must have just missed each other, that's all.'

I didn't see how she could have escaped us upstairs but I did wonder if she had a private little corner behind one of those locked doors where she could retreat and take a rest.

'Anyway, we've found you now,' I said. I felt a wave of relief that my vision of her lying on the rocks had merely been a product of my overactive imagination.

'What's all the urgency, anyway?' she asked.

'Police Chief Prescott is here and wants all the servants outside, also the names and addresses of all the gardeners who aren't here today.'

'All the gardeners?' She sniffed. 'What's all this about now, I'd like to know? Why don't they just give the poor man a proper burial and let him rest in his grave?'

'I expect the police chief will make everything clear when

177

we're all assembled,' I said. 'He's waiting for us on the lawn with the family.'

We headed out of the front door. The servants had now added to the tableau, standing uncomfortably at attention behind those seated in the wicker chairs. The chef looked distinctly annoyed, the others worried. Chief Prescott looked up as we approached. 'Ah, you've found her. Well done. Mrs McCreedy, we need the names and addresses of all the gardeners. Then one of my men will go to their homes to fetch them.'

'I doubt you'll find them at home on a fine Sunday afternoon,' Mrs McCreedy said stiffly. 'Newport men are mostly fishermen at heart. They'll be out on a boat somewhere.'

'It will be dark before long. I expect we'll find them,' he said. 'My man here has a pad and pencil. So if you'd be so good . . .'

'I only know where you'd find Parsons, who is head gardener,' she said. 'He's in charge of the hiring and firing of the under gardeners. I can give you his address.'

'Very well.' Chief Prescott was looking decidedly vexed now, as if Mrs McCreedy was deliberately holding things up – which maybe she was. Something had to explain her jumpy manner, her recent disappearance. I had thought before that she knew more than she was willing to tell us, but now I found myself wondering if maybe she had something to do with her master's death. I looked at her – a big-boned, typical Irishwoman of peasant stock. The kind I passed on the way to market every day at home. Surely such a woman would never concoct a plot to lure her employer outside and then poison him?

A young policeman scribbled down the address and then went over to the automobile. Chief Prescott waited until it had driven off, and then looked around the assembled group. 'And while we're waiting for the gardeners to arrive, we can maybe get some basic facts concerning the death of Brian Hannan. It is now confirmed that his death was no accident.' A gasp from one of the local girls. 'Brian Hannan was poisoned, and the poisoner used prussic acid.' He paused. 'I'm sure we've all come across it from time to time, dealing with wasps' nests, for example. A fast-acting poison and a horrible death from suffocation. Somebody wishes that kind of death on a man who had apparently been a benefactor to all of you.'

A breeze from the ocean stirred ribbons in the maids' caps and the women's skirts.

'So I think it behooves each and every one of you to help us find the cold-blooded killer and bring him to justice.'

'Or her,' I said.

Prescott looked sharply at me.

'Or her,' I repeated. 'It is often said that poisoning is a woman's crime.'

'Yes, but not in this case, surely.' He was clearly rattled by this. 'A man does not drink a secret glass of whiskey with a woman. Simply not done, is it? And as for making sure he fell over the cliff – well, I think that might require a modicum of strength.'

Again my eyes went to Mrs McCreedy, she who made up the beds in eight bedrooms and kept a house the size of a castle going year round. She'd have the modicum of strength all right.

Chief Prescott had clearly put me and my suggestion aside. He turned back to the group. 'So I'm asking now, is there anything at all that you saw or heard that evening that would shed light on this horrible crime. Remember, a man who uses prussic acid to kill deserves no loyalty.'

There was silence apart from the sigh of the wind that was now gathering force again. I looked out to see a bank of storm clouds on the horizon. One of the maids put a hand up to hold on to her cap.

'And I ask you again – did not one of you see Brian Hannan arrive that evening?'

'I thought I saw him, sir,' one of the maids said hesitantly.

'And you are?'

'Alice, sir. Mrs Van Horn's maid. I was unpacking the mistress's things and I just happened to look out across the courtyard and I saw a man going into the stables and it looked like Mr Hannan. Of course it was almost dark by then and I don't know him that well, and I know that he has two brothers, so I might have been wrong.'

'Thank you, Alice. Most helpful,' Chief Prescott said. 'Anyone else?'

'You might ask the servants if any of them spotted an outsider on the premises, someone they didn't recognize,' Archie said. 'And you might want to find out where someone got their hands on prussic acid in the first place.'

'I do know my job, sir,' Prescott said. 'I was getting to that. So let me ask right away – is there any prussic acid stored in this house that any of you know about?'

'There is not,' Mrs McCreedy said firmly. 'I can tell you the exact contents of the cupboards in this house. I do the purchasing and I have had no need for prussic acid.'

'I have my men doing a search at this moment,' Chief Prescott said. 'Let's see what they turn up, shall we?'

'Searching our personal things?' Terrence said. 'You've no right to do that.'

'Unless you're hiding a vial of prussic acid you've no need to be alarmed, sir,' Chief Prescott said. 'You're not, are you?'

'Of course not. I don't even know what the stuff looks like.'

'It can take several forms, as I've been told,' Prescott said. 'But to go back to the first part of Mr Van Horn's question – did anyone notice an outsider on the premises that evening?'

'I already told you about the man at the gate,' I said, 'but he couldn't get in. The gate was already shut for the night.'

'About this gate,' Prescott said. 'Is it usually locked at night?'

'It is,' Mrs McCreedy said. 'The gardeners do it when they

go home around sundown. I feel more secure when I'm on my own here knowing that strangers can't get in after dark.'

'So nobody can get in or out after that?'

'They can if they know how to,' she said. 'There is a secret way in through a small door in the wall, but a stranger wouldn't know where to look in the ivy. It's not easy to find, especially not in the dark.'

'But as I pointed out before, anybody could get in during the day and it would be simple enough to elude the gardeners, by hiding out in the wilderness or one of the outbuildings,' Joseph said.

'Yes, we understand that, sir. But the intruder would have had to come out of the stable or the wilderness to meet Mr Hannan, wouldn't he? So how about it – did anyone here notice a person they didn't recognize at any time during that day or evening?'

'I saw a woman creeping around the side of the house,' the footman said. 'I remember thinking it was strange that she hadn't gone to the front door and concluded that it was one of the local women coming to help with the serving that evening.'

'I believe I can explain that,' I said. 'I walked down the side of the house in the dark that evening. I was going to the kitchen to see if Mrs McCreedy could give me the ingredients to make my husband a soup. He was already feeling unwell, you see, and I didn't want to disturb the family.'

'Could the woman you saw have been Mrs Sullivan?' Prescott asked.

The young footman looked at me and then nodded. 'Could have been.'

I had been wrestling with my own conscience about the person I had seen that evening. Now that prussic acid was involved I realized I could keep quiet no longer. 'I saw somebody,' I said. 'When I was passing beside the flower beds I saw the French doors open and a man came out. He looked around then set off, walking past in the direction of the wood, and the gazebo for that matter.'

'And that man wasn't Brian Hannan?'

'I don't know,' I said. 'I never met Mr Hannan. I suppose it could have been, but it didn't look like the man I saw in the photographs. He seemed to be taller and slimmer. I thought at the time that it was Mr Terrence Hannan.'

'It most certainly was not me,' Terrence said angrily. 'I can tell you exactly where I was all that evening. I was playing with my small nephews, which I'm sure they will be only too happy to confirm, and then I went to my room to change for dinner. We met for sherry in the music room and waited for Uncle Brian to arrive so we could go in to dinner. We all became rather annoyed and hungry when he did not show up. Finally we decided to go in to eat. After dinner I sat smoking with the other men. Archie tried to get us interested in playing whist, but we were all rather tired from the journey. I read the paper for a while then went to bed.'

He cast me a glance letting me know that he was hurt by my accusation.

'Do we actually know what time frame we are looking at?' Father Patrick asked quietly. 'Can a doctor tell the approximate time of death?'

'Only approximate,' Chief Prescott said. 'It's still an inexact science.'

'So we couldn't, for example, be looking at some time late at night or early the next morning?'

Chief Prescott shook his head. 'Definitely before midnight the doctor says, most likely before nine o'clock. Of course with the body lying half in water, it makes such estimations more difficult.'

There was the crunch of feet on gravel as one of the constables came toward us. 'I've found it, sir,' he said. 'I believe I've found the prussic acid you were looking for.'

'Good man,' Prescott said. 'Where was it?'

'In the shed next to the stables,' the constable said. 'A little packet of it in a jar on a high shelf.'

'You didn't touch it, did you? We'll want to test for fingerprints.'

'I had to lift it down, sir, but I used my handkerchief, knowing what you'd told us.'

'Can anybody throw light on why there would be prussic acid in the shed?' Prescott asked.

Nobody answered. Prescott shrugged. 'Let's go and see, shall we?'

He set off across the forecourt. Some of us got up to follow him. The servants hovered behind, not sure what they were supposed to do. The constable flung the shed door open, like a conjurer producing a rabbit from a hat and Prescott went inside.

'I put it back in its original position for you to see, sir. Up there. That jar on the top shelf. That's the one,' the constable said proudly.

'I see. Clearly visible, isn't it?' He poked around, looking from side to side like a dog looking to pick up a scent. A workbench ran around the walls and under it were shelves and cupboards. There were also shelves above containing plant pots, jars of seeds, tools, and hung on hooks against the wall was fishing tackle. I remembered that young Sam claimed to have gone fishing that morning, when he spotted the body. Had that been a clever way of explaining possible fingerprints in the shed? I turned to look at the boy, who was standing at the back of the group, close to his grandmother. He couldn't be more than seventeen or eighteen – raised in the Lower East Side and then taken to work by his great-uncle as a messenger boy. Surely such a youth would not possess the knowledge or sophistication to think about alibis and fingerprints. If he were going to kill his great-uncle, he'd have bashed him over the head, or pushed him off the cliff. And yet . . . He was the one who led us to the body, something murderers are known to do.

Chief Prescott worked his way around the shelves and cupboards, opening each one cautiously, using his handkerchief. When he reached the far recesses of the shed we heard him say, 'So that's where it was.'

He came back out to us. 'I've just found where Mr Hannan kept his stash of alcohol. There's a bottle of whiskey and one of gin, plus a bottle of tonic water. And there's a space where I suspect the tray and decanter had stood.'

'Ah, so that's where he kept it,' Joseph said. 'We thought as much. That means presumably that the gardeners were in on his secret. He probably paid them to keep quiet.'

'We'll have to ask them when they arrive,' Prescott said.

'So it's possible that one of the glasses had the poison put in it right here in this shed,' Archie Van Horn said slowly, as if still thinking this through.

'Probably not, sir. Doing that would risk that Mr Hannan would take a drink and die too far from the cliff. No, I surmise that the poison was administered at the last possible moment.' He closed the shed door behind him. 'I want this place sealed off,' Prescott said. 'And I want one of you to get Sergeant Rawlins out here. He knows about fingerprint testing. Is there a telephone on the premises?'

'There is,' Joseph said. 'Mrs McCreedy will show you.'

'Go and telephone headquarters and have Rawlins brought out here,' Prescott said.

The constable he was talking to looked alarmed. 'I ain't never actually used a telephone, sir,' he said.

'It's not hard, man. You just pick up the receiver and speak into it. Ask the operator to connect you with the police station. Go on. Get on with it.'

As we were coming away from the shed, the automobile

arrived, with Parsons, the head gardener, and one other gardener sitting in the backseat. My friendly fellow was missing.

'I'm sorry, sir,' the police constable said as he climbed out of the auto, 'but the other man, Ted Hemmings, was out fishing today. We've left word that he's to come here as soon as he gets back.'

'No matter,' Prescott said. 'Which one of you is the head gardener?'

'That would be me, sir.' Parsons stepped forward. 'Frank Parsons, sir.'

'We've just discovered a jar containing prussic acid in your garden shed. Can you tell me whether you knew it was there and what it might have been used for?'

'Knew it was there? Of course I knew it was there. I was the one who bought it,' Parsons said. I noticed his temperament had not improved since the last time I saw him. 'I got it last year when we had a wasps' nest in that big cedar tree and Mr Hannan told me to get rid of it before the family came for the summer.'

'So the prussic acid has been up there on the shelf for anybody to see?' Chief Prescott asked.

Parsons gave him a withering look. 'I don't know about that. Who'd come in the shed except for the other gardeners?'

'This young man came in yesterday morning to find fishing tackle,' Prescott said, indicating Sam. 'And I now know that Mr Hannan kept a private supply of whiskey and gin in that little cupboard under the counter. So I suppose any number of people might have spotted the prussic acid on the shelf.'

'Up there on the top shelf? You'd have to be tall and poking around where you've no business to be in order to spot it among all the other garden things up there.'

'This presents a sobering thought, doesn't it?' Prescott turned back to look at us. 'It means that we can narrow the list of suspects, most likely to someone who is now present.'

Twenty-Three

I saw a swift glance pass among those standing outside the shed. Irene shuddered and drew her shawl around her.

'Preposterous,' Joseph said.

'And not necessarily,' I added. 'An outsider could have come prepared and brought his own cyanide with him. It may be a complete coincidence that you've found some on the shelf.'

'My thoughts precisely,' Archie said, nodding heartily. 'This sounds to me like a well-planned crime. We had all only just arrived when it happened. The murderer would not have waited on the supposition that the jar containing the poison was still on that shelf. It could have been thrown out or used while we were absent.'

My estimation of Archie Van Horn rose. Until now I had thought him one of those not-too-bright sons of the Four Hundred.

'Well, we'll know soon enough, sir. We'll be sending this jar to look for fingerprints on it, and we'll be taking fingerprints from everyone here.'

'What do you mean, "taking fingerprints"?' Mrs Flannery's voice trembled.

'Nothing to worry about, ma'am. Unless you're guilty, that

is. It's simply a matter of pressing your fingertips onto a pad of ink and then pressing the inky fingers onto a sheet of paper. As simple as that. Now I suggest you all go into the house so that my men know where to find you. I want another word with the gardeners. Oh, and nobody is to think of leaving the area at this juncture. Nobody.'

'We have a business to run, man,' Joseph said. 'Do use a little common sense. Why would I have wanted to kill my brother when we had been so successful together?'

'And I could never do a terrible thing like that,' Mary Flannery said. 'Poison my own dear brother? Never. None of us would. We respected him and we loved him.'

'Then you have nothing to upset yourself about, ma'am. If your fingerprints don't show up on that jar or packet, we can assume that none of you is guilty and you'll all be free to leave.'

One by one they started to drift away. I touched Prescott on the sleeve. 'I have to get back to my husband,' I said. 'I've already left him long enough as it is. But I'll be in the cottage if you want me.'

'It's all right, Mrs Sullivan,' he said in a low voice so that the others couldn't hear. 'I can safely rule out you and your husband from the investigation. In fact I'm now of the firm belief that Mr Hannan wanted your husband here because he suspected that something like this might happen. I just wish he'd given your husband more of a clue. Right now we've got nothing to go on.'

I left him and made my way back to the cottage. As I crossed the lawn I realized that I had never actually had that tea, to which I had been invited, and I have to confess that I sneaked an éclair as I passed. I would have sneaked one for Daniel too but I didn't think he'd be up to it. The moment I started to think about him, I began to worry. Had I left him for too long? Was he all right? Would the girl have checked on him often enough?

I found myself walking faster and faster until I was almost running by the time I reached the front door.

'Martha?' I called.

She appeared from the kitchen. 'Yes, ma'am?'

'How is Mr Sullivan?'

'Sleeping like a baby last time I looked in,' she said.

Sleeping like a baby. My heart lurched. What if he had slipped away and she hadn't even noticed? I ran up the stairs and burst into the bedroom. Daniel was lying there looking so peaceful and still. Holding my breath I tiptoed up to him. Was he breathing? I put my face down close to his and had just given a sigh of relief when I felt faint warm breath on my cheek when he opened his eyes.

'What?' he asked, starting in alarm.

'I'm sorry.' I had to smile at his shocked face. 'I came back and you were so still and peaceful that I had to find out if you were still breathing.'

'If you wanted a sure way to scare a fellow to death, then put your face two inches from his,' he said. I noticed he was still breathing heavily as he spoke, as if he'd just run a race, but his eyes no longer had that awful hollowness.

I sat on the bed beside him and stroked his cheek. 'You're looking better already,' I said

'Where were you?' he asked 'I woke up and you weren't here.'

'I was out to tea,' I said.

'Out to tea?'

'The family invited me to join them for tea on the lawn.'

'That was nice for you.'

'I didn't get my tea as it happened. We had just started when Chief Prescott arrived and made the startling announcement that the body contained traces of cyanide.'

Daniel raised his head, attempting to sit up. 'Cyanide? Good

God. That's something I wouldn't have expected. So he was poisoned and then the body dumped over the cliff.'

'Or more likely he was standing near the cliff when he drank the poison and collapsed over the edge. That would explain the shattered glass among the rocks.'

'Fascinating. I wonder what Prescott plans to do next.'

'You lie back.' I pushed him gently down. 'You're not getting involved in this. You're to rest, remember and get your strength back. Chief Prescott is taking everyone's fingerprints and seeing if they match up on the packet or jar containing the cyanide.'

'Ah, so they've found that, have they?'

'They have found a jar, containing some cyanide in the shed. That doesn't necessarily mean that that particular lot of poison was used. However, if anyone's fingerprints can be detected on it, then we'll know.'

Daniel closed his eyes, thinking. 'The boy said he'd taken fishing tackle from the shed, didn't he? And he was the one who found the body. That's always interesting.'

'I know. I thought the same thing. Someone should check into him. I thought I might befriend his grandmother who is clearly upset by all this. She might inadvertently share some revealing facts about her grandson. We do know that he had become a Junior Eastman. Who knows, maybe he was following orders from Monk.'

'Or he had an ax to grind against his great-uncle. Maybe Hannan was making him toe the line and he resented it. Sometimes that's all it would take.'

'But do you think a boy like that would be savvy enough to use cyanide? It's not an easy substance, is it? And highly dangerous for anyone who breathes the fumes, I remember reading.'

Daniel was silent for a while, considering this. 'No, I can't see a boy using that method – unless some adult had instructed him and that wouldn't be the way that Monk Eastman would dispatch an enemy. I think of it as a more, shall we say, refined type of murder? And you're probably right and they'll find that the cyanide in the packet here has nothing to do with the crime.'

I looked out of the window and the long shadows stretching across the lawn. The clouds were almost upon us. I wonder if they'd mean another storm.

Daniel put a hand on my arm. 'Maybe we should abandon all this speculation. It's not your case, Molly. Not mine either. So don't get involved. Leave it to the local police.'

'But you said he was an idiot.'

'Maybe, but it's still his province, not ours. Especially if it turns out that somehow corruption in New York is involved.'

I frowned, trying to make worrying thoughts that flitted around my brain slow down enough so that I could voice them. My eyes strayed toward the great black shadow cast across the lawn by the castle and I realized what had been worrying me all along. 'This may sound silly, but I can't get it out of my mind that Brian Hannan's death is somehow linked to the death of his granddaughter.'

'The little girl? How could that be – apart from both of them falling off a cliff.'

'That's one thing,' I said. ' "Exactly the same spot," I heard one of them say.' I turned to face him. 'There's something strange about it, Daniel. Something not right. This refusal to speak about her. I mean if you'd lost a beloved child, wouldn't you want to remember her fondly sometimes? Wouldn't you want to look at her picture sometimes? Would you really act as if she never existed?'

'What are you trying to say?' He was frowning at me.

'That there may be a secret this family is keeping from us—'

'Oh, I'd believe that all right,' Daniel cut in. 'I'm sure the

Hannan brothers have plenty of things they'd like to be kept hidden. What New York politician has not been involved in corruption and graft. And then there are shady business practices . . .'

'No, not that kind of secret. I meant to do with the death of little Colleen.'

He looked at me suspiciously. 'What are you trying to say? You think that maybe it wasn't an accident? That she was murdered too, and her body dumped like her grandfather's?'

'I bet they didn't do an autopsy to show whether she was poisoned.'

'Interesting,' Daniel said, 'but a little far-fetched.'

'Then why not speak about her? Why have they all been scared into silence?' I stood up suddenly as a wild thought flashed across my mind. 'Or how about this? What if she's not really dead?'

'But we saw her grave.'

'What if there's nobody in it? Listen, Daniel. We know how much Brian Hannan liked perfection. All his family had to dress well at all times. He has expensive and beautiful things around him. What if Colleen fell from the cliff and wasn't killed, but badly disfigured. They could have kept her shut away all this time.'

'Now that is definitely far-fetched.' He smiled.

'What about the face I saw at the window? I know I saw it, Daniel. So it was either a ghost or a real person. Either way there was somebody up in that turret and everyone is denying that there is even a way up to that part of the house.'

'So what are you trying to tell me now – that she came down from her prison and murdered her grandfather because he'd kept her locked up?'

I shrugged. 'When you put it like that it does sound a little crazy, I'll admit.'

Daniel was still smiling, the sort of smile one gives to humor a child. 'How old would she be now? Twelve? A twelve-year-old child finds cyanide in a shed, lures her grandfather out to the cliff with alcohol, pops the cyanide into his drink, then pushes him over the cliff. Think about it, Molly.'

'Very well, I agree that doesn't sound possible. But I have a gut feeling that there's something strange going on. You'll see. Something they know about Colleen's death that they are not telling us. Mrs McCreedy knows something, and she's frightened.'

'Then all the more reason for you to stay well away.' His fingers gripped around mine. 'Molly, I know you pride yourself on your detective skills and I'm sure you want to show me that you're as fine a detective as I am. Well, I'm not doubting your skills, but sometimes I doubt your judgment. So I'm telling you now, as my wife, don't put yourself in harm's way. Those people have made it quite clear that we are not welcome here and they want us gone as soon as possible. If they know that one of their family members is a murderer, all the more reason for us to respect their wishes and leave them alone.'

'Yes, Daniel,' I said in simpering wifely fashion, making him laugh.

'You can't fool me with this sudden meekness.' He reached up and ruffled my hair, then took my face in his hands and pulled me down to kiss him. 'You're a good woman, Molly Murphy,' he whispered, as I nestled my head on his shoulder. 'And I want to keep you around for a long while.'

I felt his heart beating against mine and gave a little prayer of thanks that he was still alive. My first task now was making sure he recovered quickly and fully, and I'd leave Chief Prescott and his men to pursue this murder investigation, however tempting it was to join in. I closed my eyes and fell asleep against Daniel.

Twenty-Four

In my dream I thought that an audience was applauding. Then I opened my eyes and realized that the rain had come – a hard pattering against the thatch that sounded remarkably like clapping. I got up and looked out of the window and thought I saw a flash of lightning out to sea. At least we were snug in our little cottage tonight and didn't have to go anywhere. Martha tapped on the door at that moment.

'I'm off home then, Mrs Sullivan,' she said. 'I've heated up the soup like you wanted, and there's cold ham and tongue and some salad for you at the table in the dining room.'

'Thank you, Martha.' I followed her down the stairs.

'I'm glad he's feeling better, ma'am,' she said as we reached the front hall. 'Mrs McCreedy said this morning that she thought the poor man was done for and we'd have a second death on our hands.'

She took her shawl down from the hook.

'Tell me, Martha,' I said. 'How long have you worked for the Hannan family?'

'About five years, ma'am.'

'So you weren't here when that terrible thing happened to little Colleen?'

'No ma'am. We heard that a tragedy had befallen a child on

the estate and then we saw the funeral, of course. But that's about it. When they came in the summer they brought all their own servants from the city with them. Mrs McCreedy and the gardeners were the only locals they employed, and frankly the Hannans were not looked upon with much favor among the people of Newport. Newly rich upstarts – no better than ourselves, not old money like the Rockefellers.'

'I see,' I said. 'Well thank you for your help, Martha. It's been a big comfort to me.'

'We changed our minds later,' she added as she opened the front door. 'Mr Hannan was a generous man. He paid well.' She opened the door and looked out. 'We're in for another wild night, I can tell. Best hurry home before it starts in earnest.'

I watched her go out into the rain. I had just shut the front door again and was on my way to the kitchen to see about Daniel's soup when the front door opened.

'It's me again, Mrs Sullivan. There are some people outside the gate. I could hear them talking softly in the darkness. Should we tell them at the big house, do you think?'

'What kind of people?'

'Hard to tell in the dark, but I heard one say, "There has to be another way in." And knowing what just happened to the master, I thought I should tell someone.'

I took down my own cape. 'Quite right,' I said, although I suspected that her return to find me had more to do with her own unease than with her sense of duty. 'I'll come and see if you like.'

'Oh, go carefully, ma'am. They might be armed.'

'It's not as if it's the middle of the night,' I said. 'I don't think we can be in too much danger.' But even as I said it I realized that Brian Hannan had probably died in the early evening hours and nobody had seen anything.

However, I put on a good show of bravery as I walked ahead

of her toward the gate. The rain had died down to a gentle patter on the dry leaves. At first I couldn't see anybody but I soon picked up a rustling just behind the wall.

'Have you found a door yet?' came a shrill whisper.

'There had better be one. I'm not about to climb over the top,' came a whisper in reply.

'They're trying to get in.' Martha grabbed my arm. 'Shouldn't I run and tell the gentlemen at the house?'

I inched closer to the gate and peered out. I caught a movement of light fabric, contrasting with the darkness of the ivy. It seemed to be a skirt, moving in the breeze. The words white lady flashed into my mind. The boys swore they had seen somebody running across the lawn. Maybe their ghost had been all too real – a real person who had managed to gain access once and was now back again. The thought struck me that news of Brian Hannan's death would have reached New York by now and that these intruders were most likely newspaper reporters, determined to get a scoop. Suddenly I wasn't afraid, just angry.

'What are you doing out there?' I demanded. 'If you want to see the Hannan family you can telephone them to make an appointment. Or you can return in daylight.'

'It's not the Hannan family we want to see.' One of the figures came out of the ivy and started to walk toward me. 'We understand you have a Mr and Mrs Sullivan staying on the property. It's them we've come to visit.'

And out of the shadows stepped my dear friend and next-door neighbor Elena Goldfarb, usually known to her friends as Sid. She was followed by Miss Augusta Walcott, of the Boston Walcotts, who went by the nickname of Gus. I saw delight and recognition flood their faces as they saw who I was.

'Molly, my dear,' Gus said, running toward me, arms open. 'I am so glad to see you.'

'We came as soon as we got the telegram.' Sid was one pace

behind her. 'We thought you wouldn't want to be alone at such a difficult time. How is Daniel? Are we too late?'

'Over the worst, thank God,' I said. 'He survived the crisis last night and I think he's going to be all right.' To my own surprise these last words came out as a great hiccupping sob and tears welled up in my eyes.

Gus extended her hands to me through the bars of the gate and I took hold of them. 'Oh, that's wonderful news,' she said. 'We were so worried all the way here. The wretched train moved at a snail's pace.'

'Molly, can you please let us in?' Sid said. 'I'd like to give you a hug and there are bars in the way. I feel like a prison visitor.'

I swallowed back the tears. 'Wait a second.' I turned back. 'Martha, come and give me a hand with this gate.'

Together we raised the peg that locked it and dragged it open.

'For some reason the gate is always locked at nightfall here,' I said. 'But come in, do. You don't know how happy I am that you're here.'

'Molly, dearest. As if we'd stay away in your hour of need.' First Sid then Gus enveloped me in a big hug.

'I'll be off home then, Mrs Sullivan,' Martha said. 'Seeing as how these are friends of yours.'

'Oh, right. Yes. Thank you, Martha,' I said. Together we shut the gate behind her.

'So everyone is imprisoned for the night?' Sid asked.

'There is another door, apparently, but I haven't been shown where it is,' I said. 'Come inside, do, before the rain picks up again.'

'Oh, we got good and soaked getting into the cab and then walking up to the house, didn't we, Sid?' Gus said. 'But there's no harm in a little rain. We didn't wear our best hats.'

And she laughed.

'We're not staying in the big house,' I said, steering them away from the main gravel drive to a small flagstone path.

They stared up at the massive dark shape beyond us. 'Oh, I remember this, don't you, Sid?' Gus said. 'We laughed about it. We called it the Evil Castle.'

'And we wondered why anybody would choose to build a new house to look so old and uncomfortable.'

'It was to remind Brian Hannan of his homeland, I understand. And to remind everybody else that he'd come from a peasant cottage and could now afford a castle.' I turned back to them. 'So you've seen it before? I remember that you stayed in Newport last summer.'

'Of course we've seen it. We could hardly miss it, could we, Sid?' Gus said. 'My cousin's estate is next door and our windows looked straight at the monstrosity.'

'Wait – your cousin's house is next door? You don't mean the house built like a Roman temple, do you?'

'Exactly.' They laughed.

'What a coincidence.' I led them up to the cottage door. 'Here we are. Cozy but cramped.'

'How awfully quaint.' Sid laughed again. 'Not only does the man build the most uncomfortable-looking castle but he's added the peasant cottages around it too. Has he imported an Irish bog or two for the peat?'

'We shouldn't laugh about him,' I said, suddenly remembering. 'The poor man was murdered two days ago.'

'Mercy me,' Gus said. 'Daniel nearly dies of pneumonia and your host gets murdered. And you thought you were here for a quiet week on the seashore.'

'I know.' I opened the front door. 'As I said, it's rather cramped, so I'm not sure how we'll manage with sleeping arrangements . . .'

'Molly, don't worry about us,' Sid said. 'It's all sorted out.

Gus telephoned her cousin the moment we received your telegram, and the upshot is that we are most welcome to camp out in marble luxury next door. The housekeeper there will take care of our needs and we shall be free to look after you and Daniel.'

'That is wonderful,' I said. 'Here, let me take those wet coats.'

'How very dinky.' Sid was already poking her head in doorways. 'A real Irish cottage. And supper already laid out on the table.'

'I'll take you up to see Daniel and then we can eat,' I said. 'We should go quietly just in case he's sleeping.'

But he wasn't. He opened his eyes in surprise as we came in.

'Daniel, dear. Look who has come to be with us,' I said.

'Now I suppose I'm to get no peace from a pack of women,' he replied, but his eyes were smiling.

'I can see you are on the mend, Captain Sullivan,' Sid commented.

As for me, I felt as if a great burden had been lifted from my shoulders. My husband was getting better and my dear friends were here to support me. Everything would be all right after all.

Twenty-Five

I awoke to a great crash and leaped up, my heart thumping. Was it someone hammering on my door, or trying to break in? Part of my brain was already calculating how long it had been since I'd been allowed an undisturbed night's sleep. Daniel beside me murmured in his sleep but didn't wake. Instinctively my hand went to his forehead and I was relieved to feel it pleasantly cool. I grabbed my robe and tiptoed to the stairs. At that moment the room was bathed in a flash of light and I realized that the crash I had heard was only thunder from the storm that had been threatening. I went over to the window and watched as lightning flickered out to sea. Thunder rumbled again nearby and the heavens opened in a veritable downpour. I stood for a while watching it until the thunder died to a distant murmur and the rain abated.

I was about to go back to bed when I saw something pale moving through the bushes. I peered out into the blackness of the night wishing for more light, trying to work out what I had seen. Then it appeared again, closer this time. There was no mistaking what I saw: a person dressed in white was dancing in the rain. The boys' white lady. I was downstairs in an instant and ran toward where I had seen it. It, or rather she, must have heard me coming or sensed my presence because it ran lightly

199

across the lawn to the tower and then simply disappeared. I followed, my feet cold and tingling on the wet grass. I reached the tower and searched diligently. No sign of her. Nowhere she could have gone. I felt the hair on the back of my neck standing up as I tried to come up with a reasonable explanation. I had to conclude that there had been a ghost after all. The ghost of a young woman. Who was she and why had the family never mentioned her?

I dried myself off and climbed back into bed, snuggling against Daniel in an attempt to bring back warmth to my cold, wet body, but sleep wouldn't come. A dead child who must not be spoken of – a young woman in white who was never mentioned, and now a murder. Daniel had always said to me when speaking of investigations, 'First find the connection.' What had happened at this place, to this family that they were keeping from the rest of the world? And who was the mysterious woman in white? I was determined to find out.

At first light I was still awake. Daniel beside me was breathing peacefully but noisily. However, it was no longer the rattling rasping of someone who was suffocating in his own fluid. I got up and dressed silently, then I let myself out. It was a lovely still morning with the promise of a fine day ahead. Birds were chirping in the trees. A squirrel ran across the grass, then up the nearest cedar tree when he spotted me. I headed straight for that tower and started to pull apart the ivy, looking for a hidden door. After a long and diligent search I was forced to the conclusion that there wasn't one. The ivy here had really been allowed to take over in this part of the house, growing thickly and unbroken around the base of the tower.

I extended my search to the castle wall on either side. The ivy was not so rampant here. But neither was there any kind of door or opening through which a person might have slipped. My figure in white had definitely not run around to the front door or to the back of the house. I would have seen her against the darkness of that building. I stared up in frustration. The first windows seemed to be in the upper floors and they were closed. I was about to give up when I noticed a tendril of ivy on the ground. Of course it could have been brought down by the force of the storm, but I parted the ivy close to where it lay. No, I hadn't missed the door, but what I did see was a solid trunk of ivy tree stretching upward and dappled daylight shining down on me. It might just be possible for someone young and agile to climb up inside the ivy at this point. I had no idea where she would be going, but it was worth a try. I hitched up my skirts and was tempted to remove my pointed and impractical shoes. After I slipped on the wet ivy a couple of times I did remove them, leaving them hidden under the ivy.

Then I hitched up my skirts in a most unladylike manner and up I went. It really did seem as if there was a route upward. As I climbed higher the ivy branches became more fragile and I worried about it supporting my weight and pulling away from the castle wall. I was high now – at least two stories up, but nowhere near at the level of the turret itself. I hesitated, wondering where this would lead and whether I was risking my life for nothing. But then I found a couple of ivy leaves that were crushed, as if someone had gripped the branch right there.

So I kept on going and came at last to a small window, hidden from the outside world by the ivy. It was closed but I tugged at it and it swung open. It was arched like a castle window with tinted leaded panes. I peered inside and saw a narrow stairway going up and down. It was no easy challenge to squeeze myself and my skirts through but after a heart-stopping moment when a tendril of ivy did come away from the wall, I made it. I found myself standing on the staircase. In one direction it descended into darkness. On the other it went up, hugging the castle wall.

There were no doors that I could see. The narrow stair was enclosed and cut off from the rest of the building.

So up I went, my heart beating faster in anticipation of what I might find. It must lead up into the tower. It was dimly lit with that one window of tinted yellow glass and then no other form of light for quite a while. At the top I came to a doorway. It was shut. I turned the handle, rattled it, but it must have been locked from the inside. Frustration welled up in me. I was so close and I wasn't about to give up now. I knelt down, trying to put my eye to the keyhole, but the key must have been in it as I could see nothing. I realized in annoyance that I hadn't yet put my hair up. A good hairpin might have been able to dislodge that key. I didn't relish climbing all the way down again and then back up with the right tools to gain entry, but I was prepared to do it if that was what it took to find out the truth.

Let me tell you that going down was harder than climbing up. I slithered, got my skirts caught, scraped my toes, and was generally thoroughly vexed by the time I reached the ground. I found my shoes and went back to the cottage, carrying them in my hand. Once back at the cottage I removed my wet stockings and underskirt, giving me one less layer to encumber me. I wished I had dared to pack my bicycling bloomers. How much easier it would be if ladies were allowed to wear them on a regular basis. Then I found a small knife in the kitchen drawer and took a sheet of writing paper from the desk. Thus armed I recrossed the lawn. The sun was now coming up over the ocean, painting the water with lovely streaks of gold. I felt a renewed sense of urgency. Gardeners would be arriving. People in the house would be up and around. Young Sam might want to go fishing, if the shed was unlocked.

I reached the ivy unseen and slipped inside. The second climb seemed to take forever and I wondered at one point whether I had taken another route upward and missed the window. But there it was at last and I climbed through more easily with one less layer of clothing to hinder me. Up the stairs I went, slid the sheet of paper under the door and then used the knife to push out the key. I heard it drop with a loud clunk and hoped that I had positioned the paper correctly. I held my breath as I pulled it out carefully and was delighted to see the key lying on it. In a few seconds I turned the key in the lock and the door swung open. Before me was a good-sized, rather large Spartan room with bare floors, dotted here and there with braided rugs. It was lit by another arched window, this one paned with clear glass so that I could look out at the grounds and the gate. On the far wall was a fireplace but no fire was lit and over it was a painting of Jesus with the little children. In one corner of the room was a bed, unmade, with coverlets half falling to the floor and over it a large crucifix. The other furniture consisted of a small table with two chairs, an overstuffed chair – rather the worse for wear – a small wardrobe, and a cupboard with a doll and teddy bear sitting on top of it. In the middle of the floor there was a dollhouse and a big rocking horse in the corner. A child's room. I felt a wave of fear run through me. A child's room kept as a memorial to a dead girl? But the bed had been slept in and the dollhouse was open with a baby doll in a cradle sitting on the rug.

I looked around for an occupant but the room was empty. There was a door on the far side. I found myself tiptoeing over to it. The bare boards creaked as I crossed the room and I held my breath. But the door only opened onto a sort of anteroom with a sink, a tin bath, a small stove, and various foodstuffs on a shelf. That was all. So where was the person who lived here? Had she gone down the stairs to other rooms where she spent the day?

I came out of the anteroom and was about to walk back to the door when I heard a low voice.

'Otay wee awa n baba, Coween.'

'Wee awa.'

All my thoughts of ghosts came back to me. Then I realized that the sound was coming from under the bed. I crept toward it and lifted the comforter that was about to fall to the floor. Looking back at me was the face I had seen in the window, the face I had seen on the portrait in town. Her big eyes were staring at me in pure terror and I noticed that they were not bright blue, as in the portrait, but were greenish brown. I also realized, of course, that she was not four years old, but a girl of eleven or twelve with long light-brown hair. The hair was still plastered to her forehead the way it would be if she had been out in a rainstorm and had not dried or brushed since. She was still wearing a white nightgown but I couldn't tell whether that had dried on her or was a fresh one. After her initial frozen shock the girl was now looking around like a trapped animal for a way of escape.

'Don't be afraid. I won't hurt you,' I said gently. 'I'm a friend.'

She stared at me, silent, unblinking.

'I saw you dancing in the rain,' I said, smiling at her. 'That must have been fun. And you put a flower in my hair when I was asleep, didn't you?'

She was staring at me, unblinking, not giving any sign as to whether she heard and understood what I was saying or not.

'Are you Colleen?' I asked.

Still she didn't reply or move.

'Colleen?' I asked again.

A tentative smile crossed her face. She picked up a big rag doll with yellow hair that had been lying on the floor beside her. 'Coween,' she said.

I was confused. 'The doll's name is Colleen?' I asked. 'Or your name?'

It was her turn to look confused now, her eyes darting, ready for flight. 'Coween,' she said again, holding the doll close to her now.

'And what's your name then?'

She was starting to inch away from me. I could tell she wanted to get out from under the bed so that she had room to escape. Suddenly I saw her eyes shift from me and open wide in terror.

Mrs McCreedy stood behind me and in her hand was a knife.

Twenty-Six

'I knew I couldn't trust you from the very beginning,' she said in a threatening voice. 'You with your poking and prying where you've no right to be. Well, I hope you're satisfied now because you've just condemned her to death.'

I scrambled to my feet, standing in front of the child to protect her. All kinds of thoughts were whirling through my brain. Colleen had never died at all. This crazy woman had kept her hidden away and captive all this time. The child on the floor whimpered and attempted to crawl away.

'It's all right, Kathleen, love,' she said gently. 'You'll be safe, don't worry.'

'Kathleen?' I frowned. 'Not Colleen?'

'Coween.' The child scrambled under the bed to pick up the doll and then backed into a corner.

'I'm not going to harm her,' I said. 'I saw her outside running around in the storm last night and I had to find out who she was.'

'Outside? Don't tell me she's managed to get out again, has she? I wonder how on earth she did it this time.'

'She opened the window halfway down the stair and she climbed down the ivy. I followed her route. That was how I got in.'

'But I leave the door locked.'

'Somehow she managed to open it,' I said.

Mrs McCreedy shook her head. 'She used to be such a docile little thing. She'd play happily with her toys and eat her food and that was that. But recently she's grown restless. I found she'd got out once before but I thought we'd taken care of that.'

'I think she's been outside several times while I've been here,' I said. 'The two boys reported seeing a ghost, and I was asleep in a lawn chair when I heard singing in a strange language and awoke to find a flower in my hair.'

'I told the master it wasn't going to work much longer and we'd have to decide what to do with her,' she said. 'Is that why he brought you here? He wanted to show her to you and see what you'd recommend?'

'Mrs McCreedy, I don't know what you're talking about,' I said. 'And please put away that knife. I'm not a threat to anybody. I don't know why Mr Hannan invited Daniel and myself here and I don't know who this child is or anything about her.'

She looked down at the girl who was now sitting on the floor, hugging the doll to her, humming to herself as she rocked back and forth.

'Go back to your playing, Kathleen. Everything is all right. You can tell Colleen everything is all right.'

Then she took my arm none too gently, her fingers digging into my flesh, and led me across the room and into the little scullery area, closing the door behind us.

'I could kill you now,' she said. She was standing between me and the door, the knife still in her hand. 'Nobody knows about this place but me now that the master is dead. Plenty of cubby-holes to hide a body.'

'My husband knows where I was going,' I said, trying to sound calmer than I felt. 'And I don't know why you'd want to kill me. I told you I meant no harm.'

'It doesn't matter what you meant, the harm has been done. They'll find out about her and then it will be all over for the poor little thing.'

'Why should it be?'

'Because they'll send her back.' She sounded close to tears. 'After all I've done for her all these years to keep her from harm.'

'You called her Kathleen,' I said slowly. 'She's not Colleen?'

'Colleen is dead,' she said flatly. 'You knew that. You've seen her grave.'

'Then who is she?'

'Kathleen's her name. She was Colleen's twin.'

'Colleen had a twin sister? Then why is she kept up here rather than with her family?'

She leaned closer to me. 'Because she killed Colleen. She pushed her sister over the cliff.'

'But she was four years old. She couldn't have known what she was doing.'

'I'm afraid she knew, all right. She was observed, you see. Creeping up behind her sister and then giving her that awful push. She was always the strange one, poor little thing. Colleen was the most adorable little girl you could ever imagine – blonde curls, blue eyes, dimples, and a disposition to match. Everybody adored her. And Kathleen, well she had the same features but without the prettiness, if you know what I mean, and her hair was mousy while her sister's was golden, and she was sullen and stubborn and withdrawn. She hung back when Colleen ran into your arms. How do I put it – she simply wasn't as lovable.'

'So you think she got rid of her more lovable twin?' I asked.

'I know she did.'

'What did she say about it? Was she sorry? Did she think it was an accident?'

'We don't know. At that moment she stopped speaking. I don't believe she remembers a thing about it, and she's even forgotten she had a twin. It's as if she blotted the whole thing from her mind. As you can see she calls that doll Colleen and she speaks to it in gibberish, but that's the only time she speaks. Not a word to me, although she may nod now and then.'

'So whose decision was it to have her locked away up here?' I asked.

'After it happened her mother was fearful for her little boy and for the one she was expecting. She didn't want Kathleen in the same house anymore. So it was agreed she'd be put in an institution for the mentally impaired. They found one in the Connecticut countryside and off she was shipped. It was agreed that she'd never be mentioned again.'

'That's terrible – a four-year-old child condemned because she was jealous of her popular twin and did something stupid on impulse.'

She shrugged. 'You have to understand how they all adored Colleen. Miss Irene and Mr Archie doted on her. And so did the master. She was the light of his life. But he was a fair man, a just man. Miss Irene couldn't bring herself to visit her daughter, in fact a doctor told her that it would be more disturbing for the child to see her family. But Alderman Hannan, he went up to see her, and he was horrified. This place was supposed to be a humane institution and they were paying well for the privilege of keeping her there, but he said the patients were treated like animals. They were like animals – unkempt, crawling around on the floor, stealing each other's food. He saw Kathleen retreating further and further into herself, giving up on life. He knew if he left her there any longer she'd die. So he had these rooms built secretly within the tower. He made them soundproof and a stair going up within the walls. I'm the only one who has the key and knows the way in.'

She paused, breathing heavily, and she toyed with the knife in her hand. For a moment I wondered if she was still considering using it on me and I glanced around for something to defend myself with.

'Didn't her parents ever want to check on her?' I asked after a silence.

'They believed that the alderman visited her regularly – which he did, of course – and reported back to them. But if you ask me, I think they preferred not to be reminded of her.'

'How do you manage to keep her a secret?' I asked.

'Most of the year it's no problem,' she said. 'It's only me and Kathleen and she's been an easy child until recently.'

'What happens when the family is here?'

'Then I change her routine,' she said. 'I give her medicine to make her sleep all day and then she's up at night.'

'No wonder you wanted to get back when you came to Daniel the other night,' I said.

'I don't like to leave her too long when people are here.' She glanced at the door. 'I've had to put the fear of God into the child. I've told her that the bad people will take her away back to that dreadful place if they find her here, so she has to be as quiet as a little mouse. I hate doing it, but it's for her own good. Poor little mite looks down from her window and doesn't even know it's her own brothers running around down there.'

'They saw her the other night,' I said.

She sighed. 'I feared it would happen eventually. Usually it's no problem because they bring their own staff with them all summer and I can watch over Kathleen, but this visit – well, it's completely thrown me. Even before the master's death I felt that something bad was about to happen to us.'

I didn't quite know what to say. She still had the knife in her hand. She seemed to be considering things too because she said, 'You don't think, do you . . . ?'

'That she had anything to do with his death?' I shook my head. 'If he'd just been pushed off the cliff then I'd consider the possibility, although I doubt that she's strong enough. She's small for her age, isn't she?'

She nodded.

'But I can't believe that a child of limited mental abilities, who doesn't even communicate, could plan a murder that involved putting poison in a glass of whiskey. How would she know that her grandfather drank whiskey? Can she even read? I don't see any books. How would she know where poison was kept or even what it did?'

'My thoughts too,' Mrs McCreedy said, 'but that's not how they will look at it. When they find out she's here, she'll be the one they want to pin it on, you mark my words. Because if it wasn't her, then likely it was one of them and that's too worrying to think about.'

'Maybe the police will soon find out who really killed him and then she'll be safe,' I said.

'Maybe not.' She turned the knife over in her hand. 'I don't know what to do, Mrs Sullivan. You're a nice enough woman, I daresay, but I don't see how I can let you go.'

I realized then that she had been pushed to the verge of madness. I had to tread most carefully. 'I told my husband about finding a way up through the ivy into the tower,' I said. 'He knows I'm here. Besides, I can tell you're a good Catholic woman. You couldn't kill someone and then live with yourself. Added to which I'm a trained detective. I know how to defend myself pretty well.'

She threw the knife down on the table. 'Then help me,' she said, 'because I don't know what to do. You don't know what she was like when she came here. A terrified little animal, that's what she was. Crawling around on all fours and scurrying off to hide under furniture if I came near her.'

211

'I realize that it's a problem,' I said. 'And I'd like to help her if I could.'

'Then go away, go back to New York City with your new husband, and forget about us. Say nothing and she'll be safe.'

'Look, I'll do what I can,' I said. 'I also have to remember that I'm married to a police officer. I'll have to share this knowledge with him and he may feel that we have to report her presence to the Newport police.'

'Then the family will know and it will be all over.' Tears were now running down her fat cheeks. 'He wanted to protect her. He made sure the family never found out she was here. I'd be letting him down as well as her.'

Tentatively I touched her arm. 'I will try to do all I can to protect her, I promise.'

'Yes.' She wiped tears away with the back of her hand. 'And we can pray, can't we? We can pray that there is justice for the late master and for this little mite too.'

Kathleen was playing with her dollhouse as we came out of the kitchen area. She didn't look up, instead went on singing nonsense in a sweet, high voice. 'Na baba do, Coween.'

I squatted down beside the girl. 'You have a nice dollhouse, Kathleen,' I said. 'Are the dolls having their tea?'

She looked up at me with a puzzled expression then went back to her tuneless humming, moving the furniture around and ignoring me.

'You should go,' Mrs McCreedy said, pulling me to my feet. She half pushed me to the door.

'Did she ever speak normally?' I asked.

'I hardly saw her before the – the tragedy,' she said. 'They came with their nanny and were mostly up in the nursery. But I remember she and her sister were very thick, whispering and hugging together, but from what I hear she was quite normal in most ways.'

'Do you understand her? Does she use real words?'

She looked back at the girl on the floor. 'Sometimes I think I understand her – at least some words – but then others it's total gibberish.'

A sudden thought struck me. 'I have a friend in New York who is an alienist – a doctor of the mind. He studied in Vienna with Professor Freud who is discovering such interesting things about dreams. Would you like him to take a look at her? Maybe he'd be able to unlock the mind she has shut from the outside world.'

Her eyes darted nervously. 'I don't know about that. The last doctor condemned her to the asylum. Why wouldn't this one do the same?'

'He's an intelligent, compassionate man. I believe he might be able to help her. Wouldn't you like her restored to normality?'

She shook her head violently at this. 'No, I would not. As long as she didn't know what she was doing, then it would only be some kind of asylum for her. If she was proved to be sane, well then it could well be jail, couldn't it?'

'Surely not, at her age. Even if she knew what she was doing, a four-year-old has no real concept of death, of killing someone. It was an impulse and you can see what it has done to her.'

'Whatever it is, it won't be for the better, poor little mite.'

She unlocked the door and led me down the stairs. I stepped aside and allowed her to go first. To tell you the truth, I thought she might be tempted to give me a shove and get rid of me in what would look like an accident. I could see her point. She had protected the child for eight years and now all her hard work was about to be undone. When we reached the window she stopped.

'If you don't mind, I'd like you going back the way you came,' she said. 'I'd rather you didn't discover the way out of here. If you honestly don't know how to get in and out, then you can't give us away by mistake, can you?'

She stood watching as I hitched up my skirts and eased myself out of that window.

'Now I'm making sure it's good and secure,' she said after me. 'You'll not be getting in this way again, no more will she be getting out. I'll be making sure she takes her medicine to make her sleep until everyone has gone.'

I heard the window slam shut behind me and climbed down, getting a couple of good scratches along the way.

Twenty-Seven

At last I was on the ground and went back to the cottage without encountering anyone. Martha had just arrived and was humming to herself in the kitchen.

'Lovely morning, Mrs Sullivan,' she called. 'Been out for an early walk, have you?'

'That's right,' I said, hoping she wouldn't notice that I was barefoot and surely had bits of ivy sticking out of my hair. 'I'm going to take a bath before breakfast. Is Captain Sullivan awake yet?'

'Not when I peeked in,' she said.

I went up to see for myself and found him still sleeping peacefully. Then I made a decision. Daniel would undoubtedly tell me that I had to inform the police about Kathleen. I didn't like the idea of keeping things from him, but I saw all too clearly that she would make a perfect scapegoat – a crazy child who has already killed once. How perfect. Case closed. I needed to buy myself some time. And to seek advice for once. I had never been too good about asking for help or seeking advice, but this time there was too much at stake and friends, whose opinion I valued, were within reach.

I wasn't going to wait for Sid and Gus to wake up, then have their usual leisurely breakfast before they came to visit. I made myself look respectable, put on shoes and stockings and then told Martha I was going to pay a call on the next-door neighbors. As I walked I smiled at the term. Next-door neighbors – Irish castle to Roman marble palace. You'd hardly pop next door for a cup of sugar in these parts!

As I came out of the gate and turned into the road I glanced at the colonial house across the street and saw those lace curtains drop back into place. Even at this hour the occupant was either vigilant or nosy, depending on how one saw it. I resolved to pay her a call on my way home.

The Roman marble palace next door had even grander gates than the Hannan residence. These were gilt tipped with tall classical statues on either side. Luckily there was a little door to one side. It opened easily and I let myself into magnificent formal gardens and a broad driveway leading to the white columns at the front of the house. It was breathtakingly beautiful, although personally I'd not have liked to live in a place that looked like a mausoleum. I went up the marble steps and rang the doorbell.

The woman who answered looked most surprised to see me. 'Miss Augusta and Miss Elena are in residence, madam,' she said, 'but they are not ready to receive visitors at this hour. They haven't even come down to breakfast yet.'

'Don't worry, they are used to my dropping in on them at strange hours,' I said. 'I am their next-door neighbor back in New York and we often take breakfast together. If you could just let them know I am here and it's rather urgent.'

'If you say so, ma'am. Whom should I say is calling?' she said, displaying considerable reluctance.

'I'm sorry, I didn't bring my card with me.' I said it half joking, but she nodded as if she was accepting my apology just this once. 'But it's Mrs Daniel Sullivan.'

'If you'll please come in and take a seat,' she said, ushering me into a circular marble hallway with statues in niches and a curved marble stair ascending to a marble balcony above. She indicated an uncomfortable-looking marble bench. I sat.

It was cold and drafty in that marble hall and I found myself wondering about the rich and why they would want homes that were neither comfortable nor friendly. The sound of the housekeeper's feet on the marble steps made me look up. Her demeanor had changed.

'Mrs Sullivan,' she said. 'Miss Augusta and Miss Elena would be delighted to join you in the breakfast room as soon as they have completed their toilettes. Please follow me.' And she led me to a delightful room with large arched windows giving incredible views onto the ocean. Sun streamed in and there was the smell of coffee and bacon. A row of silver tureens sat on a white-clothed sideboard along one wall – an awful lot of tureens for two people, I thought.

'Do help yourself,' she said. 'I'm afraid the choice is a little sparse today, but I wasn't given much warning of Miss Augusta's arrival, and frankly one doesn't expect family visits at this time of year.'

I took a plate and opened the first tureen to reveal scrambled eggs, then bacon, sausages, smoked haddock . . . I felt the housekeeper's presence looming behind me and couldn't decide whether she was making sure I had everything I needed or she was worried that I'd walk off with the silver.

I turned to her. 'Have you been with the family long, Mrs—?'

'Sweeney, ma'am. Mrs Sweeney. And yes, I've been housekeeper here since the family first built the home in '88.'

'I'm staying with the family next door,' I said. 'The Hannans.'

She pursed her lips. 'Are you, ma'am? They've been saying Mr Hannan was killed, is that right?'

'That's correct. He fell from the cliff. Very tragic.'

'I'm sorry to hear that, ma'am. My condolences if you were a friend of his.'

I smiled. 'I take it the family here is not great friends with their neighbors?'

'Begging your pardon, ma'am, but you can't just make a lot of money and then expect to fit in with families who have been brought up to wealth. That's not just how it works. Mr Hannan might have been rich, but he'd never have belonged here in Newport. He was never invited to the parties, you know. Mrs Astor wouldn't even acknowledge him in the street.' She paused. 'I'm sorry, I should never have spoken my mind, you being a friend and all.'

'Actually I never met Mr Hannan. My husband has had business connections, that's all.'

'Ah, well in that case, you'll understand why I feel the way I do. God rest the poor gentleman's soul. It must be a shock for the rest of the family, although what they are doing here in October is past me. Whoever heard of one of the cottages being occupied after Labor Day? See what I was saying about good manners and fitting in? You can't buy breeding.'

I took my plate to a place at the table and poured myself coffee. Mrs Sweeney didn't offer to pour for me and I tried to remember if it was usual for the rich to serve themselves at breakfast. Footsteps on the marble floor outside announced the arrival of Sid and Gus. Gus came toward me, arms open.

'Molly, dear. How nice of you to come and share breakfast with us. How is dear Daniel?'

'I left him sleeping peacefully,' I said. 'And I didn't just come to visit to be social. There is something urgent I wish to discuss with you.'

'Let us just help ourselves to coffee and then fire away,' Sid said. I noticed she poured her own coffee, then lifted one tureen after another, closing each with a shudder.

'Just toast, I think,' she said. 'You don't perhaps have any croissants, do you, Mrs Sweeney?'

'We do not, I'm afraid.' Mrs Sweeney's expression made it quite clear that she hadn't a clue what croissants were and that she would never serve them if she did know.

Sid took a slice of toast and sat down beside me.

'What did you want to discuss, Molly? You're looking worried.'

'Let's wait for Gus,' I said. I turned to Mrs Sweeney. 'Tell me, Mrs Sweeney, I presume you heard about Mr Hannan's grandchild who fell from the cliff about eight years ago?'

'We did hear something about it,' she said. 'Such a shame. Sweet little thing, I remember.'

'Did you ever meet her sister?'

'Sister? There was more than one child?'

'She had a twin.'

'Ah, that explains it then. I saw her a few times and once she was smiley and friendly and then the next time she was silent and shrank behind her nurse. So they were twins. How interesting.'

'But you never heard the details of her death?'

'No, I can't say that I did. As I said, this household was not on social terms with the Hannan family.' She looked around as Gus sat on the other side of the table. 'Is there anything else I can get you, Miss Augusta.'

'No, thank you, Mrs Sweeney. This all looks splendid,' Gus said.

The housekeeper gave a little half-bow, half-nod and went.

Gus gave me an exasperated look. 'We did tell her that we don't like a big breakfast, but I don't think it sank in. Now, what is so important that it needs to be discussed at this ungodly hour, Molly?'

I told them exactly what had happened to me – the white figure in the night, my climb to the tower, and what I had discovered there.

'How frightfully thrilling,' Sid said. 'A hidden child who murdered her twin. How terribly gothic.'

'Sid, it's not a subject for amusement.' Gus gave her a disapproving frown. 'You can see that Molly is distressed.'

'I am most concerned about it,' I said. 'The housekeeper is terrified that the girl will be sent back to an insane asylum when it's discovered she's in the house. And she's sure they'll think she murdered her grandfather.'

'Because she pushed her sister over a cliff at the age of four?' Sid said. 'What child has not wanted to get rid of an adored sibling? I know I often wished I could make my brother disappear. Has she demonstrated more murderous tendencies since?'

'She has only been with the housekeeper and seen her grandfather occasionally,' I said. 'She seemed a docile, timid little thing to me.'

'Then why would the family want to pin the crime on her?' Sid persisted.

'Because she makes a perfect scapegoat. And the family would rather think that she was the culprit rather than one of them.'

'What a charming family,' Gus remarked as she reached for the marmalade. 'To know there might be a murderer in their midst and yet to let a child take the blame for it.'

'This is only what Mrs McCreedy fears,' I corrected hastily. 'She may be quite wrong, of course. They may want to do the right thing and find the true culprit. Although from what I witnessed of them, they were most anxious to find a mysterious outsider and thus exonerate themselves.'

'Only natural,' Sid said. 'Nobody wants to believe there is a black sheep in their own family, especially not a murderer.'

'So you can see my dilemma.' I looked first at Gus and then at Sid. 'I should tell Daniel about the girl, and he would undoubtedly want me to report it to the police. Then the family will know and it will all be over for Kathleen.'

'But how do you know whether she is guilty or not?' Sid asked. 'You say she can escape from her tower at will. Who is to say she didn't give her grandfather a timely push.'

'That much I could believe, but not the part with the cyanide. Think about it, Sid – to find a jar containing cyanide in a shed, be able to read the label, know what it is, and slip some into his glass of whiskey – no, I can't go along with that. She's still a little child, Sid. She sits hugging her doll and talking to it in gibberish.'

'Did you say she calls the doll by her sister's name?' Gus looked up suddenly.

'She does.'

'Then she's probably speaking to it in the language of twins.'

'Is there such a thing?' I asked.

Gus nodded. 'Oh, yes. I went to a lecture about it recently. It appears that twins frequently communicate with each other in a secret language known only to themselves. You say it was gibberish but I expect her language has its own vocabulary and syntax known only to her twin.'

'Fascinating,' I said. 'But I don't know how one would unlock the key, when she doesn't speak apart from that.'

'It would take a specialist,' Sid said.

'I was thinking of asking Dr Birnbaum to see her,' I said. 'He is the expert on diseases of the mind, isn't he?'

'And what would you hope he'd accomplish?' Sid asked. 'To have her proved sane? If she's sane, then she knew what she did and she's evil. If she's not sane, then she's not responsible. So think carefully before you tread, Molly.'

'I know. It's such a great dilemma. I don't know what to do.'

'I don't wish to sound callous,' Sid said. 'But this really isn't your problem, Molly. Haven't you enough to worry about with your husband's grave illness? Surely your first duty is to him.'

'But you know me. I can't sit by and let an injustice happen.

221

But I shouldn't keep my discovery from my husband and the law, should I?' I looked at them again. 'Tell me, what would you do if you were me?'

'As I see it,' Sid said slowly, 'if you really want to do something for this girl, then do it. You're right that you shouldn't keep anything as major as this from your husband. However, you don't have to tell him at this exact moment. In fact it would not be wise. He's been gravely ill. You would not want to upset him with startling news like this. So for his own good you decide to keep the news from him.'

I had to laugh. 'Sid, you are devious.'

'Just pragmatic. And in the meantime, if you want to rescue this girl, you could find out who really killed Brian Hannan.'

'And how would I do that?'

'You're a detective, aren't you? You've solved difficult cases.'

'But I've kept my eyes open and tried to quiz family members and got nowhere so far.'

'Then you need to find out who had the best reason for wanting him dead.'

'But that would mean going to New York and poking around in his business and Tammany Hall and the family home . . .'

'You could do that,' Sid said, sounding enthusiastic now. 'We're here. We'll watch over Daniel for you. And you can talk to your Dr Birnbaum at the same time. See what he has to say.'

'I would like to do that. But as for finding the true killer – I wonder if the family members really know and are just clamming up, or that they don't know and they are frightened to find out?'

Gus had been sitting silent for a while. Suddenly she said. 'Did anyone actually witness this child pushing her sister off the cliff?'

'I believe so.'

'Pity,' she said. 'Because if they didn't, then maybe the same person has killed more than once.'

I stared at Gus across the table. Morning sunlight now streamed in through the long windows, making Gus a silhouette against the brightness. 'You're suggesting that a family member killed the little girl, then Brian Hannan?'

'One has to wonder if they are not somehow linked. The same area of cliff, you said. Two family members dying in the same manner. And then there is the reason that Brian Hannan invited you to be able to observe his family. Had he discovered some disturbing fact about a family member and wanted Daniel to confirm it?'

I stared at the ocean beyond Gus, watching a sleek white yacht sailing far out to sea. 'He did say one thing. He said to Daniel that he thought he might have got it wrong. But he never explained what "it" was.'

'What if "it" were the circumstances surrounding his granddaughter's death?'

'But why would that come up now, after all this time?' I asked. 'What could he possibly have discovered that made him question what happened when she died?'

'You're the detective,' Sid said. 'You can find out.'

'I don't see how I can,' I said. 'I have no authority to question the family and, even if I did, they wouldn't tell me anything.'

'Then go to New York. Mr Hannan might have left some kind of clue there – he might have confided in a friend or an employee.'

I shook my head. 'Daniel might be furious if he knew I was doing my own investigation,' I said.

'Daniel need never know. If you find out anything valuable you turn it over to the police, anonymously if necessary. The local policeman is a hero and justice prevails,' Sid said.

'He might notice if his wife is missing for a couple of days,' I pointed out.

223

'Take the early train tomorrow,' Sid said. 'There is a fast train at six o'clock. The cottage owners take it when they have to attend to business in New York. You'd have a full day there and be back that night.'

I gave a nervous laugh. 'I can't be expected to solve a crime in a day. Even Sherlock Holmes couldn't do that.'

'No, but you might find out something that puts you on the right track. We'll go over to amuse Daniel.'

'And how will you explain my absence?'

'We'll think of something,' Sid said with an expansive shrug.

'How about poor Molly was exhausted after nursing you through your crisis so we're giving her a day off,' Gus suggested. 'What could be more simple?'

I nodded. 'He might accept that. So I'll go tomorrow then, if Daniel continues to make sufficient progress for me to leave him with a clear conscience.'

'And in the meantime have you talked to the family members about the child's death? Have you observed their reactions?'

'They've been forbidden to speak of her. All traces of her have been removed from the house.'

'All the more reason to do so now,' Sid said. 'Ask them questions and you'll jolt them out of their complacency. They may say things they didn't mean to.'

'Sid, it's you who should be the detective, not I.' I laughed.

'I think I'd be rather good at it,' Sid said.

'I'm not having you risking your life, the way Molly has,' Gus said firmly. Sid patted her arm.

'So tell us.' Sid leaned toward me. 'If it's a family member, whom do you suspect?'

'I really don't know.'

'Go through them, one by one.'

'All right,' I said. 'Archie Van Horn and his wife, Irene. She's Brian's daughter. Brian doted on her. Only child. She wouldn't have pushed her own daughter over a cliff or killed her beloved father. Archie wouldn't have killed the goose that laid their golden eggs.'

'Who else can we eliminate?'

'Brian Hannan's sister Mary and his brother Patrick. She is a comfortable middle-aged woman. A simple soul. Loves her grandson. Wouldn't know about poisons. The same goes for Brian's brother the priest, Father Patrick. Rather shy and unworldly. He'd have no reason to want his brother dead.'

'See we're eliminating people left, right, and center,' Sid said. 'Who else can we strike off?'

'Joseph Hannan's daughter, Eliza,' I said. 'She's the sort of person you'd like. A do-gooder. You may even know her. Works among the poor, and in the temperance movement.'

Sid laughed. 'No, I can't say we're big proponents of the temperance movement, are we, Gus? We enjoy a good wine too much.'

'But I think we can strike off Eliza. I can't see any reason she'd want to kill her great-uncle.'

'Which brings us to the likely suspects,' Sid said. 'How many of them are there?'

'Well, I suppose Joseph Hannan, who was Brian's brother and business partner. Daniel suspected the company was involved in some shady deals and Brian had recently left the running of the company to Joseph. Perhaps Joseph didn't want Brian to know what he'd been doing.'

'But that wouldn't tie in to the little girl,' Gus pointed out.

'Maybe it doesn't tie in,' I said. 'Maybe Colleen's death was as described and the fact that Brian was found in the same spot is purely coincidental.'

'Go on with the suspects,' Sid said. 'After Joseph Hannan?'

'His son, Terrence. He's a likable young man. A lot of fun at parties. Reminds me of our friend Ryan O'Hare – witty, debonair.'

'But—' Gus said.

'But I wouldn't say trustworthy. Likes the easy life. Doesn't want to work. And I think I saw him slinking from the house around the time that Brian was murdered. At least he's tall and slim and his father is a good deal stockier.'

'He'd be a good suspect,' Gus agreed. 'Uncle was forcing him to work, maybe cutting off his funds, so he seized the moment.'

'I've got a wonderful idea,' Sid said. 'Go to see Brian's attorney, Molly. What if Brian was about to change his will – cutting out Terrence, for example. That would force the family member to take action before the new will was signed.'

'Good thought,' I said. 'I'll look into it.'

'Have we finished? Is that the entire Hannan family at last?'

'There is a great-nephew, Sam,' I said. 'Also a likely candidate. His own family situation is not the best – drunken and useless Irish father, beats up his mother. Sam was involved with a gang, so Brian Hannan took charge of him and has put him to work as messenger boy in his business. He was the one who discovered the body and Daniel says that murderers often draw people to the scene of the crime.'

'Yes, he sounds suspicious.' Gus nodded.

'It's hard to say,' I said. 'I can't believe any of them could have had anything to do with the little girl's death. And they all seem genuinely shaken about Brian Hannan. Maybe it was an outsider after all.' And I told them about the man who had appeared at the gate, wanting to know if Brian Hannan had arrived yet.

'It seemed clear that he had followed Mr Hannan from New York,' I said. 'But the police were not able to find him the next day. Maybe he went back to New York on the early train.'

'Of course Hannan was a public figure, wasn't he?' Gus said. 'Such people do expose themselves to crackpots.'

'But what about the tray of liquor and the two glasses,' I said. 'Brian Hannan was clearly going to have a drink with somebody he knew.'

Sid patted my shoulder. 'Go to New York and find out what you can, Molly. Otherwise you'll never be satisfied.'

Twenty-Eight

I felt guilty as I hurried back to Daniel. I had left him longer than I intended to. What if he'd awoken and needed me and I wasn't there? What if he'd taken a sudden turn for the worse? I glanced at that house across the street as I reached the gate. I'd have dearly loved to interview the person behind those drapes, but I had to check on my husband first. I opened the cottage door to the smell of bacon frying. An hour ago it would have been a delicious aroma. Having just had my fill of breakfast, it had lost its appeal.

'I'm back,' I called to Martha.

She looked out of the kitchen. 'Breakfast is ready when you are. I told Mr Sullivan that you'd gone out for an early morn-ing walk and that I'd have a good meal ready for you on your return. He didn't want much himself. Just a boiled egg and toast. I told him he needed to build up his strength again. He's still looking awful peaky.'

I turned and ran up the stairs. Daniel was sitting propped up in bed. He did still look rather frail. The healthy tone had gone from his skin and his eyes were still a little sunken. But he gave me a grand smile as I came into the room.

'Ah, there you are. I wondered where you'd gone.'

'Out for a little walk. It's such a lovely day and you were

sleeping like a baby, so I left you in Martha's capable hands,' I said.

'She was trying to stuff me full of food,' he complained. 'I told her I had no appetite.'

I looked at the boiled egg, only half eaten with the yolk now congealed down the side of the shell.

'You should try to eat and build up your strength, Daniel,' I said. 'And I'm going to see if we can get you downstairs and out into the good sea air later today.'

'All right.' He nodded halfheartedly and my heart lurched. The doctor had warned that there could be relapses. I had expected him to bounce back to his usual robust self. He was too passive, too lethargic.

'I'm going to ask the doctor to have another look at you today,' I said.

'What good could he do, old quack,' Daniel muttered. 'Don't worry, my love. I'll be all right in a few days. Just give it time.'

'Old quack or not, I still want him to come and see you,' I said. 'No arguing. And I'm making you another boiled egg and going to feed it to you myself.'

He didn't protest, which made me even more worried. The normal Daniel would have told me in no uncertain terms that he was not about to be bossed around by his wife. I went downstairs and made a good show of enjoying a second breakfast. Then feeling like a stuffed goose, I set out for town and the doctor's surgery. I decided it was still a little early to make a formal call across the street, so I walked briskly into town and found the doctor's residence.

The door was opened by his wife. 'I believe my husband was planning to stop by and check on your husband, Mrs Sullivan,' she said. 'But I'll leave a note on his desk to make sure that he does. So don't worry.'

I left and went to find a newsagent's shop for a copy of the *New York Times*, then a greengrocer for some grapes. As I passed the harbor I had to stop and take a look at the waterfront before I returned to Daniel. I suppose in a way it reminded me of home with its busy fishing boats, gulls crying overhead, sounds of winches, shouts of men, and the smell of fish and brine and seaweed. I stood there for a while, taking it in, trying to enjoy the scene while thoughts raced around in my troubled brain. As I walked back through the town I looked in the art gallery window and saw that Colleen's portrait was no longer there. I opened the door and went inside. The same young man came out from the backroom.

'Has the portrait been sold?' I asked.

He looked around. 'Portrait?'

'The little girl and the lamb. We looked at it a few days ago.'

'Oh, that. I believe the artist came and took it back. I don't know. Maybe he had found his own buyer.'

'And I remember you said I could find the artist down by the harbor. What was his name again?'

'Ned Turnbull,' he said. 'Not a bad painter, but he needs to adopt a more modern style, if he wants to sell. It's all Impressionism these days.'

I couldn't find a logical reason why I wanted to talk to Ned Turnbull and found out who might have bought his painting, so I turned my steps reluctantly in the direction of the cottage and Daniel. It was almost eleven o'clock when I reached the gates of Connemara. A respectable hour to pay a social call. So instead of entering those tall iron gates, I changed direction and went up to the front door of the redbrick colonial house. I knocked, having no real idea what I was going to say. It was opened by a crisply starched maid.

'Can I help you?' she asked.

She looked so prim and severe that words failed me. Luckily

at that moment a voice called out from a nearby room, 'Who is it, Maude?'

'A lady, Miss Gallinger. I haven't yet ascertained what she wants.'

'A lady? Well, don't leave her standing on the doorstep. Invite her in.'

'Please come in, ma'am. What name shall I say?'

'Mrs Daniel Sullivan. I'm staying at the house across the street.'

I was ushered into an attractive front hall, decorated with hunting pictures, a curly hat stand, and an old wooden chest.

The maid went ahead of me through the doorway on the right. 'A Mrs Sullivan, ma'am. She is staying at the house across the street.'

'Of course she is,' said the voice. 'Show her in, Maude.'

And I was invited into a charming sitting room. The furniture was very old and well polished. The sofa had comfortable cushions on it and the chairs needlepoint antimacassars. It smelled old – a mixture of beeswax, woodsmoke, and lavender water. A tiny old woman, wearing a white lace cap of a style that had long gone out of fashion, was seated in a high-backed chair near the window. Her face was smooth and pink, without a wrinkle in sight and her blue eyes were still bright.

'I've been watching you,' she said. 'I am Miss Gallinger – Catherine Swan Gallinger to be precise.'

'Mrs Daniel Sullivan,' I said, taking the bony little hand she extended to me and shaking it gently for fear it might shatter. 'Molly Murphy Sullivan.'

She beamed. 'I'm so glad you've come to visit. How kind. I rarely get visitors these days. Do sit down. Maude will bring us some coffee, or would you prefer lemonade?'

'Coffee would be lovely, thank you,' I replied as I took another high-backed chair close to her. 'And it's good of you to

231

see me. I've wondered about this house every time I've passed it. Have you lived here a long time?'

'I was born here, my dear. My father was a sea captain, as was his father before him. He was lost at sea and I remained as companion to my dear mama. She died many years ago and it's been my house ever since. I'll die here soon and am content to do so.'

I nodded, wondering how to put what I wanted to ask. Again she gave me the right opening. 'So you're staying at the haunted castle, are you?'

'Haunted?' I asked. 'Why haunted? Have you seen a ghost there?'

She had a delightful melodic laugh. 'Oh, no. It's just what we old-timers called it when we saw it being built. Why would anyone want to build a haunted castle? we asked ourselves. But then I probably shouldn't make fun of it if you are connected to that family. And it has had more than its share of tragedy, in its few short years, hasn't it?' She pulled back the lace curtain to take another look at it. 'First the granddaughter and now we understand that Mr Hannan has died tragically. I watched all those policemen coming and going. Tell me, do they suspect foul play?' She was looking at me eagerly.

'I believe they do,' I said. 'Miss Gallinger, you are—' I paused, fishing for the right words – 'you are so well positioned here to see who goes up and down this street, and I imagine you have a lot of time on your hands.'

She gave that musical laugh again. 'A polite way of saying I'm a nosy old lady. But you're quite right. Looking out of my window and catching glimpses of other people's lives is about all I can do these days. We can no longer afford a carriage so I can't go out. And I can only take a few steps. So I have to live vicariously.'

'The evening that Mr Hannan was killed,' I said. 'Did you see him arrive?'

'Oh, yes. He came in a hansom cab from the station.'

'How do you know it was from the station?'

Another laugh. 'Because I recognized the horse. That cab picks up passengers from the trains.'

'What time was this?'

'It was just dark. Around seven thirty, I'd say. I had not yet been summoned to dinner and I always dine at eight.'

'You are sure it was him?'

'Oh, yes. I see rather well for my age and I saw his face in the lantern light as he paid the cabby.'

'Was he alone?'

'Yes, quite alone. He went in through the gates but he didn't go to the house. I believe he went off toward the outbuildings.'

'You didn't see anyone else arriving either before or after him, did you?'

'I saw a young man. Skinny, not well dressed. He came not too long afterward. He tried to get in to the estate but the gates were locked. He spoke to someone through the gate but he was not admitted. So he went away again.'

'He didn't try to get in by another way?'

'Not as far as I could see. It was quite dark by then, remember, but I think I spotted him walking back into town.'

'And after that?'

'After that the dinner gong went.'

Coffee arrived along with slices of rich fruitcake. The maid poured for us.

'Miss Gallinger, did you see anyone come to the house earlier in the day who wasn't a family member?'

'Only you and a man I presume is your husband. Good-looking fellow, isn't he?'

'Yes, he is,' I said. 'But he's been ill since you saw him. He came down with pneumonia.'

'I suspected something of the kind, didn't I, Maude?' she

asked. 'When they sent for the doctor in the middle of the night I knew something was wrong.'

Clearly she didn't miss a thing. I tried to think what else to ask her. 'You heard, presumably, about the little girl who died, didn't you?'

'The one eight years ago? Oh, yes. I heard about that. Such a shame. She was a pretty little thing, and friendly too. I could walk in my garden in those days and she used to wave to me through the gate. She blew me a kiss once.'

'And her sister?'

'Always two steps behind the other child, and certainly not as friendly. There's something wrong with her, isn't there? That's why he brought her here to live and had the special quarters constructed for her?'

I stared at her in amazement. 'You knew about that?'

'Oh, yes. How could I fail to know when I watched the workmen going in and out, bringing supplies in after dark, and they weren't local men either. He brought the child in after dark too, so I realized she was supposed to be some kind of secret.'

'Do many people know about her?'

'Only myself and Maude, of course. I am not one to gossip, so I have never seen fit to mention her to visitors.' She took a sip of coffee, then looked at me, bright eyed. 'Is that why you've come to see me? You hope I might have seen something that sheds some light on two baffling deaths?' Before I could answer she went on, 'Oh, yes. I never did quite accept that the child's death was the tragic accident they claimed it was. Children are resilient you know. They don't fall easily and if they do fall they don't die easily. So unless she landed wrongly and broke her neck, I don't believe our cliffs are tall enough to kill anybody.'

'What are you suggesting?'

'It did cross my mind that she might have been dead before she was thrown over the cliff.'

I sat in stunned silence. I could hear the coffee cup rattling in my nervous hand. My brothers and I had fallen occasionally while we clambered on the cliffs at home and had seldom come away with more than scrapes and bruises. Of course a strong push from her sister would have sent Colleen plummeting down, and could have killed her, especially if she was facing away from the cliff edge and fell onto the back of her head. But what if she also had been poisoned first? Not that we'd have any way of finding out now, would we? I couldn't see the family agreeing to unearthing her remains. I sensed Miss Gallinger staring at me while all this went through my mind.

'I can see you have questioned this too,' she said. 'Are you a family member, my dear?'

'No, my husband was a business associate of Mr Hannan, that's all. No connection to the family.'

'If you don't mind my saying so, you seem extremely interested for one who has no connection to the family.'

I smiled. 'You are very astute. If you really want to know, I'm afraid the girl will be blamed for her grandfather's death. And I'm also afraid that the local police won't manage to find the true culprit.'

'And you think you will have a better chance of doing this than a policeman?' She cocked her head on one side, like a bird.

'No, of course not.' I laughed, feigning modesty.

'You may well do better than our local police,' she said. 'Prescott was only made chief because of family connections. He hasn't exactly demonstrated any great skills that I have witnessed. Good luck to you, my dear. I like a resourceful woman. I always felt I should have been able to make much of my life if I hadn't been saddled with Mama.' She pulled back the drapes

235

and peeked out of the window. 'I believe you may have visitors,' she said, and indeed Sid and Gus were walking up the street toward the front gate.

'You're right,' I said. 'These are my friends from New York.'

'Staying at the Roman Palace, no less,' she said dryly. 'My, but you move in exalted circles.'

'The Roman Palace is owned by my friend's cousin,' I said. 'She's a Walcott.'

'Well, she would be, wouldn't she?' She reached out and patted my hand. 'You'd better run along then. But I'll keep my eyes open for you, just in case there is anything else to be seen.'

'Thank you.' I smiled at her fondly. 'I have enjoyed talking with you. I'd like to come again.'

As I went to go she said, 'That family, they are great ones for secrecy, aren't they? Such a lot to hide. All those comings and goings through the little door in the ivy.'

I turned back quickly. 'Really?' I asked. 'Who, for example?'

'The brother, for example.'

'Joseph Hannan or the priest?'

'Not the priest. The one who resembles Brian Hannan. Always slipping out – or helping a young woman to slip in.' She grinned wickedly. 'And his son too. Slipping out, slipping in at the oddest hours.'

'I suspected that,' I said. 'He seems like a devious one to me.'

'He went out that evening, you know. I was going to bed, looked out and I saw him. About nine thirty or ten.'

'Interesting.'

I saw Gus and Sid opening the gate and going through. I knew I had to leave but I didn't want to abandon this treasure trove of information.

'And I'll tell you another one,' Miss Gallinger said. 'The young woman. The daughter, isn't she? Very beautiful, but also quite devious. She used to slip out a lot. In fact the day that

236

the girl died, I don't believe her mother was even there.' She paused for effect. 'I never did find out where she went. Do tell me if you ever learn, won't you? I should be most interested.'

'I will,' I said. 'But I really must go now.'

'Of course you must,' she said. Then she called after me, 'Take care, my dear. I suspect that the Hannan clan are not the nicest of people in some ways. It's never good when people acquire money and don't know what to do with it.'

Twenty-Nine

Sid and Gus were just closing the front gate behind them when there was a clatter of horse's hooves and a cab came up the street toward us at a lively clip. As I watched it came to a halt outside the gate. The cabby climbed down to assist the passenger and out climbed Daniel's mother.

'Holy Mother of God,' I muttered. That was all I needed right now. But of course I hurried across to join her like a dutiful daughter-in-law.

'Mrs Sullivan. How good of you to come,' I said.

'As if I could stay away with my boy lying at death's door,' she said. 'Why are you not at his side?'

'He is a lot better than when I sent you the telegram,' I said. 'Still not his usual self, but at least that awful fever has broken.'

Gus and Sid had come over to join us as Mrs Sullivan paid the cabby and the cab departed.

'You remember my mother-in-law, don't you?' I said. 'Mother Sullivan, you remember my two bridesmaids, Elena Goldfarb and Augusta Walcott.'

'Of course I do. I suppose you are here because your family owns one of the cottages, Miss Walcott?' Mrs Sullivan was all charm and politeness.

'We're here to support Molly,' Gus said. 'She was so worried about Daniel and we thought she needed company.'

'How very kind of you. Molly, you are lucky to have such considerate friends,' she said. 'But don't let's stand here. Take me to my boy.' I opened the gates and ushered them through. 'My my,' she said. 'What an imposing-looking place. Not that I'd want it for myself . . . drafty inside, is it?'

'Rather gloomy,' I said, 'but we are not staying there. We are in the little guest cottage on the property. It's rather cramped, as you'll see.'

I led them up the path and the thatched cottage came into view.

'Good heavens, now why would anyone build an old thing like that,' Mrs Sullivan said. 'No wonder Daniel got sick. I'm sure that thatch harbors all kinds of insects and diseases.'

'Mind how you go,' I said as I led her up the stairs, with Sid and Gus bringing up the rear.

'Look who I found on my way back from town,' I said, ushering them in to Daniel.

Daniel's eyes widened. 'Ma, what are you doing here?'

'Your wife sent me a telegram that you were at death's door. I came as soon as I could,' she said. She sat on the bed beside him and took his hand. 'How are you, my dear? You don't look well at all.'

'Certainly feeling better than I was yesterday,' Daniel said. 'It was good of you to come.'

'I'll stay and help Molly take care of you now that I'm here,' she said. 'You need building up, that's for sure. What have you been eating?'

'Very little,' I said for him. 'He doesn't want to eat.'

Mrs Sullivan patted his hand as if he were a child. 'Don't worry, his mother knows what to tempt him with. If your wife will show me to my room, I'll go straight down to the kitchen and make you your favorite things.'

'I'm really not up for waffles and that kind of stuff, Ma,' Daniel said.

'Then I'll poach an egg just the way you like it, and some stewed fruit, maybe? With a vanilla sauce?' She nodded with satisfaction when he didn't answer. 'Come on then, Molly. Where am I to sleep?'

'I'm afraid there's just one small bedroom through here,' I said. I opened the door. It did look dark and gloomy, with the window opening at the back of the house onto pine trees.

'It will have to do,' she said, the disapproval clear in her voice. 'I'm surprised they didn't invite you to come up to the castle when Daniel became ill.'

'They have their own problems at the moment,' I said. 'The owner of the castle, Alderman Hannan, was found dead two days ago.'

'God rest his soul.' She crossed herself. 'What a shock. Heart, was it?'

'No, a fall from the cliffs.'

'I thought I overheard someone in the train talking about the alderman's death, but I didn't realize it was the man who owned this estate. They were saying what a good thing it was for Tammany Hall. Apparently he was supporting one candidate to head up Tammany but the rank and file wanted another man – silent Charlie Murphy, I believe they called him. Alderman Hannan was dead set against this Murphy and everyone feared a rift. The two men opposite me said that his death was a god-send. I thought that was a funny way to put it, don't you?'

I nodded. 'Strange. But then Tammany politics have always been strange, haven't they?'

'They've done plenty for the Irish, so we can't say too much against them.' She looked up as Sid put her bag on the chair beside the bed. 'Thank you, my dear. Now show me where the kitchen is and I'll get started.'

'We have a local girl who's been cooking for us,' I said.

'Splendid. Then she can help me.' With that Mrs Sullivan marched down the stairs and into the kitchen. I pitied Martha. I went back upstairs to find Sid and Gus standing talking to Daniel.

'Don't worry, Captain Sullivan, we are not about to tire you with idle girlish chitchat,' Sid said. 'But do let us know if there's anything we can do, other than keep dear Molly company.'

'You're most kind,' Daniel said, 'and frankly there's nothing I do need at the moment. I confess to feeling as weak as a kitten.'

'Well, isn't this turning into a merry party,' I said, joining them.

'Why on earth did you have to send a telegram to my mother?' he asked with a resigned sigh.

'The doctor told me to prepare for the worst and to notify your loved ones. I thought she ought to know,' I said. 'I didn't expect her to show up here.'

'You obviously don't know my mother well enough yet.' He managed a tired smile.

'Anyway, I've seen the doctor's wife and he will include you in his daily round,' I said. 'Maybe he can make you up a suitable tonic. But in the meantime, what about some fresh air? Could we assist you downstairs, between us, or at least put you beside the open window?'

'I don't think I could tackle the stairs yet,' he said. 'But I could sit in the window if it would make you happy.'

We moved the little armchair and then helped him across to it, surrounding him with pillows and rugs. When we'd finished he had to laugh. 'Look at me, I look like a ninety-year-old.'

'I brought you a copy of the *Times* when I was in town,' I said. 'And some grapes and oranges.'

He took the newspaper. 'I might manage a grape,' he said.

'And you remember the portrait of the little girl,' I said. I wondered why I found it so hard to use her name.

'In the gallery? You didn't buy it, did you?'

'No. It had gone. The man at the gallery said that the painter had taken it back. He thought maybe he had found his own buyer. I thought it might be interesting to find who had wanted to buy the picture at this exact moment.'

Daniel wagged a finger at me. 'Molly, what are you up to? Remember I warned you about getting involved in a case that doesn't concern us. The local police are handling it and we should leave it to them, however annoyingly slow they seem to be. Now you women please leave me to enjoy my newspaper.'

As we went down the stairs Gus whispered to me, 'He's not looking well yet, is he, Molly? I hope sitting in the chair is not too much for him.'

'I am concerned about him,' I agreed. 'That's why I asked the doctor to visit again today, although I think I agree with Daniel that he's an old quack.'

'At least you'll be free to come and go as you please with his mother watching him like a hawk,' Gus whispered to me.

I shook my head. 'I rather think my job will be to give him enough rest and keep her occupied. I wonder how long she'll stay?'

'We can help too, if you want to go back to New York first thing tomorrow,' Sid said. 'Much as I dislike rising before eight, we can make the sacrifice and come here in time for you to catch the six o'clock train.'

'You're very kind, but you heard what Daniel just said. I really don't want to upset him now.'

'You want to find out the truth, don't you?' Sid asked.

'Of course I do, but Daniel is my husband, and he has been

very ill. I must think this through and see what the doctor says when he comes.'

A few minutes later a harried-looking Martha came to tell me that Daniel's mother had taken over the cooking and was there anything else I'd like her to do?

'I think it's better if we let her keep busy,' I whispered and she grinned. Then she looked up. 'Doctor's here,' she said and went to answer the front door.

'Now what are you doing out of bed?' the doctor asked when he came into the bedroom and saw Daniel in the armchair by the window.

'I thought sea air might be good for him,' I said.

'Ye gods, woman, he's had an infection of the lungs.' The doctor frowned at me. 'A cold wind could do more harm than good. And he's not strong enough to be sitting up yet. Take his other arm, Mrs Sullivan, and we'll get him back to bed where he belongs.'

The doctor's face was somber and he made *tut-tutting* noises as he listened to Daniel's chest with his stethoscope. He looked up at me. 'There is still fluid on the lungs,' he said. 'Lots of hot broth and hot tea to loosen that fluid and help him to cough it up. Good nourishing broth. Maybe an oxtail. And I'll write you up a recipe for a tonic, and see if the pharmacist has a cough mixture containing licorice and slippery elm.'

'But he's going to be all right, isn't he?' I whispered as soon as I had led him out of the room. 'He is on the mend?'

'To that I give a cautious affirmation,' he replied. 'As I told you before, I've seen enough relapses to know that one can't always predict the outcome. Plenty of rest, Mrs Sullivan. Complete quiet. No excitement like letting him read a newspaper. He can be propped up in bed to help him breathe more easily, but no getting out of bed until I say that he's ready.' He opened the front door. 'I'll be by again tomorrow.'

And then he was gone. I went back up to Daniel's room. 'That man took my newspaper,' he said grumpily. 'And I was rather enjoying sitting in the window.'

'I suppose we ought to do what he says,' I said.

'At least give me my newspaper back.'

I handed it to him with a smile. 'But if you read anything disturbing you are not to get excited.'

'Old fool,' he muttered. 'And now my mother here too. I've got to make an instant recovery, Molly, so that we can go home to our own house. When did he say I'll be well enough to travel?'

'You certainly aren't up to taking a train yet,' I said. 'An automobile would be even worse. No, I'm afraid you'll just have to do what the doctor says and rest and eat good food to get your strength back.'

He sighed. 'With my mother forcing food down my throat.'

'Don't worry,' I said. 'I'll tell her what the doctor says you are allowed. And as to that, he's said oxtail soup and calf's-foot jelly. So as soon as you're comfortable, I'd better walk back into town to buy the ingredients and to have your prescription filled.'

He gave me a tired smile. 'Nobody can say I don't have an energetic wife,' he said. 'I hate to put you through all this.'

'For better or worse, remember?' I said. 'I'm glad to have something to occupy me.'

'An excuse to leave the house, you mean.'

'That too.' We smiled into each other's eyes.

I went down to the kitchen. 'Oh, Mrs Sullivan, don't go to too much trouble,' I said. 'The doctor wants Daniel to have oxtail soup and calf's-foot jelly. I'm off to town to buy a calf's foot and an oxtail.'

'If you say so,' she said stiffly. 'It's a pity I didn't think of it. I've a jar of calf's-foot jelly at home. But that's no problem. I won't mind making another one.'

I found Sid and Gus sitting on the bench outside the front door. 'I have to go into town again,' I said. 'Do you want to join me?'

'Shouldn't one of us stay with Daniel?' Gus asked.

'His mother is there, and Martha too. And we won't be long.'

'Then a walk sounds delightful.' Gus got up and slipped her arm through mine. 'Poor Daniel. I hope he can cope with a mother and pneumonia at the same time.'

'I left him reading the paper,' I said. 'I'm sure we can walk to town and back before he finishes.'

We had a pleasant walk into town, carried out our commissions, and then I took Sid and Gus to the waterfront. The scene looked especially charming in the slanted fall light and Gus immediately wished she had brought her paint box.

'There's a young man painting over in the dock,' Sid pointed out. 'I wonder if he's any good?' I saw where she was indicating. He was not unlike Daniel – broad, healthy looking with a mop of unruly dark hair. I plucked up courage and went over to him.

'You wouldn't be Ned Turnbull, would you?' I asked.

'The one and same. What can I do for you ladies?' He gave us a charming smile. 'I've a variety of paintings of the harbor to sell. Reasonable prices.'

'I wanted to ask you about another painting,' I said. 'The little girl with the lamb that had been hanging in the gallery on Farewell Street until a few days ago. The man at the gallery said the artist had taken it back so I wondered if you'd found your own buyer for it.'

'Were you wanting to buy it yourself?' he asked.

'It was very charming,' I said noncommittally. 'Has someone just bought it?'

'No, I took it back,' he said. 'I decided to keep it after all. Sorry, if you were thinking of buying it.'

'Actually I was more interested in the child who is the subject of the painting. Colleen Van Horn, wasn't it?' I waited for him to say something. The smile had faded and he was staring at me almost belligerently now. I continued, 'I was thinking: it must have been painted just before she died. So I wondered if you were commissioned to paint that picture.'

'Not exactly. I saw a likely subject and painted it. She was a natural.'

'So you know the family personally?'

'Used to,' he said. 'How about yourself? Are you a friend of the family?'

'In a way,' I said.

'That's me too. A friend of the family, in a way. And I'm sorry, but the picture is not for sale. Now I must get back to work before I lose the light.'

He went back to his painting, ignoring us completely.

Thirty

We arrived back at the Hannan estate to find chaos. Police were guarding the gate, keeping out men in derby hats and ill-fitting jackets whom I identified instantly as newspaper reporters. Obviously the news of Brian Hannan's death had now reached New York.

They fell upon us as we approached the gate. 'Are you family members? Did you know Brian Hannan well? Is it true that they are calling his death foul play?' The questions flew from all sides, while they stood, pad and pencils ready.

'We're just visitors,' I said. 'No close connection with the family so I'm afraid we can't answer any questions.'

'Were you staying here when he died?' one asked. 'If you were, my newspaper has authorized me to pay one hundred dollars for a first-person account.'

Tempting as this was I declined politely and indicated that the policeman should open the gate for us. Of course they had not seen Sid and Gus before so I had explaining to do before they would finally let us in. It was only then that alarming suspicions arose.

'Nothing new has happened, has it?' I asked. 'No new tragedy while we've been out?'

'Not that I know of, miss,' he said. 'But my chief can

247

probably set you to rights. He's in there talking with the family now.'

The gate clanged shut behind us and we walked briskly toward the cottage. I couldn't shake the worrying thoughts and had to stop myself from breaking into a run.

'Molly, slow down,' Sid called. 'I'm sure Daniel is just fine.'

As the cottage came into view I saw someone standing at the front door. It was Chief Prescott and he was facing Daniel's mother. She was half his size but she was holding the fort admirably.

'I don't care who you are. The doctor said no visitors and no excitement and I'm going to make sure he gets his peace and quiet,' I heard her say as we went up the path. Chief Prescott turned to see us coming and I saw relief flood over his face.

'Mrs Sullivan. How good to see you. I had wanted a word with your husband but this lady doesn't seem to understand that this is a crime investigation and that I have to speak with people, even if they are sick.'

'I'm sorry, Chief Prescott,' I said, 'but my mother-in-law is quite right. The doctor did forbid any kind of excitement or stimulation. My husband is still very weak and not out of danger yet. Is there anything I can help you with? Would you care to come inside?'

'I don't believe so, Mrs Sullivan. Actually I wanted your husband's opinion on the latest developments – policeman to policeman, so to speak.'

'He may have recovered enough to speak with you tomorrow,' I said. 'Has something else occurred? I saw that the place is crawling with your men.'

'They are just to keep the newshounds at bay,' he said. 'I'm afraid word got out to New York that the alderman had been poisoned. I'm not sure who spilled the beans. My men were instructed to remain silent. It must have been one of the family.'

He was looking at me in a way that indicated he thought maybe I was the one who squealed. 'These things have a way of leaking out, don't they?' I said, eyeing him coldly. 'I can't shed any light, I'm afraid. I've hardly spoken with the family,' I said.

'I have just come from interviewing them and I have the impression that they are deliberately being unhelpful. They are very good at claiming to know nothing and providing the alibi for each other. It's like facing a brick wall.'

'So what are the latest developments?' I asked. 'Not another death?'

'Nothing like that. But we've ascertained that the prussic acid we found in the shed was used for the crime. At least we can surmise that it was because both the packet and jar were wiped clear of fingerprints. Somebody didn't have time to put on gloves and had to make sure there was no incriminating evidence. So I would have to surmise that it must have been a family member or one of their staff – because what outsider would know that there was prussic acid in a shed?'

'I agree,' I said. 'Unless he went into an outbuilding to hide until dark and noticed the jar containing the prussic acid on the shelf.'

'Rather a long shot, don't you think?' His smile was condescending. 'A man comes here with the intention of killing Brian Hannan but hasn't thought out the method until he spots the prussic acid on a shelf? I don't think I could go with that.'

'You're probably right,' I agreed. 'It is a long shot.'

'So if I could just speak with your husband for a few minutes. He'd want to be apprised of this, I know.' He was now attempting to open the front door.

He was beginning to annoy me. I suppose it was the condescending smile that did it. 'I will pass along this information to my husband as soon as he seems well enough,' I said.

He hesitated. 'I had hoped he might share a little expertise, you know. He's obviously faced murders more frequently than I have. I can only remember two other deaths since I've been police chief and one of those was a drunken fight between sailors. I'm going to have to play one family member against another to extract a confession, Mrs Sullivan. I think they must know more than they are telling me. But they are remaining stubbornly close-lipped and I can't keep them all here indefinitely. I got an earful from Joseph Hannan about how I'm wrecking his business by keeping him here.'

'If you like,' I said cautiously, 'I was thinking of going to New York myself tomorrow. I'd be happy to visit Brian Hannan's office on your behalf – not officially, I realize. But I could ask some questions and see if Brian Hannan had confided in his secretary any concerns about his family.'

'Mrs Sullivan, I couldn't possibly . . .' he blustered, completely off guard. 'I mean to say that kind of thing . . . if word got out . . .' He was grinning now. 'I'm sorry, but I can't ask a woman to do this kind of work. I'm sure it's very good of you to want to help, but your place is looking after your husband.' He touched his cap to me. 'I will return tomorrow then, and hope your husband will be well enough to speak with me. In the meantime please understand that it is not your place to interfere in a police investigation.'

I swallowed back what I wanted to say to him. He was happy to use my husband but not me. I found my gaze going up to the tower. Now I was even less inclined to spill the beans about Kathleen. The thought went through my mind that I might find myself in trouble for withholding evidence and keeping what I knew about Kathleen from the family and the police. I wondered if I was letting my impulses rule my head again for no valid reason other than my pride had been wounded. It wasn't as if I was any nearer to solving this murder than Chief Prescott.

Gus and Sid moved closer to me as he walked away.

'I don't think that man is likely to be solving anything in the near future, do you?' Sid said.

'But you heard what he told you, Molly. He warned you against going to New York and asking questions,' Gus muttered.

'When has that ever deterred Molly in the past?' Sid grinned. 'My thoughts are that if you don't get to the bottom of this, then no one will. You have to prove beyond a doubt that the girl is not responsible.'

'Easier said than done,' I said. 'I really don't know what to do. I don't like to leave Daniel and I expect he'll be furious when he finds out.'

'So you're going to sit back and watch them drag off a child to a mental institution, are you?' Sid demanded.

'You're right. Somebody needs to find out more and the only way of doing that is to speak to people who know the family. And it would also be helpful if Dr Birnbaum took a look at Kathleen. So I'll go. But what on earth can I tell Daniel so that he's not suspicious?'

'We'll think of something,' Sid said. She stared out across the lawns. 'Ah, there is one of the suspects right now, skulking through the bushes – now she's bending down. Probably burying some evidence. Go and find out, Molly. The suspense is killing me.'

I could see a dark shape among the bushes. As I got closer I was surprised to find that it was Eliza. She was on her hands and knees.

'Hello,' I said. 'What are you doing?'

She jumped at the sound of my voice. 'Goodness, you startled me, Mrs Sullivan. If you want to know, I'm burying a dead bird. It flew into the window and died. The gardeners were about to throw it on a bonfire but I thought it deserved a proper burial.' She smiled up at me. 'We always used to bury dead pets in this part of the grounds when we were children. Terrence was always killing things—' She paused when she saw my face. 'Not on purpose, you understand, but he would have mice and rats and things as pets and then he'd lose them or hug them too hard and there would be another funeral And I have to confess that the funerals were as much fun as the pets had been.'

She straightened up and brushed earth from her skirts. 'Such a disturbing time, isn't it? It suddenly made sense to revert to childhood.' She looked up at me. 'I don't suppose you've heard but they say it was the prussic acid sitting on the shelf in our shed that was used. That could only mean one of us, couldn't it? I can't bear to think about it.'

I nodded. 'It is horrible, isn't it? You don't have any suspicions yourself, do you?'

'None at all. My father and Uncle Brian didn't always get along, but poison wouldn't be my father's modus operandi. If he wanted to get rid of his brother, he'd hire a gangster to do it on a New York street. Besides, for all their disagreements I think my father realized how much he needed Uncle Brian. Brian was the levelheaded, practical one.'

'My husband says you always have to ask the question "Who benefits?"'

'And the answer to that would be nobody, I'd say – unless he's left all his money to one person, which I'm sure wasn't the case. Uncle Brian was extremely generous to all of us – especially to Irene and Archie of course. But he was trying to groom Terrence to take over the firm, he hired young Sam in the hopes of making something of him. He was even generous to my mother's charities.'

'But he ran the family like a dictator, didn't he? He expected you to live up to his standards from what I've noticed.'

'Well, yes,' she agreed.

'So if someone was not behaving in a way he thought fit, might he have threatened to cut off that person?'

'I suppose so,' she said, frowning now. 'It's hard to say because money has never meant much to me. But Terrence needs a good deal of it. So does my father. And Irene and Archie. But none of them would have poisoned him. It's too grotesque to think about.'

'And you didn't see anyone leaving the house around seven thirty the night Mr Hannan was killed?'

'We were all together, waiting for dinner. Irene went up to check on the children at one stage, I believe. Terrence went to find a bottle of wine. But that was all.' She shook her head again. 'I can't believe it. There must be another explanation. Somebody knew the poison was there. Somebody sneaked in. But not one of us.'

She bent to pat the earth down firmly.

'Tell me what happened the afternoon that Colleen died,' I said.

She almost lost her balance as she stood up, stepping away from me as if to defend herself. 'Who on earth told you about that? I thought it was a family secret. We never mention her anymore.'

'But you were there. You can recount the events.'

'Why would you want to know?'

'Because it might have some connection to your uncle's death.'

She shook her head vehemently. 'That's absurd. It's just not possible.'

'Nevertheless, humor me,' I said.

She frowned. 'Who are you, exactly? Why are you snooping into our family affairs? Why did my uncle invite you here with us? Do you know something we don't?' Her face was flushed with anger suddenly.

'Look, I just want to help, that's all. Don't you want to know who killed your uncle? My husband is a detective and he always says there are no coincidences in life. If two people were found in the same place at the bottom of a cliff, then maybe the two deaths are linked.'

Eliza shook her head. 'I shouldn't be telling you this. Uncle made us all promise . . . but Colleen was pushed over the cliff by her twin sister, in a fit of jealousy. Horrible but true. We witnessed it.'

'Did you?' I asked. 'Did you actually see one twin push the other over the cliff?'

'I didn't, but we were all sitting together at tea and other people saw it.'

'Tell me about it,' I said. 'You were all sitting on the lawn, in the same area where we had tea yesterday?'

'Not far from there.'

'So you all had a view of the cliffs?'

'I didn't,' she said. 'We were sitting in a circle. I had my back to the ocean.'

'So who exactly saw the deed being done?'

She frowned. 'I'm not sure. The first thing we heard was this awful, awful scream. We jumped up and somebody shouted, "She pushed her. She pushed Colleen."

'And we all rushed to the cliff edge. Kathleen was standing there, staring down at her sister's lifeless body. People grabbed her. "What happened? Did you do that to your sister?" someone demanded. But she just kept staring down as if she didn't hear them. And I gather she never spoke another word. Her mind must have gone, poor little thing. I like to think her mind went before she did the deed, so that she wasn't responsible for her actions, because until then she'd been a nice enough little thing.'

'Tell me about her before that.'

'I always felt a little sorry for her,' she said. 'Colleen was so pretty and so lovable and so outgoing. Just because Kathleen was shy and hung back, they thought she was stupid. But I always felt she was deep. She observed. She thought things through. And she seemed content to let Colleen have the limelight. That's why I was so surprised that she deliberately pushed her sister, because one thing seemed certain to me and that was that the twins adored each other. They were more like a unit than like two people. They even spoke in their own funny language, you know. It sounded ridiculous but it made sense to them.'

'Can you remember who saw Kathleen push her sister?'

She frowned, thinking. 'All I remember is the scream, then a man's voice saying, "She pushed her," and then tables were overturned, there was chaos, and we were all running to the cliff edge.'

'Was the whole family together at tea?'

'I believe so. We usually gathered for tea on warm afternoons. Uncle Brian, Aunt Mary, my mother, Archie. I think my father arrived later. Yes, because he asked, "Is the tea still hot?" I don't remember Terrence, and I'm not sure about Uncle Pat – but yes, he must have been there because he was first to the cliff after the scream. I believe he was the one who said, "She pushed her." Then Irene came running up from somewhere when we heard the scream.'

'And Sam?'

She paused, then shook her head. 'No, Sam was not there and when he finally joined us, I remember that he looked – well, flustered.' She turned to stare at me. 'What are you trying to prove? That one of us pushed the child off the cliff? It's absurd. She was adored. We all loved her. Her death almost broke the family apart. Irene's never been the same since. Uncle Brian suffered deep melancholy . . . in fact I believe that was what started his drinking.' She started to move away from me. 'No, Mrs Sullivan. You should leave this alone. Bringing it up to this family would only open old wounds and frankly you are barking up the wrong tree.'

Thirty-One

I set off for New York City in the gray light of dawn. I had slipped out of bed without waking Daniel and dressed in the bathroom. I had mentioned to Mrs Sullivan the night before that I was going to see if I could arrange transportation to get Daniel back to New York, as I felt he'd recover faster in his own bed. She agreed with this sentiment and promised to take good care of her son until I returned. Sid and Gus had agreed to come over to keep Daniel company if necessary, so I felt he was in good hands.

It was a pretty journey along the coast with wisps of fog clinging to marshes and inlets, flights of wild duck rising into the dawn sky and small fishing boats going out to the ocean to be swallowed into mist. On another occasion I would have enjoyed just watching the scenery go by, but I was wound tighter than a watch spring. I was taking a huge risk, going to New York with no particular destination in mind and with little hope of accomplishing anything. When I thought of the family I had to agree with Eliza. Brian Hannan was more valuable to them alive than dead. Again I toyed with the idea of the outsider. There was still that man at the gate. He had obviously come from New York and seemed to have followed Brian Hannan from there. But if he wanted to see him so badly why

not see him before he left for Newport? Was it possible he had
been sent to kill Alderman Hannan by someone who wanted
him out of the way?

I considered Tammany Hall and that overheard remark that
they were relieved Hannan was no longer around to meddle in
the election of Charlie. Had Charlie Murphy sent someone to
follow Brian Hannan and make sure he never returned to New
York? It seemed like a good possibility, but one that I could
never hope to prove. That would have to wait for Daniel. He
had the influence and the clout to get the truth out of tough
Irish political bosses. I would be brushed away like an annoying gnat.

So what did I really hope to achieve in New York? I took out
my little notepad and pencil. The alderman's house, perhaps?
Would they know of any family upsets, and more to the point,
would they tell me? I could maybe find out from Alderman
Hannan's attorney who would inherit and whether he had
recently made a new will. I could find out from his office
whether there were any recent problems in his professional or
political life. But the more I thought of it, I always came back
to the family. There had to have been a good reason that Brian
Hannan summoned his entire family to a deserted beach town
in the middle of October and just happened to invite a top New
York police detective at the same time. He had wanted Daniel
to observe something or help him figure out something that
weekend, I was sure.

'I think I might have gotten it wrong,' was all I had to go on.
No indication what 'it' was. But something to do with his family.
And it occurred to me that if he'd confided in anyone it would
have been to his secretary or attorney. I'd try both of them.

I arrived at the Grand Central Terminal at the same time
as thousands of workers and businessmen. After the quiet of
Newport the noise and smells of the city were overwhelming

and I fought my way through the crowds to the station for the elevated railway. I had decided that my first stop should be at the alderman's mansion on the Upper East Side, since that was my only destination in that direction. Also I was a little early to visit his office. So I hopped aboard the Third Avenue elevated railway and alighted at Sixty-seventh Street. The alderman's house was on Sixty-sixth, just across the street from the Astors. He had certainly moved into the realm of the Four Hundred, and judging from the magnificent facade of the white-trimmed brick mansion, he had made more money than most of them. I adjusted my hat and took a deep breath before I rapped on the front door. The maid who opened it ushered me into a small anteroom where I was joined almost immediately by the butler, Soames. I introduced myself to that very proper English gentleman and explained that I had been the alderman's guest. I had come to town and suspected that they had heard little about what was going on at the cottage.

'It is most gracious of you to pay us a call, Mrs Sullivan,' the butler said. 'As you can imagine the entire household has been in a state of shock. We could scarcely believe the news when the policeman came to the door. Is it true that the master was murdered? Have they found out who did this awful deed yet?'

'They have not. My husband, who is a New York police captain, would have been able to assist more fully in the investigation, but he is recovering from pneumonia,' I said and decided to stretch the truth a little. 'So he sent me down to the city on his behalf, in the hope that either you or the alderman's office staff could shed any light on the sad business.'

'Me?' Mr Soames looked perplexed. 'In what way does he think I should be able to help you?'

'He wondered if the alderman had received any threats recently.'

'Threats? From whom, Mrs Sullivan?'

'I don't know – someone with whom he has crossed swords in business or politics?'

'I only know what goes on in this establishment, and I think it highly unlikely that anyone would come to threaten him in his own home.' He held my gaze. 'Is that what the police think? That an adversary followed him to Newport to kill him? Why not do so here? The alderman often took a walk in the park in the mornings before work. A perfect chance to kill him if one was so inclined.'

'Had he seemed worried recently?'

'I am only his butler, not his confidant,' he replied stiffly.

'Mr Soames, I know that loyalty to your employer may prevent you from speaking your mind to me, but I'm sure you want his killer found as much as the rest of us do. If there is any small thing you can think of – anything at all in his last days that made you feel the alderman was worried, or upset?'

'He did seem – preoccupied as he prepared to leave. As if he had a lot on his mind.'

'Had he shared with you his reason for summoning the family to Newport at this time of year?'

'My dear Mrs Sullivan. I am his servant. And he was a man who kept himself very close. But he did say, "You are lucky to have grown up in an orphanage, Soames. Families are a pain in the neck."'

'So some family member had been on his mind. Any idea which one?'

Mr Soames shook his head.

'Had any of them been to call on him here recently?'

'Not that I can think – oh, but wait. Mr Archie came by on Thursday last and was annoyed to find that the master had already left for Newport. I asked whether I could take a message and he replied, rather rudely, "No you damned well can't. It's too late." And he stalked off again.'

'Was that sort of behavior unusual for him?'

'Oh, yes, Mrs Sullivan. Mr Archie is usually such a well-mannered young man. I was quite shocked, I can tell you.'

I got up to take my leave. 'Thank you, you've been most helpful and my condolences on the loss of your employer.'

He pressed his lips together, fighting back emotion, before he said, 'We in this household thank you for your efforts, Mrs Sullivan. We pray to God that you find the person responsible. Alderman Hannan will be sadly missed.'

Of course he will, I thought as I walked away. All those people have now lost their livelihood. I made my way back to the El through a carpet of fallen leaves. It was a crisp fall day and I passed well-dressed people, out for their morning constitutional. They nodded politely as we passed and I wondered if any of them were Mr Archie's parents. Why had I never considered him before? A young man with usually perfect manners, who had had to endure the tragedy of losing his beloved daughter. What possible reason could he have for murdering the one who financed his pleasant lifestyle? Unless his father-in-law had found out something about him – some guilty secret? A mistress, perhaps? And was threatening to cut off his allowance.

I filed this information in my already cluttered mind and went to see the one person I hoped could actually achieve results in this case – my old friend and alienist Dr Birnbaum. The Third Avenue El took me down to Ninth Street and I headed for familiar territory. Dr Birnbaum usually stayed at the Hotel Lafayette, just off Washington Square. I asked for him at the front desk and was told that he had not yet left his room. The clerk indicated it would be most unseemly for a young woman to wish to go up to a gentleman's room, but consented to take Dr Birnbaum a message.

He returned instantly and addressed me in a rather more courteous manner, saying that I should wait in the hotel restaurant where the good doctor would join me for a cup of coffee shortly. I was ushered through to a pretty room with checked tablecloths and bright French china. I found that the early rising had given me an appetite and worked my way through several breakfast rolls and a cup of coffee before Dr Birnbaum appeared. As always he looked dapper, immaculately groomed with his neat little blond beard and mustache. He clicked his heels and bowed in that Germanic way when he saw me.

'Miss Murphy, or should I say Mrs Sullivan, what a delightful surprise.' He took my hand, then seated himself opposite me. 'To what do I owe this early morning call?'

I told him, trying to put everything as clearly as possible. He listened, not looking at me but toying with the crumbs on the table. Only when I had finished did he look up at me.

'A most fascinating case, Mrs Sullivan. The relationship between twins has always intrigued me. And a separate language . . .'

'So you will come and see her?'

'I'm sorry,' he said, 'but I could only examine her at the request of her parents. She does have parents and a family, doesn't she?'

'But they haven't even visited her in years. They believe her to be in an insane asylum. I could take you up to her so that they'd never know.'

He shook his head this time. 'Mrs Sullivan, I am required to follow a strict code of ethics in my profession. Much as I would like to see the young girl, I reiterate that the parents would have to invite me first.'

'If she had been confined to an asylum?'

'Then I could only see her at the invitation of the director of the institution.'

I sighed. 'If you saw her, do you think there is anything you could do to help her?'

'I couldn't say that without observing for myself. From what you tell me the shock of her sister's death has put her into a catatonic state from which she chooses not to emerge. Maybe I could bring her out of it, maybe not.'

'But do you think it's likely that she really did kill her sister deliberately, when one of the relatives tells me that they adored each other?'

He smiled sadly. 'Children sometimes do things on impulse, things that they regret later. I remember that my brother killed our puppy because it bit him. He knocked it across the room because his hand was bleeding and he was angry and scared. He hadn't mean to kill it, however, and wept bitterly. Perhaps one twin said something that annoyed the other, making her react and give the other girl a shove, not realizing how close they were to the clifftops.'

'But do you think it would be possible that she actually did mean her twin to fall to her death?'

'Oh, yes,' he said. 'It would be quite feasible. You say the other girl was popular and pretty. She might have had anger building up inside for a long time. Or it might have been an impulse on the spur of the moment, lashing out the way children do. Of course, she regretted it instantly but it was too late.'

'And do you think that was the action of an insane person?'

'Oh, no, quite the opposite. I think that would have been the action of a normal child. I think we have all wanted at times to be the only child, to rid ourselves of annoying siblings. Only this one acted, with devastating consequences.'

'Then let me ask you one more thing,' I said as he sipped his coffee. 'Do you think that such a child, a child whose mentality seems to be frozen at the age of four, could also manage to poison and kill her grandfather?'

'To poison? I think that unlikely. Tell me, was the child known to be devious, sneaky?'

'Not that I heard. Shy, sullen; but not sneaky.'

'I have to say that poison requires a degree of sophistication that would probably be beyond a child such as you have described. How would she know where poison was kept? How would she know the correct amount? And you say it was potassium cyanide? My dear Mrs Sullivan. It was more likely to have killed her when she handled it. Just to inhale it or to get some inadvertently on her fingertips could be fatal.'

I felt a tremendous wave of relief. I had never believed that Kathleen had killed her grandfather, but to hear this confirmation was wonderful. I don't know why I was fighting so strongly on her behalf, but I have always been a champion of the underdog. The question now was – had she really killed her sister?

Thirty-Two

I left Dr Birnbaum and went straight to Alderman Hannan's office. It was on Broad Street, near the new Stock Exchange building. I had found that out easily enough by chatting with Mary Flannery who lived not far away on Water Street. I didn't know the number but it would be easy enough to ask for directions when I got there. Another ride on the El and I alighted at Hanover Square station. Men in tailed coats hurried up and down the steps between the marble pillars of the Stock Exchange building. I walked along Broad Street, examining the brass plates on nearby walls and found that the office was in another new building, a veritable skyscraper all of twelve stories high. And Alderman Hannan's office was on the twelfth floor. I rode the elevator with some trepidation. I don't think I'll ever get used to those things. That creaking, grinding little cage going slowly up a dark shaft inspires in me an unnatural terror and I was breathing hard when the attendant slid open the door for me and said, 'Top floor.'

The office was busy in spite of the absence of its owner. Two young men were working away at typewriting machines, making such a clatter that I had to shout when a female receptionist asked me what I wanted. I told her that I had just come from the estate in Newport. Her eyes widened. Typing ceased miraculously. 'You were there? Then you know all about it? We've only heard what we've read in the press.'

'Yes, I was there,' I said. 'I took the train down to New York this morning and wondered if I might have a word with Mr Hannan's private secretary?'

'Is it true then?' the girl asked. 'They are saying that he was poisoned. Is that really true?'

'I'm afraid it is,' I said. 'I had to come down to the city so I volunteered to help the local police with their investigations.' I neglected to add that the local police had turned down my offer. 'So if I might have a word with Mr Hannan's secretary, maybe he could shed some light on this awful business.'

'I hope you can, ma'am,' she said. 'We all worshiped Alderman Hannan. We want his killer caught and punished.' She moved closer to me. 'Do they think those Tammany boys had anything to do with it? There was an awful ruckus only last week up here in the office, with everyone shouting and Mr Hannan saying that he couldn't be bought. And the men stomped out saying that he'd be sorry. So I just wondered. I know how those Tammany thugs work sometimes.'

'Annie, you shouldn't be talking like that,' one of the typists said, turning away from his machine. 'That kind of talk could get you in trouble.'

'I don't care. It's the truth, isn't it?' She looked at him defiantly.

'So men from Tammany Hall were actually up here in this office threatening him, were they?' I said. 'Had he received any other threats recently? He was a public figure, after all.'

Before she could say any more a frosted glass door from the inner office opened and a young man stood there. Everything about him was stiff and efficient from his collar to his haughty expression.

'Miss Shaw?' he said. 'May I ask what is going on? This

person is not from the press, is she? Who let her in? Remember I told you that we speak to nobody until we are given instructions from the family.'

I crossed the room to him, holding out my hand. 'I am most certainly not from the press. I am Mrs Sullivan, wife of Captain Daniel Sullivan. I believe you may have written to us last week on behalf of the alderman to invite us to stay in Newport. I have just come down from the estate and I thought you might have been told very little about the tragedy.'

'Mrs Sullivan.' The haughty look melted from his face and he looked absurdly young and embarrassed. 'I am Donald Brady, Alderman Hannan's secretary. It was good of you to think of us. Frankly we have heard absolutely nothing except for the scant information in the newspapers,' he said. 'Would you care to step into my office?'

He held the door open for me and I went inside. The room was sparely furnished with an oak desk and filing cabinets. Clearly Alderman Hannan did not believe in spending unnecessary money. Mr Brady pulled out a straight-backed chair for me. 'Do sit down. Can I have Annie bring you anything? Coffee, water?'

'No thank you. I have just had coffee and I have a lot of business to cram into today. But I wanted to talk with you first.' I pulled my chair closer to his desk. 'I don't know if you have heard yet but it has been determined that the alderman was poisoned, with cyanide taken from his own garden shed.'

'We heard a rumor.' His face was white and shocked. 'But it's too terrible for words. Who would want to do such a thing? He was a good man, good for the city of New York. Look how many men he employed building the new subway.'

'I would like to find out who did this as much as you,' I said. 'The police chief seems to think it was a family member. They, of course, are saying nothing and all seem shocked by the death. My husband and I think the alderman must have suspected something, or he would not have invited a well-known New York police detective to be present at the same time as his family. So I wondered – did Alderman Hannan ever mention to you why he was inviting my husband up to Newport?'

He shook his head. 'Mrs Sullivan. I am merely his secretary. He dictates to me. I write the letters and he signs them. He does not discuss his business with me.'

'Pity,' I said. 'So you would have no way of knowing if anything was worrying him?'

'Something was,' he said. 'He was quite out of sorts for the past couple of weeks. I took it that his anger might have had something to do with the subway tunnel collapse. You heard about that, did you? A sad occurrence – and several men were killed. Mr Hannan was furious. He thought that maybe someone had been using substandard materials. He and his brother had an argument right here in the office. He said, "If I find out you've been cheating the company, lining your own pockets at the expense of men's lives . . ."'

'And what did his brother say?'

'He said, "You can't threaten me. You forget I'm a partner in the company. You have no right to speak to me like that." And he stormed out. But right after, Mr Hannan had me set up an appointment with his accountant.'

'I see,' I said. 'And where might I find this accountant?'

His face became immediately guarded again. 'Mrs Sullivan, this is private company business. I couldn't let outsiders be privy to what Mr Hannan did or said.'

'Mr Brady,' I said carefully. 'From what I've observed I don't believe the local police have a chance in hell of finding out who killed Alderman Hannan.' I saw him visibly flinch at the use of such strong language coming from a woman's lips. I didn't care. If he needed jolting a little to make him reveal things to me, then I'd jolt. I continued. 'I'm sure he invited my husband there for a reason. My husband is now on the spot and the local police can use his expertise. Unfortunately he has been quite sick and is still unable to travel, so I volunteered to undertake this journey for him. I realize all this is unofficial and the New York police really can't get involved, but Captain Sullivan is your best chance at seeing justice done for your employer.'

It was a good speech. I was rather proud of it myself, even if it did stretch the truth a little. I saw Donald Brady's Adam's apple going up and down above his stiff collar.

'Of course I would like justice for Alderman Hannan,' he said. 'I'd like to do anything I could to help. I'll give you the accountant's name, but I can't guarantee he will divulge any company secrets to you.'

'I understand.' I watched as he wrote an address on a piece of paper in fine fluid penmanship, and then blotted it dry.

'Would you happen to know if the alderman changed his will recently?' I asked.

He reacted to this with surprise. 'I have no idea. If he did, he did not ask me to contact his attorney.'

'If you would be good enough to add his attorney's name,' I said, pointing to the piece of paper, 'at least I could speak with him. If the police chief thinks a family member responsible there has to be a good reason.'

He was looking more and more uncomfortable and wrote grudgingly.

'One last thing,' I said. 'Would you know if the alderman has received any threats at all recently? I understand that there has been a falling out at Tammany Hall. The alderman was against the choice for the new leader.'

'He was,' Brady said. 'He thought this Murphy was prone to corruption and would want to feather his own nest. Clearly Murphy has paid off enough men to get himself elected.'

'Do you think it's possible that someone from Tammany Hall might want the alderman out of the way?'

I could see he hadn't considered this possibility. Then he shook his head. 'I think that Charlie Murphy would be elected with or without the alderman. And poisoning wouldn't be their style either.'

'Any other threats?'

'No. The alderman was well liked. Who would want to . . .' He broke off suddenly and I saw his expression change. 'There was a young man came in here a couple of weeks ago. Very angry he was, because his brother had been killed in the subway cave-in. Apparently the brother had left four small children and a widow. Alderman Hannan offered him money as compensation and the young man flung it back in his face. Then the alderman had him escorted out. The man yelled that he'd get even some way and people like Hannan Construction could not think they were above the law.'

'What did this young man look like?'

He thought for a moment. 'Ordinary looking. Skinny. Dark hair. Little mustache.'

'Did he wear a derby and a rather ill-fitting coat?'

'He did.' Mr Brady nodded.

'Then I'd wager he was the same one who showed up outside the estate in Newport right about the time the alderman arrived,' I said. 'You wouldn't happen to know his name, would you?'

'I think I would.' Mr Brady went over to a filing cabinet and extracted a file. 'We have the names of all those killed in the subway accident. Let me see . . .' He ran his finger down the page. 'Hermann. That was it. He said his name was Joshua Hermann.'

'And his address?'

'I couldn't tell you his address but the man who was killed

in the cave-in was Frederick Hermann and he lived at Thirty-eight Hester Street.'

'Thank you,' I said. 'I shall pass along this information to the authorities.'

He looked alarmed. 'Are you suggesting that Hermann followed the alderman out to Newport and then killed him?'

'I'm just examining all possibilities, rounding up as much evidence as possible for my husband,' I said. 'Tell me, did you have much to do with Mr Terrence Hannan, and with the alderman's great-nephew Sam?'

'Very little,' Brady said. 'Mr Terrence stopped by at the office occasionally, but the other young man – I believe he was employed down at company headquarters. Since Mr Hannan has been involved in politics he has left most of the day-to-day running of the company to Mr Joseph Hannan.'

'And Terrence?'

'I understood he was being groomed to take over some day,' Mr Brady said. 'Although I don't think the alderman felt he was altogether satisfactory. He was too much of a dilettante.'

While he had been speaking my attention was drawn to the door behind his desk, the door that must lead to an inner sanctum.

'Would you mind if I took a look at Alderman Hannan's office?' I said. 'I presume that is his office behind you?'

'It is, but I can't see any reason . . .' He moved so that he was guarding the doorway.

'Can you think of any reason why not?' I demanded, my patience now wearing thin. 'It's not as if the alderman is going to come back, is it? I only want to help and if he scribbled a note to himself, something that's now residing in the wastebasket . . .'

'Mrs Sullivan, I have the baskets emptied twice a day,' he said primly. 'His desk is always kept immaculate. So is his filing system. Alderman Hannan likes everything just so—' he corrected himself, 'I mean he liked everything . . .' And his voice faltered. 'I still can't believe that he's gone,' he ended quietly.

'All the more reason to find his killer,' I said. 'Would you rest quietly knowing that you could have helped but instead let his killer walk away a free man?'

'But I don't see how . . .' He was clearly upset now. 'I mean his office is quite pristine. No paper in wastebaskets . . .'

'Then you'd have no objection to my looking,' I said. I pushed past him to the door and opened it. It was, unfortunately exactly as he had described and I had no idea what I had hoped to find there. Men do not rise through Tammany Hall to the rank of alderman and leave around incriminating slips of paper that might name their killer. I stood looking at the polished mahogany desk with its matching Italian red-leather blotter, inkwell, and penholder; the file cabinets; the portrait of the alderman at his investiture; another portrait of him shaking hands with President Roosevelt. I wandered around the room, feeling Donald Brady's breath down the back of my neck. Would there be anything to be gained by searching through all those drawers of files? Surely Donald Brady did the filing and he'd know what was in them.

I noticed that a thin film of dust had already accumulated on the polished surface of the desk. Then my eye was drawn to the leather-bound blotter.

'How often do you change the blotter?' I asked, trying to make out the words that had been blotted onto it.

'As soon as it is full,' he replied. 'The alderman was never one for waste.'

I leaned over the desk and tried to make out the words. It was as I had suspected – the secretary wrote the letters and Mr Hannan merely signed them. On the maroon sheet I could discern the alderman's signature several times, but not much else. There were some scribbled figures, but I had no way of knowing what they were. And on one side of the maroon blotting paper a small list of words. I took my notepad from my purse and tried to make sense of them, as of course they were scribbled backward in the Alderman's bold hand.

Berlin
Salem
Granville
Cambridge
Brandon

I read out the words to Brady. 'Do these mean anything to you? Was the alderman maybe planning a trip to Europe? Or maybe something to do with Massachusetts? There are a Cambridge and a Salem near Boston, are there not?'

He shook his head blankly. 'I have never heard him mention any of those places to me. If indeed they are places. Isn't there a new songwriter called Berlin? Brandon and Granville sound more like names.'

I nodded. 'They do indeed.' I paused. I had heard one of these words recently, but in what context I couldn't remember. A name someone had mentioned in connection with the Newport cottages? Maybe the owner of one of the neighboring homes? I frowned then shook my head. 'But they mean nothing to you? Not a list of people the alderman had to meet, or deal with in some way?'

'I just told you, I don't recall a mention of any of these names.'

'When did you say you last changed the blotter?'

He frowned. 'Let me see. It would have been about a week before he left to go to Newport. He had a whole slew of dictation for me the day before he went, but just ordinary business letters, nothing of note.'

'So those words were important enough to jot down within the last week that he was here.'

'I suppose so,' he agreed grudgingly.

'I'll ask the family about them when I return to Newport,' I said. 'But in the meantime, I should be getting along. I've a lot to accomplish in one day before I return to Newport.'

He opened the door for me then followed me to the outer office. 'You will let us know as soon as you have any news, won't you?' he said. 'And please tell Mr Joseph Hannan that we are awaiting instructions on several matters to do with the business.'

'I will tell him,' I said. 'I presume he'll be running the business now, unless the alderman left everything to another family member in his will.'

'Even if he did, they were partners,' Brady pointed out. 'To be sure Mr Joseph was the junior but he'd still be involved in the running of the company.'

I held out my hand to Brady. 'Thank you for your help,' I said.

'I wish we could have come up with more,' he replied. 'But he was all efficiency at the office. If anything was happening in his life outside of his work, we'd never have heard about it.'

'I'll do my best,' I said, and went down the stairs, wondering where on earth to go next.

Thirty-Three

I spent a frustrating hour visiting first Alderman Hannan's accountant and then his attorney. The former told me in a cold and patronizing voice that he did not intend to discuss Hannan company business with anyone, least of all an unknown woman. For all he knew, I could be yet another member of the press, digging for scandal.

I assured him I was not only staying at the estate at the invitation of Alderman Hannan, but that my husband was a New York policeman. Didn't he want to help solve Mr Hannan's murder? I inquired. If the police came to him, naturally he would answer their questions, he replied impassively. Until then . . . and he personally escorted me to the door.

The attorney was even more frustrating. His clerk informed me that he was not in the office, in fact he had gone out of town, and he couldn't say when he would return. I came out onto Pearl Street and stood, letting the commerce of the city flow around me, wondering what else I could do. So far I had come all this way and accomplished very little. Dr Birnbaum would not visit Kathleen. If Donald Brady knew anything, he had not divulged it to me. The accountant wouldn't even speak to me. I was tempted to go to police headquarters and find out which officers had been working with Daniel on the investigation into the tunnel collapse and whether negligence had been found, but Daniel would not be happy that I was investigating without authority, and had kept salient facts from him. Besides, I couldn't expose him to ridicule by his peers, that he now had his wife do his work for him.

So reluctantly I turned in the other direction, toward Hester Street and the address of the former Mr Frederick Hermann who had died in the tunnel collapse. Hester Street was all bustle and noise as usual, a jumble of pushcarts, crying babies, grubby children dodging in and out, laundry flapping. I steered my way through the crowds and entered the stairwell of a tall, grim tenement building. The smell was the same as in all those buildings – lack of good plumbing mingled with the lingering odor of various ethnic foods – garlic, cabbage, boiled fish, fried chick peas. I wasn't sure what I was going to say to his widow when I knocked on the door of the third-floor apartment, and all thoughts went from my head when the door was opened by none other than the young man I had seen at the gate in Newport.

'Yes?' he demanded. Then he squinted, frowning at me. 'I know you, don't I?' he said. 'Weren't you the woman I spoke to at the gate? Did they send you down with more bribes to keep me quiet?'

For once words failed me. I was suddenly all too aware that I might be facing Alderman Hannan's killer and I was alone with him on a dark third-floor landing that smelled of boiled cabbage and bad drains.

'I came because you might be the one who can help us,' I said. 'You must have heard that Alderman Hannan was killed.'

'I did hear something about it,' he said. 'Fell off a cliff, didn't he? Good riddance to bad rubbish.'

What on earth do I say next? 'Then you must realize that the Newport police are looking for you as a possible witness,' I said.

'Why would they think that?'

'Because you came to the gates of the house at about the same time that Alderman Hannan arrived,' I said. 'It is estimated that he was killed soon after that. So we wondered . . .'

'If I came up there to kill him?' he demanded. He took a step toward me and I realized that a steep flight of steps was right behind me. One good shove and I'd go flying down it.

'We wondered if you saw anyone on your way to or from the house,' I said. Even to me it sounded weak. Suddenly I decided to stop beating around the bush. I was in a tenement building, for the love of Mike. If I screamed, doors would open on all sides. 'Why did you go there?' I asked. 'You must realize that it looks bad for you.'

'And who is going to identify me?' he demanded. 'Who is going to say I was there, apart from you?'

'It won't do any good to threaten me,' I said, sticking out my chin more bravely than I felt. 'I've already talked with the police about you, and Mr Hannan's secretary gave me your address. They all know I was on my way to speak with you.'

I saw the air go out of him like a deflated balloon. 'You're right,' he said. 'I've thought about that. When I heard he had died, I knew it would look bad for me. I just hoped that nobody would be able to identify me.' He sighed. 'I should never have gone up there. I've always been too impulsive.' He glanced back into the room. 'Do you want to come in? I've no doubt that there are half a dozen ears glued to their doors at this moment, listening to what we have to say.'

I hesitated. *Will you walk into my parlor,' said the spider to the fly?* And yet my instinct was to trust him. The matter was decided by a small blond head poking out of the door and saying, 'Uncle Josh. Whatcha doing?'

He wasn't likely to kill me in front of children. 'Thank you,' I said and accepted his invitation. The room was well furnished by tenement standards, and trust me, I have seen enough of the other kind. A table, chairs, even an armchair by the stove, curtains at the window, a print from a magazine on the wall. This was a well-cared-for home.

'You live here too, do you?' I asked.

'I moved in to take care of Trudi and the kids,' he said. 'This is no city for a woman alone.' He pulled out a chair for me and I sat. I was conscious of three small faces watching me from a backroom doorway.

'I'd offer you coffee, but I'm not sure where she keeps her things,' he said. 'She's out, working in one of the garment shops. Seeing as how I don't have a job at the moment, someone had to bring in money.'

'I'm sorry,' I said.

'Not nearly as sorry as I am,' he said. 'My brother and I were both working on the subway, you know. Then it caved in, my brother was killed, and I was laid off. Work stopped until the investigation was completed. No money to tide us over, just good-bye and see you later.' He pulled up another chair and leaned closer to me. 'I was planning to kill him, you know,' he said in a low whisper. 'Because it was shoddy materials that caused that cave-in. I've worked on enough construction sites. I know about these things. I took a look at that collapsed tunnel. I could tell they had skimped on the rebar and poured the walls too thin. I tried to get people to listen to me, but I was warned to back off – roughed up, in fact, by Hannan's bully-boys. I got the feeling that the Hannan brothers were not going to be held responsible for anything, because of who they were. So I followed him to Newport. I thought it would be easier to get him alone out there. Then he had a vehicle waiting and he took off and I lost him. And when I found the house, the gates were locked. I suppose that brought me back to my senses. I couldn't even find a way into the damned house.'

'What did you do then?'

'I turned around and went home. Pathetic, isn't it? I feel like such a fool.'

'And you didn't see anyone else anywhere near the house?' I asked.

'It was dark,' he snapped. 'And all I wanted to do was to get out of there and back to New York. It was foolish on my part to think I could do anything to harm people like the Hannans. But I tell you one thing. I'm glad he's dead. I hope his family is suffering the way Trudi and the little ones are. The way I am.' He looked directly at me and I saw tears in his eyes. 'We were twins you know. There's a special bond between twins. I feel as if part of myself is missing now.'

'I'm sorry,' I said. 'My husband was part of a police task force looking into the tunnel collapse. If they can prove negligence or even corruption, then I'm sure you'll get compensation.'

'It won't bring him back, will it?' he said.

'No. It won't bring him back.' I stood up. 'Mr Hermann, I'll probably have to give your name to the police and they'll come and question you, but I'll delay as long as I can. Maybe they'll have found the real culprit by then.'

'Thanks,' he said. 'Because if they throw me in jail, then who will look after these little ones?' And he pointed toward the towheads in the doorway.

So I had established one thing – we could cross Joshua Hermann off the list of suspects, and since he was the only outsider who had been observed, again it was narrowed down to family. I couldn't think of anyone else I could question, I made my way back to the station. With any luck I'd be back in Newport in time for tea.

As the train huffed and puffed its way along the coast I thought again about the family. Brian Hannan had had a falling out with his brother Joseph. Presumably Joseph was to blame for the substandard materials that caused the subway collapse that Daniel was investigating – and that was why he was so anxious to get Daniel out of the cottage. And that might also have been just one incident that led Brian Hannan to discover his brother had been cheating the company. But would that have made Joseph kill his brother? They were partners, after all. Brian couldn't just throw his brother out. So my thoughts moved on to Terrence and then to Sam and I remembered something that Eliza had said. When Colleen fell from the cliff Sam had come running up late, looking guilty. If only Daniel was well enough, I'd leave the questioning of Sam to him. Men are so much better at extracting confessions from young boys.

My thoughts then turned to Kathleen. What would happen to her now that her protector had gone? Surely the rest of the family members would want her back in the asylum. How could I ever persuade them to leave her where she was in Mrs McCreedy's care, or better still, to let someone like Dr Birnbaum see if he could help her.

It was only when I was on the train that I realized I had failed to do what I had claimed as my reason for going to New York – find a way to transport Daniel back home. That would look suspicious. So when the train came into Newport, I made first for the harbor and inquired about passenger ships that sailed to New York. I found there was a regular service up and down the coast and I could book a cabin with ease. My conscience thus cleared, I threw caution to the winds and took a cab to Connemara.

There were still a bevy of reporters milling around the gate. I had to push my way past them. Policemen were still guarding the gate, but they recognized me and let me in. I noticed more police outside the main house. Had something else happened? My heart beat a little faster as I walked up to the front door of our cottage. What if Daniel had taken a turn for the worse and

I wasn't there? I started walking faster and had almost broken into a run by the time I pushed the front door open. It was dark in the hallway and it took time for my eyes to accustom myself to the light and to see the figure standing at the bottom of the stairs. He spun to face me and I saw that it was Sam.

Thirty-Four

'What are you doing here?' I blurted out.

His eyes darted nervously. 'She said I could,' he said.

'*She?*'

'The old lady. I smelled the baking and she said I could come back when it was out of the oven.' He glanced back into the kitchen. 'When I get scared I like to eat.'

'What are you scared about?' I tried to sound casual.

'You know. All the things that have been happening. Uncle Brian and now this. I want to go back to New York but the policeman says we have to stay.'

Mrs Sullivan's head poked around the kitchen door. 'Oh, Molly, you're back. Just in time for tea. And this young man too. I can see he needs fattening up and I've just been baking all of Daniel's favorites – my soda bread and buns and Barmbrack.'

'Daniel is all right, isn't he?' I asked.

'Oh, yes. Making splendid progress now he's had a chance to eat some proper food,' she said. 'He was talking of coming downstairs and sitting outside for a while. I gather the family is taking tea on the lawn. Well, poor things, I expect they are really shaken up by the latest developments.'

'What's happened?' I asked.

She leaned closer to me. 'It turns out that the owner of the place, the one who was murdered, was keeping his insane granddaughter up in that tower, and all this time the rest of the family thought she was safely in an asylum.'

I was finding it hard to breathe. 'How did they find out?' I asked.

'The man's lawyer came to read the will and, as I understand it, there was a large sum of money left for the care of this granddaughter, provided she was looked after properly in a family home. I don't know the rest of the details but that's what Martha told me.'

'It's Kathleen,' Sam blurted out. 'You know, the one who pushed her sister over the cliff. Nobody knew where she was. Uncle Jo sent a telegram to the asylum where they thought she was and they sent a telegram back saying she had been taken away years ago.'

'So how did they find her?' I could hardly make the words come out.

'They found Mrs McCreedy,' he said. 'One of the maids found her early this morning when she was cleaning. She was lying on the floor dead. She'd fallen from a trapdoor and broken her neck. So Terrence and Uncle Jo got a ladder and they went up and do you know what they found? Kathleen had been living up there all this time and we never knew. So of course then they reckoned that she'd pushed Mrs McCreedy just like she did her sister.'

'And where is Kathleen now?' It was all I could do to remain calm and not go rushing over to her.

'She's still up there and there are policemen guarding her until they can come and take her away,' he said. He had his arms wrapped around himself, shivering as if he was cold.

'And your friends are with her,' Daniel's mother said. 'The two women who were your bridesmaids. Apparently she can only communicate in a strange language and they are experts in such things.'

I gave a huge sigh of relief. Sid and Gus were with her. I was half-amused, half-impressed that they had conned their way to Kathleen, claiming to be experts. They'd make sure nothing terrible happened to her for the time being – until I could prove that she didn't kill Mrs McCreedy. I wanted to go to them right now but my husband came first. 'I must go and see Daniel,' I said.

Mrs Sullivan grabbed my arm. 'He doesn't know anything about this and he shouldn't be told. No sense in upsetting him when he's still so weak.'

I nodded agreement.

'And young Sam here better get started on his tea,' she added. 'Tell Daniel I'll be bringing a tray up to him in a few minutes.'

Sam brightened up instantly at the word tea. He was through the door of the kitchen and had grabbed a bun before I started up the stairs. Daniel was sitting propped up by pillows and his face lit up as I came in, making me feel a flush of warmth and gratitude.

'There you are,' he said. 'I wondered where you had got to.'

'I was scouting out ways to have you transported back to New York safely,' I said. 'You're not up to traveling by train yet.'

'And what did you find?' He took my hand in his as I sat beside him.

'There is a regular steamship service. I can reserve a cabin as soon as you feel strong enough to be moved.'

'That's good.' He took a breath as if speaking was still an effort. 'I thought for one awful moment that you were running around doing your own bit of detecting. There are still Prescott's men all over the place. Do you know if they've made any progress?'

'I've only just returned,' I said. 'I have no idea what the police are doing here until I go and ask them.'

'Then find out and report back to me.' He squeezed my hand. 'I'm feeling strong enough to be nosy again.'

I turned to kiss him. 'You're as bad as I am.'

He took my face in his hands. 'Some honeymoon this has turned out to be, hasn't it?' he said. 'But don't worry. I'll try to make it up to you.'

'You already did.' I gazed at him lovingly. 'By not dying. Now I've got my whole life ahead with you. That's all I need.'

His lips came toward mine in our first proper kiss for days. The moment was spoiled by footsteps coming up the stairs and his mother appearing in the doorway. 'Here we are, son,' she said. 'Some of my soda bread. That's just what you need to build you up.'

I stood up, still holding his hand. 'I'll leave you to it then,' I said. 'I'll report back as soon as I find out anything.'

Mrs Sullivan shot me a warning glance as I went past her. I paused in the kitchen to help myself to a slice of soda bread. Sam had already decimated the plate of cakes.

'She's a good cook,' he said. 'Mrs McCreedy used to be a good cook too. She made jam tarts.' And that bleak sadness returned to his face. I remembered what I had been told.

'Sam,' I said cautiously. 'When your cousin Colleen died, you weren't on the lawn with everyone else. Your cousin Eliza said you came running up, looking guilty.'

His young face flushed bright red. 'How did you know about that?' he said.

I ignored the question. 'So what had you been doing?' I asked. 'Why weren't you with the others?'

He grimaced. 'All right, if you really want to know – I'd been in the kitchen, helping myself to cakes,' he said. 'She told me not to touch them, that they were still cooling, but I snuck in when everyone else was sitting on the lawn. Then I heard this awful scream and everyone was yelling. It was horrible. I really liked my little cousin. We used to play together. I've always felt, you know, that I might have been able to save her if I'd been around.'

'You believe that Kathleen pushed her, do you?'

He looked up, surprised. 'Of course. How else could she have fallen backward over the cliff? And Kathleen never said a word after that. That had to mean she was guilty, didn't it?'

'I don't know,' I said. 'I'd like to find out.'

'She pushed Mrs McCreedy today,' he said. 'Nobody else could have done that.'

That was true enough. I wanted to believe Kathleen innocent, but nobody else knew that she had been hiding up in the tower.

I left him to his eating and made my way across the grounds. Two policemen were standing at the door to the house. They barred my way. 'I'm sorry, ma'am, but nobody is to go in at the moment. The chief and the doctor are still up there.'

'And my friends are still with the young girl?'

'I don't know about that,' he said. 'I just know that I have orders that nobody is to go inside. You'll find the rest of the family out on the lawn, I believe.'

He folded his arms, making it quite clear that he was not going to let me past that door. So I had no choice but to go to the lawn and join the family. I wasn't sure they'd welcome an outsider at a moment like this, but they appeared almost jolly as I approached them, chatting away and passing food. Eliza looked up and spotted me.

'Mrs Sullivan, do come and join us. Have you heard the latest news?'

'I've been out all day,' I said. 'I just returned to find more newspapermen and the police won't let me in the house.'

'That's because poor Mrs McCreedy was found dead,' Eliza said. She motioned to the maid to pull up a chair for me. I sat. 'And you asked me about our cousin Kathleen. Little did we know that she's been in the house all this time. My uncle Brian had a suite of rooms made for her up in the tower and apparently Mrs McCreedy was taking care of her, until now.' She leaned closer to me. 'I can tell you it's a load off everyone's mind.'

'That your uncle has been providing for her so well?'

'No!' she said scornfully. 'That it's now obvious who killed Uncle Brian. She pushed her sister over the cliff, and then her grandfather, and now her caregiver . . .' She paused. 'Poor little thing,' she added. 'She's obviously out of her mind. Uncle Brian left a large sum of money for one of us to take care of her, but now, after this, she'll have to be locked away, won't she? She's clearly not safe.'

I looked around the group. Irene's eyes were red as if she'd been crying, but other than her I could read the relief in their faces. It wasn't one of them, it was a deranged person. Life could return to normal. I accepted a cup of tea from a maid.

'You've heard the shocking news about Brian's granddaughter Kathleen, I suppose,' Joseph Hannan said as he noticed I had joined them. 'What was he thinking to keep a dangerous lunatic here in the house, where she could have escaped and done harm to her brothers? We are just debating what should be done with her. She's obviously not responsible for her actions but the police will want her locked away.'

'I was about to suggest that there was a very pleasant nursing home in my former parish in Cambridge,' Father Patrick said.

'I didn't know you had a parish in Massachusetts, Uncle Pat,' Terrence said.

'No, not Cambridge, Mass,' Father Patrick said. 'A little town in the Hudson Valley. I was also once in Salem, New York – not a witch to be seen.' And he smiled.

I had taken a mouthful of tea but couldn't swallow it. I forced it down, burning my throat. Now I remembered. On the night when Daniel was close to death and Father Patrick had chatted pleasantly to distract me from my worry, he had mentioned his little church in Granville.

Thirty-Five

It was all I could do to sit there, my expression composed, sipping tea with them when every fiber in my being wanted to leap up and do something. I studied Father Patrick's innocent serene face. Why had Brian Hannan written a list of the parishes in which he had served just when he was summoning Daniel and his family to the estate in Newport? It might be quite innocent, of course. He might have been talking with his brother and asked, 'So how many parishes have you been in now?' and jotted down the list as Patrick dictated them. One does that to remember. But it was the only clue I had from Brian Hannan's office.

I found my gaze going up to the tower. Could Kathleen really have pushed Mrs McCreedy through an open trapdoor to her death? I had to conclude that it was possible. What if Mrs McCreedy had taken away her favorite doll, or stopped her from doing something she wanted to, and the trapdoor was open? I had no idea why that would be, when there was obviously a proper staircase that led to the tower from the lower levels of the house. I stared at the ivy, wondering if I dared risk climbing up that way again, and if I made it undetected to the window, would I find the door guarded by a policeman?

I decided I couldn't risk it and compromise my husband's integrity. Prescott might jump to the conclusion that Daniel had sent me up there to snoop. Even as these thoughts passed through my head, I saw the front door open and Chief Prescott himself emerged from the house. He headed straight for us. 'I'm afraid the girl is completely unresponsive,' he said. 'She's lying curled up under her bed and refuses to come out. I have left one of my men and the two young women who have experience with the language of twins with her, but I'm not sure . . .'

I rose to my feet. 'Chief Prescott,' I said. 'I happen to know a doctor in New York who is a specialist in diseases of the mind. He studied with Professor Freud in Vienna and might find a way to communicate with the girl. If you and the family agreed, I could send a telegram to New York, asking him to take a look at her.'

'That's very kind of you, Mrs Sullivan,' he said. 'Unfortunately I think there is little anyone can do. In the eyes of the law she is a menace to society and will have to be locked away. We'll try to make it as humane as possible, but as for reaching into that troubled brain . . . I just don't think it is possible.'

'It would be kinder not to,' Eliza said. 'One would not wish to bring her back to face the reality of what she had done.'

Chief Prescott came over to me. 'I wondered if your husband might be feeling well enough for a visit today? Although I fear that the case may have solved itself in the meantime.'

'Yes, I think he might wish to hear everything that has transpired since his sickness,' I said.

'Then if you'd be good enough to accompany me,' he said. 'I don't want any unpleasantness with his mother, who seems to be guarding the door like a watchdog.'

'Of course,' I said. 'Please excuse me.' I nodded to the company and left.

When we were out of hearing I asked the chief, 'Do you know if my friends have made any progress in being able to interpret her language?'

'I don't believe she has spoken a word since the body was found,' he said. 'She is curled up like a wounded animal, poor little thing. One can't help feeling sorry for her, even if she does possess this monstrous side to her.' He leaned confidentially closer to me. 'I've only just been told that she killed her sister. One has to wonder if she also found a way to kill her grandfather. Sometimes these diseased minds can be fearfully cunning and clever when they want to be.'

'I presume you found no evidence that anyone else had been near that trapdoor and could have pushed the housekeeper?'

'Nobody else knew of its existence,' he said scornfully. 'The family members were all shocked to find out that the child was in the house.'

'But it might not hurt to dust for fingerprints,' I suggested. 'If anyone was up there . . .'

'Remember that the murderer of Brian Hannan left no obvious prints,' he said. 'If anyone else was up there, he'd have been careful.'

'He or she,' I corrected. 'We can't rule out that a woman was involved.'

'Since it appears that a frail twelve-year-old girl has managed to push a hefty woman to her death, I suppose we can't rule out a woman as a murderer,' he agreed, 'although I'm afraid this latest death is all too horribly simple. I suspect that the housekeeper was about to tell the world about her secret charge and the girl tried to stop her the only way she knew how. If only those two women experts can interpret her speech, maybe we'll find out what was going through her troubled brain.'

We reached the cottage door. I led the way and again bumped into Sam in the hallway.

'Hello, my boy, what have you been up to?' Chief Prescott asked.

Again the look of panic on Sam's face. 'Just eating some cake, sir,' Sam mumbled. 'I'm on my way back.'

He pushed past us and almost ran down the path.

'That boy has something to hide,' Chief Prescott said. 'Maybe I'll take him aside and put the fear of the law into him.'

Daniel's mother came out of the kitchen. 'Don't tell me you're back again,' she began to say to the police chief, then saw me. 'Oh, Molly, it's you. This man keeps trying to see Daniel.'

'I think Daniel is now well enough for a visit,' I said, 'and I'm sure he'll want to be brought up to date with everything that has happened.'

'If you think so.' She gave me a look of resigned disgust. 'You are his wife, after all.'

'Yes, I am. This way, please,' I said brightly and escorted the police chief up the stairs. As I had surmised, Daniel was pleased to see him. I decided that the police chief would speak more freely if they were alone.

'Don't tire him out, Chief Prescott,' I said. 'I'll leave you two to talk.'

And I bowed out of the room. *New York*, I thought. I needed to go back to New York to find out about that list of place-names. But I could hardly leave Daniel again. Who could I send in my place? I wondered if any of the Hannan family clan could be considered an ally, then I remembered Eliza's relieved face when she said, 'It wasn't one of us.' No. They'd want Kathleen to be guilty and this nightmare to be behind them.

I went into the drawing room and took paper from the desk, then I wrote a note to Sid and Gus. *I need to speak with one of you on an urgent matter. Could one of you be spared for a while?*

I blotted it and took it to the policeman at the front door. He agreed to deliver it and a few minutes later Sid appeared.

'Molly, you're back. I suppose you've heard the news. What

a sad, sad business. She seems such a sweet, gentle, pathetic little thing. And she's inconsolable about the housekeeper.'

'I tried to persuade them to invite Dr Birnbaum to examine her,' I said.

'What an excellent idea.'

'But they rejected it,' I finished. 'I think everyone wants to believe her guilty.'

'And you still don't?'

'I really don't want to. I know all the evidence points to her, but something else came up when I was in New York. A list of place-names on Brian Hannan's desk – and they seem to be places where Father Patrick Hannan has been a priest. I'd really like to go back to the city and check them out, but I shouldn't leave Daniel again.'

'So you'd like one of us to do it.' Sid had a great way of reading my mind. 'I'd be happy to. To tell you the truth, I'm finding being with that child most disturbing. Gus is so much better at this sort of thing and, if anyone can get through to her, Gus will. So tell me what you'd like me to do?'

'I'm not quite sure,' I said. 'I have a list of five place-names and I suspect they are all in the Hudson Valley. Could you check the archives of the *New York Times* and the *Herald* and see if these names turn up in any context in the last year or so?'

'I can do that,' Sid said. 'What sort of context are you looking for?'

'I really don't know,' I said. 'But Brian Hannan wrote that list for a reason just before he came here.'

Sid nodded. 'So any mention of these five places during the past few years? I've a good day's work ahead of me then. And if I find anything I'll telephone the house here.'

'Wonderful,' I said.

'I'll go and tell Gus,' Sid said. 'I'm sure she'll understand.'

'And if she wants me to keep her company with Kathleen, I'd be happy to do so if the police will let me,' I said.

A flight of seagulls wheeled overhead crying. We looked up at the tower.

'You know what Gus and I thought before this happened,' Sid said speculatively. 'We wondered if the child's death all those years ago was an accident and somehow Brian Hannan blamed himself for it. How about this – the girls were in his care and he wasn't paying attention and allowed the tragedy to happen. Perhaps it was a simple accident but in a moment of weakness he allowed the blame to fall on Kathleen. He's lived with that guilt ever since and summoned everyone here to make a full confession and set things right.'

'That's a lot to swallow,' I said.

'No, I think it's quite logical,' Sid said. 'And somebody killed him because they found out the truth and now knew he was really to blame. And then we thought what if they all decided to punish him for his negligence, so they lured him here. Do we actually know that he invited them and not the other way around?'

'No, I don't think we do,' I said. 'The excuse was a yacht race that Archie Van Horn was competing in, but I don't think we ever knew who invited whom.' As I said it I remembered Archie's bad behavior when he had called upon the alderman and made a note that it was his yacht race that had lured them all here. Maybe there was something to what Sid was postulating.

'There you are then,' Sid said. 'The death of Brian Hannan was a joint affair, a family plot. They'll keep it a closed family secret.'

'Do you still believe that, now that Mrs McCreedy has been killed and all evidence points to Kathleen?'

'I'm not sure,' Sid said. 'I can't help feeling that an important point is missing. I can believe that Kathleen killed Mrs

McCreedy. I could believe that Kathleen pushed her grand-father off a cliff. But what twelve-year-old child of simple intelligence, who has been locked away all her life, would know how to put poison in his whiskey glass? That is the crime of a sophisticated person and one who knew Hannan's habits.'

'That's what I've been saying all along,' I agreed.

'So what do you think this list of place-names might have to do with anything?' Sid asked.

'I'm not sure. Maybe it's nothing of importance, but they were there on his blotter and must have been written in the last days before he came here. They were the only words, apart from his signature, that I could make out. So they had to have some importance.'

'I'll head back to New York then, and see what I can dig up,' Sid said with her usual confidence. 'Then maybe we'll be wiser. What do you suspect these place-names will tell you?'

'I've no idea,' I said. 'We may be chasing straws, but Kathleen has nobody else on her side but us. We owe it to her to find the truth if we can.'

'Yes we do,' Sid agreed. She hugged me. 'I'll be off then. I'll telephone you as soon as I find something.'

Then she went back into the house, leaving me alone with the sound of the surf and the cry of the gulls.

Thirty-Six

Daniel seemed quite animated after Chief Prescott's visit.

'It seems I've been missing out on a lot,' he said. 'And I owe you an apology, Molly.'

'You do?'

'I didn't believe that you'd seen a face at the turret window and it turns out that the girl was up there all the time.' He shook his head. 'What a foolhardy thing to do – to keep an unstable child in such close proximity to her family all this time. Brian Hannan always appeared to me as such a sensible man, but he paid for this mistake with his life.'

I almost said, 'If the girl did it,' but I swallowed back the words. No sense in sharing my doubts with Daniel at the moment. It would only mean I'd have to confess to doing my share of investigating and I didn't want to upset him.

'I wonder if I'll feel strong enough to get up and take a look at that tower for myself tomorrow,' he said. 'I'd be most interested to see the child and the trapdoor.'

'You're not to get up until the doctor says you can,' I reminded him.

'That old quack? What does he know about anything? I'll get up when I feel like it, in fact I'm going to try walking a little now. Give me your hand, Molly.'

'Are you sure?' I held out my hand tentatively.

Daniel swung his legs over the side of the bed, then pulled himself to his feet. 'There, you see?' he said. He took a few steps across the room. 'I'm doing splendidly. Back to normal in no time.' Then he swayed. '*Whoops.* Feeling a little dizzy. Room swinging around.' As I went to steady him, he went limp and collapsed to the floor.

'Daniel!' I shrieked and dropped beside him. My scream brought Mrs Sullivan running.

'Oh, dear sweet Jesus, you've killed him!' she exclaimed, pushing me out of the way to reach him.

I felt a pulse. 'No, he just fainted,' I said. 'Help me get him back to bed.'

Together we lugged him with some difficulty. As we were finishing the operation he opened his eyes.

'What's going on?' he murmured.

'You fainted,' I said. 'Now I hope you realize that you're not well enough to get up yet. You scared the living daylights out of your mother and me.'

'That's interesting,' he said. 'I don't remember fainting before.'

'And I don't want you to do so again.' I tucked bedclothes around him angrily. 'You nearly died, Daniel. You have to take things slowly. First you sit in a chair for a while, then you try walking.'

'But if I don't hurry up, I'll have no chance to be a part of this investigation.' He sounded like a petulant child.

'Dang the investigation,' Mrs Sullivan said. 'You're just like your father. He could never stop acting the detective, and look where it got him. Dead before he was sixty.'

'You can't blame me for feeling frustrated,' he said. 'I'm not used to lying still and being waited on while the local police need my help.'

'I'll keep an eye on things for you,' I said.

This brought a chuckle, and a warning look. 'I bet you'd love an excuse to get involved, but you're not going to. You stay well out of it, do you hear? Old Hannan knew there was something wrong, didn't he? And look what happened to him.'

I thought it wiser not to mention that Sid was on her way to New York, investigating on my behalf, and certainly not that I'd been up in that tower and seen the child for myself.

'I'll see to your dinner, son,' Mrs Sullivan said, patting his cheek. 'How about my chicken and dumplings? You need to get your strength back.'

'And I should go and see how my friend Gus is doing,' I said. 'Sid had to go back to New York in a hurry, so Gus may want to come and eat dinner with us.'

I put on my cloak and went out. The night wind had turned cold, reminding me that this was indeed October. I needed to walk and to think. If Sid's research tomorrow turned up nothing, then what did I do next? I couldn't confess to Daniel that I had unearthed shady business practices at Hannan Construction, that I had found the identity of the man at the gate, or even the Tammany threats. Even if he were well enough to listen, I rather felt that they were meaningless. Maybe Sid and Gus's theory about the family luring Brian Hannan to his death was not so outlandish after all. I wondered if that lawyer was already on his way back to New York. I would have dearly loved to know if Brian Hannan had been about to make any changes to his will.

I paused, listening to the sound of the wind in the pine trees and the underlying thump of the waves below. Why did one or more of them want him dead? Need him dead so badly that they were willing to take a terrible risk? And how could it tie in with Colleen's death? It seemed to be now that there had to be some connection. The moment that Kathleen's presence was revealed, someone had found it necessary to kill Mrs McCreedy. Either that, or Kathleen really had killed her caregiver for betraying her presence.

I had to see Kathleen again, and I had a good excuse. I went to the policeman at the front door.

'I take it that Miss Walcott is still up with the girl in the tower?' I said. 'Has anybody taken dinner up to them yet?'

'I wouldn't know about that, ma'am,' the young constable said.

'I'd be happy to take them some food, if you'd allow me into the kitchen.'

He looked at me, weighing whether my motives were pure, no doubt.

'I am a guest here,' I reminded him. 'Alderman Hannan invited me. I should be able to go in and out of the house as I choose.'

'That was before two murders,' he said. 'Chief Prescott says nobody comes in and out and we've got to keep an eye on the family at all times. We even have a constable keeping an eye on their bedrooms at night.'

'Then I'd be saving you extra work if I took food up to my friend and the little girl, wouldn't I?' I said.

'Why are you so keen to get up there? Morbid curiosity to see a child murderer, is it?'

'Certainly not.'

'You wouldn't be the first,' he said. 'You should see the way the people mill around when we've a murderer in the jail. Just to catch a glimpse of him.'

'I assure you it's not morbid curiosity. It's purely concern for my friend up with the child, that she is not forgotten at mealtimes. She's been up there alone long enough.'

'One of our men is with her,' he said. 'But I do see your

point. Very well, then. You can take them up food, but I'm having you escorted straight down again.'

He called another constable to guard the door for him, then led me back to the kitchen, where the chef gave me two plates of food, a glass of milk for the child, and one of water for Gus. The constable gallantly offered to carry it for me and told me to follow him. Then to my surprise he opened the door across from the kitchen. It was the same door where I had so startled Mrs McCreedy and I realized now that she had just come down from Kathleen's room. Down a long dark passage we went, then up a long, equally dark stair.

'I don't know how the old woman managed going up and down this all day long,' he grunted to me. 'The least that that Hannan guy could have done was to put in an elevator. All the newer houses have one now, you know. All the rage, it is.'

He stopped talking as the stairs went on. Finally we reach the window through which I had climbed, then up the last flight to the door to Kathleen's rooms. It was firmly shut and my constable tapped on it before it was opened by yet another policeman.

'This lady has brought up their supper,' he said. 'All right for her to bring it in? The girl's not likely to be dangerous, is she?'

'See for yourself.' The constable opened wide the door to reveal Gus sitting on the floor with Kathleen lying with her head on Gus's lap. She was sucking her thumb and had her arm around the big rag doll she called Colleen. Gus looked up, smiled, and put her finger to her lips.

'She's almost asleep, I believe,' she said gently.

'I've brought you some supper. I thought they might forget you,' I said, as the constable put the tray on the table.

'Thank you. Most kind of you,' Gus said. 'I must admit it seems as if I've been up here a fearfully long time.'

'Has nobody else been to see Kathleen?'

'That pompous policeman. Of course he got nowhere. He terrified her and she went to hide under her bed.'

'But her family hasn't come to see her yet? Not her parents?'

Gus shook her head. 'Perhaps the police have forbidden them to,' she suggested, as usual looking for the kindest explanation and dismissing the more logical one that they wanted nothing to do with her.

'Are you planning to stay with her all night?' I asked.

'I thought I might,' she said. 'As you can see, she has really taken to me. Poor little soul, she was terrified. And do you know what? I don't believe anybody has touched her or hugged her all the time she has been here. Or sung to her. You should have seen her face when I sang a lullaby. She looked as if an angel had just stepped out of Heaven.'

'You have a way with children,' I said.

'I seem to.' She smiled again and stroked Kathleen's hair.

As I talked I pulled over a low table and put the two plates on it, so that Gus could eat without changing her position or disturbing the girl.

'Not particularly exciting fare,' Gus commented, prodding experimentally with her fork. 'Or am I getting what the servants eat?'

'I got the impression that the chef is sulking or in mourning. Perhaps he fears he's going to lose his job.'

'Then he should be working harder to impress.' Gus prodded at the meat. 'This joint was cooked yesterday, I'll wager. And reheated.'

Nonetheless she began to eat. The smell of food reached Kathleen. She sat up, started in fear when she saw me, and grabbed at Gus.

'This nice lady won't hurt you,' Gus said. 'See. She's brought you food and a glass of milk. Do you see? Labby.'

Kathleen scrambled to her feet, took the glass, and drank greedily.

'What does "labby" mean?' I asked.

'Her word for milk, I believe.'

'So you're making progress with her speech?'

'A little.' She put down her fork. 'She hasn't said much – in shock, the poor little thing. But I have observed her interacting with her doll and a speech pattern is beginning to develop. Quite interesting. Not like our grammar at all. I plan to make notes and give a dissertation to the science club at Vassar.'

Kathleen had now fallen upon her food like a savage. Clearly manners had not been taught. I got the impression that Mrs McCreedy had been caretaker but had believed what her employer had told her – that Kathleen was a dangerous imbecile and thus not worth educating.

'Eat nicely, Kathleen,' Gus said and demonstrated putting the fork daintily into her mouth. Kathleen complied.

'I don't believe she is mentally impaired at all,' Gus said.

Suddenly there were screams outside. Kathleen leaped up and rushed to the window and looked down. 'Mima!' she whimpered. 'No boo Mima.'

'I think that's what she called Mrs McCreedy,' Gus said. 'Mima.'

We looked out but couldn't see where the scream had come from. Kathleen was shaking now. She scurried back to Gus and buried her head in Gus's skirt.

'It's all right,' Gus said calmly. 'You're quite safe. I won't leave you.'

The policeman had come over to us. 'You should leave now,' he said. 'You don't have permission to be here.'

'I'll be back in the morning then,' I said.

'We'll be just fine,' Gus said as she stroked Kathleen's hair. 'I'm going to stay with you, Kathleen, and we'll be quite safe.'

301

I left them curled together. I was escorted back down the long stair, through the dark passage, and out to the front door. As I came out into the dying evening light two white shapes ran past me, followed by a third. One of them screamed again and I prepared to leap into action until I saw that it was the two boys, playing some kind of tag. And chasing them was Eliza.

Thirty-Seven

The wind rose again that night, howling though the trees and around the cottage. I snuggled close to Daniel and felt safer wrapped in his arms. But even in the safety of my own bed I couldn't shut off the thoughts. Kathleen had looked out of the window and seen something that had made her think of Mrs McCreedy. Had she seen Eliza chasing the two boys? Had the sight of Eliza alarmed her? Surely not Eliza, who seemed so pleasant, so normal, so kind? I didn't know what to believe anymore.

By morning the storm had blown through and we woke to mist. I could just make out the ominous-looking shape of Connemara, looming like a giant castle of nightmare, which I suppose it was. Mrs Sullivan was already bustling around, making Daniel's breakfast and bossing Martha who had just arrived. Suddenly I couldn't wait to get away from all this.

'I'm going into town to book us passage on one of those steamers,' I said to Daniel. 'It's no good for either of us to linger here. We need to be back in our own home.'

'You're not happy at the way my mother is taking over.' Daniel smiled. 'I can understand that. But she does mean well, you know.'

'She wants to look after her precious darling boy and doesn't believe his wife is capable of doing it.'

His smile broadened. 'Wait until the babies come and you'll be glad for her assistance,' he said. 'But I have to confess that I've had enough of being waited on like an invalid. And between ourselves I've never been a big admirer of soda bread.'

I dressed, had breakfast, and went to the castle but this time I was not admitted. I was told that breakfast had been taken up to the young prisoner and her attendant and that nobody else would be allowed up there until Chief Prescott arrived. So I walked into town and booked a cabin on a ship sailing in two days. I thought Daniel might be strong enough by then, if a cab took us to the dockside. I hated to leave Connemara and Kathleen with nothing solved, but at this moment it appeared that Gus had a better chance of reaching the child than I did. If Sid's investigation in New York turned up nothing, then I could see no way to prove Kathleen's innocence or to find Brian Hannan's killer. Ned Turnbull was painting on the dockside as I passed. I hesitated, wondering if there was anything he could tell me about Kathleen, anything that he had noticed when he presumably spent a considerable time with the twins, painting Colleen's picture. But as I turned in his direction he gathered up his brushes, lifted his easel, and moved off. I returned and waited impatiently for a telephone call. Morning turned to afternoon and still she didn't call.

The morning mist had melted away to a fine day. The boys were out on the lawn, trying to fly an improvised kite. Other family members strolled. It all looked so peaceful and so normal like any other family on holiday. It was hard to believe that this was a house of tragedies and that a young girl was locked away upstairs, perhaps on her way to an institution for the insane, perhaps even to jail. Then I spotted one of the young police-men coming toward the cottage. I went out to meet him and he beckoned to me. 'You're wanted on the telephone, ma'am.'

He escorted me to the house and then down the hallway to

the library where the telephone was to be found. I picked it up and put the receiver to my ear. 'Hello,' I began hesitantly.

'Molly, is that you?' came the voice through the crackles of distance and several exchanges.

'Yes, it is I. Is that you, Sid?'

'It is. Listen, I've been through the archives of the *Times* and I've found something that may be of interest. Just over a year ago a young girl was found dead in a field in what were described as suspicious circumstances in Cambridge, New York, and a month ago a little girl was found drowned in a pond near Granville. A long way from her home. Too far for her to have walked alone. Coincidence maybe, but both girls were of similar age and appearance—'

'They were both fair-haired?' I asked.

'Yes, and around six years old.'

I could hardly breathe.

'Is this important? Does it mean anything to you?'

'I believe it does,' I said. 'Thank you.'

'I could go back further in time to see if the other names appear in the newspapers,' Sid said.

'No, I think this is enough to go on.'

'Then I'll come back to you. I don't like to leave Gus holding the fort without me. Is she all right?'

'Doing very well, I believe. Kathleen has really taken to her and it seems Gus is really beginning to unlock her speech.'

'That's Gus for you. Who could not warm to her?' A pause for a louder crackle. 'On my way then. Tell Gus to be careful, won't you? And you take care too. If someone has killed several people he will be desperate.'

The line went dead before I could say, 'He or she.'

I hung the mouthpiece back on its hook and turned to see someone standing behind me. It was Terrence and he was leaning casually against the doorjamb.

'Telephone call from home, Mrs Sullivan?'

'Uh – yes, from my neighbor,' I replied, wondering how much of the information I had actually repeated was overheard. Not much, I thought, except that Gus was having success with Kathleen.

'Allow me to escort you back to your cottage,' Terrence said. 'One can't be too careful at the moment, can one?'

'Oh, I'm sure I can find my way without help,' I replied. 'After all there are plenty of policemen around.'

'You never know,' he said. 'We were all here when my uncle was murdered and yet we knew nothing.' He held out his arm to me. 'Besides,' he repeated, 'I enjoy escorting attractive women.'

I had no choice. I told myself that it was daylight, there were policemen within reach if I screamed, and I had been known to deliver a good kick where it hurt before now. We walked down the hall and the policeman opened the front door for us. We stepped out into sunshine.

'Lovely day again,' Terrence said. 'Strange to be having all this fine weather when none of us feels like enjoying it. Amazing about little Kathleen, don't you think? All this time and we never found out.'

I sensed that he was rattling on nervously. Then he lowered his voice and said, 'You mentioned that you saw me leaving the house the night my uncle died. I'd rather you forgot about that, if you don't mind.'

'Why?' I faced him defiantly.

'Because I was meeting someone I'd rather the family didn't know about.' He released my arm and turned to face me. 'Look, I have a small problem with a drug habit. Not something I'm proud of, but one sort of slips into it. And once one is hooked . . . well. I owe a fellow quite a lot of money. And he's been sending some nasty types to make sure I pay up. Uncle

Brian was keeping me short of cash, so that I learned the value of money, he said. But it's dashed embarrassing, and now all this has happened, I rather suspect that it will all come out into the open and I'll be in deep trouble with my father. So any little you can do to help . . .' And he gave me that engaging smile.

I resisted his charm. Why was he telling me this now? Was it that he didn't want me to suspect him of a more serious crime? He'd almost certainly benefit from Brian Hannan's death, wouldn't he? And as for Colleen and those dead girls in upstate New York . . . what could be easier than paying a visit to his priestly uncle from time to time in various charming spots along the Hudson Valley?

I was relieved when I saw the thatched roof of the cottage through the bushes.

'And you've been presumably helping yourself to money from the business to pay for your habit?'

'Maybe from time to time,' he said with an easy shrug.

'And ordered substandard materials?'

'Good God, no. I'd never do a thing like that.' He looked at me sharply. 'That's what caused the collapse, was it? Substandard materials?' He sighed. 'If you want to know, that sounds more like my father. He keeps a rather expensive mistress. He thinks Mama doesn't know, but of course she does. Everyone does. Such a farce.'

And he laughed.

'Thank you for escorting me home,' I said. 'As you can see, we've arrived safely.'

He nodded. 'By the way, Mrs Sullivan, I just wanted to ask,' he said in a low voice. 'Your husband – is he getting better?'

'He is, thank you.' I smiled. 'Why, were you wanting to court the merry widow?'

'Nothing like that, although you are the most attractive woman I've met in a while. But I wondered about this sudden pneumonia. If someone could poison Uncle Brian, is it possible that the same person wanted to make sure your husband, the famous detective, was not available to help with the investigation?'

'An interesting thought,' I said. 'But in this case we both got drenched in a storm and he caught a chill that went to his chest.'

'I'm glad to hear that. I've been worrying for both of you,' he said.

Then he bowed and turned on his heel. I watched him walk away. A nice lad, I thought, and a brainy one too. If only he'd put his talents to good use he'd be a great asset to the Hannan company.

I entered the dark hallway of the cottage, and stood alone, trying to process all I had learned in the past moments. Two little girls dead in two New York towns. Someone in this family who killed little girls. But how would I ever find out who? I wasn't like the police. I couldn't drag them one by one into a dark cell and threaten them with being locked in the Tombs or with being roughed up until they confessed. If only Gus could reach Kathleen and rekindle her memory about what happened to her sister. But she had shut that horror firmly away to the extent that she no longer believed she had a sister. Colleen was a big floppy rag doll with yellow hair.

Then a thought came to me. That portrait of the adorable child just before she died. I went upstairs to find Daniel's mother sitting at his bedside, while he was pretending to be asleep, I suspected. 'I have to go into town on an errand,' I said. 'Is there anything you want me to buy for you?'

'Thank you, dear, but we have all we need, I believe,' she said. 'You just run along. I'm taking good care of my son.'

At any other time that would have riled me no end. Today I was glad of it. As I came out of the house I spotted Miss

Gallinger at her window. She waved and beckoned me. I really didn't want to stop, but I could hardly refuse her. So I went in, telling her that I could only stay for a few minutes. Of course she had seen all the police activity and wanted to know what was happening. I filled her in on the details of Kathleen, refused tea, and said I had an urgent errand in town.

'So silly, these policemen,' she said as I walked to the door. 'They never get it right, do they? If they allowed more women to be detectives, they would know instinctively who was guilty and who was innocent and the world would be a better place.'

I wondered about this as I walked into town. Did women make better detectives? Did I instinctively know who was guilty and who was innocent? I had always felt that Kathleen had no part in her sister's death, but as to the guilty – I could not tell which one of them had put cyanide in Alderman Hannan's glass, or who had pushed Mrs McCreedy from that trapdoor. But it did occur to me that whoever did it would now try his hardest to get at Kathleen, just in case she could incriminate him. I sensed the urgency and quickened my pace.

Ned Turnbull was painting away on the quayside, with some admiring tourists behind him. He stopped, produced a painting from his canvas holder, and held it up for them. They nodded, then haggled and money was produced. The tourists went away and Ned stuffed the money into his pocket. I seized the moment to pounce.

'Mr Turnbull, about that painting of Colleen Van Horn.'

'I told you. It's not for sale,' he snapped.

'I don't want to buy it. I want to borrow it for about an hour. Is that possible?'

'Why?'

'I want to save her sister's life. You do still have the picture, don't you?'

309

'Oh, yes, I have it. How do I know I'll get it back if I lend it to you?'

'You could come with me, if you like and bring the picture yourself.'

'Oh, no,' he said. 'I'm not going near that place and seeing them. Don't ask me to do that.'

'What do you have against them?' I asked.

'Nothing. It's not their fault.'

'What's not their fault?' I was confused. I sensed a powerful emotion in him, almost ready to explode, and wondered for a moment if he might strike me.

'Nothing. None of your business. Okay, you can borrow the picture as long as you bring it back safely and promise you won't leave it with any of them.'

'I promise,' I said.

'Then come with me. It's in my workshop.' He gathered his things and stomped ahead of me, his big seaboots making a thumping sound on the cobbles. I followed, trying to keep up with his giant strides. What had made him so angry with the Hannan family? Had they tried not to pay him for the painting? Or not paid the agreed price? I thought of old Miss Gallinger and her assertion of women's intuition. What exactly was this emotion that I was sensing and suddenly a word came into my head. *Jealousy.* And I thought what old Miss Gallinger had said about Irene slipping in and out through the secret door in the wall.

'You were in love with Irene Hannan,' I blurted out as he paused outside a bright red door to take out his key.

He spun to face me, his eyes blazing. 'Who the devil told you that? Did she?'

'Nobody told me. I figured it out for myself.'

He turned the key and kicked the door open. Then he went inside ahead of me, throwing down his things on a scrubbed pine table. He didn't invite me in but I followed anyway.

'I loved her since we were kids,' he said. 'They used to come here before her father had the house built. They'd rent an ordinary place and she'd come to watch the boats. We'd play together. Then she was sent off to finishing school in Europe. And then I heard that she'd married a snooty Dutchman, one of the Four Hundred. But when I saw her again, I knew right away that she still loved me.'

'She slipped out to visit you,' he said.

'She was always so careful,' he said. 'How did you find that out?'

'She wasn't careful enough. She was seen. But don't worry. None of the family knows.'

'I always thought that those girls were mine,' he said. 'Twins run in my family, you know, and Colleen . . . she had a look about her, when she was puzzling something out . . . well, I could see myself in her.' As he spoke he took out his brushes and mechanically cleaned them in a jar of turpentine that stood on the table. 'You don't know what a torture it was, knowing she was so close and yet only being able to see her once in a while. Hoping to catch a glimpse of the little girls . . . It was like a dream come true when Old Hannan commissioned the portraits. He was going to have one painted of Kathleen too, but of course Colleen came first. She always did. I had to come to the house every day. It was like being in heaven. And then that awful thing happened.'

'She was with you at the time, wasn't she?'

'How do you know that? What are you, some kind of witch?'

'No, I'm a detective, actually, and if you want to know, it was a guess. Someone told me that Irene wasn't with them at tea. She came running up when she heard Kathleen's scream.'

'I haven't seen her since,' he said. He picked up a filthy rag and dried one of the brushes on it, his back still toward me. 'She wrote me a note saying that she could never see me again. She felt so guilty, you see. If only she'd been there, she could have saved Colleen. And her father added insult to injury by bringing back the painting. They no longer wanted to be reminded of her. I didn't want to be reminded either. It was locked away for years. Then I needed money and decided I might as well sell it. But I couldn't. Wait there.'

He went into a backroom and returned with the painting. 'Here,' he said. 'Take it. You say you want to help the other twin? Isn't she in a mental home? That's what Irene told me.'

'She's at the castle,' I said, 'and she's accused of killing her nurse. She's blocked out all memory of her sister and I thought if she saw the portrait, it might reawaken her memory.'

'So she's not mad?'

'I don't know. But I don't think she killed her sister, and I want to help her.'

'Here you are, then.' He handed me the portrait. 'Anything to help her.' And as I took the painting from him he added, 'How does she look now? Anything like Colleen?'

'Very much like Colleen, I would say.' I could read his expression – wary, not daring to hope for something he couldn't have.

Thirty-Eight

The heat of the day and the weight of the painting started to grow on me as I walked back from town. I was delighted then when I heard the honk of a horn behind me and an automobile drew up, enveloping me in a cloud of dust. As I brushed the dust away, coughing, I saw Police Chief Prescott sitting behind the driver.

'Mrs Sullivan. Do allow me to give you a ride,' he said. 'I'm on my way to the house now.'

The driver jumped out and opened the rear door for me, taking the painting and helping me up the step.

'Have you been purchasing art?' Chief Prescott asked. 'I understand we have some fine painters in the area.'

'No, I've just borrowed it,' I said. 'I'm hoping to conduct a little experiment.'

'Really, what kind of experiment?'

I lifted the painting for him to see.

'Good heavens,' he said. 'It's the child in the tower.'

'It was her dead twin.'

'The resemblance is striking,' he agreed. 'What do you plan to do with it? Surely not show it to the family at this time. Wouldn't it only cause more grief?'

'I want to see if we can reawaken Kathleen's memory about what happened to her twin.'

313

He looked wary. 'What would that achieve? Do you want her to be burdened with the knowledge of what she did? Isn't it kinder to leave her in oblivion?'

'Chief Prescott.' I put down the painting and turned to face him. 'Do you want this case solved or not? I don't believe this child is responsible for anything that has happened here.'

'How can you go on insisting that? What about the housekeeper?'

'I don't think she killed the housekeeper or her twin. I'd like one chance to prove her innocence – that's all I'm asking.'

'What do you plan to do, Mrs Sullivan?' he asked warily.

I told him and he listened, frowning.

'Most irregular,' he said, 'and I can't see what you could hope to achieve.'

'What harm could it do?' I said.

'What harm? What about the harm to the child? What if the shock is too much for her and pushes her into madness for life?'

I nodded. 'I have considered that. I know we'd be taking an awful risk but I see no other way to save her. If nothing is achieved then the poor child will spend the rest of her life locked away, shut off from love and affection, among the mad. I'll do anything in my power to prevent that from happening. If you're a just man, you would not want another horrible mis-carriage of justice, would you? If it was your daughter, would you want her locked away in a madhouse?'

'No, of course not,' he spluttered. 'But then my daughter has not been in a catatonic state for eight years.'

'Maybe your daughter did not witness a shocking crime to the one she loved best. Ten minutes, Chief Prescott. That's all I ask.'

He sighed. 'I don't really see how this will bring us to the truth, but I suppose it can't put her in a worse position than she is in already.'

'Thank you. You won't regret it. And your men should be standing by unobtrusively, just in case . . .'

' "In case"?'

'In case the true murderer is revealed.'

We reached the gates. They were opened for us and we drove through, the tires crunching on the gravel drive.

'Could you make sure that tea is served and everyone is summoned to the lawn?' I asked him as we alighted. 'And could I please go up and explain my plan to Miss Walcott?'

He looked at me and rolled his eyes. 'Mrs Sullivan, do you interfere like this in all your husband's criminal cases?'

I smiled. 'We haven't been married long enough to tell yet. But I will say this – I have been successful before when the police have failed.'

With that I went into the house and up the long stair to Gus and Kathleen. When I entered, Kathleen was playing with the dollhouse and Gus was sitting behind her, taking notes.

'Hello, Molly,' she said, looking up as Kathleen scurried to cling to her skirts. 'Any news from Sid yet?'

'She's on her way back here, and she's made some interesting discoveries.'

'I've been doing rather well myself,' she said. 'I think I've made a good start in unlocking her language. Of course I can't really tell. I've tried speaking to her in her own tongue, but she just looks confused and won't answer.'

'Gus, I think we have one chance to help her escape this nightmare for good,' I said. 'This is what I want you to do, if you're up for it.'

I led her away from Kathleen and whispered into her ear. As I unfolded my plan, she drew away from me, looking horrified.

'Are you mad?'

Kathleen scurried under her bed at the sound of Gus's raised voice. Gus lowered her voice and leaned closer to me, her eyes still on the cowering child. 'Haven't you thought what it might do to her? Hasn't she suffered enough?'

I took Gus and led her into the other room. 'It's the only way,' I said. 'The one chance we have. I have no other way to prove who really killed her sister. And as things stand, they'll come and take her away however much you try to defend her, Gus. She'll be locked up in a madhouse for life.'

'But what you're suggesting might really drive her mad,' Gus hissed back at me.

'Isn't it worth a risk to try and save her, even if it is going to be traumatic? And the very least we'll get is justice for her dead sister. She'd want that, wouldn't she?'

Gus looked at me, long and hard. 'You've let your emotions take over before, Molly. The results haven't always been good.'

'I know that,' I said. From the window I heard sounds on the lawn below as chairs and tables were being carried out. 'But I really believe this is our one chance to reawaken her memory, if she has kept the details of that traumatic event locked away until now.'

'We're not alienists. Either of us, Molly,' Gus said. 'I like to think I know what I'm doing with the child, but I really don't, and neither do you.'

'But since they won't let a real alienist get involved, it's up to us, isn't it, and we both want what's best for her, don't we?'

Gus sighed and started to walk back into Kathleen's room. 'Come on out, precious,' she said. 'It's all right. Gus is going to take care of you, no matter what.'

And she knelt down beside the bed. 'I'll get her ready to come down when you say,' she said quietly.

I hugged her. 'Thank you. Let us hope for a miracle, shall we?'

I went back down and chose my position with care among the trees. One by one the family emerged from the house.

'What on earth can he be doing now?' Joseph was blustering to Father Patrick. 'They've already searched our rooms once. What more do they think we are hiding?'

'At least tea is ready and waiting for us,' Father Patrick said. 'And my favorite little cakes too. You see, there is a good side to everything.'

'You have to say that because you're a damned priest,' Joseph snapped. 'You always were a holier than thou little prig, weren't you?'

They took seats on the lawn. I waited among the trees, hardly daring to breathe. At last the rest of the family was there.

'Why have the chairs been moved here today?' Irene demanded. 'This is too close to the ocean. Too breezy for me. Archie, have the servants move them back where they usually are.'

'That annoying police fellow had them put here, I suppose,' Archie said. 'I can't wait to go home, back to a normal life. Why are we still here – we know what happened now and the poor child isn't responsible for her actions.'

Among the trees I saw a movement. Gus and Kathleen had arrived. I signaled and waited. A few minutes later I saw a flash of white skirts as they came toward me through the under-growth. As they stepped out onto the lawn, Kathleen caught sight of the people sitting there and gave a little scream of horror, and at the same moment I stood up from behind a bush, holding the painting up in front of me.

I couldn't see what was happening, but suddenly terri-fied screams filled the air. I came forward with the painting. Kathleen grabbed Gus, trying desperately to drag her away.

The family had all risen to their feet.

'What on earth's she doing down here?' Archie demanded. 'Who brought her out? Can't you see how it will upset her mother to see her like this? Take her back immediately.'

'The poor child. Why are you trying to frighten her in this way?' Father Patrick said gently, going toward her.

Gus stopped him, shielding the child.

I dropped the painting and ran toward them. Kathleen was cowering behind Gus as Father Patrick came toward her. With one hand she clawed at Gus's sleeve, with the other she flailed at the air as if warding off an attack. 'No, no!' she shouted. 'No boo Coween.'

'It's all right, child. Nobody is going to hurt you.' He reached out his hand as if to touch her gently. 'She should never have been let out. Let's take her back to safety. Can't you see how distressed she is?'

I put myself between him and Kathleen. 'She's distressed because she recognizes you and she remembers now that you killed her sister,' I said.

'What utter nonsense. The child's babbling the gibberish of a diseased mind.'

'Miss Walcott has made remarkable strides in understanding her speech, which is the language of twins, the language she used to speak to Colleen.' I knew I was stretching the truth; conscious of the family members closing in on us, I addressed them as much as Father Patrick.

'You accuse me of killing her sister?' he said, his normally gentle voice now high and taut. 'I adored Colleen. We all did.'

'Did you love the other little girls you killed?' I asked. 'Those little girls in Granville and Cambridge?' I looked around the faces of those who were frozen in a group around us, staring with a mixture of horror and fascination. 'That was why your brother summoned us all here, wasn't it? Because he had finally figured out the truth.'

'Your mind is as diseased as this child's,' Patrick Hannan said. 'I don't know exactly who you are but your meddling is causing this family great distress.' He glanced up at the policemen who were now making their way across the lawn toward us. 'Officers, this woman is mad. Please remove her.'

'It's no use, Father Patrick,' I said. 'I went to Brian Hannan's office, you see, and I saw what he had written. He had figured out for himself why your bishop moved you from parish to parish so frequently.' I stared at him defiantly. 'That's why you had to kill your brother, wasn't it? You had to kill him before he revealed what he had found out to the rest of the family and had you put away.'

'He told me he'd spoken to my bishop,' Patrick said, 'When he said he was calling the family together to decide what to do with me, I had to stop him. We'd used that cyanide on a wasps' nest last summer. I met him and told him I wanted to talk privately first. And I offered him a drink.'

The family members stood there, staring with expressions of horror and disbelief. Archie Van Horn was the first to move. 'You killed my daughter?' he shouted. 'You killed Colleen?' He started toward the priest, his eyes blazing.

'I didn't mean to, I swear.' Patrick stepped back, almost sobbing now. 'She was like a little angel. I just wanted to touch her, to hold her in my arms. But she started to scream and I put my hand over her face, and when I took it away she was dead. I didn't know what to do . . .' He looked around from one face to the next, hoping for understanding, I suppose. 'I must have panicked. The cliff was right there. I pushed her body over, hoping to make it seem like an accident. I didn't think anybody would see.'

'But Kathleen saw, didn't she?' I demanded. 'And the shock drove her mad.'

'I'm so sorry,' he whimpered. 'I didn't mean . . .'

'And what about those other little girls?' I demanded as he stood with his face in his hands, shaking. 'Didn't you mean to kill them either?'

He looked up at me then, his face surprisingly innocent and serene. 'Oh, yes, I ended their lives quite deliberately. I realized when I had killed Colleen that I had done her a service. She was a little angel and I had made sure she'd gone straight to Heaven, uncorrupted by the world.' He looked around us for understanding. 'They were all little angels, you see. Beautiful children. Uncorrupted. I was just making sure they went straight to Heaven, before they could be sullied by the world. I was helping them.'

I realized then that he wasn't sane. Out of the corner of my eye I saw two policemen closing in on him. Suddenly Patrick's demeanor changed. He darted forward, grabbed at Kathleen, and pushed her in front of him. She gave a whimper of terror as his hand came around her throat.

'Stand back!' he shouted. 'If you come any closer, I'll throw her over the cliff.'

'Don't do this,' I pleaded. 'It can't help you in any way. Think of all those years you spent as a priest. Think of all the good you've done. You're essentially a good man, I'm sure you are. You don't want to harm her.'

'It doesn't matter any longer,' he said calmly. 'You can only go to Hell once and I condemned myself to that fate when I killed Colleen.'

I tried to think what I could say to reason with him. Two of the policemen were still attempting to inch toward us. Patrick Hannan dragged Kathleen until they were poised at the very edge of the cliff. 'I said stay away or down she goes. Get back with the others and don't attempt to stop me. I'm taking her with me.'

The position in which he held her left us no chance to tackle him.

'It's no use, Father,' one of the policemen said. 'You can't get away. The place is surrounded with our men. Now let the little girl go and give yourself up. Don't bring disgrace to the Holy Church.'

I didn't think they were handling this too well. Patrick Hannan's expression became wilder. His eyes darted nervously.

'Give myself up to a filthy jail?' Patrick demanded, his voice now high and tight again. 'Or to the electric chair? Never.' He started to drag Kathleen along the cliff edge, making for the stand of pine trees. Kathleen coughed and choked as his arm wrapped tightly around her neck.

'You're choking her!' Gus shouted. 'Let go of her neck.'

He released his hold and she stood there, coughing, her hand at her throat. Before we could do anything she turned and hurled herself at him, uttering a dreadful, unearthly cry. Kathleen's head hit her uncle square in his stomach knocking him backward. He gave a gasp as the air went out of him and they both went over the cliff together.

Thirty-Nine

There was a gasp of horror from those who stood watching helplessly. I believe I screamed. Then from the crowd there was a loud cry of 'No! Not Kathleen!' And Irene Van Horn rushed toward the edge of the cliff.

Father Patrick Hannan was lying on the rocks, eyes open and staring up at us while a river of blood flowed from his shattered head to mingle with the water in the rock pools. Kathleen lay lifeless on top of him.

'Oh, no. Kathleen, my little girl!' Irene wailed as one of the policemen grabbed her arm before she too went over the edge. At the sound of her mother's voice Kathleen stirred and tried to sit up. 'Mama?' she called plaintively.

Archie, Terrence, and the policemen were already slithering down the cliff nearby to reach her.

'Careful, sir,' one of the policemen warned as Archie went to scoop her up into his arms. 'She may be badly injured. You should wait for a stretcher.'

Archie and Terrence were on their knees beside the little girl.

'Does it hurt you to move, sweetheart?' Archie asked. 'Are you badly hurt?'

Kathleen looked at him with wonder. 'Papa?' she said.

A makeshift stretcher was brought down from the house

and she was carried up to safety. Remarkably she only suffered a cut knee. Her great-uncle had broken her fall. And more remark-ably, she began speaking again. Hesitantly at first, but it was as if the great weight she had carried for eight years had been taken from her shoulders. And now that the family knew the truth and the terrible injustice that she had suffered, they couldn't do enough for her.

I found myself alone as they carried Kathleen back to the house. Suddenly I wanted to feel Daniel's arms around me. I made my way back to the cottage. Daniel was sitting up in the chair in the bedroom. He looked up expectantly when I came in.

'What was all that commotion about? I heard shouting and screaming. What was it?'

'Patrick Hannan. The priest. Kathleen's memory returned and she recognized him as the man who killed her sister and threw her body over the cliff,' I said.

'The priest. Well I never.' He said. 'And to think I missed out on all the excitement. You were there, you lucky devil. Come and sit beside me and tell me all the details.'

His jovial tone was too much for me. 'It wasn't funny,' I retorted angrily. 'How can you be so callous? This was a horrible man who killed little girls and . . .' My voice cracked. 'And he grabbed Kathleen and threatened to hurl her over the cliff. Then Kathleen threw herself at him and they both went over.'

And to my embarrassment I burst into tears. Immediately Daniel had enveloped me in his arms. 'It's all right. You're safe now. I've got you,' he murmured. 'Are they both dead, Patrick and the little girl?'

'He is. She landed on top of him and he broke her fall. Only justice really for what he did to her sister,' I said, swallowing back my sobs.

'And how did they find out he killed her sister?'

'I did a little investigating of my own. I found out why Brian Hannan invited us here.'

'I might have known,' he said. 'You never can leave well enough alone, can you? You get yourself involved and then you wind up in trouble.'

'I solved your case, Daniel Sullivan,' I said as anger replaced tears. 'I found that Patrick Hannan had been quietly killing little girls in each of his parishes. Brian Hannan discovered that too, and that was why Patrick had to kill him.'

Daniel took my face in his hands. 'Molly, what am I going to do with you?' he asked tenderly. 'How can I make you behave like a normal wife and leave investigating to those whose job it is?'

'You weren't able to do it,' I said. 'And Chief Prescott certainly wasn't up to it. Somebody had to find the truth before poor little Kathleen was blamed for these murders too and shipped off to an insane asylum.'

'So you did it.'

'Yes,' I said, as I realized with pride what I had accomplished. 'Yes, I did.'

So Kathleen was restored to the bosom of her family. At my suggestion Dr Birnbaum was summoned and suggested that her introduction to normal life be a gradual process. So a trained nurse was hired and Gus volunteered to be with Kathleen during the first difficult weeks. She was very proud of what she had accomplished.

'I was telling Sid that maybe I should go to Vienna and study with Professor Freud, so that I could work with traumatized children,' she said.

'That would be wonderful,' I agreed, 'but I'd miss you.'

Gus shook her head. 'Sid doesn't want to go. She says there is so much to be done in New York and she doesn't really like

Austrian food. So I'll content myself with being Kathleen's protector and guide.'

'And you will write that paper on the language of twins to read at Vassar,' I reminded her.

'Yes, of course I'll do that.' She looked quite excited.

The next day I went out to return the portrait to Ned Turnbull and recounted the events of the afternoon to him. 'So she's going to be all right, is she?'

'I hope she will, Ned,' I said. 'Her grandfather left a lot of money for her care and I understand that Irene and Archie want her to come home to them.'

'Yes,' he said slowly. 'I suppose that is for the best.'

I handed him the painting. He looked up at me. 'Give it back to Irene,' he said. 'I think she'll want to remember her daughter now.'

As we packed up to leave Irene herself came to visit me at the cottage. 'You gave me back my daughter,' she said. 'I can never thank you enough.'

'I'm glad I could help.' I smiled at her because I could see she was struggling to tell me more.

'I behaved so badly,' she said at last. 'I wanted to believe that Kathleen killed her sister, because then I couldn't have prevented it, even if I'd been where I was supposed to be. I couldn't bear to see her because she reminded me of what a rotten mother I'd been and how much I loved Colleen . . . how I loved Colleen better than her.'

'I do understand,' I said. 'And I know why you felt so guilty.'

She looked up sharply. 'Of course. The portrait. Ned told you?'

'No. I guessed.'

She sighed. 'My father forced me to make a good marriage, you know. But Ned and I – you can't just stop loving someone, can you?' Then she smoothed down her lovely silk gown and got to her feet. 'I'm going to make it up to my daughter. The doctor says she can lead a perfectly normal life in time. It will be fun bringing her out into society. She's a pretty girl, isn't she? Who would have thought she'd turn out so pretty?' And she left.

As Kathleen's speech returned she was able to tell us the truth about what happened to Mrs McCreedy. She had watched Patrick as Mrs McCreedy spotted the open trapdoor. She had watched as he crept up behind the caretaker and then given her a mighty shove to her death. Kathleen had rushed back to hide under her bed and Father Patrick had never known he had been observed. We'd never know exactly why he had to kill Mrs McCreedy. Had she caught him trying to sneak up to Kathleen? Personally I think he wanted to make Kathleen appear guilty of a second murder. A coldhearted man indeed! What a lot of traumatic memories that child would have to work through before she could start to live a normal life. I was glad that Dr Birnbaum and Gus would be helping her.

Sid, Gus, and Daniel's mother left to go home and Daniel and I finally had the place to ourselves until the ship arrived. We sat together on the lawn, looking out at the whitecaps on the ocean and I thought how lucky we were that we had our whole lives ahead of us now. When Daniel was forced to take a rest I found time to visit Miss Gallinger and give her all the news. She was most excited to hear what had transpired.

'So I was right then, wasn't I?' she said. 'The child was already dead when she went over the cliff. I remember how resilient one was as a child. I fell off that cliff once. And you see, now her sister survived the fall too.'

We took tea together and she thanked me profusely. I'd obviously given her something to talk about with her maid through the long winter evenings ahead. I saw her watching me wistfully from behind the lace curtain as I left.

* * *

On the day of our departure Daniel and I were driven to our boat in the family motorcar. As soon as the steward left our cabin, Daniel took me into his arms.

'At least you can say that our honeymoon wasn't dull,' he said. 'I hope we can look forward to a more peaceful life together in the future.'

'Peaceful lives can be awfully boring.' I smiled up at him.

'What am I going to do with you, Molly Murphy?'

'Just love me for what I am.' Then I asked abruptly. 'What do you think you're doing?'

'What I haven't been strong enough to do for the past few days,' he said firmly.

'Are you up to it?'

He started to laugh. I laughed with him and we didn't even hear the toot of the siren as the ship slipped away from its berth, back to New York and our new life.